Dear Doug,
Congrats on
I hope Xander + M show
you love is way more than
skin deep.

Rock on,
♡ Arell
Rivers
S

PRIDE

Sins of the Fathers, Book #3

ARELL RIVERS

PRIDE

Book 3 in the **SINS OF THE FATHERS** series

ARELL RIVERS

Editing:

Theresa Leigh, Velvetfire Press

Trenda Lundin, https://www.facebook.com/ItsYourStoryContentEditing

Rebecca Hodgkins, https://www.rebeccahodgkinseditor.com

Proofreading:

Angel Nyx, https://www.facebook.com/ProfreadingBayouQueen

Roxanne Blouin

Cover design:

Dar Albert, Wicked Smart Designs, https://www.wickedsmartdesigns.com

❀ Created with Vellum

Thank You!!

Thank you so much for taking the time to read PRIDE! I really hope Xander and Madison steal your heart!

The next installment in the Sins of the Fathers series awaits!

Rock on,
Arell

Breaking News: NYC's Golden Boy Takes A Walk

This "Breaking News" about Xander Turner hardly deserves such a title. Then again, the mere mention of Xander's name has always made my ladybits tingle, no matter that he never gave me a second glance when we were in school. But when the news anchor announces he's out of the high-profile marketing position in his now-infamous family's business, my wayward thoughts shift to my struggling PR agency. I want him. Ahem, to save my firm.

Much to my shock, Xander accepts my job offer. Not only does his sexy face and business savvy bring in the clients, but he adds a layer of fun and creativity I hadn't expected. He even makes the transition from uptown shark to downtown employee seem effortless. Soon I come to realize that Xander's more than just his looks. A hell of a lot more.

When the paparazzi catch wind of our unlikely pairing, will their ruthless pursuit give my agency more exposure, or will NYC's dog-eat-dog media industry tear apart all we've built?

"Pride achieves almost nothing but destroys a lot." ~ *Abdulazeez Henry Musa*

Xander

I f possible, my eyes would hurl daggers at my father. "How could you take money from such a little prick, Dad? Hudson acts like he *owns* us."

Standing behind his desk in his home office overlooking Central Park, my father fumes. "Look, I know he's an asshole, but Gold Fleet Capital's money is green, and we needed the infusion. But he had no right to fire you. Here I am trying to save VOW³ Media through the damn bankruptcy, and this weasel pulls a stupid stunt like this." He fixes stormy blue eyes on mine. No questioning my parentage. "And you fell for it, Xander. You should've made him file the damn lawsuit."

Patrick Hudson, head of VOW-cubed's creditor's committee in our company's bankruptcy, breezed into my office not thirty minutes ago, wielding a draft motion to reject my employment contract. Gave me the impossible option: quit or be fired, publicly, by the court. No choice really.

A frisson of fear runs up my spine. I am going to get my job back, right? "You'll have this straightened out soon, though? I mean, it's our family's company. I deserve to be there."

In an ugly tone, Dad replies, "I don't know, Xander. Don't you think I *deserve* to work at the place I built? And what about your uncles, Ward and Ogden? Do we *deserve* to be stuck in our respective homes, wearing stupid ankle monitors?" He lifts his pant leg to reveal the device slapped on him and my uncles by the government at their bail hearing.

"Dad, I—"

My father cuts me off. "Looks like you're going to have to do what the three of us have been doing since that goddamn Gala. Suck. It. Up."

I shift my weight between my feet. He can't leave me to hang in the wind. "You're filing a motion to dismiss soon, and then we'll all be back at our desks. Everything will return to normal."

"That's the idea. But nothing's going according to any damn plan." He moves some of the papers on his desk and holds up a daily. "If you had stayed with Darcey Abbott like I told you to do, the media would be happily reporting your upcoming nuptials and maybe Hudson would've been more circumspect." He taps on a photo of her with some guy. "Look. She's on some football player's arm now."

At my former fiancée's name, my stomach clenches. Swallowing to keep the bile from escaping my esophagus, I respond, "Good for her." I was fucking fired, and he's getting on my ass about her?

"Should've been you. Fuckin' gorgeous with a pedigree a mile long."

What is she? A thoroughbred? My reflexive defense of the woman dies when I remember her throwing my Tiffany ring at me after Dad and his partners were arrested at the Tinsel and Tatas Gala. Which she followed up with a venomous article in *Spill It Magazine*.

Dad flings the daily onto his desk as if it bit him. "I bet you could still get her back. All you'd have to do is grovel a little. Maybe buy her a car or something. Women like that shit. And the press would eat it up. Lord knows we need some good news reported about our families now, other than in our own magazines."

Her rejection seared me to the core. We *were* media darlings.

Until that awful night five months ago. When everything came crashing down.

Dammit, I thought I was in love with her. Caught up in the heady whirlwind our combined lives brought. Dazzled by her beauty. Not to mention the sex.

It's been five months since I had any of that, too.

"Not. Going. To. Happen." My voice is laced with steel.

"Well," his head jerks back.

Dad's surprise at my standing up to him is evident in his posture, which turns rigid. I've always done what he told me to do, as proven by *almost* becoming the first Executive Vice President of VOW-cubed when I got engaged. If only the FBI hadn't come in and ruined my whole life—professionally as well as personally. To which Hudson just did a final swift kick.

Anger surges. I've run the company, mediating between my father and his partners, ever since the indictments. Hell, right before Hudson showed up, I sent them a PowerPoint deck outlining a new strategy about how to engage readers. Not once did any of them express their gratitude over my impossible situation. All my life I've followed Dad's advice to the letter, including getting engaged to his choice of my perfect wife—which *his* arrest dissolved. What have I gotten for my obedience? A broken engagement and no job.

And when did he ever say he was proud of me for all my compliance? I can count the times on one hand. At my acceptance into his *alma mater*. At my college graduation, for following in his footsteps and not because I made the Dean's List once. He even said the word when I graduated from NYU Business School five years ago because my degree enhanced VOW-cubed's resume. The last time? When Darcey accepted my wedding proposal. I snort. Seems like I only earned accolades from Dad when I followed his instructions.

My body tenses. "You know what? Nothing I do will ever make you proud of me, will it? I'm out of a job at *our* family business and all you have to say is suck it up and buy Darcey a car? This affects my entire life, and it all started with whatever you did to get arrested."

He growls, "I do not have to listen to this shit. Get. Out."

Assuming bravado I don't feel, I echo his pitch. "Gladly."

My heartbeat takes off into the stratosphere as I stalk out of his sanctuary. Unseeing, I pass a wall of windows framing the Park. When I cross into the family room, Mom greets me. "Everything okay, honey? I thought I heard raised voices." Her eyebrow shoots upward even as her arms open wide for me.

I enter her embrace—if palms hovering over each other's shoulders and air-kissing both cheeks counts. "No. It's not by a longshot."

"Oh." She pastes a smile on her face and steps away from me. "Well, I'm sure your father can fix it."

"We'll see." My body shakes with pent-up anger at the situation I'm in, fear at my unknown future, disappointment about Dad's reaction. My forehead crinkles. Make that fury at his suggestion I get back together with Darcey. Not wanting to share my feelings with Mom, I murmur, "I have things to do. I'll see you soon."

She offers a small wave. "Bye. Don't be a stranger."

After I smack the elevator's call button, their housekeeper appears at my side holding my coat. "Here you go, Mr. Xander."

Taking it from her, I reply, "Thanks, Luna."

Giving her a wan smile, I shove my arms into the sleeves and stride to the cab. As the doors close, I exhale. Shit. I need to return to the office and clean out my stuff before Hudson posts it on eBay. Exiting the grand marble lobby of my parents' apartment building, I hop into the family's SUV that I presciently asked to wait for me and instruct the driver to take me back to VOW-cubed.

Despite the fact she's been gone for nearly three decades, I picture Grandma Lucia giving me a hug like she used to do when I was a child. Can almost smell her lilac perfume. If only she were still with us, but breast cancer robbed the world of her presence when I was only five.

Now, at age thirty-three, I'm unemployed. Unmoored. Aimless. Needing to talk with someone who can talk back, I reach for my phone and call my lifeline. "Theo. I need you."

"Be there as soon as I can, bro."

Theo's always been there for me, as I have for him. Son of

Ogden Hansen, Dad's best friend and one of his partners at VOW-cubed, we were raised together like one big family. God bless a man who answers a distress signal without asking even a single question.

Returning into my office, my open palm sends the empty cardboard box Hudson "gave" me flying. A beat later, I deflate. What am I going to do?

I snake over to the windows, tracking the ants and toy cars below my fifty-second-floor view. I'm lost inside my mind when Theo enters the room. He picks up Hudson's cardboard box and places it on the low coffee table. "Talk to me." After a long moment, my brain kicks into gear and I lay out the day's gory details while collecting personal items from my office. "What did your dad say?"

"Basically told me to figure it out—his plate is full. Then he went off on how I should reconnect with Darcey as it would bring much-needed positive headlines."

"I hope you told him to get the fuck out of your love life."

"I did." My hand lands on a picture of Theo and me from the Tinsel and Tatas gala, which was snapped an hour before our lives fell apart. After showing it to him, I deposit it in the box of keepsakes. A ping from my cell phone catches my attention. Checking the screen, I roll my eyes.

"Who was that?"

"Not who. What. A stupid reminder about my b-school networking event tonight."

He holds up a framed certificate from the Chamber of Commerce to which I shake my head. Won't need it in the unemployment line. "I think you should go to the business school event."

I pause from adding another piece of memorabilia into the box. "Why? So I can be the poster boy for out-of-work losers?"

He approaches me. "No. Because you have to keep your chin up to show Hudson he doesn't faze you in the least. And you never know—you might get a lead on a job opportunity."

I turn my head away, my eyes landing on a sanitized piece of artwork, which is typical of VOW-cubed's decorating style. "Not how I want to spend my Thursday. Cold appetizers and watered-down drinks aren't on my agenda, especially after—"

He places his hand on my shoulder. "I understand. But what better way is there to show Hudson that he means nothing to you than attending this NYU thingy? Plus, shove it in your father's face, too."

Theo's words hang like a cloud bubble over my body. "News hasn't leaked about my leaving here, so I guess it would also be good to keep up appearances."

He checks his watch. "How long until the party starts?"

"Doors open at seven." Seems like I'm going to a party. I rub the back of my neck. "Can you help me pack first?"

"You got it."

***

My Rolex reads seven-thirty as I get out of the limo to attend the b-school's networking event at the trendy restaurant downtown. Despite Theo's best efforts, my mood is decidedly sour.

I cross the sidewalk and walk toward the front door, which is lined by reporters. Of course it is. With effort, I force my "pleasant face" mask into place and take a few steps. Offering a nod as I pass them, I stop to answer a couple of the more innocuous questions— and sideswipe the more probing ones.

"*Xander, how are your father and his partners holding up?*" I respond to this softball by putting the most positive spin on it as possible. "They're working hard to clear their names."

"*Xander, what's the atmosphere like at the office?*" I can take this one. "We're very busy keeping up with deadlines." Yup. My leaving VOW-cubed isn't public knowledge.

"*Xander, any truth to the rumors that the execs at VOW-cubed don't see eye-to-eye on whether to cut a deal with the Southern District of New York?*" What the fuck? I keep my smile schooled and focus on a different reporter who asks, "*Xander, do you feel your degree helped in your career, or did having the last name Turner do that all for you?*" Christ. I deflect with my response, "Education is always a positive enhancement. I was thrilled to earn my business degree from NYU and use the strategies I learned in class every day."

Okay, enough. I stride past the rest of the gauntlet and am gratified when I reach the door. Half-turning, I wave to the press and step into the sanctuary of the restaurant. Sans paps. Thank fuck.

I pause at the threshold to allow my vision to adjust to the dim, ambient lighting inside. A moment later, I approach the hostess. "Can you please direct me to the NYU Business School event?"

The woman, approximately five or six years my junior, glances up from the reservations book and her eyes glaze over. While I've been getting this reaction from women since I was a teenager, it's beyond annoying today. It's only a face. I have to keep playing the game, though. Not allowing my mask to falter, I force a smile.

The young hostess blinks, then her tongue swipes her plump lips. "It's, ah, in the Eastman Room." Her finger, complete with white nail polish with crystals on it, points off to the right.

I nod and take one step in that direction when her voice stops me. "Although, I could make it worth your while to skip that stuffy event."

Brazen. Never one of my turn-ons. And certainly not going to work now. "Thanks, but I've been looking forward to tonight for a long time. Have a good evening." I dip my chin while maintaining eye contact, then take measured steps toward the room she indicated. Drawing nearer to the entrance, I prepare for the crush of this networking event and dredge up my façade as an Assistant Vice President of Marketing. God, I hope Jesse is here. He said he was coming, although that was weeks ago.

I check in, donning a sticky name tag with Xander written in black Sharpie. Somehow, I doubt anyone will need to look at it.

The room is about three-quarters full when I enter. B-school alumni are a sociable lot, and tonight's similar to the other events I've attended—pre-indictment. As I travel deeper into the room, I ignore my classmate's whispers behind my back. I've gotten used to this treatment over the past couple of months, but it still stings. *I* did nothing wrong.

When I turn toward the bar, Madison Welch crosses my field of vision. The short, roundish woman wears a pair of black pants with a black shirt. Her blond hair's down, like usual. We never socialized when we were in school, but her rep as being scary smart intrigued me—especially since no one's ever accused me of the same. She started her own PR firm a few years ago, which I have to admit is cool. Being able to work with a wide variety of clients rather than being relegated to only VOW-cubed, always fascinated me. It never was an option.

Before.

Our paths have crossed over the years, but we're barely acquaintances. Saw her at the Tinsel and Tatas Gala before all hell broke loose. Even thought about reaching out to her agency to find out if they could help us out. *Not your problem anymore.*

"Glad to see you showed!" Jesse Dimon punches my shoulder.

I spin around and give my best friend from school a bro hug. My mood picks up—at least the evening's taken a turn for the better.

Even if my future is still unsettled.

2

Madison

I pull my hair across my cheek, putting a few strands into my mouth. Stephanie tips her martini glass to me. "Have you heard Xander Turner is supposed to show up tonight?"

For a second, my knees threaten to stop accepting my weight. Thankfully, I bounce on my heels and maintain my balance. Xander is one of those BPs—Beautiful People—who are nice to everyone because they can be. He's rich and adored and powerful in the City, even if his father is under house arrest. Not to mention he's gorgeous as all get-out. Dark hair, blue eyes, over six feet tall, and with this goatee that makes mere mortal women beg for his favors. I'm so tongue-tied around him—anything beyond pleasantries is unimaginable.

I sample my mojito. "I'm shocked he'd be able to come out to a school get-together. Seems like he has much bigger things on his agenda."

"Truth," Stephanie says, toasting me. Our glasses clink, and I take another sip. Stephanie leans in closer. "But, damn, I hope he does show up. Nothing like some eye candy to make a networking event interesting."

He's all that and a bag of chips, for sure. "I'll believe it when I see it." Moving on, she brings up a local charity she's been volunteering with, Friends For Fun, which pairs up successful adults in a variety of fields with underprivileged kids. It's along the lines of a Boys and Girls Club and is headquartered where I live, in Brooklyn.

"Wow. Sounds like an amazing charity, Stephanie. I'd love to help them out."

"It is pretty awesome. I heard they're going to be looking for some assistance on the PR and marketing front soon, so I'll let you know when the RFP is going out."

RFPs—Request for Proposals—have become as necessary to me as air. "Please do." All of a sudden, Stephanie's eyes widen, and she almost faceplants into her drink. I place my hand on her forearm. "What's going on?"

Without moving her glass, she whispers, "The rumors are true. He's here. And he's as damn gorgeous as ever." She swallows. "If not more so."

No need to ask who she's talking about. I resist the urge to spin around and check out the hunk of gorgeousness in the room. I learned at an early age not to put myself out there since no one that hot would think of giving short, round, scarred me the time of day. Friends. I'm friends with the BPs of the world. And I guess the word "friend" should be more like "acquainted with." I tug on the end of my hair.

"Do not turn around, Madison, but it looks like he's heading in our direction."

"I'm sure there's someone over here he's interested in talking with," I whisper back, my gaze searching the room for anyone worthy of a BP greeting.

"There you are." A hand taps my back. Spinning, I come face-to-face not with Xander, but with Jesse Dimon. We met in b-school and hit it off immediately—as friends. He's hot in his own right, although he doesn't touch the Xander Turner Hotness Meter in my opinion. Since he's one of the sweetest men I've ever known, I open my arms wide and he pulls me in for a fabulous hug. Too bad there's never been any chemistry between us.

I step back and punch his upper shoulder. "Jesse Dimon. Great to see you, buddy."

"It's always a good day when I can hang out with my favorite school chum." He sips a Guinness and looks at Stephanie. Since she was a year behind us, I introduce them. "A pleasure."

A red-faced Stephanie tips her glass toward him.

"Actually, I was looking for you." Jesse pins me with his green eyes. "I'd like to pick your brain about some marketing stuff. But before I do that, do you know Xander Turner?"

Oh crap. He's going to introduce me to the god of NYU Business School? No way will I let him know we've been introduced at least five times throughout the years, as I'm positive Xander won't remember me. Why would he? The only reason I breathe the same air as him is because we're in the same town.

I lick my lips. "I don't think so." True statement.

Jesse turns around and waves toward our group. Like in the movies, Xander materializes from a group of people. His drool-worthy frame crosses the room, making a beeline for us. *Holy moly.* He'd give my all-time favorite male model, David Gandy, a run for his money. Of course, Mr. Gandy wins since he has a British accent, but still.

My heart rate kicks up the closer Xander gets to us. *Play it cool, Madison. He won't remember meeting you tomorrow, like he doesn't remember our prior meetings.*

When he stops next to Jesse, my friend says, "Xander, this is the famous Madison Welch, PR goddess extraordinaire. Madison, this ugly guy here is Xander Turner, of VOW-cubed fame."

I extend my arm toward the newcomer, determined to treat him like any other person. Even if we have met several times before. "Nice to meet you," I smile. "I graduated five years ago. You?"

Xander shakes my hand, causing a ripple of electricity to scream up my arm, but I force myself to let go after the proper number of seconds has passed. "I graduated then, too. I remember you from classes. Happy to see you again."

He remembers me? I tuck this delightful piece of information away. "Likewise, buddy." Buddy? Everyone is a buddy. Don't forget.

His pouty lips tick up. "I like your pin. Is that a frog?"

For some reason, his compliment sounds insincere. Ma gave me this frog for my twelfth birthday, and it reminds me you have to kiss a lot of them before you find your prince. I keep trying, but they're all frogs. And there aren't too many of those amphibians around either.

"Why, yes it is. My mother gifted it to me." My chin kicks up a notch.

"Oh, it's cute."

Cute? It's much more than *cute*. Biting my tongue at the retort dying to come out, I introduce Stephanie to Xander.

Once they exchange greetings, Jesse dives into the deep end. "Now that I have two fantastic marketing minds together, I'm ready to pick your brains."

With difficulty, I focus my attention away from the model standing before me and toward my true friend. "What's up?"

"Well, I'm at a plateau and need to break through," Jesse begins. "You know I have this handmade furniture company that I've been working on the side for the past few years, right?"

Both Xander and I nod while Stephanie fades to the background. While Jesse's day job is in compliance at a bank, his heart and soul are in woodworking. "I hope it can become my full-time business," he continues. "I love using my hands and creating something beautiful out of the ordinary. Can you give me any pointers about what my next steps should be?"

This I can handle. My business is all about PR. I straighten my spine to reach my full five-foot-two-inch height. "Of course. PR is a way of spreading the wealth and connecting people to products and ideas that will enhance their lives. And your creations, I'm sure, provide a beautiful enhancement to anyone's life." I whip out my cell. "What's your website?"

Jesse looks down at the floor. "I haven't gotten around to creating one yet."

I touch his muscular forearm. "Hey. No worries! It only means you're starting from scratch and won't make the same mistakes others have. This is a good thing."

His eyes dart back up and meet mine, their multi-faceted hazel appearing greener today. Probably due to his dark green button-down. "It is?"

My hands raise as if in surrender. "Yes! It's easy to get a nice website these days. I'll bet you'll have one ready to go by next week." I continue on about ideas for each page, then move on to opening a shop on Etsy, getting involved on Facebook, Instagram, as well as setting up a newsletter.

After five minutes of running my mouth, Xander chuckles. "Damn, woman. You're a one-person PR machine." He offers me a brilliant smile.

My breath stutters—I had almost forgotten he was listening. All my thoughts scatter under his beauty. While men aren't supposed to be beautiful, Xander's the poster child. I lock eyes with Stephanie, who nods. Women everywhere are fucked if they have to interact with him. Or pray to be.

I clear my throat. "I'm sure you would've offered the same advice to Jesse here."

Xander swallows amber liquid from a low ball glass. Nothing frou-frou about him. "Maybe some. But you've really got a handle on it."

His compliment slides over my body like ice cream on a hot summer's day. Not that Xander's ever eaten anything so decadent, judging from his body. My mouth opens. "Well, uhm, thanks."

"And your take on PR is refreshing. Spreading the wealth to connect people with things they need. I always think of publicity as another avenue for promotion. Your way is a lot more relaxed. Positive."

I grasp some of my hair from my right side and trail it across my lips, not daring to meet Xander's eyes. "I like to think we're helping others, rather than pushing stuff on them they don't want."

The liquid in his glass swirls as he moves his wrist in a fluid motion. "Like how people need the information contained within our magazines—in lieu of us forcing our content on them."

"Exactly. You're enhancing people's lives with facts. Or décor that will improve their space by making it more functional or pretty." My words stop when I make the mistake of gazing directly into Xander's dark blue, perceptive eyes. In fact, all of my bodily functions cease.

"I can work with that. Very insightful," he compliments.

"Great."

Stephanie wraps her arm around my shoulders. "Madison here is really amazing. It's ideas like these that keep her clients coming back." She squeezes me and steps back.

"I bet," Xander replies.

I appreciate her building me up in front of Jesse and Xander, especially since what she's saying isn't true. My client roster covers the bills, but nothing extra. I recently lost Ellen, who did all my pitches, because her husband got a job in Seattle. I may be insightful according to Xander Turner, but a good orator I am not, as my past ten failed pitches prove. If I don't find someone to replace Ellen soon, I worry about how viable my business can remain. It's not like VOW-cubed Media is in the market for a new PR firm.

A guy I've never seen before approaches our little group, holding his fist up to Xander's for a bump. "Long time no see. How are you doing, man?"

"Hey, Zeke, I'm good." He bumps his knuckles, then returns to us. "I gotta talk with this guy here. Nice meeting you Stephanie." Xander offers a short hug to Stephanie and turns to me. "Madison." Thinking quickly, I hold out my fist to him like Zeke just did. We contact, then he disappears.

Jesse stays behind, and we discuss his business some more. After a few minutes, Stephanie's called over to another group and excuses herself. I help Jesse develop a workable plan for his new business. While I'd never think of billing him for my time, I'm filled with positive energy for doing a good deed.

As I'm walking home from the subway, I review everything that happened at the event. Hanging with Stephanie is always fun, and I'm so happy she's doing well at her headhunting firm. Given her human resources background, I'm not shocked.

I have faith Jesse's new furniture business will take off. He's got a good head on his shoulders.

Then there's Xander. My feet continue on their path back to my apartment, going at a faster clip. We actually exchanged words. Had a real conversation. I managed to string more than one sentence together. And he complimented me. Twice. Both of which didn't mean anything in the larger scheme of things, but were nice to hear anyway.

That and five bucks will get me a cup of coffee. And no one to handle the pitches for my Agency.

I sigh as reality returns. A BP's casual comments won't change my life. Plus, I doubt I'll see Xander Turner again.

I pull some hair into my mouth.

Time to refocus on what truly matters.

3

Xander

Pounding on my door rouses me. Theo's voice assails my ears. "Open up. I know you're in there!"

I pry my eyes open and swing my legs over the side of my bed. Slipping into my workout shorts, I stumble to my front door and unlock it. Letting him open it himself, I make my way to my kitchen and pick up a carton of orange juice from the fridge.

The door swings open. "Figured you'd be lazing about this Monday morning. Since we're both out of work, I thought I'd stop by so we can go for a run together."

I almost drop the container. "What did you say?"

He grins. "I wasn't about to stay at VOW-cubed if you weren't around, so I quit." He shrugs. "Amelia's thrilled. Says I can focus on writing my biography of Uncle Daniel."

I blink several times. "You quit because of me?"

"Damn straight. Best decision ever."

"What did Uncle Ogden say?" I can't imagine his father would be too happy to lose the last remaining second generation from the company.

"I submitted my resignation to my manager." He sips the coffee he brought with him. "You know my father. Always one for the rules." He laughs. "Honestly, this was long overdue. I'm excited to give my book my full attention. And until it's published, I still have a good chunk of my trust fund to tide me over."

"That's great." I walk over to the window, which overlooks Central Park. My building is parallel to my parents', with the same fantastic view. Used most of my trust fund as the down payment, and with a heavy monthly nut. But the address can't be beat.

Sighing, I remember when I received my million-dollar trust fund when I turned twenty-five, like each of us kids. At least I got the money. Ward's twins, plus Theo's younger brother and sister, and my younger sister are still waiting to reach the magical age. Will our fathers' arrests stop them? My eyes shut.

"Wait. Don't you have some of your trust fund left?"

I turn toward him. My shoulders rise. "A little." I do a quick calculation and confirm there's a few months saved in my emergency fund.

"You're a smart guy, Xander. You have a great head on your shoulders and have been the leader of this family forever." Theo punches my shoulder. "Maybe you could start your own marketing company? You have the chops for it."

My lips tip up. Could I be like Madison? In my mind, Dad mocks such a "provincial" idea. Whoa—after our last conversation, who cares what he thinks? Not me. Righteous indignation converts into doubt in my ability to create my own business, since I've never tried to do anything like it. "I'll mull it over."

"I have faith in you." He points to me. "Okay, enough of this dilly-dallying. Go put on a shirt and your running shoes. Chop, chop."

Amazement over what Theo gave up for me overwhelms. I detour in his direction and give him a tight hug. Then, I get dressed and we start the six-mile jogging loop around Central Park, going at a brisk pace. Ignoring the zoo and the hordes of people lining up at the Met, my brain swirls over the possibility of starting my own marketing company. Not even the smell of popcorn from vendors surrounding the reservoir diverts my mental pro and con list. By the time we pass the fountain and are on our way back to my apartment, I've decided the cons win. For now. I'll look for a job at a firm to understand the lay of the land, then start my own. Possibly.

Sweaty, we return to my apartment where I offer Theo a pair of sweats and a t-shirt. While he showers in the guest bathroom, I use mine. Cleaned up, I enter the kitchen to make two breakfast protein shakes. Even though it's nearing afternoon.

Once the blender does its job—at least *it's* gainfully employed— Theo joins me, saying, "Alexa, turn on NewsTime." Holding up our glasses to each other, we toast to being out of work and gulp the green shake.

And I almost spit it out when Hudson's whiny voice fills my apartment. "I met with Xander Turner last week and gave him two options: quit or be fired. For once, he made the smart choice to voluntarily leave the company." In horror, we watch the trainwreck, which apparently has been playing on a loop, until Theo turns off the television.

"That interview was whack," he says, shaking his head.

I collapse onto the sofa, my hand rubbing the back of my neck. "Now the whole world knows I'm out of VOW-cubed."

He sits next to me. "Did you have any other choice?"

"No. Although Dad yelled at me for not making Hudson file the lawsuit."

"Fuck him. He's the one wearing the ankle monitor, not you."

"You're right." I shift my weight between my hips. "I didn't want to have to hire lawyers and possibly suffer even worse press if I lost. Plus, that would've diverted my focus from the company, which needs undivided attention." I suck in a breath. "From someone else now."

His palm runs over his trimmed beard. "How do you feel about not working there anymore?"

I contemplate his question. I'm no longer fighting fires from all directions—the employees, the advertisers, the bankruptcy court. Not to mention dealing with Dad, my uncle and Theo's father, otherwise known as the VOW-cubed execs, who disagree on virtually every idea. Tiptoeing through that minefield was fraught with unexpected skirmishes. Come to think of it, these past few nights were the best sleep I've had in months. "You know? While I have no idea where I'm going, I'm actually sort of happy not to be at VOW-cubed."

"Glad to hear you say that. Believe me, something is right around the corner for you, and it will be beyond your wildest imagination."

After he leaves, I place our glasses into the dishwasher, my mind mulling over the next steps. My life has gone to shit after that fateful Tinsel and Tatas gala. If only Dad would tell me where to work next.

Hold up. Dad's steamrolled over my life since day one. It's my turn now. Taking stock of what I've amassed throughout my thirty-three years on this planet—this apartment, my wardrobe, tons of well-connected friends, media that fawns all over me—I'm golden.

I need to talk with someone who's made it on their own. Theo's only starting out on his path. While he encouraged me, he's not in a position to give me pointers. Same for Jesse with his fledgling furniture business.

PR genius Madison Welch pops into my mind, whom I dismiss. She's so *downtown*. Besides, she doesn't have the aura of success I aspire to, given her unstyled hair and stature that's as round as it's short. Plus her off-the-rack clothing.

Sebastian. Yes! My younger brother defied Dad and became world-renowned in the culinary field as Chef Bash. He must have some wisdom to impart. I grab my phone and hit FaceTime.

My brother appears on screen wearing his chef's hat and an apron over his bare chest. His signature style. "Yo, Xander, how's it going?" He takes off the hat and runs his fingers through his dark hair. Which matches mine, although he wears it longer.

"I didn't mean to interrupt the great Chef Bash," I tease. Dad hates it when we refer to him like that.

"We're on a break while the kitchen assistants prep the ingredients for the next recipe, so it's a good time. We just recorded our one-hundredth episode for YouTube."

My lungs expand at his achievement. "Congrats, bro. That's actually why I called you."

His eyebrows rise. "To congratulate me on recording shows? What's up?"

Sebastian knows me too well. "I am happy for your success, truly, but I'm calling to let you know that I quit VOW-cubed."

His mouth falls open, replaced by a smirk. "Didn't see that one coming."

"Well, long story short, the asshole head of the creditors' committee issued me an ultimatum. Either quit or he'd file a motion to oust me. I took the path of dignity."

He drops his chef's hat and claps. "Good choice."

More like *no* choice, but I don't go there. Offering him a feeble grin, I dive into the deep end. "Let's just say my conversation with Dad about it turned into a major blowout. Was he always so uncaring about us? How did you make your own way in the world without his help?"

His face morphs into a toothy smile. "Finally. I knew you'd break away eventually. Or, at least I hoped you would."

"You did?"

"Hell, yes." He mimes being on the phone to someone off-screen. "I only have a few minutes before I need to get back into makeup, so I'll be brief. We both know, or you're finally coming to realize, that Dad never gave two shits about us kids. We were a means to an end for him. A box to check off." He mimics holding a pen and making a checkmark. "So long as we did what we were told, without deviation, he bestowed his precious approval. Heaven forbid you make a left turn, though."

I remember when Sebastian was a model for a hot minute, and Dad booked him for one of our magazines to portray life as a chef. Which led him into a different field. "Like you did after the magazine layout. That certainly didn't end up the way Dad intended."

He chuckles. "You're right there. Only after I garnered over one million followers as Chef Bash did he reach out for another spread in the magazine. Which is in the trash now, given the indictments."

"Yeah." His planned article was scrapped when resources at the magazine became too stressed.

Another person comes into view and Sebastian nods. "Sorry, I have to go. Listen to your heart, and you'll be great." The screen goes black.

Guess I better find a marketing agency to join.

4

Madison

I boot up my computer and place my purse into my drawer. The past two weeks have been hell—the only bright spot when I actually spoke with Xander Turner at the b-school event. And that's only because how can anyone be stressed with such raw gorgeousness in front of them? I wish his golden touch had rubbed off on me.

At least I made three pitches for new clients. If I land any of the three, my concerns over my Agency will go away—for now. *If only Ellen hadn't moved across the country.* "Shut it. I tried my best."

Redirecting my nagging doubts about my presentations, I begin my Monday morning routine. When I pull up my emails, ones from all of the potential clients wait in my inbox. "When it rains, it pours." No one responds. Of course no one does since it's barely after seven.

I inhale and open the first email. "Thank you so much for your presentation, but we've decided to go with another firm." Not bothering to read it any further, I hop over to the second potential client, which contains the same bad news. I swallow and move my cursor over the third email.

And pray.

Clicking, I read, "We're interested in working with your agency, however, our budget has changed and we don't have the funds at this time. We will keep you in mind for the future."

Shoot. Effectively a third no. A sad chuckle leaves my mouth. Rejected three times and I've not even been fifteen minutes in the office.

I swivel my chair to stare out the window. From five stories up, I watch people strolling on the sidewalk on Fifth Avenue. Although I'm way downtown on Fifteenth Street, I made damn sure my Agency was on the illustrious boulevard. It's a bonus that I'm near Union Square, with its restaurants and amazing farmers' market. I love this neighborhood and my office space.

I don't want to have to give it up.

What would my employees do?

Despite being a thirty-year-old business owner, I want my mother.

Since she's at home in Kansas, I can't see her in person. Knowing she's a morning lark, I do the next best thing: pick up my cell and call her.

"How are you doing, sweetie?"

My chest is so heavy I lean forward and rest my forehead on my desk. "Oh, Ma. Since Ellen moved away, I've had to make my own pitches. I saw three potential clients over the past two weeks." I take a deep breath. "I just found out I didn't get any of them. And that's on top of another long string of rejections."

"Maddy. How awful. I'm sure you tried your very best. You're always so prepared."

"Thanks," I reply without animus. She is right. I was very prepared, but my tongue grew five sizes as soon as I walked into each of their conference rooms. "For all of them, I was my typical bad speaker. When I wasn't stumbling over my words, I was fumbling with the PowerPoint. My ideas were solid, but I couldn't present them worth a damn. Ellen would've reeled one of them in, I'm sure."

"Don't be so hard on yourself. Look at you! You have your very own PR firm in the Big Apple. How many other people can boast that feat?"

"Yeah, but for how much longer? If I can't get more clients, I'm going to have to close the doors." Pushing away from my desk, I stride over to the bookcase and turn on the television. NewsTime comes up. I mute the sound.

"I don't want to hear you talk like that. Aren't I speaking with the same woman who skipped not one, but TWO grades in elementary school?"

I plop down into my chair. "Kindergarten doesn't count, Ma."

"It's a required grade. And you tested out of it. Then you skipped third grade, too. No one in our small town has ever done that before. Or since."

I wave my hand. "That was long ago. No one here cares about my elementary schooling." My fingers grab a few strands of hair that cover my scar and pull them across my cheek. Without direction, my lips open and close around the locks.

"Do they care that you graduated high school at age sixteen? And moved to New York City—where you didn't know a single soul —after college, when you were only twenty? For heaven's sake, you couldn't even drink!"

I shrug. "Again. Those facts aren't important now. It's all about what I can do for the next client."

"Don't sell yourself short. You can do anything you set your mind to. Your father and me, plus your brother and sister, brag about you all the time. You're brilliant and have channeled your talents to helping people. Tell me, the clients you work with, aren't they happy with your ideas?"

"I guess so."

"You only guess? Didn't you read me that email from one of your clients who raved about your ideas and how you implemented them so their profits doubled in one month?"

I smile, remembering the exuberant email. "The Espositos. They were thrilled with my work. Their Soho deli is doing even better now."

"See? And what about the other client who invited you to their big shindig celebrating Valentine's Day?"

Memories of attending the event, complete with spotlights outdoors focused on the lingerie boutique, fill me with warmth. I loved getting the most exposure possible for the East Village store. I'm working with them now to boost their online presence. "I do love Sexy Unmentionables." Even their name rocks.

"So what if you've run into a string of bad luck recently? Your clients are thrilled to work with you. And why wouldn't they be? You're brilliant!"

I called Ma for a reason. I sit taller. I can do this. "Thanks. I really needed to hear this today. My firm isn't a good fit for everyone. Hell, one of the rejections said it wasn't me, but their budget, and they'll keep my Agency in mind."

"And I bet they will. You got this, sweetie."

I disconnect the call with a smile back on my face and optimism dancing in my soul. My work helps a lot of people. I'm ready to slay all the dragons and turn this ship around. Standing, I unmute the TV, which is showing a still of Xander Turner. My mouth goes dry. He is, by far, the hottest male specimen I've ever encountered.

The chyron announces, "Breaking News: NYC's Golden Boy Takes A Walk." How is this news? Don't we all walk in the City? The reporter states Xander quit his job at VOW-cubed. *Whoa. He didn't mention he was going to quit during the b-school event.*

A montage of images play. In one, Xander's expression isn't his normal resting face. It shows him appearing definitely annoyed with whatever the gaggle of reporters is asking him. Poor guy. I can relate. At least only *I* know about my three rejections, while the whole world now knows he's unemployed. Although, his situation seems to be his choice. I'm sure he'll land on his feet within a hot minute. Someone that sexy will be scooped up in a heartbeat.

For a nanosecond, the prospect of hiring him to take Ellen's place flits through my mind. Which immediately short circuits. I snort. Several reasons exist why this isn't even a remote possibility.

First, I'd never be able to talk with him coherently.

Second, I couldn't afford his salary.

Third, I'm a nobody and he's, well, a god among mortals.

If only I were taller and skinnier and prettier. My palm steals to my cheek. And unscarred. Then maybe I'd be more of a blip on the City's radar.

Shaking my head, I turn off the television and return to my chair. If I don't get myself in gear, my firm is going to fly over the edge. No more time for foolish nonsense about my gorgeous classmate.

I have a solid two hours' worth of work behind me when the door flings open and Dev makes his entrance. Love him, he's always upbeat and positive. I can use some of that now.

My administrative assistant plunks a takeaway cup onto my desk. "Here you go. One Caramel Frappuccino, no whip." He pretend-clinks his own takeout cup against mine, which I'm certain contains a double espresso. Because he needs more caffeine in his life.

I can't repress a smile. "Thanks." I remove the top and blow on the ambrosia, taking a gentle sip. "Perfect."

"I aim to please."

Instead of retreating behind his own desk, he settles his hip against the side of mine. "So, how was your weekend? Do anything fun?"

Fun? "Not if you count watching Netflix and eating ice cream."

His eyebrows pull together. "You need to get out more. What's a gorgeous doll like you staying in when this amazing City is your playground?"

"I get out. I also went out for brunch on Sunday." By myself. For take-out. I don't share this tidbit with him, though.

"That's better." He blows on his brew and takes a sip. A couple of minutes later—halfway through his espresso—Dev pops off my desk and turns the TV back on. "So, tell me, what's on the agenda for today?"

I pause in bringing my drink to my mouth. "I emailed you a list of things to do. I'm going to focus on finding potential clients this week." Sounds businesslike.

Dev nods and leaves for his desk while my other employees stream through the door. We exchange hellos, then they disappear down the hall to their own offices. Each one of them makes me proud that I've gathered enough clients to need them. This fact spurs me on to find more work.

"Geez, no wonder you have no social life." Dev strolls back into my office, holding a printout of my email. "Did you think up all this work for me to follow up on over one weekend?"

My mouth opens on a yawn, which I belatedly hide behind my palm. Shrugging, I reply, "I was on a tear."

"You can say that again." His eyes widen. "How on earth did you complete four client strategies on top of all this other stuff?"

"Lucky, I guess?" Not to mention motivated. These plans will lead to more work, which leads to more income. Of course, each project is necessary. I'm not bilking our clients.

Dev walks around my desk. As I'm reviewing the site that lists open RFPs, I let him peer over my shoulder. His index finger points to the screen. "How many of these interest you?"

"I'd say most of them. I could help them achieve their stated goals, with innovative ideas. If only—" I clamp my mouth shut. No need to worry him. I carry enough worry for the both of us.

"I bet you could. Your ideas are the bomb. But—" He doesn't complete his sentence.

I yawn again. And take the bait. "But what?"

Dev lowers to his knees in front of me, taking my hands in his. "Don't take this the wrong way, but you need help. You look like shit. Have you thought about hiring someone else to replace Ellen?"

I yank my hands out of his and cross my arms across my chest. "Thanks," my clipped tone conveys my thoughts about his comment. My hand grabs some of my hair and cups my cheek with it, hiding my scar more fully.

He rises to his full height. "I wasn't trying to offend you. I worry about you." His expressive brown eyes plead with me to believe him.

He's never reacted to my appearance with the repulsion I'm

used to, which is one of the reasons I hired him in the first place. He's always been supportive. My shoulders hunch—he is a good guy. "And I appreciate it, Dev. I really do. I'm doing everything I can to bring in new work."

He taps my shoulders, which lower into their rightful position. "I know you are. I also know how much you hate public speaking. Ellen was the face of the Agency, and you two worked well together. Why don't you try to offload that chore to someone else? So, maybe, you could get some sleep."

NewsTime replays its piece about Xander's quitting VOW-cubed. Ignoring the drool-worthy images, I focus on my assistant. "I know you're right. Ellen was fantastic, and she was here for almost three years. But I can't snap my fingers and *poof!* the perfect candidate will appear. I don't have the bandwidth to deal with it now."

Dev nods in apparent understanding, his eyes bouncing away from me to glance at the television. His arm snakes out toward the TV. "Hire him. Seems like he's in need of a job."

I follow his pointer finger to the television, where an upset Xander awaits. Damn. He is fine. Coming to my senses, I retort, "I might as well try to hire George Clooney." Or David Gandy.

"Just sayin' his mug would look mighty nice around here." He offers a wicked smile, complete with a wink.

I flick my wrist. "Go. Get out of here. You have a long list of to-do's."

Dev opens his arms wide. "All good?"

As if I could stay upset with him. "Of course. Now, go, or I'll change my mind."

He gives me a salute and returns to his desk.

I try to focus on my screen, but my eyes betray me and I rewatch Xander's segment until the end, then shut off the television. Is Dev onto something here? Ellen was a pretty woman, and we both had our sneaking suspicions her looks upped the firm's appeal and helped us land some difficult clients. Xander's objectively a million times better-looking than Ellen ever was.

His woes at VOW-cubed don't seem to have anything to do with him. All the negative press surrounding his father and *his* partners doesn't reflect on the son's ethics or morals—that is, if they even broke the law. People are arrested all the time for things they didn't commit. Look at the recent news cycle about convicted murderers found later to be innocent. Besides, don't I tell my clients that the only bad press is none at all? His presence could amp up the profile of the Madison Welch PR Agency.

My mind wanders back to the b-school event and how alive I felt standing in his orbit. He practically radiated an energy that drew everyone in and held them in his thrall. *Not me.* Other people were wrapped up in him. The fact he resembles my favorite model doesn't figure into this equation. Heck, Dev was drawn to him and he only saw him on television. And Xander definitely doesn't play on Dev's team. Although I bet my admin wished he would.

I close my eyes to block out my wayward thoughts. Xander might be the answer to my prayers. If he's actually looking for a new job. Minus a few zeros he's used to from a VOW-cubed salary.

He probably isn't.

This idea is nuts.

I force my attention back to my computer and continue my search through the RFPs. I land on a most unusual one—a wolf preserve in upstate New York. A shudder screams throughout every limb and my fingers run over the scar left behind by a nasty pit bull when I was only five. I'd been in kindergarten for only a couple of weeks when the attack happened on a class trip to a petting zoo, causing me to refuse to return to school. As a result, Ma got me tested and I was able to jump to first grade.

For some reason, Xander's face pops up in my mind. I bet he wouldn't be afraid to confront the wolves. Heck, he's so damn gorgeous, they'd probably acknowledge him as their alpha. I force myself to read the description of their needs and know the Agency could provide excellent service to them. But *I* can't. No matter how much I sympathize with their plight.

Dev bounces into my office. "Here you go!" A brown paper bag lands on my desk. "Turkey and sprouts on a wrap with mustard. And an apple." He makes a face. "Don't know how you eat that."

My stomach rumbles despite his description of my boring lunch. "You're too good to me."

Dev plants his ass on my desk again. "I am, aren't I?"

His grin is contagious, and I smile up at him. "And humble." I pull out my sandwich and smooth the bag down as if it were a placemat.

"Hey, listen. I didn't mean to insult you before. I only have your best interests at heart and I can tell you're drowning here."

"I know. And I appreciate it." I unwrap my sandwich and divide it into two. The diet I started today tells me to only eat half of a meal, so I dutifully re-wrap the other half. I pick up my lunch and take a nibble—remembering to slow down my natural tendency and devour it in three bites. After I swallow, I reply, "I'm still thinking about what I want to do. Circle back with me at the end of the week."

"You got it, boss." He hops off my desk. "I better get cracking on that humongous list you gave me. Can't be thought of as a slacker."

Alone again, I finish my sandwich way too quickly. How can I best help the Agency? Clearly, trying my hand at pitching isn't doing the job. I glance at the blank television screen.

Dare I?

What's the worst thing he could say? No?

My heart does a double-flip as I contemplate taking Dev up on his suggestion. Xander is qualified, and out of a job. But I don't have his number.

Although he and Jesse seemed pretty chummy at the b-school event. Before I can talk myself out of this stupid idea, I grab my cell phone and call my friend. If he has Xander's number, I'll consider it a sign from the Fates I'm meant to reach out to him. And if he doesn't, I'll return to the drawing board.

Without a sexy new employee.

5

Xander

I get out of the limo in an area of the City I haven't visited since I was going for my MBA. The shops are downscale from those I'm used to in the Upper East Side, where I live—or even in midtown where our offices are. Correction. Where VOW-cubed offices are located. Not mine.

Which brings me to the reason I'm in this neighborhood. I replay the phone call I had with Jesse, when he asked if he could give Madison Welch my number. He acted as if I wouldn't remember her. I didn't correct his mistaken assumption, but I did allow him to pass on my info.

While my eyes scan the dingy sidewalk and streets, my lips turn downward. Coming here every day—to *work*—gives me the heebie-jeebies. I'd leave, but the limo's already down the block. I refuse to make a spectacle of myself and draw attention to the fact I'm downtown.

I stride by another bodega before reaching One-Hundred Sixteen. I pause and look up, counting twelve stories. Far cry from my fifty-second-floor office overlooking Central Park, which wasn't even on the top story of the skyscraper. I square my shoulders. This is only a practice job interview. I'm sure more requests will come in and I want to be on top of my game.

Someone walks out of the building wearing casual clothing and I slip inside, running my palm down my blue tie that matches my eyes. Darcey loved this tie and always commented on it.

Why did I think of that bitch now, before going on my practice interview?

Shaking my head, I approach the front desk and give my name and identification, where I receive a stick-on badge reminiscent of the b-school event and am directed to the fifth floor.

Fifth floor? I could run up the stairs. Deciding I shouldn't show up to an interview sweaty, I take the elevator and enter the Madison Welch PR Agency.

"May I help you?" a young girl singsongs from the desk directly in front of me. She must be sixteen, but appears at least three years younger than the legal working age.

With my professional mask firmly in place, I approach her. "Hello. I have a meeting with Madison Welch."

The girl gives me the usual once over. "Lucky her." When I don't respond, she continues, "I'll call her to let her know you're here." Her hand lands on the headset. "May I have your name?"

"Xander Turner."

She nods and places the call. "Madison will be right out. Please take a seat."

"Thanks." I wander over to the small seating area, which has two chairs and a tiny coffee table covered with magazines. Some business ones, while others are City-centric, like *Spill It Magazine*. I don't bother to pick any of them up, instead unbuttoning my navy blazer and palming my phone. I know how things like this go. It's a tried-and-true power play. Ask the interviewee to arrive a half-hour before you plan on meeting with them. I'm guilty of doing the very same thing.

I pull up a game and am in the second round when a female voice reaches my ears. "Xander. I'm so sorry for keeping you waiting. A client called unexpectedly."

Surprised at Madison's almost punctual appearance, I slide my phone back into my pocket and rise. "Believe me, this wasn't a wait." I offer her a friendly smile. My eyes land on her interesting pin, which looks like a dragonfly. Pretty. After the NYU event where she acted all weird when I complimented her on her frog pin, I keep this observation to myself.

She pulls her hair across her cheek. Using her left arm, she motions into the office proper. "Why don't we talk inside?"

I nod and let her lead me into the corporate office. I pass by a small room bracketed by window walls with a desk outside of it, plus a small hallway that leads to a few other offices. The walls are decorated with framed photographs of people and stores, some with handwritten notes. It's jarringly comfortable. When we enter what seems to be the only conference room, a guy jumps to his feet. His hair is platinum white.

"Oh, hello there."

He approaches me, standing half a head shorter than me, but still towering over the vertically-challenged Madison. When she doesn't introduce us, I extend my hand. "Hi, I'm Xander Turner."

We shake. "I'm Devlin Tate, but everyone calls me Dev. I'm Madison's administrative assistant."

"Nice to meet you."

He steps back and claps his hands. "There's water and a carafe of coffee over there." He motions toward the opposite wall. "Help yourself." At my nod, he adds, "Well, I'll let you two get to it." He rushes out of the room.

"Dev's a fantastic assistant. I'm lucky to have him," Madison jumps into the vortex left by her employee. "Water? Coffee?"

My mouth feels as dry as the Sahara. I've never been one prone to nerves, but this whole situation is outside my comfort zone. "Water would be great, thanks."

She passes me a bottle, and we slide into our seats around the oval conference room table. Oval. Given the size of the room, it was a wise choice, although I've never attended a meeting at one. I open the cap and take a swig, trying to find my Zen. Placing the bottle onto the table, I give Madison my undivided attention.

"So, uhm, I'm very glad you decided to come in and meet with me. I hope you didn't have any problems finding the office?"

I bite my tongue, choosing not to tell her the family limo dropped me off. Instead, I say, "No. It was pretty straightforward."

Her gaze bounces around the room—to windows looking into another brick building— and finally lands about three inches above my head. "Great. So, I'll get right to it. I heard you may be, uhm, in search of a new position. I'd like to discuss you coming to work with me. Here."

No idle chit-chat. I like it. Donning a smile, I reply, "I'm flattered you thought of me. What type of role are you looking to fill?"

"A Senior PR Rep." She inhales. "In addition to routine publicity matters, your primary duties would include making pitches to potential clients. Of course, I would oversee the creation of the strategy, but you'd be the face of the Agency."

This is a lot to unpack. I've never done public relations before. Seems like she's throwing me into the deep end. "You want me to do pitches?"

Madison nods. "Yeah." She clears her throat. "Yes. I've seen how you handle yourself in group settings, and how comfortable you are with public speaking. I want," she opens a water bottle and takes a sip. "I'm looking to fill a position a wonderful employee just vacated because her husband got a job in Seattle and she had to move. She did all of my pitches, and her record was fifty-five percent."

"So you're looking for a closer?" I've never considered myself to fit this role, but I did sign a majority of the advertisers for the VOW-cubed magazines. I bet the skill set is transferable.

She shrugs. "In a sense."

How can this position sound intriguing? *Get a grip, Xander.* I continue with the charade. "And once I bring in a new client, who will service them?"

"Ellen kept a select few for herself, but mainly passed them along to one of the other reps."

I nod. "How often do these pitches come up?" I can't imagine it's more than one a month.

"Usually two a week, sometimes three."

My mask slips as I'm shocked by her number. "Wow. I didn't

expect that many." I take another sip of water. "What's the average budget from each of these clients?"

"It varies, of course." She passes her water bottle between her hands. "They're in the low or middle four figures or so."

Now I get it. I would've expected the budgets to be mid-five figures. At least. "No wonder you pitch so often."

Her voice takes on an edge of defensiveness. "I'm working up to higher budgets."

Only a practice interview, Xander—no need to insult her. I raise my hands. "I wasn't passing any judgments."

She accepts my explanation with a quick head bob. "Anyway, given the number of pitches, you can understand why I'm looking for help."

Madison sits back in her chair. Her hair flies away from the side of her face and I notice a discoloration on it—perhaps a birthmark? In b-school, there was talk about something on her cheek but I never paid too much attention. Ignoring whatever it is, I ask, "How many of these pitches would you expect me to do?"

She covers the mark with some hair. "All of them."

Holy shit. I understand why this Ellen wasn't able to work on any of the accounts she brought in. "Don't you like to meet your clients before you bring them into the office?"

"Oh, I attend most of the pitches."

Then why doesn't she simply do them? I keep this thought to myself, as her posture has morphed to match the defensive tone. Changing the subject, I ask, "Can you explain what all is involved with servicing your clients?"

Visibly relaxing, Madison launches into a complete dissertation of how she helps her clients with PR. Must admit, her approach is admirable. Her roster seems to be loyal. The longer she talks, no matter how improbable, the more intrigued I become with her Agency. And I can almost make ends meet with her financial package in addition to my trust fund.

One last elephant in the room remains. "I have to say, Madison, this all sounds extremely interesting to me. If I'm honest, I've been jealous of you for a while now."

Her head whips toward me, and we establish solid eye contact for the first time. Her blue eyes are a much lighter shade than mine, brimming with intelligence. "*You*, you've been jealous. Of *me*?"

"I thought it would be cool to work with a variety of different clients, rather than be in-house to the magazines. I was stuck in the family business, and I knew it, but admired your entrepreneurial spirit and ability to be on different projects." All of this is true. Perhaps this job would be a good proving ground? But it's so … *downtown*.

She tucks her hair behind her right ear, exposing what now appears to be more of a scar than a blemish. A nanosecond later, she pulls the locks forward again, her cheek disappearing under a veil of blond hair. "I don't know what to say."

"I didn't mean to embarrass you. I was only stating the truth." While I'm enjoying this interview, I'm sure I'll be fielding plenty more suitable offers soon. Might as well continue with one more practice question for her. "Which leads me to another truth—are you really serious about wanting me to work here, considering all the press documenting my every movement in unflattering terms these days?"

She returns her hands to the table and steeples her fingers. "I'm in PR you know. Obviously, your family's business is being hounded by the media. But now that you're no longer working for VOW-cubed, I fail to see why reporters would continue being so interested in you. After all, you're not accused of doing anything illegal."

Like Dad. Madison doesn't complete her sentence. She's polite like that. Reassuring her, I say, "And I won't." I pull the water bottle to my lips and sip. "My father and his partners didn't do anything wrong, either, and I'm sure the charges will be dropped soon. They're going to be filing a motion to dismiss the indictment."

Madison nods once. "See? The lack of a story will make reporters move on to more exciting pastures."

Then I'll return to VOW-cubed, and everything will be normal again. But it still could take months, and I need to find something to do until then. Uptown. "Thank you. And thanks for inviting me in to discuss this position. I'd like to think about your offer, if that's alright with you?"

"Of course." She pushes away from the oval table and stands to her full, diminutive height. "I appreciate your coming in today. Would you like me to show you around the office?"

Manners require my assent. "Please." I follow her down the hallway, and she waves to her reps. Everyone seems friendly. And relaxed. I'm the only one in a suit. As we're walking to the front, I ask, "Your office is business casual, huh?"

"Oh yes. Unless there's a client meeting, then we wear proper business attire. Everyone has a suit or two hanging in the coat closet." She points toward a closed door. "I can't understand why working in comfortable clothing is a negative."

Makes sense, although VOW-cubed always required a degree of formality. Surprising myself, I agree Madison's philosophy is smart. "I bet your reps are more creative in clothing they prefer."

"Exactly." We reach the front, outside the receptionist's desk. "I really liked chatting with you today, Xander. I hope you'll consider my offer—among all the others I'm sure you're entertaining—and get back to me with a *yes*. I think we'd have a good time working together." She raises her fist.

I oblige her with a bump. Not very professional. More like buddies at the gym. "I promise to let you know soon."

J esse hands me a bourbon and sips on his own Guinness. We scored a high top at a busy bar uptown since we got here before the rush. "You're a lucky bastard, you know that, right?"

I shake my head at my friend. "I don't see how you can even call me that. I'm an unemployed son of an indicted businessman, who's trailed by the paparazzi everywhere I go." Case in point, I tilt my chin toward the sidewalk where five reporters are stationed.

"You're handling it like a pro, though." He raises his pilsner. "Mr. Cool."

I return the gesture with my glass. "Ha! I wish. I want to shake them by the throat most of the time." Like when I arrived here and had to navigate through the gaggle outside. They asked me myriad questions about Dad and VOW-cubed, as if I still worked there and had any insider knowledge. Not like my father and uncles ever shared too much with me when I *did* work for them.

"Well, you keep your emotions hidden."

I sip my drink and bang my glass against the table. That's me. Never let them see your highs or lows—my mantra since the Tinsel and Tatas Gala. I take a longer drag of my bourbon.

Swallowing, I state, "I asked to meet you here because I met with Madison the other day."

His eyebrows raise. "So you took the interview?"

"Yeah. And she offered me a job." My finger circles the rim of my glass. How do I frame this? "It's a totally different experience from anything I've ever known."

"I like her office. It's relaxed, but crackling with creativity, you know?"

I tilt my head. "You've been there?"

"Hell yes. I was there for the ribbon cutting a few years back and stop by every so often when I'm in her neck of the woods. Usually on the weekends."

"I'm shocked she works the weekends. Doesn't seem the type." At his questioning look, I add, "She seems much more relaxed than being a weekend work warrior."

Jesse chuckles. "Don't be fooled by her upbeat demeanor. Inside, she's a true shark willing to take on the world."

I tuck this tidbit into the back of my mind. I could call Madison Welch many things, but a shark isn't one of them. "I'm not sure I'm going to sign on the dotted line, though."

"Really? What other offers are you considering?"

That's the crux of my issue. I've reached out to friends and other business associates, but no one seems to have any openings. I tap the edge of my glass. "None at the moment. But I'm not sold her firm's a good fit."

He pauses in bringing his beer to his mouth. "Madison's building a solid PR agency. You've mentioned to me before how much you'd like to work with different clients instead of being stuck with the magazine advertisers. What's stopping you?" He tips his drink.

"For one, them." I point toward the reporters. "Plus, the—culture—down there is so foreign from anything I've experienced."

He takes a handful of pretzels and munches. "So what you're saying is that you're too good for her."

I lean back as his words land a direct strike. That's not it at all. I've only worked at VOW-cubed, located in midtown, with offices spanning five floors. Hell, my corner office was on the fifty-second floor with a view of Central Park, while hers is on the fifth floor near Union Square. Her clients have almost minuscule budgets. Dad wouldn't hesitate to tell me taking this job is a giant leap downward.

My friend interrupts my woolgathering. "You know, I've implemented some of the ideas she gave me at the b-school event. They've been right on the money. Meaning, I'm already starting to see a small turnaround in my furniture business. If this trajectory continues, I'll be able to quit the bank in a matter of months."

"You're making that much?"

He smacks the side of my head. "No, stupid. I'm not replacing my salary, but I have money saved. I'm thinking my side hustle will pull in enough for me to make a full-time run at it soon."

Jesse's following his dreams of working with his hands rather than behind a desk. Madison's already living her truth. And me? Without VOW-cubed, I'm adrift. "I'm happy for you, man."

"Don't you want to be a part of a company helping others achieve their dreams? Or would you prefer to stay in publishing?"

"Publishing is all I know."

"You got your MBA from NYU. If I remember correctly, you took a shitload of marketing classes. You're qualified to explore beyond the walls your father erected around you."

His statement is reminiscent of my conversation with Sebastian. I'm ready to bust out of those damn walls. "You're not wrong."

"I think you're in the catbird seat. You have a fantastic offer handed to you on a silver platter. Madison's one of the smartest people I know, and I have faith in her." He pushes my shoulder backward. "Just like I believe in you."

I swirl the amber liquid. Jesse's one of my best friends. I can afford to show him some vulnerability, knowing he won't share it with anyone. "You do?"

"Hell yes."

"I wish I felt the same." I tap my glass on the high top. "I'm not sure I'll be any good at this PR stuff."

"Dude, you won't know until you try. From what I gather, you were pretty ace with advertising at VOW-cubed." He finishes his Guinness.

I scoff. "I was selling ad space and working with clients on their campaigns. Public relations is much different."

Jesse motions for our server to bring the check. "Madison clearly thinks your skills are a good fit. And I trust her instincts implicitly."

Backed into a corner, I retreat to humor. "Says the compliance officer who's throwing it all away to make tables." I hold up my hands to let him know I'm only teasing. *His* skills are amazing.

He blows on his fingers. "Yeah. I'm the bomb." We both laugh. "And, on that note, I need to get going. I have an early morning appointment with my hammer before I have to leave for the office." The server drops off our check and he pulls out his wallet.

This is the time when I usually tell him that I'm covering the tab. But with my uncertain income staring me in the face, I keep my mouth shut and grab my wallet. We split the bill, no matter how uncomfortable it makes me.

As he leaves, he says, "Keep me posted. Can't wait to hear what you decide."

Alone at the table, I continue sipping my bourbon and pondering the possibility of working with Madison to get some experience under my belt before opening my own firm. Drink finished, I check out the window, where a gaggle of paps lies in wait. For me.

Pulling out my phone, I text Jimmy, our family's vehicle concierge, to request a car. When the limo pulls up, I take a large breath and slip my mask back in place. Must never show any weakness or I'm toast. They need to believe I'm living my best life, with or without a job.

Leaving the bar, I ignore the shouts for my attention. Ensconced inside the vehicle, I lean against the headrest. Like always when the weather's overcast, traffic is fierce. Horns blaring, lights preventing more than an inch of movement for blocks. About ten minutes from my apartment, I ask to be dropped off. The walk will do me good.

My mind whirls around Madison's job offer. The salary's low but my emergency fund will supplement it. Should I take it?

Not like I have any other options.

I wait for the light to change and a rumble of thunder pulls my attention away from my own problems. Tilting my head upward, I scan the now-black sky filled with rain-laden clouds. *Great.* I always beat the rain home, though.

I pick up the pace, passing by upscale boutiques, food markets, and museums. Across the street is Central Park. I bet Madison lives in Brooklyn. Not that there's anything wrong with the borough at all. Some stellar restaurants are there. But Manhattan is where everything happens—parties, clubs, galas.

Like my desert of interviews, I've not been invited to many of them lately.

Jesse's high on Madison. He likes and trusts her, and her ideas are helping him move forward. Should I take the job to learn how to run my own company? Uptown, of course, with clients wielding bigger budgets.

A streak of lightning crosses the sky, immediately followed by thunder. The clouds open up, drenching me in an instant. Soaking wet, I dash the remaining block to my apartment.

Memories of being hailed as NYC's "Golden Boy" mock me. This better not be a sign.

6

Madison

"I am delighted to accept your offer. Looking forward to starting on Monday."

Re-reading the text from Xander, I fan my cheeks. The past days of waiting and worrying evaporate under the hope he can come in and switch things up around here. If nothing else, he'll be able to make our pitches sound even better. How could he not? Whatever comes out of his mouth is automatically bumped up two notches, considering the delivery vehicle.

I picture him walking in through the office doors, all tall and dark and sexy as sin. *Stop it, Madison. He's going to be your employee.* Sighing, I amend my thought. Tall and dark and will have every potential client eating out of his hand. *Better.*

Still sexy. A smirk passes my face.

My ringing phone pulls me out of my daydream. Picking it up, I answer, "Hey, Stephanie. How are you doing?"

"Great," she responds. "Want to come with me to the mall? I don't want to go by myself."

"You know what, that sounds like fun." I deserve a little treat for landing my first whale of an employee. Stifling my giggle, I reply, "Meet you in an hour."

Strapping my purse crossbody, I stop by Dev's desk. "Meeting Stephanie for some retail therapy and then I'm going home. Have a great weekend."

"You too. Enjoy!"

With my assistant's jaunty words, I leave the office and take the train to Brooklyn. Inside the mall, by an upscale lingerie chain, I meet up with Stephanie. After browsing their gorgeous underwear sets, I pick up new blue cotton panties and matching bra. Of course, I had to rummage to the back of the rack for mine, while Stephanie's perfect 34B was up front. Packages in hand, we go to a department store to try on some clothes neither one of us could ever afford, laugh at each other's bad jokes, and generally have a wonderful afternoon.

Sitting in the food court, Stephanie moans about her Kung Pao Chicken. "Here. Want to try?" She offers me her fork filled with the delicious-looking food.

I shake my head. "I wish." I hold up my half tuna salad sandwich. "I'm trying to stick with the diet plan."

"Hope this one does it for you. I've given up."

She swallows her Chinese food, which journeys into her perfect figure. Can't imagine why she thinks she needs to lose any weight. "Says the size eight woman sitting across from me."

"Used to be a four. I'm much happier with these extra pounds."

If only. Because Stephanie's four inches taller than me, her frame hides many sins. I take a small bite of the tuna.

She gives me a quick glance. "I have some news." Her fork dives back into the large pile of food on her Styrofoam plate. "You know I volunteer with Friends For Fun, right?" At my nod, she continues, "More kids are signing up. So—they're putting together an RFP for a PR firm to recruit more adults to help out."

"Oh really?"

She takes a sip of her soda. I'm sure it's not the diet sitting in front of me. "I took the liberty of telling Vanessa, who runs the charity, all about you. She'll keep an eye out for your bid when the time comes."

"You did? Wow. Thank you so much." I suck my zero-calorie

soda through my straw and then drop my own bomb. "Which I'll discuss with my new employee on Monday, who will be doing the pitch."

"Oh really? She's replacing Ellen?"

I bring my cup in front of my face to hide my smile. "Yes, he is."

Stephanie's mouth drops open. "A him?" Her shoulders fall. "Please tell me he isn't going to be more interested in Dev than you."

I giggle and place my forearms on the table. This is fun. "He's straight. And you know him."

Her head tilts. "Who is it?"

I inhale. "Xander Turner."

"Holy hell!"

At her scream, everyone around us stops talking and turns toward us. "Shhh," I admonish. "People are looking at us." My fingers run through my hair to ensure my scar's covered.

She leans forward. "You hired *the* Xander Turner? From b-school?" She extends both of her hands, palms up. "Touch me. I need your mojo."

Shaking my head, I take another bite of my sandwich. "I saw he quit his job, so I knew he was open to a new opportunity. I asked Jesse to get me his number and invited him in for an interview. He accepted."

She takes three more bites. "Sounds too easy. C'mon, give me more than that."

"Seriously, that's all it is. But I will say, he wore this amazing navy blue suit to the interview, which matched his eyes." I sigh. "I'm going to be his boss, so no, there will be no sexual harassment suits brought against me." *As if.*

"If for nothing else, he'll sure brighten up that drab office."

"Hey. My office is not drab. It's cozy."

She laughs. "And Xander's not good-looking, he's freaking fine."

I lift up my fork. "Touché." Hers clinks against mine and we finish our lunches.

"I need to be heading home. Thanks for coming here with me."

She holds up her few bags of clothing that actually fit her and were in her budget. "I had a blast."

"Me, too." I hold up my bag from the lingerie store plus another from a cheapy jewelry store containing my new pin, a leaf with a dew drop on it that reminded me of home. We stand and someone walks by, their perfume wafting feet in front of her. "Rats. I forgot I need to pick up more perfume."

"Can't imagine what triggered this thought."

I shrug. "No idea." We smile at each other. "I'll stop by the fragrance counter on my way out. You don't have to come with me. Let's do this again soon."

"Definitely." Stephanie opens her arms and we exchange a quick hug.

At the perfume area of the mall's anchor department store, I pass by several booths until reaching Dolce and Gabbana. Standing by the poster of my favorite model, I pick up a bottle of "The One" and spritz it onto my wrist. It's the perfect scent—the advertising describes it as "bergamot and mandarin, notes of lychee and peach, and ending with a delicious deep vanilla." I sniff my wrist and agree. A clerk comes over and I request a bottle, and she indicates she has to get it from the back.

While I wait, I lift my hair off my neck and wave my hand in front, trying to alleviate the heat in here. Why are all malls either too hot or too cold?

Tucking my hair behind my ears, I pull up Instagram. To torture myself, I click on Xander's profile and scroll through his drool-worthy photos My next swipe turns up his engagement photo. I know their engagement ended later that night with the arrests, but they both are so happy here. *To have someone look at me with that expression.* None of my boyfriends ever approached this level of love, even post-orgasm. No. All of the guys I've been with have been introverted and nerdy. I square my shoulders. Nothing wrong with those qualities. Just wish I could get a little taste of the love shown here.

The clerk returns and I click my phone off. Once I pay, I push my hair out of my face again and turn. A couple in the aisle pushes a stroller, so I wait for them to pass. The boy in the stroller, about two, points at me. At the top of his lungs, he yells, "Look! Yucky!"

My entire body seizes. I pull my hair to cover up my scar, but the damage has been done. Others in the mall turn toward the ruckus, causing me to want to disappear into the floor. For their part, his parents shush their son, and the mother offers me a sympathetic glance. The husband murmurs, "Sorry," and they triple-time it away from the perfume counter and the "yucky woman."

I should be used to this reaction since I've had this scar before I jumped over kindergarten. But I'm not. Pain and embarrassment and desolation war inside my body while my pulse escalates. Escape. I need to get out of here.

The clerk reappears and points toward another booth. In a soothing tone, she whispers, "We sell some amazing creams for scars."

I want to yell at her that I've tried all of them, multiple times. None of them do anything, no matter the cost. Cocoa butter, five-hundred-dollar creams, even olive oil. Nothing. Still, hope springs eternal. Because I can feel tears welling behind my eyes, I give her a quick nod and scurry in the direction she indicated. Maybe this time will be different.

At the counter, I ask about the lotion and suffer the indignity of having to show the rep my scar. Thankfully, she doesn't comment on the mark left behind so many years ago. She bends down and gives me this snake oil. That's not fair. I've never tried this cream. So, I turn over my credit card, add it to my bag, and dash out of the mall.

When I get home, I throw my new underwear set into the laundry, put my new perfume next to my almost empty bottle, and bring the cream into my bathroom where I slather it over the ugly scar. Chocolate. I deserve something delicious to help ease the pain of this afternoon. Placing the jar into the medicine cabinet, I retreat to my kitchen and remove the makeshift lock I put in place when I started this new diet a week ago. When the pantry is open, I survey the variety of chocolate bars waiting for me and take a few with me to the sofa. Turning on the television, the Hallmark channel comes up. Two gorgeous, tall, unblemished people gaze into each other's eyes. Pretty soon they'll be kissing.

No way would anyone look at me like this in a million years. Like Xander looked at his ex-fiancée. What good-looking guy would ever deign to adore such a short, fat, scarred woman like me? Xander's stunning face pops into my mind and I banish him from my realm of the ordinary. Such fantabulousness has no place in my world. I switch the channel to music and let the sounds of calming yoga music wash over me.

As I'm diving into my second—or is it third?—chocolate bar, my phone rings. Without any interest, I check the screen and my sister's name appears. I always answer calls from my family, no matter what I'm doing. Wallowing in self-pity notwithstanding.

"Hey, Macy. How are you doing?"

"I'm good. You know how things go out here in Kansas. Everything stays the same."

Swallowing the last bit of my chocolate bar, I reply, "Sometimes status quo can be good. How's Randall doing? And the kids?" Her husband's a truck driver, so he's not home for long stretches at a time. Which leaves my sister with their two kids, but Ma and Pops help out, so her family's well taken care of.

"They're doing fine. They're enjoying school, which is such a relief."

Noticing some chocolate on the pad of my pinky, I lick my finger. "What's not to like when you're in second and fifth grades?"

She laughs. "You're right. Plus, Randall called and he should be home in a few days."

"That's good. How long will he be home this time?"

"I'm not sure, but at least a couple of weeks. So that gives me plenty of time to tell him the news." She takes an elongated pause. "I'm pregnant again!"

A lightness zooms throughout my body. "Oh wow. Congratulations! I knew you wanted to have three kids like we had growing up."

"Exactly. I think a family of three is the perfect amount."

While she shares her good news, I return to the kitchen and snag another candy bar. I'm excited for her. She always wanted to be a mother, and now she will be three times over. Wish she could send some of that pixie dust my way. Perhaps it's only stationed over Kansas?

"Have you told Ma yet?"

"No way. You know she can't keep a secret!"

Her impassioned response lures me out of my personal doldrums and brings a true smile to my face—my first real one since the toddler screamed in the mall. "You're right. Remember the time we were trying to have a surprise birthday party for Pops? She lasted maybe a full day."

We break into laughter.

"And that's"—Macy catches her breath—"Why we never tell her anything unless we want the whole neighborhood to know."

"Absolutely." I chuckle again. "I'm very happy for you guys. What do you hope it is?"

"We already have two girls, so of course, Randall will want a boy. I'll be happy so long as the peanut is healthy."

"C'mon. Don't you want a little boy? Mark has a boy and a girl —you don't want our brother to be the only one to have both genders do you?"

"Fine," she huff-laughs. "I do want a boy, too. They have such cute baby clothes."

"Thought so," I snap off another square of chocolate. "What can I do? Do you need anything?"

"No, I'm good. I wish you could be here for when I tell Randall and our parents, but I get you're a busy New York City gal now."

I savor the melty chocolate. "Sorry. I'll take a trip home for the BBQ cook-off this summer."

"Oh, great! I'll be early in my third trimester by then. That'll be perfect!" She blinks a few times before asking her usual, dreaded question. "Have you gone on any exciting dates lately?"

A picture of Xander floats through my mind, which I banish. "Nah. Married to my work, you know." Our conversation continues for a while, then we hang up with more congratulations on her pregnancy.

Sneaking another candy bar, I flop onto my sofa. I'm genuinely happy for my sister—I'm well aware of how much she wants a third child.

But … When will it be my turn? Will I ever meet Mr. Right here in the City? Should I move back home and try my luck there?

Xander's text calls to me again. Even though I realize we'll never be more than friends, he makes me want to stay here. Boys back there don't come close to being half as handsome. Besides, the big clients are here.

But can a Kansas transplant ever find her barbeque in the big city?

7

Madison

I finish reading the draft and call Bonnie into my office. When she sits down, I cut right to the chase. "Your ideas are fantastic."

Her face morphs from concern to elation, pushing her glasses higher on her forehead. "You really think so?"

My head bobs so fast my hair skims against my shoulders. "I do." I point to my screen. "I never would've thought of partnering with a bakery."

Her chin lifts. "Thanks. I'm proud of this plan. The synergies between the companies will be excellent." She takes off her glasses and cleans them on her shirt. "Now to figure out which bakery would be the proper fit."

I run through our roster of clients and land on one. Once I say the name out loud, Bonnie replaces her glasses. "Oh, I didn't think of them. They'd be great. Let me talk with Elisabeth to see if they'd be interested." She hops up and leaves my office.

Happy with this turn of events, I stand and stare out my window. New York City is coming alive with the change of seasons. Well, if you count five straight days of rain as Spring. But where I'm from, rain is a harbinger of good crops and the promise of summer. Kansas positivity is ingrained and refuses to be quashed.

I've spoken with all my employees about the status of their cases, and everyone's doing great. Our clients are getting fabulous service. If only there were more of them.

Which leads me to my newest hire. Xander. Over this week, I've introduced him to everyone. Even took the whole office out to a welcome lunch. I've given him pointers about how to find clients and had Dev sit with him for tips. Xander still wears suits to work—which fit him better than material has a right to do, *not that I'm looking*—but he's been leaving his jacket in his office. Loosening up. Fitting into the culture here. All good.

However, I haven't seen anything from him. No emails or proposals. Although it's only been a week, I shouldn't put off checking in on him.

Before I cross my office, I give myself a pep talk. *He's just a guy. Pants on one leg at a time. Great. Now I'm thinking about his legs. And muscular thighs.* Inhaling, I leave my office and walk down the hall, stopping before his door.

"Knock, knock."

"Come in!"

With a final deep breath, I enter his space. Neat piles of paper line his desk. Behind it, Xander sits with a pen in his mouth and fingers flying over the keyboard. His dark blue gaze meets mine. *Damn.*

"Hey, I was about to print out my proposal and bring it in to you."

Lightness fills my limbs. "Oh, great. I was stopping by to see how you're settling in."

He removes the pen and brilliant white teeth emerge from beneath his pillowy lips. "I'm loving it." He presses a key, presumably to print his document. Pushing away from his desk, he stands and my neck extends upward to maintain eye contact. "Let me go to the printer and I'll meet you in your office in a few."

Mouth dry, I manage a nod and leave him to it. I walk toward my office, berating myself for thinking about my employee in any manner other than professional. Dev pops up from behind his desk.

"Hey, Madison. I'm going out to get lunch. Want me to pick up your turkey sandwich?"

I shake my head. "That diet is so last week. How about roast beef and provolone on a roll?"

Dev takes down my order. "Gotcha. And nothing against turkey, but that seemed kinda bland."

"We'll see. I'll probably be on to my next diet soon." Xander's motivating. I take a step toward my office. "Oh, Xander's on his way here for a meeting. Why don't you ask him for his lunch order too?"

Dev nods. "Sure thing. I'll put it on the company card." He offers a sly smile. "Two lunches in a week with Xander, huh?"

I better nip this in the bud. "No. Not 'two lunches' with Xander. If I remember correctly, the entire office was there for the first one."

He waves his hand. "And now?"

"We're reviewing his first proposal. My guess is this won't be a five-minute meeting. It's lunchtime. I'm being pragmatic."

He taps his pencil against his teeth. Which are white, but not the same level of whiteness as Xander's. "Pragmatic, right. Nothing like a little eye candy for dessert."

I huff a laugh and leave my assistant. How could I respond to that comment anyway? In my office, I survey the mess of papers and straighten up. Not that I'm trying to make a good impression on Xander, but his organized space said "professional" to me. No wonder he was a big-time exec at VOW-cubed.

I'm topping a stack of documents with a paperweight my niece made for my thirtieth birthday last month when Xander walks into my office. He crooks his finger toward Dev. "Gave my lunch order to your assistant. Is that okay?"

"Yeah. I asked him to get it since we'll be working through lunch." I motion at my guest chair. "Have a seat. I'm excited to see which project you selected and to hear your proposal."

He strides across my office and hands me a stapled document, opens a button on his blazer, and sits. He doesn't need to be so formal, but damn.

He begins, "So, I did what you told me to do and reviewed the various websites with RFPs. I was surprised at how many people are looking for help out there."

"Yeah. They're crying out for guidance daily. And we're here to provide it."

"That's great." He directs his attention to the paper in front of him. "After going through all of the requests, I selected the most impressive one of all—the Mahigan Preserve."

A frisson of awareness runs up my spine. Please tell me he didn't choose who I fear he did. I swallow. "Is it upstate?"

He nods. "Yeah. It's part of the Native American tribe up there."

Shit. "The wolf preserve," I murmur.

"That's the one! You saw their request?"

I sag against my chair. "I did."

Oblivious to my thoughts, Xander barrels forward. "The RFP spoke to me. Their mission is to care for the environment and all living creatures who reside here. They treat everything—from worms to bears—as needing to be nurtured. And their current project is to protect wolves. They have five on the property now and are looking to double their number over the next few months."

"Admirable."

He doesn't take a breath. "It is, right? And what's even better is the owners of the Mahigan Preserve are a couple who's descended from the Onondaga Wolf Clan. This tribe believes the wolf is intelligent, non-aggressive, friendly, and with the ability to make strong emotional attachments. According to their lore, wolves are considered what's called a 'medicine being', meaning they're associated with courage, strength, loyalty, and success at hunting." Xander's face has transformed as if he were a child in a toy store for the first time.

I lean forward, in thrall to his description. "You know, that is fascinating. We can play up the 'strong emotional attachment' angle."

"That's exactly where I went with this proposal." He shakes the papers on his leg, then dives into his suggestions.

Despite my hatred toward all things dog, I find myself drawn into his inventive ideas. He's presented about half of his pitch when Dev arrives with lunch.

"Hate to interrupt such important discussions, but if our Madison here doesn't get her fuel, it won't be pretty." He laughs, and Xander joins him.

Thanks, Dev, thought you were on my side. I bury my sentiments and don a smile. "That's right, boys. Thank you for picking up lunch, Dev."

My admin winks at me and exits the room. Pointing to my table, I ask, "Want to eat in here? Or go to the break room?"

"Here's fine. I used to work at my desk all the time at VOW-cubed." His cheeks fall, and he busies himself with setting out our sandwiches on my table.

I unwrap my roast beef, and he opens his turkey. *Shoot. I probably should've gone back on my diet.* When I see some cheese on his, I feel somewhat better. We eat in silence for a couple of bites. "How are you liking how we do things downtown?" Innocuous question. I mentally pat myself on the shoulder.

His tongue swipes some mayo off his lip. Mayo. Not a diet food. "It's different down here. More, ah, authentic. I'm surprised at how much I'm enjoying it."

"That's great. Don't get me wrong, I love to visit uptown, but I'm more comfortable on a daily basis down here. Have you been to the Union Square farmers' market? It's unique to this area."

"Not yet. I'll check it out."

He finishes his half sandwich in one huge bite. *Wow.* While I nibble on mine, he wipes his hands on a napkin. "You should. The GreenMarket is held every Monday, Wednesday, Friday, and Saturday year-round, depending on the weather." We both glance out my window. "Hope you'll be able to try it soon."

Pulling the sandwich away from his mouth, he says, "Union Square is around the corner from here. I'll hit it up before work one day." He takes another bite.

I finish up half of my sandwich at the same time Xander savors his last morsels. Deciding to save my other half, I wrap it back up while he opens a small bag of chips. Salt and vinegar. Not my favorite or anything. When he crunches, my eyes can't stop straying to the bag.

"Want some?"

He flicks his wrist and the open bag appears before my face. Guess I wasn't too subtle. This is what friends do. They share food. And since I've never met a chip I didn't like, I nod. "Thanks." I slip my hand inside and take a small handful. Don't want to appear like a food hog or anything. I put one at a time into my mouth.

"So dainty." He takes his own handful and shoves them all into his mouth.

Caught up in his lightness, I open my mouth and drop the remainder of my chips into it.

"That's more like it," he says around potato chips.

"I try," I manage to say before a piece of a chip lands on the table. *Oh God*. Embarrassed, I swipe the evidence into my hand.

"Those suckers are hard to keep in your mouth aren't they?" I dart my eyes toward him, and he's sporting a grin. "But worth every calorie."

"That they are."

He offers the bag to me again, but I retain my self-composure and wave him off. "Nope, they're all yours."

Like every guy I've ever seen, he holds the open bag up and shakes the remaining chips into his mouth. Once he swallows, he asks, "So tell me, what do you think about my proposal for the Mahigan Preserve so far?"

As I'm sipping my diet soda, I hold up my finger. I don't want to dissuade him on his first outing, so I choose my words with care. "It was an interesting choice. I really enjoyed learning about the Native American connection."

"It's compelling." He digs into the white bag and I expect him to pull out a cookie or some other bakery sweet. Instead, an apple appears in his hand. "I love their devotion to the environment, and saving wolves is a worthy endeavor. When we get a little further into my presentation, you'll see how fascinating wolves are." He takes a huge bite into the juicy fruit and swipes a droplet from the side of his mouth.

Like an ordinary person.

I open the bag Dev gave me and eye the macarons. My favorite. Maybe I can have one? I hold a green one up and turn the bag in his direction. He shakes his head so I pop the one into my mouth and close up shop. No need to draw attention to my less-than-Darcey figure. Especially after our potato chip escapade.

"I'm looking forward to hearing all about them." *Not.* But his enthusiasm is contagious.

Thirty minutes later, we're back at my desk and Xander's finishing up his presentation. "Wolves are strong, highly intelligent, and independent creatures. With them, respect is about acceptance of each other. A human's approach, demeanor, and attitude all truly matter as to whether you're welcomed by the pack or not. I think these themes are universal. My idea is to create a campaign centered around these gorgeous animals, and how interaction is a two-way street. By keeping them safe, we'll enhance our own environment."

His passion is spellbinding. "I love that."

Xander looks down at his papers. Is he embarrassed? Nervous? Unsure of the value he's providing? In a low voice, he says, "I want to pitch these ideas to the Mahigan Preserve. What do you think?"

Considering his work is top-notch, I reply, "I think this is a fantastic proposal you've put together. It's well thought out and creative. I bet your ideas will be well-received and the good people at the Preserve would be fools not to hire you."

I'm almost blinded by the smile and energy bouncing off the man across from me. "You think so? Don't you have any changes you'd like to make?"

Other than not pitching the client? I was against them because, well, they're all about wolves. Which are basically big dogs. But something in his demeanor reaches out to me, begging me not to dampen his enthusiasm. I hold up his proposal. "I do have a few subtle tweaks, yes, but not too many. You did a fabulous job." Smiling, I extend my fist. "You might have a future in this industry."

Our knuckles bump. "That means a lot to me." Xander glances at the clock on my wall to his right. "Wow. I didn't realize how late it was getting. I'm meeting up with Jesse and a few other people at a club in midtown. Want to come with us? Jesse can't stop talking about how all the ideas you gave him are working great."

All that talent and polite, too. *You're his boss.* "Thanks for the offer, but I still have tons to wrap up here." I swivel my head from side to side, taking in all of the neat piles around me. Tons might be an understatement.

He stands, causing me to scramble to my feet as well, not that it makes a difference considering our height difference. "I'll let you be, then. I appreciate your spending so much time with me today. I look forward to your comments about the Preserve."

He turns. The entirety of Xander Turner is a sight to behold. "Please tell Jesse hello from me. And I'm glad my ideas are working for him."

Giving me a nod, he strolls out of my office. My eyes meet Dev's, who gives me a thumbs up. I squint toward my admin, who rubs his nose. Because I can't help myself, once Xander's down the hallway I call out to Dev, "Isn't it time for you to go home?"

"Why yes. It is. I was so wrapped up in your meeting I almost forgot."

"There was nothing to see in my meeting."

"A guy can dream."

Shaking my head, I return to my office. I need to get a better handle on my admin.

And my misguided response to my newest employee.

8

Xander

At nine o'clock, I saunter into the club Jesse and Theo agreed on and stroll into the VIP area. A bunch of my friends are seated on the sofas, overlooking the dance floor beneath us. Classmates from high school sit off to the right side and from college to the left. Because neither of my friends has arrived, I grab a bourbon from the bar and walk to the right.

I approach the group, which consists of some guys who were on the football team with me back then, some women I've dated, and others I haven't. I wait for someone to greet me. When they remain involved with their own conversations, I ask, "Hey, how's everyone doing?" One of the women I've never dated responds, "Hi, Xander. Didn't know you were going to be here."

"I'm meeting up with Theo and Jesse."

"Oh." She takes a sip of her drink and starts talking with another woman at her right.

Snubbed? Nah, she probably was rapping with her friend long before I arrived. The football crew doesn't give me a warm welcome either. Instead of staying here, I slip over to the other side and take a seat by some of the people I hung out with during college.

"Oh, hey there, Xander," my freshman year roommate says, holding up his glass.

Much better. "Hey." I clink my bourbon to his drink. "What's up?"

"All the normal stuff. We were talking about potential accounts to add to the store's roster."

He works for an upscale gentlemen's clothing boutique. "A few of the most prestigious brands advertise with us. Let me know if you need an introduction." As if a word cloud hung over my head, I realize my mistake. I spoke in the present tense. *Fuck.*

My brain scrambles to figure out how to fix things, but I'm too slow. "I'm acquainted with all the advertisers at VOW-cubed. Thanks." He returns his focus to the people he was talking with before I arrived.

I shift my weight between my hips on the upholstered chair. After tugging my long sleeves downward, I murmur, "That's great."

Drawing another sip, I glance to my other side. My stomach clenches. I dated the woman seated there for a few months at the end of college. We had a wonderful time together, as she was one of the few women who treated me like a normal guy. She hinted about taking our relationship further, but Dad urged me to drop her. After all, I was on my way to VOW-cubed, and she was thinking about a career in the museum industry. Dad felt she wasn't a good fit for my goals. The thought brings me up short.

"Hey, Kellie, how are you doing?"

She whips her head toward me. "Oh, Xander, I didn't see you sitting there. I'm doing great." She holds out her left hand, where a large diamond graces her ring finger. "Got engaged a month ago."

"Oh wow. Congratulations." Looks like she got what she wanted after all. "Who's the lucky fellow?"

"He's in charge of the Frick Museum."

"I've been there. Liked it." I wait a beat. "So where are you working these days?"

"I'm at the Met." The Metropolitan Museum of Art is the pinnacle of the museums in the City, in my opinion. "I'm the Assistant Director."

"That's awesome. I knew you were interested in working for a museum during college, and it seems you've realized your dreams."

She brings a glass of white wine to her lips. "I love it there. Things are beyond amazing."

"Happy everything's working out for you." And not for me. Being publicly ousted from VOW-cubed wasn't on my bingo card. Ever. Working downtown wasn't on my radar, either. Yet, here I am, living both. I shift my weight again.

You enjoy working for Madison.

What?

Kellie jumps to her feet without continuing our conversation. "Excuse me. My fiancé just walked in." She floats over to the guy who gave her the ring, they embrace, and then start talking with some people.

My former roommate is in a heated discussion with someone about the pros and cons of three-piece suits. I used to engage in such debates, but now I'm not inclined. Especially since the Madison Welch PR Agency doesn't have a dress code and all of my co-workers wear jeans or trousers to the office.

Where's Theo or Jesse?

Getting to my feet, I meander throughout the VIP area, exchanging pleasantries with acquaintances. I'm never drawn into conversations, nor do I have the need to interject myself into some. For the first time I can remember, I'm unwanted and uninterested.

Thankfully, Theo's brown head appears at the entrance to the VIP area. I raise my hand, he gives me a nod, and we meet at the bar where he orders his favorite, Dark 'n Stormy. I refuse a second drink, considering I'm nursing this and am only about halfway through. In the past, I would've knocked this one back and gotten another, but seems more frugal to hold off.

He bumps my arm. "How are you holding up?"

"I'm good. Started working for the Madison Welch PR Agency this week." I rise to my full height.

He tips his glass to his lips. "Let's go over there." He points to a rare, unoccupied table. As we walk, he asks, "How's it going? Do you like it?"

I consider his questions. "You know? Shockingly, I do. I mean, it's downtown with a view of encroaching buildings and we're on the fifth floor." My lips twist. "Seriously."

Theo raises his glass in front of his lips to hide a smile. "Is the office nice at least?"

I pause for a moment. "It's comfy. Madison has photos of employees and clients on the walls. And the other people who work there are pleasant." I sip my bourbon. "It's a collaborative environment. Madison even told me today about some farmers' market everyone goes to that's like a few blocks away."

"Wow. Light years from VOW-cubed."

"You could say that again. There isn't even a dress code. My coworkers wear *jeans*."

He chuckles. "Sounds like my kind of place."

His comment reminds me I've been hogging our conversation. "So tell me, how's the writing biz going?"

He taps his glass onto the table. "It's great. Scary as shit. No income is a wake-up call, for sure. But between my savings, trust fund, and Amelia's salary, we're fine."

Those are three things I don't have. Not that I'm interested in finding my own Amelia, though. After Darcey, I'm done. Don't need such a headache ever again. "That's good. How far along are you in your book about Uncle Daniel?"

"I'm about a quarter of the way into it. He's been wonderful—"

He stops talking when Jesse joins us, Guinness in hand. "Dudes. Sorry for being late. Got caught up working on my social media campaign and lost all track of time."

"Not a problem at all. I've only been here for," *what feels like ten hours*. I check my Rolex. "An hour. And Theo got here about fifteen minutes ago, so we're all good." We exchange handshakes.

Theo and Jesse met each other through me a few years back, and we get together every so often. I'm not sure Theo's up to date with Jesse's plans. "Our boy Jesse here is thinking about leaving banking to dive all-in on his handmade furniture business. How are things coming along?"

He looks between Theo and me and grins. "They're going great for 'Handmade by JD.' I created business and marketing plans and I'm working up some prototypes of things I'm going to sell. This feeds my soul, you know?"

Theo slaps him on the back. "Congrats, man. I like the sound of that."

He's so happy, his positivity is contagious. I add, "Me, too."

"I even hired someone to design my website, and it's almost completed. I've been scouting locations for my shop, and I'm hoping I found something in Brooklyn."

Sharing his excitement is a contrast to the cold shoulders I'd received over the past hour. "Cool. I'll have to check it out when everything's a done deal."

Jesse accepts our good wishes and focuses his attention on Theo. "But enough about me. Xander told me you quit working at VOW-cubed after our boy here left the family business." His hand brushes my shoulder. "What have you been up to?"

Theo repeats what we were discussing, adding in more color about his conversations with Uncle Daniel. In my mind's eye, I can picture my uncle talking with Theo, all bombastic excitement and gesticulation. He and Theo always were close.

Like me and Grandma Lucia, who passed before Theo was born. Theo's lucky to still have him. My maternal grandmother died of breast cancer when I was five but lives on in my heart and I know she's been looking out for me. I wonder if she had anything to do with guiding me toward Madison right when I needed a job?

Jesse punches my arm. "So tell me. How are things working out at Madison's shop?"

"As I was telling Theo, it's so different from all the stuff I've done before."

"Considering you only worked at VOW-cubed, I get it. I love Madison, though. She's a big softie." Jesse takes another sip and licks the dark liquid off his lips.

A softie? Madison is smart as a whip and has cultivated her Agency into a family-like atmosphere—or at least what I imagine a positive family atmosphere would be. In my Turner world, we're all independent and only get together for major holidays. Not out of dislike for each other, more like we're too busy with our own lives. Mom always tries to bring us together, but Sebastian's off in his own culinary realm building up a YouTube following while Halle's a wedding planner blessed with a ton of clients and responsibilities.

"Her office is very different. Don't get me wrong, everyone works their butts off, but it's a more comfortable environment."

"That sounds good. I guess at VOW-cubed, there were too many employees to create that sort of camaraderie."

Theo and I exchange glances. He shrugs. "Yeah."

If Dad and his partners wanted to, there were options they could've taken. Like having a monthly get-together in a conference room where business talk was off-limits. But they never acknowledged the workers as anything more than widgets to perform a function. "Madison's place is very different from high-powered corporate America."

"Not to mention, Madison's cool."

Jesse's comment draws Theo's attention. "Tell me more about Xander's boss."

Jesse raps his pilsner onto the table. "She was in b-school with us, although Xander here never was around when she was. I've always liked Madison. She's funny but doesn't show that side of herself to many people."

I remember the whole potato chip incident in her office and chuckle. "She does have a great sense of humor. I like her as a boss. Today I had to give my ideas for my first proposal about a wolf preserve upstate. She gave me free rein to select a potential client to pitch, and then let me do a dry run with her."

Jesse laughs. "Sounds like my idea of torture."

On the other hand, Theo cocks his head. "Interesting how she allowed you to choose and didn't direct you to the one she wanted you to make."

"Right? Can you imagine Dad letting me do that? It was like pulling teeth with the three execs when I tried to pitch an internal idea to them, never mind it was my own father and uncles." I focus my attention on Jesse and give him the skinny on the PowerPoint I prepared for VOW-cubed right before I was fired.

Jesse shakes his head. "Sounds like a toxic work environment to me."

I sit back. The need to protect Dad and the family business rises. "It was how things went at VOW-cubed. They only were looking out for the best interests of the company."

"More like their own best interests, if you ask me," Theo chimes in. "Your ideas were terrific, Xander. The execs, despite being related to us, were impossible to deal with. You may not believe me, but I think that Hudson guy did you a favor."

I place my knuckles on the table and lean toward my "brother." "Firing me was no favor."

Theo rubs his short beard. "If I remember correctly, you weren't fired. You quit."

I stare him down. Jesse jumps into the breach. "Whatever happened, it led you to Madison's firm."

Theo clamps his hand on my shoulder. "Bro, I didn't mean to make you upset about VOW-cubed. Hell, I quit in solidarity. But I think this job sounds interesting for you. Let's you explore your creative side that was being stifled at the company." He removes his hand.

I can't remain mad at Theo, especially considering he's right. "I know you didn't mean anything by what you said. I'm a bit…off from the whole situation." *To say the least.* "I think working for Madison will give me a leg up when I start my own marketing business. It's a great place to cut my teeth."

"I don't want you to hurt Madison." Jesse's sharp tone draws my attention.

My throat constricts. Taking a sip of my drink to alleviate the pain, I reply, "I have absolutely no intention of doing that. All I'm saying is after a year or so, I'll probably have picked up some good pointers about how I'd like to run my own place. She's like my mentor."

Jesse clunks his beer down. "Does she know this is your path?"

"Well, no. God knows we'd have a very different clientele. And this idea is a long way off from being put into action. I need to land my first client for her Agency and see how the process goes."

Theo asks an unexpected question. "What's this Madison look like?"

I chuckle. "She's what they like to call 'vertically challenged.' She's about a foot shorter than me."

"She packs a lot of punch in a pint-sized package, that's for sure," Jesse adds.

Theo grins. "I'd pay good money to see you two walk into a room together."

"I'm sure we'd make a sight." I picture us walking down the hallway and shake my head. "Other than her lack of height, she has blond hair and blue eyes. A bit chubby." I run my hands down my torso. "Although, I can see how you could pack on the pounds working down there. There's no gym there like at VOW-cubed and no real healthy options nearby."

"Brown bag it and get a membership with a gym for ten dollars a month. Better option than to give up your soul to the family gods." With this piece of advice, Theo places his empty glass down onto the table and stands. "Well, I'd love to hang out with you two but Amelia's waiting for me at home." He wiggles his eyebrows, shakes both our hands, and departs.

"He seems happy," Jesse notes.

"I've never seen him like this before," I remark. "Amelia's done wonders for him."

"They say women can make your life so much better. Although, I've failed to see that." Jesse finishes his Guinness.

"Me neither. All they've ever brought me is heartache. And headaches."

He lifts his empty pilsner to my glass and we tap. "Leave them to the Theos of the world. I'll keep to hooking up whenever I want. With my job at the bank and trying to get my furniture store off the ground, I don't need any more complications in my life."

I used to believe being part of a couple was the ultimate goal. Not anymore. Darcey saw to that. With a flourish, I finish my bourbon. "I hear you."

9

Xander

F inishing my pitch to the Mahigan Preserve, I stare into the eyes of its owners, Mr. and Mrs. Howell. Chauncey says, "Thank you for all of your hard work, Xander."

I dip my chin. I left it all out there on the table. In my heart, I know I couldn't have done a better job with another month to prepare. I feel like I could solve all the world's problems.

Isa pushes away from the table. "Would you mind if Chauncey and I went out in the hall to discuss what you proposed?"

Before I can respond, Madison stands. "No, no, no. You stay in here. Xander and I will give you some time to talk, as I'm sure you have a lot to consider. Please don't feel that you have to make a decision right away."

Isa pushes her long, straight brown hair away from her face. Streaks of grey in it show her experience rather than make her appear older. "Thank you."

I walk past the couple. "If you'd like to talk further, just step into the hallway and someone will get us right away."

Closing the conference room door, Madison beams at me. "You were fantastic. The Howells were eating up everything you were saying. Great job."

Euphoria zaps throughout my body. In my experience, praise in the business world has been infrequent. We cruise down the hall toward my office, and she punches my arm.

"Thank you. It felt great. And your ideas really kicked everything up a notch."

Her shoulders pull back. "Thanks. But you really did all the heavy lifting. I only tweaked a couple of things here and there."

We stop outside my office door. "So how long do you think this will take?"

"I don't know. Potential clients don't usually stick around after a presentation. I think that's a good sign."

Holding up my hand, I cross my fingers. "I hope so. I really want to work with them and their wolf preserve. It's fascinating to me."

"I hope this comes through for you." Her light blues zero in on me. "I have to say, you're a natural at pitching."

A pang of euphoria flits through my body—her accolades are better than receiving a new bespoke suit. "I'm humbled by your confidence in me." Have to admit, creating a plan and selling it to potential clients like the Howells is a rush unlike anything I've ever experienced. And my boss says I'm good at it. If I can make this work for her, imagine what I can do uptown.

"I'm going back to my office. Please give me a call when the Howells come out of the conference room. Don't expect them to hire us, though. Usually, we get about one out of every three or so clients we pitch. And never immediately after a presentation. Good job, again." The dewdrop on her leaf-shaped pin sparkles at me as she turns.

I'm still assimilating her kudos when Chauncey's head pops into the hall. "Xander," he calls. "We'd like to speak with you and Madison, if you're available?"

"Sure thing. Let me get her and we'll be right there."

He disappears into the conference room. I turn to hoof it toward Madison, who's already returning. "What did Mr. Howell say?"

My heart beats faster. "That they want to talk with us," I whisper, motioning her toward the conference room where my first-ever potential clients sit.

"I bet this is a good sign. Knocking it out of the park on your first time at bat would be fantastic."

With her words ringing in my ears, I hold the door for her to pass, then follow her inside. When we're both settled, Isa says, "I have to admit, we were excited by your presentation. You had some great ideas. Chauncey and I talked about it, and we want to hire you. We've canceled our other appointments."

Adrenaline screams throughout my body. This is a better feeling than I've ever had, even when I landed a major advertiser for the magazines. It's so much more ... personal. "You made the right choice, Mr. and Mrs. Howell. The Mahigan Preserve will be in good hands."

Madison stands and shakes both of their hands. "We're very honored you've chosen to place your trust in our Agency. We promise to exceed your expectations." I trail behind her, shaking their hands and relishing their positive responses. An hour later, they've signed on the dotted line and are on their way to explore the City.

Alone in the conference room, my boss erupts into a cute happy dance, all of her body jiggling with a beat only she can hear. "You're a good luck charm, Xander. This never happens. Rather, not this quickly."

I can't wipe my smile off my face. "That was awesome." Unable to control my energy, I pull her in for an enthusiastic hug. Recognizing she's my boss—and how perfectly she fits in my arms—I recoil. "I'm sorry. That was inappropriate."

She takes a step back, palming her cheek. With a hitch in her voice, she says, "I understand, buddy."

Reining in my rampant emotions, my weight shifts between my feet. After a silent moment has passed, I ask, "I'd like to keep the Mahigan Preserve as my own client, if you're okay with that?"

Madison's lips curl upward, flooding relief throughout my system that my *faux pas* is forgiven. "I love your enthusiasm and, of course, you can. The Howells are your client now. Let me know if you have any questions—I have faith in you."

Faith? She has faith in me? When did Dad ever say that? He issued orders, not support. I snort. How can a relative stranger offer me more praise than my own father? "That means a lot to me." Body vibrating, I pace around the oval table. Without censor, I ramble off a whole host of ideas for the Preserve.

She perches on the top of the table. "You better write these down before you forget them."

"Good idea." I snag a legal pad and memorialize my verbal diarrhea. "There. Done."

"You're a surprise, Xander Turner."

I tap my pen against my lip. "In a good way, I hope."

"Very much so." She hops off the table. "I don't know about you, but all this pitching has me starving. Want to go to the Green-Market for lunch to celebrate?"

"That's the farmers' market nearby, right?" When she nods, my stomach makes a loud noise of agreement, causing us both to laugh. "Can't wait."

Leaving the conference room, we enter my office where I drop off my papers, and then move on to hers. When we pass Dev, Madison says, "We're headed out to the GreenMarket to celebrate our new client."

"You got the gig?"

In response, Madison holds up the check. Her admin leaps out of his seat and gives her a hug. See? The Agency is filled with huggers. When he turns to me, I ward off his embrace by extending my hand, which he pumps. "Congrats. Looks like you two are a good team."

"Thanks, man," I reply.

"Well, I already ordered lunch in. A slavedriver gave me a huge list to do." He grins. "Have a good one."

Smiling, Madison exchanges her documents for her purse and we walk out of the office. Soon, we've made it to the oversized farmers' market, which is an open park dotted with dozens of tables under pop-up tents. Signs tempt patrons to buy their produce, fruits, breads, sandwiches—even pickles. Amazing smells battle for my attention. "Wow. This place is amazing."

"I know, right? It's a staple around here. Whether you want to pick up ingredients to make dinner or grab lunch now, they have it all. Not to mention a whole row of booths dedicated only to desserts."

Nothing like this exists uptown except for an occasional craft fair. "I'm intrigued by everything. What do you recommend?"

Madison plays with her hair, pushing it across her cheek. After a minute, she nods. "Follow me."

We wind our way through the market. Because she's so short, I have to keep my eyes trained on her back, which stands straight and proud. *Like her.*

Whoa!

Shaking my head at such a wayward thought, I pass by booths filled with fruits, nuts, and even homemade fresh ravioli.

Stopping at a place advertising sandwiches, a bald and rather round guy greets her by name. "Madison. Great to see you today. What can I get you?"

"You know me. I'd like your fabulous chicken breast with arugula and mozzarella on whole wheat." My boss turns to me. "What would you like? Everything's fantastic."

I check out the menu. "How about a tuna salad wrap?"

"You got it."

The clerk busies himself while I examine the rest of his booth. My fingers land on a small plastic bag of yuca chips. They can be awesome. Or terrible. My gaze meets Madison's and she makes a swift "no" action, so I drop them. Guess this is a sandwich-only booth. Good to know.

When our lunches are ready, I pull out my wallet and pay before Madison can unzip her purse. "I got this." After the money changes hands, I take the bag and we leave.

"Pickles and whatever dessert strikes your fancy are on me. The yuca chips there aren't so good—the best place for them is over there." She points to a booth about three rows away.

"Nah. That was a moment of weakness. I'm good with just a pickle. And an apple."

"You got it."

I let her pay for the rest of my lunch, and she directs us to a gap in a short wall on which people sit and eat their food. We sit down and when I hand her the sandwich, she remarks, "You're going to love this. It must be the bread, but no one makes a better sandwich here by far." To prove her point, she takes a big bite out of hers and groans.

Now that's a sound I could get around.

What. The. Fuck? Shut it down, Xander. She's your boss. And so downtown.

Shaking off my stupid imagination, I unwrap my sandwich. I'm pretty sure the delis uptown will beat this farmers' market, but I keep my mouth shut. This is its own unique experience. With a smile, I take a bite and an explosion of goodness happens in my mouth.

"Holy shit. This is good." I keep chewing.

"Told you!" She swings her feet, which don't touch the sidewalk.

In record time, we've devoured our GreenMarket lunches. Wiping my mouth on a tiny paper napkin, I say, "I have to thank you for showing me this place. It was phenomenal."

She elbows me in the ribs. "I'd never steer you wrong."

I collect our garbage and stride to the trashcan while she jumps off the short wall. My chest expands. I landed my first ever client *and* enjoyed some of the best food ever.

A woman with red hair approaches my boss. "Hey, Madison. What's up?"

I stand back, not wanting to intrude on the friends. Madison's normally open and sunny expression becomes pinched. "Hello, Kelsey. Enjoying lunch with my new rep, Xander Turner here." She points to me.

Taking my cue, I approach the pair. She's taller than Madison by several inches. Pretty, with a Roman nose and long hair. We shake hands.

Wide-eyed, Kelsey says, "Wow. I'm surprised to see you down here. Congrats on your new job."

"Thanks. Working for Madison is great." Working *for*, not with. *Remember that, Xander.*

"Madison here has a great firm."

My boss cups her cheek. What's that about? "Kelsey's modest. She has a fantastic PR agency, too."

That explains it. They're rivals. Although I'm only getting that vibe off Madison, as Kelsey seems to be genuinely happy to meet up with us.

Kelsey laughs. "There's plenty of room for both of us, that's for sure. Welcome to the neighborhood, Xander. I need to get something to eat, I'm starving. Hope to run into you again soon."

"Take care," Madison says as the redhead leaves and walks toward the booths.

"She seemed nice," I tiptoe into the silence.

Madison slants me a glare, then her expression softens. "She's nice enough although she's been winning every pitch out from under me lately." Her face morphs into a happy one. "But not anymore. Your pitch was great, the Howells loved it. I have high hopes for you."

"I'll do my best."

Her confidence in my abilities is humbling and exciting all at once. I'm here for the experience, but I also want to do a good job for Madison's Agency. Plenty of potential clients will pass on me in particular, so today's win is all the more sweet. We stroll toward the office.

She tilts her chin toward a woman walking ahead of us. "Oh wow. Stripes and plaid should never be mixed. I don't know anything about fashion, but I know that."

I chuckle. "She's doing her. Even if no one else wants to copy her style."

"You're right. Be you out loud." She laughs. "Sounds like an ad for a department store or something."

"Maybe we should copyright it, and then shop it around. World domination, here we come."

Her giggles are robust and uncaring as to who's attention she's grabbing. Which would be great if not for a camera lens pointed at us. I drop my head and put my hands up in front of me. "Looks like there are paparazzi here. Let's get back to the office." I pick up my pace, not seeing the commercial buildings we pass.

Since my initial interview for the job, reporters have stayed away from the office. Guess they were tipped off I was at the GreenMarket. Anything for a photo. At least I'm wearing a suit, courtesy of the pitch.

"Wait!" At her directive, I spin on my heel to see she's stopped in front of a store. "Come in here." She disappears inside.

Shit. If I stop moving, the reporters are going to grow in numbers. Yet Madison expects me to follow her—where the paps can't. Inhaling, I go through the door. Across the shop, she motions for me to join her. Approaching her, I realize why we're in here.

I snicker, "Hats?"

"Hey. They make great disguises in movies. Try this on." She appears as if she'd like to put a fedora on my head but realizes she's way too short, so she passes it to me instead.

I look at the hat with skepticism. "I'm not so sure about this."

"Just do it," she insists, tugging on her hair.

I roll my eyes and put it on. "There. What do you think?" I look around for a mirror, but there's nothing nearby.

"I think you look like Xander in a hat," she laughs.

I remove the fedora and toss it back to her. "Told you. Let's go before the paparazzi grows."

"No, wait. They have a ton of hats here and I'm positive there will be something that'll fit the bill." She looks around. "There!" She points at a brown newsboy cap.

I sigh. "Fine. Last one." I slap it on top of my head. "How's this one?"

Her index finger bounces off her lips. "I think that'll do the trick. For you." She surveys the options and picks up a straw hat with a rolled brim and tries it on. "We both have to be in disguise since they saw us together. Do you like this one?"

She looks adorable in the hat, I must admit. *Adorable? What am I thinking?* Shrugging aside the errant thought regarding my boss, I study her "disguise." The color of the band is all wrong. I spy a purple ribbon around a similar hat and give it to her. With a laugh, she tries it on. It actually looks good.

"That's perfect for you."

She claps. "Do you have sunglasses?"

"Not with me."

"Okay. Let's pick you up a cheapie pair. Between your hat and glasses, I bet you'll be able to slip by. And bonus! You can reuse this disguise whenever you need to. Leave it in your office."

Her enthusiasm is contagious, whether or not effective. I inspect the selection of sunglasses and pick up a pair for ten dollars. Who knew these things didn't cost in excess of two hundred?

After we pay for our purchases—rather, disguises—I give her my blazer, shove my tie into my pocket, untuck my shirt, and roll up my sleeves. "Don't be surprised if these don't work. But it was a fun interlude." It was. She thinks it's this easy to outsmart the paparazzi, but I know better. Still, it was more entertainment than I've had in a long time.

Disguises at the ready, I let her exit the store first. Engulfed in my blazer that hangs nearly to her knees, she enters the sidewalk, turns right, and walks slowly away from the store. No reporters take note of her. My turn. *Please let this work.*

Body tense, I hunch my shoulders, stoop my posture, and lope out of the store in an unnatural gait. At least six cameras are trained on the store, all of which remain in place when I follow Madison—who's staring at a store window. "Excuse me, miss, are you all alone?"

"Why, yes, I seem to be. No one's tracking my steps at all."

I do a quick survey and confirm we did dodge them. "I'll be damned. Your trick worked."

She does a little jig. "Told you." She licks her finger and touches her ample bottom. "Stick with me, kid. I'll keep you flush."

I toss my head back and laugh. "If only everything was this easy." Pointing toward the office, I say, "C'mon, let's not press our luck." We traverse the remaining block and turn on Fifth Avenue.

Only when we're inside the Agency's building do we take off our disguises.

"I'll never doubt you again. That was fantastic," I congratulate my partner in crime.

Clicking her sunglasses shut, she drops them into her purse and inspects the hat I chose for her. "I love this, Xander."

"One of my strengths. Finding women's hats."

Her smile freezes for a second. "You definitely sold yourself short. I don't remember seeing that on your resume." She laughs, although it's not as free as it was before. She shrugs out of my blazer.

"I'll have to revise it." I remove my sunglasses and sling my blazer over my shoulder. The newsboy cap comes off next, and I finger-comb my hair back into place.

When the elevator dings for our floor, I follow her into the office. "Thanks for showing me the GreenMarket. I had a good time, and want to return to explore."

"You'll find new stuff all the time. It's one of my favorite places to go in the City." She stops in front of Dev's desk. "Would you mind going over your notes for the Preserve and meeting back here in an hour? I want to get this refined as soon as possible."

I offer her a salute. "Will do." I leave the pair as Dev says something to her I can't hear and she whacks his chest.

When I arrive in my office, the dichotomy between what I had at VOW-cubed and what I have now hits me. I thought my corner office with views of Central Park made a statement. But here, now, I'm more comfortable than I've ever been. I have one window with a crap-ass view, but it doesn't matter. My desk isn't covered with five inches of "important" papers. I don't cringe when I enter, either. No Felicia, but I don't need an admin. All of us reps share a secretary and that seems to work out fine.

How has my life become this upended?

I settle into my chair and turn on the timer on my phone before putting all of my attention on the Preserve account, creating a series of actionable steps. I identify a couple of areas that need to be fleshed out and am working on them when my timer goes off. Proud of what I've accomplished, I press print and gather two copies of the document.

"Hey, Dev," I call out to her admin. Pointing toward her closed door, I ask, "She available?"

"Bonnie beat you to it. She went in about thirty minutes ago, so I'm guessing she'll be out soon."

Instead of anger at being made to wait like Dad used to make me do, I'm neutral. Bonnie's great and I'm sure she needed Madison's attention. I tap my papers on his desk. "May I use your stapler?"

"Of course." He gives it to me.

"So, how long have you been working with Madison?"

"I've been here for three years. She's awesome to work for, let me tell you. Always understanding if you need personal time, so her perfectionist ways don't feel so, well, demanding. And she's open to new ideas, even if she doesn't want to hear them."

I staple my document and return the gadget to him. "She is quite the sneaky perfectionist. With my presentation to the Preserve, her comments enhanced my proposal but they were couched in such a way as to be collaborative." *Hmmm.* So different from how things at VOW-cubed worked.

"Oh, yes. She's good at that."

The door opens and Bonnie sails out. "Oh, hey, Xander. Congrats, heard you scored a client on your first try."

"Thanks. It was an awesome experience. I'm chalking it up to beginner's luck."

"With Madison at your back, I bet it was more than luck." She holds up a document. "I'm off to incorporate her changes. She's all yours."

Dev stifles a chuckle, which garners my attention. He holds up his hands as if in surrender, then flicks his fingers to shoo me into her office.

Ignoring her admin's reaction, I pass Bonnie and knock on the doorframe. "Hey, is now a good time?"

Madison releases her hair, which falls to her shoulders. "Of course. Sorry to keep you waiting, but Bonnie needed some help with ideas for her client."

Her client. Interesting. The client belongs to the business—which belongs to Madison—but she refers to the client as belonging to her rep. Another example of how she's fostering a collegial atmosphere.

I enter her office. "No worries. I was getting to know your admin."

"Dev's the best." With a smile, she points to the guest chair. "Take a seat and let's review how you plan on implementing all your fantastic ideas for the Preserve."

Handing her a copy of my ideas, we dive in. "In order to make the Preserve a destination for city dwellers, I'd like to create a campaign that takes advantage of the movement toward saving the environment."

"Smart. I like it. Perhaps you could partner with some of the City's bigger charities?"

I hadn't thought of that. The possibilities of cross-promotion are endless. "Great idea. What do you think about somehow gamifying the experience?"

"Oh, that's superhot right now." She pauses. "And if there's a baby wolf—" She stops short.

"A pup," I supply.

"Ah. Thanks. If there's a pup, maybe we could create a naming contest."

We continue like this, bouncing ideas off each other at a rapid-fire pace. Jesse's right. Madison's smart. Like super-off-the-charts-scary smart. Some of her ideas are brilliant on their own, while others take mine and twist them to make them exponentially better.

"I really love your ideas, Xander. I think the Howells are going to be very happy they hired you."

Me? "You mean the Madison Welch PR Agency," I correct her.

She grins. "It was your pitch that sealed the deal. Your ideas were fabulous. Seriously. I only added a few details around the edges." She stands and walks so that she's leaning against her desk in front of me. "If I haven't said this before, I'm happy you chose to give this firm a chance. I know we're nothing like what you're used to."

A fleeting glimpse of pain in her eyes makes me surge to my feet and place my hands on her shoulders. Which should be as broad as a New York City avenue for all the pressure she's handling, but her frame is tiny. I admire how she deals with her employees and the quality work she provides to each of her clients. She's as capable as anyone I worked with at VOW-cubed, my father included.

"What you're building here is special, Madison. I'm honored you were willing to put all my family's crap to one side and give me this opportunity."

Her chin tips up toward mine and I'm drawn into her light blue eyes, filled with intelligence and kindness. An irresistible combination. Her lips open and she inhales, which I register as her shoulders shift beneath my hands. She sidesteps away from my hands.

What was I doing? She's my boss. She's a downtown girl, while I'm an uptown guy. Heck, she's a *woman*. I've sworn off her entire gender.

I grab up the papers filled with my scribbles. "I better get to work on these ideas. I want to have something for the Howells by next week." I race out of her office.

10

Madison

My eyelids flutter as Xander escapes my office. *What was that?* I touch my shoulder, which still feels branded by his hand.

All the air expels from my body and I sag onto my desk. *Get a grip.* So what if he won a new client in a rare first meeting decision?

So what if he loved the GreenMarket as much as I do?

So what if we had a blast buying a random disguise and evading the paparazzi?

Paparazzi—the difference between him and me right there. Reporters never would be interested in anything I'm doing, yet they hound him like fleas on a dog. I swallow and run my fingers over my scar. Forget the dog metaphor.

Which leads me to a second reason Xander would never be interested in me. His first pitch was to a wolf preserve, for heaven's sake. He chose to work with those overgrown, wild dogs. Never in a million years would I have selected that client. Add a few more million to that.

I trace my scar. Sighing, I push off my desk. He's a glorious sculpture and I'm one of the unwashed masses lined up to purchase a timed ticket.

Plopping into my chair, I glance at my screen which is booted up to the Agency's QuickBooks—reminding me I'm Xander's boss, a paycheck. Another reason this fantasy is a non-starter. Although I can't imagine he's working here for the money.

"Hey there." Dev enters my office and I straighten. Can't let him get a sniff I might be mooning over our new employee. He's already hinted, and I'm not adding any more fuel to the fire.

I walk around my desk, asking, "What's up?"

Dev picks up my new hat. "Haven't seen this before. It's cute." He plops it onto his head and pretends to strut the catwalk, with exaggerated shoulder and hip movements. His brand of crazy is exactly what I need to reorient myself.

I snatch it off his head when he passes by. "I just bought it." I've always been partial to hats since they force my hair down over my scar and I don't have to worry about it becoming more visible. The toddler's reaction at the mall the other day reminded me not to get too careless. The overpriced cream hasn't made any difference.

He puts his hands on his hips. "Well, I think it's fab." He picks up the calendar he'd dropped when he found my hat. "I want to go over your schedule for the week with you."

Work calls. No more fun thoughts about my new hat—the one Xander picked out for me. *No more thoughts about my new employee either.*

Thirty minutes later, Dev tosses the calendar onto my desk. "Okay. I think we're all set. I'll confirm all your appointments and send email confirmations before I leave unless you need me for something else?"

"You're too good for me. Take off when you're done. Thanks."

He swipes my hat and wears it out to his desk. He's nuts, but the best admin I've ever had. Sitting down, I focus on my screen and attend to the business side of the Agency. Some of my least favorite things to handle, but a necessary evil. Perhaps if Xander gets us a few more clients, I can afford to hire a bookkeeper.

A few hours later, I close down all of my spreadsheets and push away from my desk. I'm all alone here in the office as I was interrupted by everyone as they said goodbye for the day. Xander was the last one out. As soon as he left, I pulled my hair into a ponytail as it was bothering me all day. Stretching, I work out the kinks and set about packing up a few more things to handle at home.

Back in my apartment, the noises of Brooklyn comfort me. The sirens as a firetruck speeds by interrupt the quieter evening sounds of my neighbor's television. I move around my spacious two-bedroom, putting things away and changing from my work clothes into my pajamas. Mug of tea in my hand, I settle on my sofa and turn on the television instead of powering up my computer. I've worked enough today and need some downtime.

Before I can even decide on something to watch, my phone rings. Reading the screen I answer, "Hey, Mark. How are you doing?"

My brother fills me in on what's going on in his world, then asks, "Have you spoken with Macy?"

She texted me that she was telling the family today. "I have. I'm excited for her and Randall."

"I hope they get their boy this time," he agrees.

Mark and I have always had a chatty relationship. Even though he's older than me by five years, he's looked out for me, especially since I skipped two grades in school. My big protector. Although, his calls usually come with an ulterior motive.

"I was wondering if I could pick your PR brain?"

And there it is. With long-practiced ease, I ask, "What's up?" He launches into a convoluted issue his company's facing, and together we work out a feasible solution.

"Thanks, kid. You know how much I appreciate your free advice. How are things going for your firm?"

"Things seem to be turning around. I hired—" I pause. I don't want to reveal his name. Even though Mark lives in Kansas, he's clued into New York City life because of me. Plus, VOW-cubed isn't exactly a local business. "A new employee to be the face of the Agency to do our pitches. On his first try, he got the client."

"That's great, Sis. Think he has the chops?"

I picture the Howells almost eating out of Xander's hands. Everything about him screams competence. His height. His looks.

His attitude. Doesn't hurt that what he's talking about is fantastic as well. "Yeah. I think he's the full package."

Great. Now I can't stop thinking about Xander's package.

"What was the client he pitched?"

Shaking my head to clear it, I contemplate my response. "It wasn't something I ever would've chosen. A wolf preserve in upstate New York."

"Oh. Wow. You're right. I never would've imagined you voluntarily working with wolves. Do you have to visit the preserve?"

"No. Way." Like the rest of my family, Mark lived through my trauma as a five-year-old. I've never gotten closer to a dog than seeing one on a television commercial ever since.

"Guess it could've been worse. It could've been a pit bull rescue."

An uncontrollable shiver races throughout my body. "Not funny."

"Hey, sorry for the bad joke. But you know what I'm thinking? This new client may be a blessing in disguise. Maybe you should visit this wolf preserve. It might help you get over your fear."

"Not having been bitten ever would've prevented my fear from starting." My retort is swift and deadly. "I have no desire to ever set foot there." I take three deep breaths. "But, I'll gladly take their money."

"I guess that's one way to look at it." He sighs. "I wasn't trying to make light of the situation at all. Hell, I lived through it with you. We all did. But it's been a quarter of a century. It could be time for you to try again."

"Said by the man who doesn't have a permanent scar on his face."

Our conversation dies. I pick at the throw blanket across the back of the sofa.

"Listen. I didn't want to bring up a sore subject for you," he says. "You're one of the strongest and smartest people I know, if not *the* most. I hate that your fear may hold you back."

"I appreciate your concern, Mark, I really do. I didn't share my phobia with my new hire and the client has no clue. Everything will work out fine."

"I'm proud of you. Obviously, your fear didn't prevent you from reviewing the presentation and giving your input. See? You *are* brilliant."

His faith in my abilities is welcome. But before he can poke his nose into my nonexistent personal life, I end the call.

Mark was right, though. I did skirt the whole wolf issue with Xander with a deft hand, if I do say so myself.

I stand up and cross into my bathroom and brush my teeth. I stare at my reflection in the mirror, taking in my unremarkable blue eyes and round face. Pulling my frizzy blond hair away from my cheek, I expose my scar. *So ugly.*

Xander's friendly with everyone. Remember that. "You're so far below his league, Madison. Stick to your lane."

11

Xander

I take my seat in front of Madison's desk. "You found a new potential client you'd like me to pitch?"

It's been a few days since our near run-in with the paparazzi, and it's been quiet on that front since. Probably because it's been torrential downpours on the daily, although today the sun is streaming through Madison's window. Spring weather can be unpredictable, and I'm glad the gloom's going away.

"A friend of mine actually sent it my way." She taps her pen on the desk. "You met her at the networking event—Stephanie."

I search my memory bank. "Ah yes. She was drinking a martini, if I recall."

Her eyes crinkle as she smiles. "That's Stephanie alright. Dirty martini with one bleu-cheese stuffed olive always at the ready. Anyway, she's a volunteer for this charity called Friends For Fun, which helps underprivileged kids in Brooklyn. It's along the lines of a Boys and Girls Club."

In the past, I've donated to the latter, but keep my mouth shut. I nod.

"Stephanie gave me a scoop that the charity is casting about for more help on the PR front," Madison continues. She looks down at a paper, then hands it to me. "She sent this to me today, and has already spoken with the charity's director on our behalf."

I take her document and read the RFP's summary of desired services. From this list, it seems they want help expanding their reach for volunteers. "Interesting. Want me to work up a proposal?"

She nods. "Yes. I want to help this charity out. I live in Brooklyn and bringing joy to the kids who live there is a worthy endeavor."

My mind races. Everyone and their brother is going to pitch them, as charity work triggers massive interest. We need to do something different from the rest to stand out in addition to Stephanie's referral. An idea sparks. "I'm interested in helping them out, but I want to go off the normal track for our pitch."

She focuses on me like a laser. I can see her brain clicking to process what I said. "What are you thinking?"

"I don't want to create another presentation, go to their office, and do a pitch. I think we need to approach this from a different angle somehow." If only I could come up with that angle.

Her right hand slides behind her hair and lands on her cheek, with her pointer finger moving up and down. "I like your idea. Something unique to stand out from the crowd." She takes a moment. "Stephanie's already given us an in, but we need something more. Why don't we check out their website to see what they have planned?"

"Great idea." I walk behind her chair while she pulls up their site. I bend around her shoulders and point to the Events tab.

"You two make a cute couple!" Both of our heads bump up as her assistant sashays through the door, carrying something in his hand.

"Really, Dev? We're working here." Madison's tone conveys how inappropriate his comment was.

He must be a damn good admin, as I'm sure he would've been out of VOW-cubed in an instant. Besides, we're not a couple. She's my boss. I straighten to my full height.

Madison addresses Dev, "What do you need?"

Chastised, he comes over to us and plunks down a birthday card. "It's Bonnie's birthday tomorrow."

"Oh, I forgot." She opens the card and scribbles a note, then signs it. "Do you have breakfast ordered?"

"All set, boss."

"Thanks. You're forgiven." She holds up the card to me. "We celebrate birthdays around here with an office card and breakfast for everyone. You haven't been here that long, but I'm sure Bonnie would appreciate it if you signed her card."

Birthdays weren't celebrated at VOW-cubed, except for drinks after work sometimes. Never during office hours. Another way Madison makes it special at her office. I take the card from her and add my birthday wishes to it. Returning it to Dev, he leaves us without another improper comment. Thankfully.

We return our attention to the computer and I skim their upcoming events. On Saturday, they're going ziplining in the Catskills. "Yes!"

Madison asks, "What caught your eye?"

"The ziplining trip."

Madison flinches. "I was partial to their tour of a museum in Brooklyn. Why did you zero in on that trip?"

I inhale, and her strawberry shampoo invades my nostrils. *If you can smell her shampoo, you're too close, Xander.* Leaving her at her computer, I return to my seat across from her desk. "The museum won't foster interaction like ziplining. I like the idea of being with the kids and exploring something new with them. We can experience what the charity offers first-hand. Possibly rub elbows with the executives, and give ourselves a leg up. Besides Stephanie's referral, of course."

"I like how your mind works, Xander, especially the part about schmoozing with the folks at the charity in a volunteer capacity. I don't know how much help I could be, though, as I've never ziplined in my life." She chuckles. "Maybe you should ask another rep to go with you."

My response is swift. "No. It has to be you—your name is on the door of the Agency, after all." She swallows. I can tell she's scared to try the activity, but I think it's perfect. "I've done it before, and it's fun. You'll be a pro in no time."

I remember my trip to Costa Rica with Darcey, where we went ziplining through the forest. It was exhilarating flying through the trees, with monkeys as observers. I'm sure this trip will be much tamer. But fun, nevertheless. *Sans* the bitch.

"I'm not sure. I'm more of a foodie girl." Her lips clamp shut.

"You took me to the GreenMarket. I'll take you ziplining."

Her hand lands on the mouse and she clicks a couple of times. Her shoulders sag. "Seems like the trip to the Catskills is the only one they're still looking for volunteers."

"They need us. That has to count for something."

"I guess." She bites her lower lip.

What I could do to that lip. The imaginary record playing in my head screeches. *She's. Your. Boss. Plus, born-again virgin, remember?*

Shoving aside my errant thoughts, I reassure her. "I'll be with you, so you won't have to worry. I swear, after your first round, you'll love it. And you'll be upset when it ends."

She pushes away from her desk, her palm over her cheek. Picking up the mouse again, she types something on her keyboard. "There. You're looking at the next two chaperones for the Catskills trip."

Her decisiveness propels me to my feet. Rubbing my hands together, I reply, "Awesome. You won't regret this. In fact, I bet you'll say it's one of the best experiences in your life."

"If I live long enough to tell, that is."

I toss my head back and laugh. "I can guarantee it."

Catskills—thirty miles.

I pass the green sign, my excitement growing with each mile. Friends For Fun got back to Madison that their transportation is only for the kids, so we were expected to find our own way to the event. Since Madison doesn't own a car, I spoke with our family's vehicle concierge about wanting to dust off my driving skills. Jimmy recommended I take one of the SUVs so there's plenty of room for Madison, me, and our overnight bags. We decided to come prepared in case I was too tired to drive back tonight.

Riding shotgun, Madison fiddles with the radio. A new song by The Light Rail plays. "I like TLR," she remarks. "I always think of them as an updated version of Hunte."

"They're good." I tap the steering wheel in time with the beat. "Hunte's a classic, though." Wonder how she'd react if she knew I've partied with both bands? I dip my toe. "Trent and Braxton are cool."

Her head whips toward me. "Have you met them?"

"Yeah. A few times." Heat tips my earlobes. "My family has access to everything that goes on at Madison Square Garden since it's newsworthy for the magazine. I've caught a few of their performances and chatted with them at their afterparties."

"That is so cool. I swear, if I ever make it big in this City, that's one of my goals—hang backstage with rock stars." She laughs. "I didn't even realize it was an option, but I'm adding it to my list."

"Your list?"

"Yeah. Professional goals." She pauses. "I have a list for my personal life too."

A list of goals? Fascinating. "I've never thought about creating lists like these. What else is on yours?"

"Normal things, you know. World domination and the like." Chuckling, she leans forward and shuts off the radio. "No, really, they are achievable goals. How I'd like the firm to grow year after year. Clients I'd love to work with."

"Like TLR?"

"Oh no." She shakes her head. "I'm realistic. They wouldn't give me the time of day. My dream clients are local shops. Some with a few different locations."

"You undersell yourself. You have big ideas, and I think clients like TLR would be honored to work with you."

She stares at me, her intense blue eyes unwavering. "I need to work up to them first. Baby steps."

I shrug. "Just saying, I think you'd be a welcome player on their team." I take the exit for the resort area. "And what are your personal goals, if you don't mind me asking?"

She licks her lips. "Oh, the usual stuff. Fly home to visit my family more."

Her comment makes me realize I don't know much about this woman, other than she's whip-smart, funny, and sweet with her employees. All positive traits. "Where are they?"

"Kansas." She swivels in her seat to face me. "I was born and raised there and my family's still there. I have an older brother and sister—both of whom are married with kids—plus my parents."

She makes this statement matter-of-factly, like her circumstances are nothing out of the ordinary. "What made you leave what sounds like a close-knit group?"

"Oh, you know. The lure of the Big City!" Her arms windmill. Before I can ask her another question, signs for our location litter the road. "We're almost there."

"Looks like it." I navigate the SUV through the windy roads and pull into a parking lot. Getting out, I don my Gucci sunglasses. A big yellow school bus sporting a Friends For Fun sign is parked to the side. "There's the bus. They have to be around here somewhere."

Sure enough, a group of about twenty kids stands by the ticket counter. I look down at Madison, who takes a deep breath. "Let's go meet them. And don't worry, you're going to be great." We start heading toward the group.

Locating the woman in charge isn't hard, considering she's wearing a neon pink Friends For Fun t-shirt and holding a clip-board. Madison inhales. "There's Vanessa. Let's check in."

Together, we approach her and introduce ourselves. "Stephanie's been talking your Agency up. I'm looking forward to getting to know you. And thanks for volunteering today." She gives us shirts to wear with the charity's logo and asks us to help out with the mini golf nine-hole course before we take on ziplining. Madison appears to be more comfortable with this activity, judging from her eager demeanor.

We join the kids and are assigned to be with a group of ten-year-olds. I've not been around too many youngsters since I was one, but Madison's a natural. Must be because of the nieces and nephews she mentioned during the trip here.

Successfully making it through the first three holes, we move onto the next one, which features a green with different elevations. This could be challenging but the first two kids sail through without any problem, knocking their balls in at or slightly over par. I take my turn and sink the first hole-in-one of the game, causing all the kids to shout their approval. Standing taller, I flip my putter upright and lead the exultant chants, high-fiving each one of the kids with a smile stretched across my face.

"Well done," Madison notes when I return to her side.

"I didn't expect such an uproar," I admit. "But it was cool. I love how all of the kids support each other. Even me."

"They're a super group. It's great how they offer pointers to each other."

We move on through a couple more rounds. I seem to have acquired a few new shadows, all of whom are adorable little girls. One of the boys keeps giving me dirty looks and I excuse myself to approach him. "Hey," I extend my hand. "I'm Xander."

"Troy," the little boy responds.

"Are you having fun today, Troy?"

He pretends to hit an imaginary ball. Keeping his eyes trained downward, he replies, "I guess."

"Thank you for celebrating my hole-in-one back there. I think you're pretty good at this game, too."

He lifts his head, and his brown eyes accuse me. "Then why are all the girls hanging off you?"

A light bulb goes off above my head. He's jealous. I stifle a chuckle. "I don't know, Troy. Have you tried talking with them? They're very nice."

"Nah," he scoffs and swings a few more times. Remaining silent, my restraint is rewarded when he asks, "Did you talk with them?"

I nod. "I did. They're all very sweet. And I have a secret." I bend down to be even with his height.

Troy's eyes turn a deeper shade of brown. "What's your secret?"

"Girls like it when you say something nice about them. Like, compliment their hair or their clothes."

"They do?"

His tone is shocked, like no one's ever suggested such an outrageous thing to him. My heart reaches out to him, realizing no one probably has. I raise three fingers. "Yes." I direct my face toward my female shadows. "Which one of them has caught your fancy?"

Pink stains his cheeks. "Wanna. The one with the long braids."

I slant a glance toward the object of Troy's affection. "Do you like the way she wears her hair?"

"Yeah." He swings the putter again. "And she's smart. I like that, too."

"How about this? Why don't you give her a compliment when it's her turn again? Make her feel good, whether or not she makes a good putt."

Troy focuses his attention on me and gnaws on his thumb. "I guess I could tell her she's doing great."

When Madison finishes, Wanna approaches the tee. I stand, placing my hand on Troy's back. "Now's a good time to try. I bet she'll smile at you."

"You think?"

I give him a solemn nod. "I do." Giving him a little nudge, I offer him one last piece of advice. "Go give her Troy well wishes."

He runs his hand through his hair and approaches Wanna. Resting my shoulder against a pole, I watch the scene unfold as Madison approaches me. "What were you—"

I put my fingers to my lips. "Shhh."

Madison doesn't say anything else. Turning, she watches what I do, minus my silent rooting for Troy to succeed. I've never considered talking with girls before from a place of nervousness. I really hope I was able to get through to the boy. And that Wanna responds.

Sure enough, Wanna hits the ball and Troy yells his approval. Her braids fly as she turns to check who was cheering her, a shy smile crossing her face. She says something I can't hear from my distance, but Troy's response is unmistakable—he gives me a thumbs up when Wanna goes to take her second shot. I return the signal.

Next to me, Madison asks, "What on earth is all that about?"

"Top secret." I see she's dying to know more, so I add, "Man card stuff."

"But he's only ten."

"He'll be a man someday." Chuckling, I pretend to zip my lips, then divert my attention to Troy who now is helping Wanna pick up her ball. Smiling, I return my attention to Madison. "A good man."

Three pint-sized girls rush me when we reach the ninth hole. I stifle my urge for an adult beverage break—not with this group of kids. They push one girl forward. "Mr. Xander, can you show me how to make a hole-in-one?"

If only it were that simple. "I would love to give you some pointers, but I can't vouch that you'll hit the ball into the hole. Deal?"

She giggles and holds up her palm. "Deal!"

I give her the expected high five and accompany her to the tee. I correct her stance, and while the ball doesn't sink into the hole, it gets pretty damned close. "Great job!"

She hugs my legs. "Thank you!"

Smiling down at her, I ruffle her hair. "Now go and get one under par."

She skips toward her ball. Pure joy. These kids may not have much monetarily, but they have this charity to provide some amazing experiences for them. Which they're taking to heart. Growing up surrounded with all the disposable income we ever wanted, I can't remember ever enjoying something as simple as a game of mini golf the way these kids are.

"You're great with them."

I start at Madison's compliment, not having heard her approach. "Thanks. They're pretty awesome."

When the next kid finishes, Madison walks forward and puts her ball down. I offer her some pointers the way I helped out the little girl, and Madison adjusts her stance slightly. She whacks the ball and it flies through the air in a perfect arc, landing directly into the cup.

"I did it!" Madison jumps up and down with the kids surrounding her.

When the tumult calms down, I take my place. The kids yell their advice at me like I've been giving to them all morning and I pretend to take each one of their suggestions to heart. When I tee off, it follows the same trajectory as Madison's, also ending in the cup. More chaos erupts.

"You were awesome out there," Madison notes as we walk toward the booth to drop off our clubs. "Thanks for helping me. I've never hit a hole in one before."

Plucking her club out of her hand, I reply, "Stick with me. I'll show you all sorts of new things to try." Shit, that sounded wrong. "Like what's next," I add.

Her smile dims. "I've been trying to forget we're going ziplining."

Turning over our clubs and balls to the attendant, I give her some encouragement. "I'll bet you're doing a superman by the end of it."

Sounds like some sex position. What am I thinking?

Frowning, she tilts her head.

"The ziplining instructors will fill you in."

12

Madison

A group of us stands around gearing up like the instructors taught us. Now I have one more thing to worry about, and it has nothing at all to do with ziplining.

No.

It has everything to do with what's shaking in my hands—the helmet. The woman instructing us told us to pull our hair up before putting it on. I *never* pull my hair up unless I'm alone. The toddler from the mall pointing at my scar flashes before my eyes. I put the helmet down onto a chair. "No. Way."

For once, Xander isn't by me. He's over helping out other kids to put on their gear. Of course he is. He's been like a kid all day. If my stomach wasn't doing somersaults, I'd be turned on by his attitude. Turned on? *What am I thinking?* If for no other reason this thought is verboten—he's my employee. My life is a total disaster.

One of the girls in the group comes over to me and picks up my helmet. Even though she's ten, she's barely shorter than me. She's been shadowing Xander all day, and he even helped her out with mini golf. "This goes on your head, silly."

I smile at the girl. "I know, but I'm not feeling up for this. I think I'm going to sit it out and cheer all of you on from the sidelines."

She puts the helmet back down. In a small voice, she admits, "I was scared before I got here, but this place is super cool. They'll take good care of us out on the course. But you have to wear your safety stuff."

I smile at her innocence. By her age, I was too well-versed in scorn from my classmates. "I'm sure you're right."

"Is something else bothering you besides the ziplining?"

Where did this insightful child come from? When I trace my scar but remain silent, she continues, "We're all supportive of each other. Do you want me to call everyone over and give you a cheer?"

If only it were that easy. "Thanks, but I'm not sure a cheer will convince me to put on that helmet."

Her mouth falls open. "Oh! That's it? It's so easy. Just pull your hair away from your face, pile it on top of your head, and plunk it down. Like this."

Before I know what she's doing, she has all of my hair in her hand and the weight of the helmet pushes down from the top of my head. My heart rate speeds to triple time and my palm clamps down on my scar. But the damage is done.

The child pries my fingers away from my cheek. I clench my jaw, awaiting ridicule.

"Oh wow," she breathes inches from my scar. "This is too cool." She turns and yells for her friends to come over.

Cool? Out of the myriad things my scar has been called, "cool" has never been one. My hand lands on my helmet to remove it and let my hair protect me, but I'm too late. About half of the entire Friends with Fun group has surrounded me. The girl—now a ring-leader, of sorts—announces, "Miss Madison has the most amazing mark on her cheek. Check it out!"

With no other alternative, I turn to face the group, who stare at my cheek. I've not felt this exposed since the pit bull bit me. Shallow breaths come in rapid-fire.

I need to get out of here.

Now.

My eyes dart to the exit—it's too far away. I slam them shut.

"Wow! I love that!"

"You're right. How rad is that!"

"Where can I get one?"

My eyelids pop open. Surveying the girls in front of me, I blink faster than my pulse. "You," I clear my throat. "You actually like my scar?"

The group's reply is immediate. "Heck yes."

They *like* it. My mind can't wrap around their response. Not one of them was repulsed. One even *wants* a scar like mine. I shake my head, trying to assimilate their reaction, which is unbelievable to me.

"What are we missing?"

Xander's voice floats through the air on my left side. The unscarred one. One girl points to my other cheek. "Miss Madison is a badass." All the girls giggle at the swear word, while the boys who arrived with Xander move around to get a better view of my scar. All but Xander, that is. The boys respond much like the girls did, with comments about how awesome it is. The instructor calls out for them to line up and they run over to him.

Everyone except Xander.

In a tender voice, he asks, "May I see?"

Swallowing, I nod. Cat's out of the bag. Or dog's bite is. His fingers land on my chin and he turns my head to get the full view of my ugly scar. Which the kids thought was cool.

The longer Xander takes inspecting my scar, the more I want to crawl out of my body and run away. Or scratch out his eyeballs. The familiar pricking of tears welling pings my awareness. Action. This has to end.

I open my mouth, but he steals my words. "Does it hurt?"

I swallow. "Not anymore," I whimper.

"How did it happen, if you don't mind me asking?"

"A dog bit me when I was five." I swallow. "A long time ago."

His finger traces the ugly mark. "I don't think it's cool." My eyes snap to his. "I think it shows how brave you are."

I inhale, latching onto his supportive words and sending them straight into my soul. Brave? He said I'm brave. How is Xander different from everyone in my life, including my former boyfriends? I close my eyes, savoring his touch.

Unsure how to respond, I murmur, "Thanks."

His finger remains on my cheek, his silent support unbelievable. Incredible. Amazing.

"Alright. You two over there! Come on over for your final briefing." A whistle punctuates the instructor's announcement.

Xander drops his hand, motioning for me to precede him. My amazement at how my scar was received is short-lived as trepidation about what we're about to do replaces it. The instructor shows us the basics and urges us to join our group. I slip into the rest of the gear and trudge toward the kids.

Slinging his arm around my shoulders for a second, Xander says, "Don't worry. Trust the riggings and you'll be fine."

I focus on his words as we make our way to the first pole. The kids scale the ladder with ease and shout their glee as they fling themselves from this platform to the landing zone miles away, flying over lush greenery miles beneath them. Okay, not miles. Still, it's far. *Can I do this?*

"Take a deep breath," Xander reassures.

We reach the pole that leads to the takeoff spot. I look up and shake my head. "No. I can't."

"Yes, you can. You braved a dog and bear his mark, so I have every faith you can zip across this little line."

"It's not little."

He grins. "I've done ziplining through a forest, and the lines were three times this length and height. You're going to love it. I promise." He places my limp hands on the ladder.

"Why don't you go first? I'll watch."

"Good try. Nope."

The attendant yells down to me. "Come on up. The weather's great!"

Stuck, I begin the lengthy, embarrassing trek up the ladder. If only I'd stuck to my recent diet. Or the one before it. When I reach the top, which is surprisingly soon, I focus on the attendant and blurt, "I've never done this before."

The guy wearing an orange shirt grins at me. "Let me connect you and you can enjoy your first time across. Nothing like it." He keeps up a running commentary, pointing out safety features and the braking mechanism. Before I'm buckled in, Xander appears on the landing next to me.

A wave of nausea crests. Shaking my head, I admit, "You know, I can't do this. I'm sorry." Still free of the mechanism, I step back and take deep breaths.

Beside me, Xander says, "Madison, I really think you'll love ziplining. But I won't pressure you. All I'll ask is you watch me. I promise to wait for you on the other side."

I consider his words. "Fine. I'll watch. And if I don't like what I see, I'm climbing back down."

His lip quirks up into a half-grin. "I'll catch you when you arrive." Then he shocks me by giving a swift kiss to my scar. "Be brave."

My entire body buzzes at his tender kiss as he gets buckled in, gives me a jaunty salute, and zips across to the other platform. A bunch of the Friends For Fun kids cheer his arrival. When he's unbuckled, he turns and motions for me to try.

It's now or never. I check out how far off the ground we are, which really isn't that high. I hear him calling me "brave" while the kids urge me on from the landing platform. It's like insects have invaded my limbs, buzzing throughout my veins. My eyes slam shut. *You can do anything you set your mind to, Madison.* Ma's words spur me on.

With a humongous inhale, I look at the attendant and step forward. All too soon I'm buckled in.

"And go!"

Screaming, I freefall and scramble into position as if I were sitting on a chaise lounge, hurling toward the platform where Xander and the kids await. Their arms pump the air. Landscape whizzes by. The wind blows against my face. It's gorgeous and scary and exciting and exhilarating. About halfway through, I let out a whoop. This is the definition of fun.

As I approach the platform, I pull on the brake to slow down. Xander and the kids give me some room, as does the attendant.

They point to what appears to be an oversized pillow, to which I align my feet and break my ride. The attendant catches me and undoes my buckles. Once I'm free, I jump into Xander's arms.

"I did it!"

"Yes, you did. I'm so proud of you. I knew my brave girl could do it." His lips cover mine. Before I can process what's happening, the kids break us apart, cheering my successful glide across and urging us on to the next round. On cloud nine, I complete the entire course—even trying a superman position on the final trip. All too soon, this experience ends.

Walking back to the main area, all of the kids brim with positive energy, more keyed up than before the day started. Guess that's the charity's plan—they'll crash on the way home. Vanessa's a smart cookie.

At the picnic area, boxed lunches are distributed. Boys sit at one table with Xander, and girls at the other with me. At my table, the girls trade fruit and laugh, and sing rap songs. I've had a fantastic day, due in large part to the girls who saw my scar as something unique to me to be celebrated. After the second child asks me about how I got it, I screw up my courage and share the whole story.

When I'm finished, one girl remarks, "My neighbor has a pit bull, and he's super sweet. I think you were bitten by a bad dog." The rest of the children agree.

Good or bad, I'm still staying as far away from those animals as possible. But I don't share my thoughts, as the girls are now off on a big discussion of the boys. Wanna seems to be taken by Troy, and from the glances he's giving her, I think the attraction is reciprocated. Young love can be so sweet.

If only some guy would look at me with the same longing as Troy exhibits. Xander teases the boys, drawing my attention. No. Not *some* guy. My stomach twists as realization dawns with a rush like ziplining across the course. *That* guy.

His sweet kiss on my scar and the triumphant one after my first zipline replay in my head as my longing grows. *Put a stop to this nonsense, Madison. You're his boss. And since when did you grow six inches, don a gorgeous coif, remove the scar, and be worthy of his attention?*

With a sigh, I return my attention to the girls around me who are packing up their trash. I toss the remnants of my lunch back into the box and follow them to where Xander's leading cheers for the kids while they throw their garbage from an imaginary free-throw line. Stepping up to the line, as it were, I take aim and my box goes sailing. Like usual, it deviates from my intended target, but Xander gives it an assist and it lands in the pail.

"Three points," he yells, and the kids do their chant.

He dips his chin while maintaining eye contact, then focuses on the next kid. Afterward, we join the kids as they swarm the bus, receiving hugs from our newfound friends. Vanessa thanks us for volunteering, whispers she can't wait to see our proposal, and gathers them onto the bus. As it pulls away, the kids hang out the windows waving and yelling at us. Xander and I wave back.

"What a great bunch," Xander notes, lowering his arm.

Dropping mine, I reply, "It was a great day. The kids are fantastic. I'm already thinking of some ideas to use to pitch the charity."

"I am too." We start toward his SUV.

"I want to thank you, again for helping me get over my fear about ziplining. You were right. It's a great rush." No lie. I'd love to do it again.

"Stick with me, kid. I'll introduce you to all sorts of fun things."

Friends. We'll only ever be friends. I have to keep reminding myself he's a flirty guy and doesn't mean anything by his words. If only he did.

He opens the passenger side door and helps me hop up to get in. *Wish I wasn't so damn short!* I settle into my seat and click my seatbelt while he drops into the driver's side. "I'm parched. I think I told you that my family has a cabin out here, and I seem to recall there being a bar nearby. Can I interest you in a drink?"

It's not even four o'clock on Saturday. We brought our overnight bags in case he didn't feel like driving out here and back in one day. Since I have nothing else on my agenda for the weekend, I shrug. "Sure. Sounds fun."

He turns on the GPS, pushes some buttons, and soon turns into the parking lot at a place called "Libby's Crooked Watering Hole." It looks like a hobbit house. "This is so cute!"

Xander turns off the car. "And it has some great beverages, if memory serves." He opens his door. "Let's check it out."

I put my hand on the handle, shocked when he opens the door. Without saying a word, he assists me from the vehicle onto the pavement and we enter the bar. Inside, it's like we entered the Baggins house from the *Lord of the Rings*. Only this version has crooked floors and terracotta walls. And bookcases lined with board games. What an unusual, intriguing space. I wonder who does their PR?

My always unruffled companion trips. Without thought, I catch his arm and steady him. When he's back on his feet, he gives me a brilliant smile, although his cheeks are stained a slight pink. "Thanks."

Grateful it was him who tripped and not me, for once, I tease, "Glad to see you're not totally perfect."

He snorts. "Hardly."

I ponder his comment as we approach the large, wooden bar and place our orders. His work at the Agency has been stellar, although he's seemed shocked every time I congratulate him on his ideas as if he's not received praise in the past. Or worse, that he doesn't believe in himself. I observe him interacting with other patrons, exuding confidence. Is that a cover?

Drinks in hand, we survey the bustling bar, looking for seating. "There," he points to a full picnic table with two empty spots, side-by-side, at the end. When we arrive, Xander asks if we can join them and we're greeted with welcomes.

Hours pass. Questions about his self-confidence nag, but I put them on ice and enjoy our new setting. Our tablemates are funny and we even got into a spirited game of Trivial Pursuit. When I'm able to answer the final question about famous movie stars of the Golden Age of Hollywood, our team wins. Our side of the table jumps to our feet, overjoyed, while the opposing side grumbles— exuding good nature.

The screeching of picnic benches rips the air as both sides push away from the table. We shake hands with our new "friends" as they leave. Turning to Xander, I ask, "Ready? It's still relatively early if you want to drive back to the City."

Xander checks his Rolex—because, of course, he owns this expensive piece of jewelry. "You know, I'm not really feeling like driving right now. What do you think about staying over up here? We can crash at my family's cabin."

I picture a rustic, two-bedroom log cabin in the woods, complete with a brick fireplace. The image is homey, prompting a pang for Kansas. "Are you sure they won't mind?"

"Dad's on home arrest, so he can't leave his apartment, let alone the City."

It's the first time he's mentioned his father's situation, although the headlines scream about it for him. Not wanting to add salt to what I assume to be a festering wound, I reply, "Sure thing. Sounds fun."

"Great." We wave to our Trivial Pursuit teammates, and rivals, and depart the delightfully crooked bar.

Within fifteen minutes, we turn off the highway into a more residential area. We pass several average-looking houses, some of which are log cabins. Exactly what I expected.

The blinker turns on as a new song by Cole Manchester fills the SUV. I'm humming along with the catchy tune when we drive past bigger and bigger houses. Two more turns, and my humming has ceased as I'm staring wide-eyed at the passing mansions on park-like acreage. He turns into a driveway. At least I think it's a driveway and not a road. There was no street sign for it. We turn a bend and a castle appears before us.

Holy. Shit.

"This is your family's *cabin?*" I can't keep the incredulity out of my voice.

He slants me a glance. "Yeah. We used to spend a couple of weeks here during the fall when I was a kid."

They only used this castle for a few days in the third quarter? "And what did you do with this place the other fifty weeks of the year?" Talk about overwhelming. "You know, I saw a Holiday Inn down the road. I'll be fine staying there tonight."

13

Xander

The brave woman sitting next to me who faced not one, but two demons today, wants to flee. But I don't want her to leave. I've felt more alive, more *me*, with her over the past couple of weeks than I ever have in my entire life. The time spent with the Friends For Fun kids on the mini golf course and ziplining earlier? Priceless.

I grab her arm. "No."

Her beguiling blue eyes bounce between my hand and the floor-mats . "I don't belong here."

I imagine Dad summing up my companion—*chubby and short and scarred and downtown.* To which I mentally retort—*she's kind and caring and smart and brave.* She was bitten by a dog and soldiered on. She moved from her home state to make a name for herself in the Big Apple. She says my ideas are solid rather than treat them as owed to her. Or worse, deride them as stupid. I kick my inner father out of the SUV.

"Please, Madison, believe me when I say you probably belong here more than anyone who's ever walked through those doors. Let me show you around, and if you're still uncomfortable, we'll go to the hotel."

Something I said must placate her because she offers a small, "Promise?"

"I do." I also want to bottle her up and keep her in my pocket, but no way am I ever confessing to such fancy. For three important reasons. One, she's my *boss*. Two, she's definitely friend-zoned me. What's my other reason? Oh yeah, I've sworn off women.

We get out of the vehicle and I carry all our luggage through the double doors into the pitch dark house. Depositing the bags onto the marble foyer, I instruct Alexa to turn on the lights. Once the house is illuminated, I add, "Alexa, turn on my smooth jazz playlist." The sounds of trumpets and piano fill the air. Much more comfortable.

"Xander, this is probably the largest, uhm, house, I've ever been in."

"It's only a cabin. Maybe the rooms are a bit bigger than you're used to, but we've used it as a family home for years. And remember, for me, family includes Uncles Ward and Ogden and their kids, so it's a lot of people."

"Well, when you put it that way." She looks off to the distance. "That must mean there are like twelve bedrooms in here."

At least, but I don't correct her. She's already skittish enough. And it hits me—I've never had a woman recoil from the extravagances of my family's wealth before. Another level of Madison Welch to ponder.

Stopping myself from going down that rabbit hole, I offer her my arm. "C'mon. Let me give you the tour. This, obviously, is the foyer." We take a few steps and I point out Dad's sacrosanct office. Only he and his partners go in there, so we bypass the room and enter the family room. Complete with a baby grand piano that Ward's daughter, Gabrielle, insisted on having. Madison plunks a couple of the ivories.

"I played piano when I was a kid for a couple of years."

"Have at it."

She pulls the bench away and takes a seat. "I only remember this."

She launches into "Ode to Joy," missing a few notes but doing a decent job. My shoulders relax a little as I start to believe she's going to stay and not run away to the Holiday Inn. When she finishes, I clap. "You did great."

Pushing her hair off the left side of her face, her unblemished one, she stands. "You're way too kind." She closes the fallboard and returns to my side.

"There's no way I could've done that. In my book, that makes you fantastic." I tap her side with my own. "So, think you'll stick around tonight?"

She bumps me back. "You had me at the piano."

Tension releasing throughout my body, I lead her toward what's supposed to be the heart of the home, the kitchen. It's an oversized white monstrosity, filled with every trick imaginable. Rushing by me, she exclaims, "You have a pot filler." She runs her fingers over the piping.

"I'm not much of a cook. All I know is that Mom and Dad spared no expense when they remodeled." I frown. Not like we used all—or even some—of these gadgets because we always ordered in, but they look impressive. Not even Sebastian's taken advantage of any of this.

She rubs her hand across the granite island, letting it travel over the waterfall edge. "The cookies I could bake here for the holidays." Her tone is wistful.

"We're always in the City for Christmas. There's so much going on there that we don't come out here to celebrate."

Her mouth drops open. "If I had this place at my disposal, I'd never return to the City. It's like an amusement park in here. Piano, this amazing kitchen." Her lips clamp.

To me, the cabin's always been a fall getaway, like our place in the Hamptons for the summer. Which has to be twice this size, located right on the ocean. An errant thought about getting married out there pricks my memory. "Let's go. There's more to see." Without bothering to see if she's following me, I leave this part of the house and take the stairs down to the basement. "We have all the normal things on this level. A bowling alley, media room, wine cellar." I point to the various areas while giving her the tour.

Madison becomes quieter the longer the tour goes on, so I

decide to skip the basketball court—it's only a half one anyway. Returning to the wine cellar, I select a couple of bottles and we return to the main level. My fingers point upward. "Upstairs are all the bedrooms."

"I simply can't imagine living in a home this grand."

"It's just a house. And we don't live here." I hold up the two bottles I brought up. "Let's go outside. We have a fire pit out there."

"Of course you do."

Her snarky comment causes me to smile. Glad she's not as intimidated by the cabin now. Stopping in the butler's pantry, I select two wine glasses plus an electronic wine opener and an aerator, which she takes from me. Using the retractable sliding glass doors, we enter the backyard. Flipping a button, the fire pit comes to life.

"Now that is cool." Madison deposits the wine paraphernalia on the table and places her hands in front of the fire. "Feels so good."

"Are you cold? I could get you a blanket."

"No, this fire is perfect."

Accepting her response, I get to work opening the bottle of red. Checking out the label, I say, "This is a Malbec from Australia. One of my favorites."

"When you're not drinking bourbon, that is," she teases.

I catch myself smiling. Her wit is charming. "You got me there." I pour two glasses through the aerator and hand one to her as I settle in by the fire pit. Inhaling the crisp spring air, I take in the quiet. "It's so peaceful here. Hard to believe we haven't even left New York State."

She sniffs the wine, then takes a sip, her face registering appreciation. "I know. It's like I'm back home in Kansas." She tilts her head upward. "The sky's the same here. Not like in the City with all the light pollution."

Taking her cue, I tip my chin up. "You're right. The stars are the focal point out here." I sip my wine, agreeing with her unspoken approval. "What's it like in Kansas?"

She places the wineglass down on the table and swivels toward me. "It has good and bad, like any place. The food is delicious, especially the barbeque. Every summer we had a BBQ cook-off on the town square and it was like heaven came down and showed us what to expect in our next life."

"That's quite the vivid description."

"It's fantastic." Her face falls. "I haven't been able to go back for the cook-off in three years, ever since I started the Agency."

Pondering her admission, I ask, "Maybe this summer you can make a return visit?"

She tucks the right side of her hair behind her ear, exposing her scar. It isn't as awful as she obviously believes, but it's still a nasty reminder of the dog that bit her. The realization that she's learned to hide it behind her façade of being everyone's buddy whaps like a lightning bolt. Scarred or not, this woman is beautiful because of what she's overcome with nothing but grit and her own brilliance. I want to help her believe in her true beauty.

Bringing my attention back to the present, she reaches for her wineglass. "I'm planning on it." She tilts the glass to her mouth and swallows. "I really want to see my sister. She called me the other day —she's pregnant again. She has two little girls, so I'm hoping it's a boy this time."

None of my siblings, either actual or through my extended family, are married or have kids. Even though I'm the oldest, Theo's the closest one to getting married, but he and Amelia aren't even engaged yet. "Exciting," I note, reaching for my glass.

She nods. "It is. And my brother has two kids, a boy and a girl. So there's always lots of excitement when Auntie Madison is in the house."

I can picture her surrounded by her nieces and nephew like she was today with the Friends For Fun group. "I bet they have a blast with you."

"We do. The oldest ones are starting to get to be a good age, you know?"

No, I really don't know. My family never was close. To be fair, Theo and I have been thick as thieves for most of our lives. And I get along great with my brother and sister, when I see them. Sebastian's off hitting up the YouTube world while Halle's running celebrity weddings all across the globe. Her next question catches me off-guard.

"You said this is your family's house." She uses air quotes around the word family. "What are they like?"

"I have two younger siblings." I fill her in on Chef Bash and Halle's exploits. "Then, through Uncle Ward, there's the twins, Chloe and Gabrielle. It's Gabrielle's piano you were playing inside."

"Is she a musician?"

"Songwriter, actually." She's been at a piano her entire life. "She and Chloe graduate from college this year. We usually take a trip to celebrate such milestones, but haven't planned anything because Dad and his partners, uhm—" I run my fingers up and down the crystal's long stem.

When I don't continue, she asks, "And what about the one who quit VOW-cubed right after you did? Isn't that Theo? Is he part of your extended family that gets to use this cabin?"

I shake off my funk about thinking of Dad's and my uncles' indictments and focus on her question. "Yes. Theo did quit and now is writing a biography about my Uncle Daniel." I puff up with pride at his entrepreneurial endeavor.

"That's awesome."

"He and Amelia are great together. I bet they get engaged before the year ends." I let my words soak in and then continue. "He has three siblings. His older brother, Kiefer, is a plastic surgeon. His younger brother Ryder is the catcher for the NY Aces, while his younger sister, Paige, flips houses."

"Like those awesome shows on HGTV. I love them."

I make a noncommittal noise. If only Paige had more than one house on her resume. But you have to start somewhere, right? "As you can tell, we're all busy in our own lives so we don't see each other too much anymore." Needing an anchor, I finish my glass of wine.

Madison refills my glass. In a low voice, she says, "I can't imagine how difficult all this has been for you." She places her hand on my arm. Her comforting touch spreads warmth throughout my body. "I hope working at the Agency is helping take your mind off your family's situation, even a little bit."

She has no idea how much I've come to crave working for her. Receiving praise for my ideas, while previously unknown, is a thrill. As is brainstorming with my coworkers, who actually appreciate my suggestions. I decide to share a sliver of my new understanding. "Honestly, it's been a godsend. The way you choose to do business is so different from how my father set things up. I appreciate all your homey touches."

"You should be proud of all the work you're doing. You have great ideas and a wonderful gut instinct. Like today. I never would've thought to join Friends For Fun on an outing. I had a great time, met some wonderful kids, and we got to interact with Vanessa on a totally different footing than if we were in a boardroom."

I sit taller, feeling as if I grew ten feet. This is what she does to me. "Thank you. This means a lot to me. Dad isn't a touchy-feely type of guy, and his ideas were the only ones that mattered at VOW-cubed." I take another sip and realize I've never been this truthful with another person about growing up the eldest son in the Turner-Hansen families.

She pours herself a second glass. "Well, I think he was missing out on all the great contributions you could've made." She takes a small sip and replaces her glass on the table. "Do you want to talk about your father's legal issues?"

No. I want them to never have happened. Which means I would still be working for the family business and missing out on the Madison Welch PR Agency. Including outings like today. For some reason, I'm inspired to share.

"There's not much you probably don't already know. Dad and his partners were arrested at the Tinsel and Tatas Gala." My mouth twists, remembering the public humiliation of their FBI perp walk out of the event. "Since then, they've been officially indicted, each ordered to pay a five hundred thousand dollar bail, and released on home confinement. They're currently working on a motion to dismiss the lawsuit."

Her hand reappears on my arm. "Do you think they're going to win their motion?"

I shrug. "I don't know what to believe. I want to hope so, but the government's case seems to have legs. I think the prosecutors have been building it for a few years."

She removes her hand and cups her scarred cheek. "I heard they were indicted for fraud, money laundering, tax evasion, and conspiracy. Those are some heavy-duty charges."

"Yeah." Needing a distraction, I pick up the cork and flip it through my fingers. It's fatter than a pen, but it'll do. "I spoke with their attorney and he mentioned the government thinks there are two sets of books." I toss the cork onto the table. "I can't square this with how my father and his partners operated the business."

"This is so much to deal with, Xander. I can't imagine what you're going through."

Her sincerity leapfrogs over my last bit of reticence. "Honestly, quitting my job was probably the best thing for me. I've been happier working with you than I ever was at VOW-cubed. Don't get me wrong, there's still plenty of pressure at your firm, but you manage to make it more like a group effort." I'm not explaining this too well. "I want to say thank you for taking a chance on me. And I hope my family's mess doesn't backfire on you."

"There's no such thing as bad press," she giggles. "Having *the* Xander Turner be the face of the Agency sent shock waves throughout the industry. At least, in my corner of it."

This woman is kind and generous. And she believes in my ideas. She's never swooned over my face or my body. And she only looks at my high profile as a positive. Remembering my recent night out with Theo and Jesse, I realize she treats me better than most of my so-called friends.

I'm captivated by her intelligent blue eyes, her blond hair, and even her cute Wonder Woman pin. She takes another sip of wine and licks her bottom lip. My whole body urges me to do the same.

Placing both of our glasses on the table, I turn her to face me. I cup my hands over her cheeks. She sucks in her breath. Pushing her hair out of the way, I expose her scar. It's fascinating, with its gnarl of pink bumps and ridges. "You're so brave, Madison Welch."

Her lips part. I can't hold back and meet them in a slow and gentle kiss. They're so soft and natural. I move mine over hers, begging her to open to me. When she does, I wrap my arms around her and press her tightly to my body. Her lips part and I don't wait an instant. My tongue breaches the opening and explores her mouth. Her little moan spurs me on. My hand flies to the back of her head, holding her even tighter against my hardening body.

Breaking our kiss, I pull away and suck in air, filling my lungs. I kiss a line from her cheek over to her scar and kiss it too. She pulls back and stares at me, now sporting dazed eyes and swollen lips.

I offer her what I hope looks like a half-grin. The need to lay her down on this wicker sofa and have my way with her looms. It's been, what? A good six months since I had sex. With a start, I realize I want more than sex with her. She's special. I want to celebrate that.

Recriminations hit hard. *Born-again virgins do not have sex, Xander Turner.*

Besides, she's an accomplished woman, with a bright future ahead of her. What on earth does she see in me?

Sitting before me, Madison's body tightens. "This was a mistake, Xander. I'm your boss." She rushes to her feet. "Which one is my bedroom?"

All of my limbs gain fifty pounds. "Choose any bedroom upstairs. Mine is the third one on the right."

She nods. "See you in the morning." She scampers through the retractable doors and into the house.

I stare at the fire dancing across the fake stones, shoring up my defenses against this beguiling woman. She's forthright, funny, and damned smart. I love our conversations as well as working with her. Still, I need to remember what Darcey did—the *tings* of my ring hitting the floor during the Gala resound in my brain.

No woman, no matter how bewitching, can scale my defenses.

Especially when that woman just reminded me she's my boss.

I push the button and the flame dies down immediately. By rote,

I collect the empty wine glasses, bottle of wine, and the other items of trash and return them to the kitchen.

What was I thinking? I can't go there with my boss. I reach into my pocket and pull out my cell, hitting Theo's contact without pause. It goes to voicemail. As do calls to Jesse and Sebastian. *Fuck.*

Turning to the mess on the island, I throw everything away except for the bottle of wine with about two glasses still in it. I open the kitchen drawers, looking for some paper to leave for our care-takers about the wine. Nothing. *Shit.*

I don't want the bottle to go to waste, but also don't want to finish it myself. That reeks of desperation. No, the cleaning folks will be here on Monday and can take the bottle home with them. Not finding any notepads, I leave the kitchen and enter Dad's office, the one place in the whole cabin that'll have what I need.

Standing inside the empty room, visions of Dad working at this desk assail me. Whenever we came to the cabin, he and his partners would huddle in here while the rest of us enjoyed the lake or a hayride or whatever activity we chose. If only the three chairs in here could talk.

"What were you three up to?" My voice echoes off the walls.

Shaking my head, I go to Dad's desk and open the middle drawer. "Vince Turner" is embossed at the top of a notepad. I grab it and write a note for the caretakers. When I return it, the drawer doesn't close properly.

Jiggling, the drawer opens all the way revealing the culprit—a thick ledger. Why would Dad leave this here and not have it at home, or at least at VOW-cubed? I open it up and Dad's chicken scratch greets me. The year 2019 is across the top. Guess that's why. This is old stuff. I replace it and the drawer closes. Turning my heel, I leave this ghost-filled room, drop the note on the counter, and trek upstairs with my overnight bag.

Some gentleman I am. I didn't even help Madison with her bag.

I reach the top of the staircase and notice the first door's closed. She took Paige's room. I smile, thinking those two women couldn't be more different.

And I've never wanted to kiss my "sister."

14

Madison

A week has passed since our trip with Friends for Fun. Xander's been a complete gentleman ever since our evening at his parent's cabin. I snort. If that was a cabin, I'm the Queen of England.

For the millionth time since our trip, my brain replays our shared kisses in front of the fire pit. He was so careful with me, tracing my scar with his lips and tongue. My hand cups my cheek, trying to hold in his sweet touches. Too bad it ended with a distinctively disgusted expression on my employee's otherwise handsome face.

"Knock, knock." Dev bounds into my office, ending this round of "Xander and Madison Sitting in a Tree" before it landed with a thud with his repulsed look.

"Hey, Dev. What's up?"

He hands me a pile of documents. "I've gone through all the mail like you asked and marked the ones that need your attention with Post-Its."

I accept the mail with a thanks. "And the bills for our current clients?"

"They're in the paper-clipped stack on top."

"Great. You're the best."

"Never forget that," he tilts his head, causing me to chuckle.

Xander appears at my door. "Ready?"

I force my gaze toward the doorway. Nodding, I stand, shove away my instant pang of longing for my employee, and grab my blazer. We're off to Brooklyn to pitch Friends For Fun. Dropping the paperwork my admin gave me into my briefcase, I zip it up. "Hold down the fort while we're out, Dev. I probably will stay home and work from there, rather than trek all the way back into the City after the pitch."

"Good luck. Pull a Howell on them, Xander," Dev gives us his new pep talk, referencing the first client Xander ever pitched who booked on the spot.

Xander's hand lands on Dev's shoulder. "Thanks, man." He focuses his piercing blue eyes on me. "I called for a family car to bring us to Brooklyn, hope you don't mind."

For his comfort, I remind myself. Can't imagine him on the F train. "Sounds better than taking the subway," I trickle a laugh. "Let's go."

We leave the Agency, grab an elevator, and soon we're in the building's lobby. Xander scoffs. "I remember when I first came here for my interview. They gave me a hard time." He points his thumb toward the receptionists.

"Gracie and Lou? They're pussycats." I giggle, offering them a wave as we exit the building, and slip into a different SUV from the one he drove to the Catskills. This one has dark-tinted windows.

Fingering the leather seat, I ask, "How many cars does your family have?"

He shrugs. "I'm not sure. We have a limo and at least four or five other vehicles. Why?"

I shrug, adding this factoid to my mental notes of how different we are. "Just wondering." Focusing my attention on the upcoming pitch, I pepper Xander with some questions.

He fields all my queries with grace. "Volunteers will learn more from the kids at Friends For Fun than they expect. We certainly did," he concludes.

I clap. "Sounds great."

The SUV makes its way across the Brooklyn Bridge, and I watch as the City's skyscrapers give way to smaller buildings across the East River. Soon, we stop in front of a storefront with the charity's name across it. I scramble out of the SUV, looping my rather heavy briefcase across my shoulder, and approach the entrance.

Xander comes up next to me and places his hand on the small of my back. At the innocent contact, synapses fire throughout my bloodstream, which I quell. We're here to do business. *Nothing more.*

An hour later, we leave Vanessa and the board. On the sidewalk, Xander texts his family's car service concierge. A reminder of how vastly different we are. "I think you did really well in there. You fielded all of the board's questions without missing a beat."

He puts on his Gucci sunglasses, bouncing on his heels. "Thank you. It felt good."

I give him a sunny smile. "You're a natural." Stopping myself from bumping his shoulder, I continue, "I don't live too far away, so I'll leave you here. Enjoy the rest of your night."

His head whips to face mine. "What?" He clears his throat. "I was hoping we could celebrate by going out to dinner."

Celebrate his impressive pitch. A work thing, not a personal one. I hold up my briefcase. "I'd love to, but Dev gave me tons of homework."

"But you have to eat dinner."

Yeah, while I sit on my couch and pour over the documents in my briefcase. Not seated across from the most gorgeous man I've ever seen. "I can grab something at home. Not a problem."

He pulls his sunglasses down his nose, exposing his compelling blue eyes. "It'll be more fun if we eat together. I don't want to let this feeling go, and I know once I'm alone, it'll all be over."

Damn, he's making this hard. "Sorry."

Xander's shoulders fall. "Well, thanks so much for coming with me to this presentation. Our trip out to the Catskills helped me develop it, and your suggestions made it great. I hope we hear something positive from them soon."

A wistful tone enters his voice and tugs at my heart, reinforcing my suspicions that he somehow doesn't believe in himself. The need to comfort him rises. As does my desire to simply look at this man for a while longer. "You know what? You're right. I do need to eat."

His brilliant pearly whites make their appearance. "Thanks! Let's stay close, so you can get home all the faster. I know a great place nearby—The River Café." His thumbs tap on his cell.

As long as I've lived in Brooklyn, I've never once stepped foot into this pricey restaurant. "That's too expensive, and we didn't land the client yet. There's a great little Malaysian spot around the corner from my apartment."

"Too late." He holds up his phone. "Already told Jimmy our new destination."

I've only heard amazing things about this restaurant, and it's been on my list of places to try for forever. One business dinner should be fine. *Just don't stare too deeply at your companion.* I affect a grin. "Guess I can't argue with Jimmy."

The SUV pulls up and Xander helps me into the vehicle. Within minutes, we pull into the front entrance, and the valet opens the door for us. I slide out, wishing I didn't have my bulky briefcase.

"Here, let me take that for you." Before I understand what he's doing, Xander removes the briefcase from my shoulder. The bulky leather satchel looks much less so on his frame.

Instead of fighting him, I accept his polite offer and we approach the hostess stand. She gives both of us the once-over. To be fair, she almost purrs at Xander while glancing in my direction once. "Reservation?"

"I didn't have time to make one," Xander replies. "Our business meeting ended, and I realized we were in your neck of the woods. I really hope you can fit us in." He gives her one of his fantastic smiles.

The hostess wilts under his scrutiny. *I get it, honey.* "Let me see what I can do." Her pen runs down the book, and she smiles. "Perfect." She picks up a couple of menus and requests we follow her, stopping at a table by the windows with a fantastic view of Manhattan.

Slipping into my seat, I stare out the window like a kid eyeing a candy store. "Wow! What a gorgeous view!" He glances out the window as if it were nothing extraordinary. I'll never become so blasé about the Big Apple. When he doesn't respond, I blurt, "I can't believe you don't think the same."

He focuses on looking out the window again. "You're right. I don't usually take any time to check out the City, since I live and breathe it daily." He studies the view. "But it does look beautiful from here."

Vindication runs through my veins. *Score one for the girl from Kansas!* I pick up the menu, bracing myself for the prices, and am rewarded for my foresight. My eyes pop at the cost of a simple salad, extra for a protein.

Our waiter appears, offering still or sparkling water. After he pours, he rattles off a list of mouth-watering specials. All of which I'm sure are out of my price range. Salad it is.

Seems like Xander has other ideas. "The lady will have a mojito, while I'll have a bourbon. Thanks." The waiter scurries off.

I lean forward. "I would've been fine with water."

He mirrors my posture. "We're celebrating, remember?"

Adding another twenty dollars to my tab, I say, "Isn't it a bit premature? We don't know if the Agency won the account."

"Don't have faith in my abilities?"

If only he believed in himself as much as his sham cocky attitude portrays. "You were great in there. But we don't know what the other firms are presenting, though." Like Kelsey. Bet anything she has her hooks into Friends For Fun too. "In any event, I'm proud of our pitch."

The waiter drops off our cocktails and we place our orders. Of course, Xander questions my rabbit food but I stick to my guns. Once the waiter leaves, Xander raises his glass filled with amber liquid. "I think we make a great team."

"I concur." I tap my glass against his, all the while reminding myself to keep things professional.

This mojito has to be the best one I've ever tasted. We chat about the pitch and goings-on at the office while the restaurant fills up around us. Xander is his normal, charming, engaging self and the meal passes with lots of laughter.

When the waiter clears our plates, he asks if we want dessert. His mentioning my favorite sweet treat makes me want to say yes, but my waistline—and wallet—beg me to keep my mouth shut. So I do.

Xander responds, "I'll have a cappuccino. Madison?"

"A coffee sounds good to me." That doesn't have too many calories. And how much can it cost? I add another ten dollars to my running tab, to be safe. The waiter nods and leaves our table.

Xander shifts his weight on the chair. "I need to say thank you. You've been wonderful to work with. I really appreciate all of your guidance and the camaraderie you've fostered at the firm. I've never felt like I truly belonged anywhere before I came to work for you."

Even though I shouldn't be, I'm struck dumb at his admitting a lack of self-pride. He deserves to be as confident in himself as he portrays to others. "I take working for your father wasn't a pleasant experience?"

His eyes travel across the bridge and he studies the skyscrapers for a full minute. "Not really. He's a good businessman and built a great company. If I'm honest, though, I felt like I was always under his thumb. Plus, I love doing PR. I had creativity with the ads at VOW-cubed, don't get me wrong, but what you do is more challenging. And more rewarding."

And much less lucrative. I place my hand on top of his. It's our first contact, skin-to-skin since the fire pit, the buzz of which I ignore. "I'm honored you chose to join the Agency. And your work is amazing. I hardly give you any input at all. But thank you."

"I really enjoy being around you. Learning from you. Sharing—"

"Cappuccino for the gentleman and a coffee for the lady." My hand flies off his. Xander goes silent.

Sharing what? If I ever wanted to throttle a waiter, it was right now. The moment is lost. Gone forever. What was he going to say? Sharing what?

Diverting my frustration, I focus on doctoring my coffee with a packet of sugar and some cream. My eyes bounce through the full restaurant, noticing several pairs of eyes on our table. Of course, they're staring at my gorgeous dinner companion. I blow on my coffee and take a sip, keeping my gaze trained on the white tablecloth.

"I'm proud of what we're doing, M."

M. My ears prick up. No one but Ma shortens my name. I was always the precocious one, whose full name suited her. Even at age five when the dog bit me. When I skipped kindergarten, and then third grade. When I graduated high school at sixteen and college at twenty. M sounds like a mysterious and gorgeous woman, a BP who deserves to be with Xander. I stifle a snort. "You deserve to be. You're a natural."

I also hold no illusions he's talking on a personal level, but knowing he's growing into a full-fledged PR guy, with my help, has to be reward enough. I remember our kisses and correct my thought. It's *one* reward. Can this stunning man who's had every door opened to him be interested in a scarred nobody from Kansas?

He grabs my hand. "I'm learning from the best."

My heart soars. Which I reign in when I notice other patrons staring at us. I tug on my hand, leaning forward. "People are looking at us."

I tug again, but his hand clamps down harder on me. "Let them."

"Xander, please. I'm sure they're thinking why are you out with a scarred nobody like me."

He pulls my hand closer to him, causing my body to stretch across the table. "No. They're thinking why is she out with the scandal-prone scion of New York City?"

I blink. "You are not. Your father may be in some hot water, but no one should visit the sins of the father upon a son."

His white teeth make their appearance. "I want to bottle you up and keep you with me forever. If only the world worked that way. Believe me, I'm being judged for what my father and his partners are going through."

"That's not fair," I whisper.

With his free hand, Xander cups my right cheek, his thumb

glancing over my scar. "Neither is thinking a mark on your cheek besmirches your character."

I stare at his full lips, slack-jawed. But I don't remain like this for long. Xander pulls my head toward him and our lips meet in another kiss that's as searing as it's brief thanks to our waiter's clearing his throat.

We break apart and he passes us the bill. Head reeling, I reach for my wallet, but Xander gives a black credit card to the waiter without even checking the invoice. Fingers clamping onto my wallet, I say, "Here, let me give you my share."

He shakes his head. "No. I dragged you out, away from your heavy briefcase filled with work. Besides," a grin plays across his lush mouth. "It was worth every penny."

With tingling lips, I whisper, "Thank you."

Once our bill is settled and his family's vehicle concierge called, Xander walks behind my chair and helps me push away from the table. He extends his hand, palm up. "Ready?"

Wrapped in a cocoon of his tenderness, the wonderful meal, and the amazing atmosphere, I gaze into his blue eyes and give in to the temptation. Fingers intertwined, he grabs my briefcase and we walk across the restaurant. Diners at every table follow our departure. His model-worthy figure and my short, dumpy one. With every step, the glow from minutes before recedes. By the time we pass the third table, I'm trying to extricate myself from his grip.

But he doesn't let me.

No. Instead his chin rises as if he's daring anyone to make a comment. On leaden feet, I keep pace with him before his arm tenses as if it were made from the quartz countertop at his family's "cabin." His head's turned to the left, and his cheek has hollowed. I follow the trajectory of his eyes and see his former fiancée, Darcey Abbott, sitting there, a sneer drawn across her face.

I yank my hand, but he doesn't react. Rather, he lengthens his stride, causing me to walk double-time to keep up with him.

15

Xander

Darcey. Darcey was sitting there almost this whole time we were, judging by the state of her table. Her meal—remnants of a salad—sits on the table. Her new boyfriend is at her side, grinning like the Cheshire Cat. I've never met the footballer, but I wish him well. He's going to need it.

The scornful expression on her face jumpstarts my flight or fight reaction. Knowing the latter isn't possible in this setting, I activate the former. Without thought, without even acknowledging I saw her sitting there, I speed toward the door, my heart rate kicking up. The only thing keeping me at somewhat of a normal pace is the person attached to my hand.

Madison.

M.

The woman who believes in me and my talents. Not for what my family name can bring, but rather for what *I* do. My ideas. My pitch skills. *Me.*

Before we reach the hostess stand, I've gotten my breathing back under control. My steps slow to accommodate M's short stride. So what if I saw my ex-fiancée—the person who's been spewing lies to any tabloid that will listen. Since Amelia learned the truth about her, she's tried to backtrack her article from her days at *Spill It Magazine*. People know the score. At least, my true friends do.

Dad's admonishment to try to get her back sails to the forefront of my mind, as he always was her biggest cheerleader. Well, fuck that. And fuck him. I'm my own damn man and I get to choose who I want to be with. M's small hand feels amazing in mine, as did her lips before. I've never felt as accomplished as I do with her. So what if her physical appearance isn't up to some stupid societal standard? She's special, inside and out. More so than Darcey Abbott ever could dream to be.

We reach the valet stand where our SUV waits. I open the back door for her and M—panting a little—slides in, not mentioning our race across the restaurant. As I walk around the backside of the vehicle, I realize I owe her an apology. This fantastic woman needs to know what happened back there. I *want* her to understand.

Getting into the car, I ask for her address and pass it along to the driver. "I want to apologize for what just happened," I begin. "I saw—"

M's finger crosses my lips. "I know." She settles into the seat.

We pass building after building, and Darcey's disdain directed at me gnaws until I can't keep it bottled inside. "We were engaged. It ended badly."

"I know," she repeats.

Her sincere tone spurs me to share more. I've never spoken with anyone about what went down. Theo was the closest I've ever come, and even those conversations were stilted. "We had gotten engaged that afternoon. Dad had helped me purchase the ring, and I proposed during the Tinsel and Tatas Speed Skating Relay Race." For a split second, I catch the feeling of being on top of the world when she agreed.

"In the photos, you both looked over the moon."

"I was happy. I thought she was, too. I should've known it was too good to be true when she asked to have the ring reset." I loved the simplicity of the ring I chose. But she wanted something a lot more elaborate. Grandma Lucia warned me against people like her, but I was too besotted to heed anyone's caution. Especially from beyond the grave. And particularly not when the choice was making Dad prouder of me than I'd ever seen him.

Next to me, M holds up her right hand where a couple of rings sit. Without making a comment, she drops it onto her lap. "That must've been difficult."

"I convinced myself it wasn't a big deal. Well, that and the fact she didn't want to get married on the beach in the Hamptons, but rather wanted a big City wedding. I guess I didn't care about the trappings so much as who I was marrying." I turn my head away. "Seems like she was the exact opposite."

M swivels in the seat, turning my head to hers. "She clearly wasn't the right person for you. Seems like she did you a favor by breaking the engagement. No messy divorce needed." Her lips curl upward as she tries to placate me.

And you know what? It works. "You make a very good point."

The SUV stops in front of a brick building a couple of blocks away from a park. It's a nice neighborhood. Not the Upper East Side, not by a long shot, but it's comfortable. Fits M.

"Well, this is my stop. Thank you so much for the dinner. And the ride." Her fingers curl around the strap of her briefcase. "Hopefully, we'll have another client to celebrate soon."

The woman next to me is the exact opposite of Darcey. Where my former fiancée was about being covered by the media, M's about getting positive press for her clients. Darcey wanted the spotlight for herself while M wants to highlight her clients. My ex was all about herself—M is for others. Selfish versus selfless.

When M's hand lands on the door handle, I yell, "Wait!"

Her head whips toward me. "Yes?"

I don't care that she's my boss. Or supersmart. Or even "downtown." I want to spend more time with Madison. Get to know her better and find out what makes her tick, because she's unlike anyone I've ever encountered. And truth be told, I want to hold her, kiss her, and do even more with her beautiful innocence.

You're a born-again virgin, remember?

Clearing my mind of unwanted thoughts, I prevaricate, "I've enjoyed spending time with you, M." How can I extend this evening? "Is there a bar nearby where we can have a nightcap? I'm not ready for tonight to end," I conclude with the biggest truth I've ever shared.

Liquid blue eyes ensnare me. "I'm your boss, Xander."

"I know. But I don't want to get to know my boss right now. I need to learn about the woman beneath her brilliant exterior."

Her eyes round and I bite my tongue, awaiting her response. This has to be her decision. Finally, she says, "Why don't you come on up? I'm sure I have something we can drink."

I want this more than anything I've wanted in a long time. "Really?"

"Yes. C'mon."

She gets out of the vehicle and I tell the driver I'll call him back later. With a nod, he leaves, and I follow M into her building. We ascend one flight of stairs and she opens a front door. "It doesn't have a view of Central Park, like I'm sure you're used to, but it's home."

We enter the spacious apartment, Madison's special touches evident. From the University of Kansas' throw blanket over the sofa's arm to the floral plates displayed on the open shelving in the kitchen, the place screams M's name. Cozy. Welcoming. Stable.

Passionate.

After hanging my blazer on a hook by the door, I wander through the living room while she opens a cabinet in the kitchen. "I don't have any bourbon, but I do have this cabernet sauvignon." Holding a framed photo of her, Jesse, plus some other friends from b-school, I nod. Replacing it on the bookshelf, I join her in the kitchen and take a glass.

Holding it up, I say, "To a great day."

Our glasses clink, and the red liquid glides down my throat, its smooth, velvety finish spreading warmth in its wake. The perfect ending to our day.

She places her glass on the counter. "Uhm, this is my kitchen, and you've already been in my living room. I have a small dining room tucked back here." Leaving my glass, I join her as we stroll a few feet and turn a corner. "If you need to use the restroom, it's behind this door. The deck is out these sliding doors." We return to the main area of her apartment. "Back there," she points to a hallway, "is my bedroom and office."

Standing at the edge of her living room, I admit, "This is really nice. I don't think I've been in an apartment in Brooklyn before." M walks into the kitchen and retrieves our wine glasses. Taking mine from her, I correct myself. "Oh, wait. Theo's sister, Paige, flipped a house in Brooklyn last year and I did go to see her work. I can't remember the neighborhood though."

She takes a sip as my word salad envelopes the room. Licking her lips, she says, "I'm sorry you had to suffer through all of that with Darcey." At her use of my former fiancée's name, I wince. "I can tell how much she hurt you."

"It was six months ago."

"Time doesn't matter. It takes however long it takes for a heart to heal."

Spoken like someone who knows heartbreak. The need to comfort her surges and I walk over to the coffee table and deposit my glass. Turning, I stride to her side and remove the glass from her limp fingers, placing it next to mine. When I stop in front of her, I survey her confused expression.

"What are you doing, Xander?"

"What I should've done a long time ago but was too afraid." I lean forward.

She squeaks, "Oh."

Cupping my palms on her cheeks, I slide them through her blond hair, exposing her scar on the right-hand side. I give it a kiss, then plant another one on her other cheek. "You have a gorgeous soul."

Her eyes flutter shut and I swoop in to taste her again. Like at the cabin, she offers a timid moan when our lips meet. Hers are soft and warm and inviting. I slide my arms down her back and pull her into my body, all her soft curves meeting my hard edges.

I blaze a line of kisses down her neck, pull back, and start the exploration up the other side. Landing at her ear, I puff a little air and nibble on the shell. Her legs give way. Picking her up, I carry her to the sofa and lay her down.

"Xander?" Her questioning tone brings me up short.

Hovering over her, I reply, "Yes."

Her palm lands on my chest. "Are you for real?"

"I ask myself that question about you every single day."

I end this conversation by giving into my need and kissing her again. Over and over our lips meet and meld. When her lips open for me, my tongue slides into her mouth and our dance explodes in earnest.

Her tongue explores my mouth with purpose. Like she's memorizing each square inch. I reciprocate.

The fact she has a softer body than the bony sticks I've been with doesn't diminish my desire to be with Madison. In fact, it enhances it, calling out with promises of unknown pleasure. My hands fall to the bottom of her shirt, and I pull it out of the black skirt she wore to the pitch at Friends For Fun. Restraining myself from yanking and ripping all of the buttons off her blouse, I undo each one. By the time I reach the top button, I can't tell who's panting harder, her or me. But it doesn't matter.

Opening up the white cotton material, I expose her bra. The peach color hides all her secrets from me while encouraging me to learn them. My thumbs find both of her nipples and rub, which causes them to form tight peaks. I lower my head and suckle through the thin material, relishing the curves beneath me.

M arches her back, which provides me with the perfect opportunity to unhook her bra. Our mouths collide again.

The front of her breasts still covered, she places her hands on my shoulders and squeezes. My muscles jump in response and I lift myself off her soft body, undoing the tie around my neck that's become way too tight. Fingers landing on the buttons, I open my shirt like I did hers and toss it onto the floor. My undershirt comes off next.

"Wow."

Madison sits up, her eyes eating up my abs like she's never seen a six-pack before. I sit taller to afford her a better view. Suck in my abs for best effect. I worked hard for my chiseled torso, and she's visually eating it up.

Her hand snakes toward my abs. Finally, she touches me, tracing the lines separating my muscles. "You're a work of art." Her gaze flicks to mine and she leans forward, running her tongue where her fingers were. Farther south, my cock goes to full mast beneath my trousers.

Closing my eyes, I revel in her tentative, exploratory touch. In a husky voice, I admit, "God. What you do to me."

M works her way up my body, stripping her bra off in the process. While our kiss explodes, my hands weigh her boobs, brushing her hard nipples. Their weight is perfect for my palms. Everything about this woman is perfect.

I need more of her.

Moving my right hand around her back while maintaining my other one on her boob, I lower her down and settle above her. My forearms become brackets as I hold my body weight on them, inhaling her delightful scent of strawberries and vanilla.

M's hair has fallen away from her cheek and her scar is on full display. Like before, it doesn't repulse me in the least. I trace the mark with my tongue.

She presses against my shoulders. "Xander."

M using my name is such a turn-on. I kiss her nose on the way to her lips. Before I can reach my destination, she pushes harder against my shoulders. "Xander. No. Wait."

These are three words I didn't expect to hear. I raise a few inches away from her mouth, my eyebrows pulling together. "What's wrong, M?"

Her palm covers her scar, blue eyes darting anywhere but at me. "What are you doing here?" She clarifies. "With me?"

"I like you. A lot." I bend down and kiss her once more, retreating when her lips move as if she wants to say something else.

"I'm nothing like Darcey."

Don't I know it? "Thank God."

I lean over to her again, but she squirms away. "Please, can we take a break?"

Acquiescing to her request, my head drops on the sofa cushions for a few beats. She deserves to be apprised of my feelings toward my ex. When my breathing's more normal, I stand and pick up our clothing. Passing her shirt to her, she puts it on and recloses a couple of buttons.

After tossing my shirt on but leaving it unbuttoned, I give her my full attention. "Darcey hurt me, I'm not going to lie. When she threw my ring back at me, I was dumbstruck. Of course, that happened minutes after Dad and my uncles were arrested by the FBI, so it was like a one-two punch."

Her fingers snake into my hair. "I can't imagine how difficult that must've been for you."

I grab her wrist and kiss the back of her hand. Our fingers intertwine.

M continues, "She's the polar opposite of me, though. I saw her in the restaurant earlier, eating a salad."

"That's what you ate, too," I point out.

She waves her hand. "Yeah, but only because I was trying to save money." Her hand flies to her mouth as if she confessed a deep, dark secret.

"I should've told you I was covering the tab." No other woman has ever offered to pay for herself, so the thought hadn't crossed my mind. "If I had, what would you have ordered?"

"I don't know." She picks up some of her hair and pulls it across her cheek. The right side, covering her scar.

"Scallops? Beef? Chicken?" I press because I'm interested. With shock, I realize everything about her interests me.

She shrugs. "I guess the steak looked amazing."

"There. It's confirmed. You're nothing at all like Darcey, who never would admit to eating anything but rabbit food."

Plucking at the blanket across the back of the sofa, she admits, "And that's why she looks like she does. All gorgeous long hair and skinny body. Not a blemish on her face, let alone a huge, ugly scar."

Is that what she really believes? I want to crush her against me and kiss away her worries, but I know her scar runs much deeper than her cheek. "Believe me when I tell you this. You can change how you look, but she can't change how nasty she is to her core."

M sucks in her breath. "Guess I never thought of it like that."

I run my fingers through her hair, tipping her chin up toward me. "It's true. Darcey is selfish, seeking self-aggrandizement at every turn. Theo even told me she was angling to get on 'NYC Wicked Wives,' and a proposal was a prerequisite." How devious she was washes over me once again. I stare into M's eyes, believing she's nothing like my former fiancée.

M leans forward and gives me a sweet kiss. "I feel terrible you had to go through that."

All this talk about Darcey has wrung every last ounce of ardor from my body. I give her a hug. "You're nothing like her. Believe that."

She pulls back. "And you deserve a lot better than what she gave you."

She's what Dad wanted me to have. After spending time with this delightful woman, I begin to realize how wrong he was. And not only about Darcey.

Madison kisses my cheek. "It's been a long day. Why don't you go home and get some rest?"

I gaze into her blue eyes. "This was the best day ever, because we spent it together."

A slow smile overtakes her face. "See you in the office."

I text Jimmy and collect my clothes strewn about. Blowing her a kiss, I leave M's apartment, filled with her goodness. I take the stairs to the lobby.

You're not good enough for her, Xander.

God help me. I'm not willing to let her go.

16

Madison

The door snicks shut but Xander remains all around me. Citrus melding with an intriguing musk that I've come to identify with him. I pick up our wine glasses, toss the remaining wine, and rinse them out before loading them into the dishwasher. For some reason, I can't picture my upscale employee doing such a mundane chore.

I collapse on the sofa where just minutes ago, I was being held by this gorgeous man. On the floor, my bra catches my attention and reinforces how far we went in our make out session. He wanted to kiss me. Not because he was trying to make a statement against Darcey.

Right?

I replay his comments about his ex-fiancée. The woman who happened to be at the restaurant observing us all night. Satisfaction rolls through me at knowing we had no idea she was there until we were on our way out.

Without thought, I push my hair away from my face, running my fingers over my scar. Doubt at my internal pep talk springs to the forefront. Xander is blindingly gorgeous and can date anyone he wants. How do I fit that bill?

Before I can slip down that unsavory path, my phone rings with a FaceTime call from my sister. A genuine smile crosses my lips. "How are you feeling, Macy?"

"Hi, Madison! I'm doing well. Randall's home for three more weeks and my pregnancy is right on track." In the background, both of her kids run around the kitchen.

"That's great, but what did you feed your kids? Pure sugar?"

She turns her head to watch her kids and laughs. "I think you call that Grandma's Cookies. Ma dropped off her famous chocolate chip cookies right before we had dinner. Had to hide the container until they ate their mac and cheese, then all bets were off. Randall didn't help," she chuckles.

Such normality feeds my soul. I miss being a part of this little slice of life. Then again, Xander wouldn't be kissing me in Kansas. "Wish I could sneak a cookie too."

"I'll ask Ma to mail you some. You know her, she must've baked a couple extra dozen, just in case."

Sounds like our mother. Xander's musky scent crosses my nostrils and I shake my head. Don't need the extra calories. "Nah, that's okay. We have bakeries out here and I can grab a cookie if I want one."

Macy holds up a cookie, mesmerizing me with how she runs it from left to right across the screen. When I throw my hand in front of the phone, she laughs. Then bites into it. "More for me."

We catch up on family stuff. Everything's pretty status quo. "Have you gone on any exciting dates lately?"

At her usual question, I picture Xander and me in the Catskills, ziplining with the Friends For Fun group. Playing Trivial Pursuit at the crooked floor bar. Pitching the charity today, then going out to dinner. Kissing outside the cabin. My eyes land on my sofa. And right here.

"Oh, you have to spill. I can see something's going on."

Startled, I lock eyes with her. "Well, there is someone new in my life, but I don't think it's anything more than fun. He's getting over a broken engagement." Not a lie.

"Ouch. But you guys have been hanging out?"

I spill about Xander, including our kiss sessions, but I hide his identity. "But, Macy, I'm so far away from the people he hangs out with. He comes with an amazing pedigree, money, and education. Plus, he looks like David Gandy, for goodness sakes."

"Not too shabby. He must be interested in you if he's getting all up-close-and-personal. How is he at kissing?"

I rub my lips, which have returned to their normal size but still buzz from our stolen moments. My nipples pebble beneath my shirt, but I don't share this fact with my sister. "Fantastic, of course."

"Has he seen your scar?"

I nod. "Yeah. He called it my badge of honor. Even told me I could change it if I wanted to." But that Darcey's nastiness is forever.

My sister claps. "I think he may be your Randall. You need to keep this one, Madison. I totally agree with this dude, and I've not even met him. So what if you have a scar? It doesn't define you."

On the contrary, it's defined me ever since I was five. "You're wrong."

"Promise me this." In the background, one of her kids screams for her attention. "Hold on."

She puts the call on mute and addresses her younger daughter while I ponder her remark that my scar doesn't define me. My fingers trace it, knowing in my heart she's wrong. Although Xander didn't seem to care at all. And our kisses! No one has ever kissed me like I was the only person in the world before. My nipples tingle, reminding me of his touch there too.

I'm sighing when Macy returns to the phone. "Sorry, sis. Kids sometimes." She chuckles. "Now where was I? Oh yeah, I want you to give this guy a chance. He seems really into you and I know for a fact that anyone who looks like that British model can turn your head."

"I could stare at him all day."

"Tell me this. If he had, I don't know, a crooked nose, would you still be interested in him?"

I mentally break his nose. "Of course."

"How about a unibrow?"

I giggle. "Definitely."

"Then why can't he be into you with your scar? Which, might I add, you've learned to hide pretty darn well. And it's faded over time."

"Maybe you're right."

"Great! I'll take a 'maybe.' And now I have to run before the heathens tear up the place. Love you."

We disconnect and I toss my phone onto the coffee table and flop down. Is my sister onto something? Xander did seem pretty into me when we were on this sofa. Plus he kissed my scar. Choosing to believe in his attraction, I float into my bedroom and fall into a deep sleep.

At the office on Monday, I'm working on comments to Elisabeth's strategy when Dev walks in carrying a bunch of magazines. "Hey, Dev. What'cha got there?"

He glances down at his hands. "Oh, some light reading." He dumps them onto the guest chair and takes a seat in the other one. "So, how did it go with the charity on Friday?"

I push away from my computer. If I know Dev—and I do—he's going to get to his point on his own time. "It went well. Xander did a great pitch, and the board appeared to be impressed. All we can do is wait for their decision."

My admin nods. "And afterward, what did you do?"

What is he fishing for? Not about to admit I went out to dinner with an employee, I shrug. "I was in Brooklyn, so I grabbed dinner and returned home." Not the exact truth, but close enough.

His body undulates. "What restaurant did you try?"

I stand and walk around to the front of my desk. "What do you really want to know?"

The smirk he gives me sends all my Spidey senses into overdrive. He holds up a magazine, opened to a page featuring Xander and me kissing at The River Café. "Care to explain?"

I leap forward and snatch the magazine out of his hand. Sure enough, whoever took this photo captured the kiss we shared at our table, Xander's hands over both of my cheeks. Heat infuses my upper body, neck, and takes residence on my face. "Oh, shit."

"I knew it! I could tell there was something brewing between you two."

He reaches over and picks up another magazine and flips through the pages while I study the photo. I've never seen a picture of myself kissing someone before, and it's a bit surreal. My hands are on his muscular shoulders—ones I caressed, naked, later in my apartment. For his part, Xander appears focused on our kiss. My heart skips a beat.

Dev clears his throat and shakes the magazine in his hands. "Xander Turner was spied at the tony River Café, eating a cozy dinner with Manhattan spread out before him. He seemed into his dinner companion, whom we have uncovered is a Madison Welch of Brooklyn. The two had their heads together throughout most of the meal, and even shared a few passionate kisses. All this occurred while his former fiancée, Darcey Abbott, dined nearby. Turner publicly quit his job last month at VOW-cubed Media and has turned up at Welch's PR firm. Seems that the two are working more than clients." His gaze meets mine. "The article goes on to talk about the VOW-cubed prosecution. Says a motion to dismiss all of the charges is expected to be filed soon."

My ears ring. Collapsing onto the back of my desk, my mouth opens and closes several times before I can find my voice. "This isn't what it looks like."

My admin's eyebrow raises. "What? That you and Xander are bumping uglies?"

"We're not doing that." I scowl.

Yet.

Maybe never. Especially after this article.

Thank God the magazine didn't catch sight of my scar. Nor did they have any commentary about why the City's BP is slumming with me. My stomach turns as I realize these stories are coming. *Shit.*

"I need to do damage control."

"How can I help?" Xander's baritone floats through my office.

His voice lifts me off my desk. Biting my lip, I stare at the man who undressed me. Played with my breasts. Made me feel like a sexy woman for the first time in my life. And kissed me in a public restaurant for the entire world to see.

Dev jumps out of his chair. "I'm sure you two will figure out how to handle this."

Sashaying out of my office, he leaves me alone with Xander. I grab one of the magazines he left behind and hold it up. "Did you see these?"

"I saw enough. I didn't realize someone would be taking photos." He blows air out of his bottom lip, causing his hair to fly off his forehead, then descend into place perfectly. "I don't want to cause you any problems."

I wave my hand in dismissal while my mind whirs with PR possibilities to stem the paparazzi. "At least they gave my name and info about the Agency, so that's positive. We need to come up with a campaign about how to turn this to our advantage."

His lip quirks upward. "Spoken like a true PR guru."

I don't have time to relish being called a guru, as this press can't remain unanswered. "Let's see what we have to deal with."

I take the stack of magazines Dev gave me and divide it in half, giving one pile to Xander. Instead of returning to work behind my desk, I take the guest chair Dev vacated while Xander sits in the other. We flip through each one of them, gathering the complete story—as they conveyed it.

"Well," he places the last magazine onto my desk. "Looks like we have no choice but to come out as a couple." An undecipherable expression crosses his face.

"I don't think we should do that, especially since it's a lie."

My statement hangs, unrefuted. I knew it was too good to be true. He was passing the time with a willing, warm body. Warm, *scarred* body I correct myself, my sister's pep talk be damned.

He turns toward me. "M, listen to me. I wasn't fully truthful with you. Darcey's breaking our less-than-twelve-hour engagement really messed with my head. I don't know how to trust my instincts any longer, even if they're screaming at me to try for something with you."

"They are?" I blurt, unable to keep the longing out of my voice.

He leans forward, placing his palm over my scar. In a deeper voice, he replies, "Yes."

His dark blue eyes communicate he means every word. Needing to process this turn of events, I pull away from his intoxicating touch. "Then we can take things slow. And since we're not in a relationship, we can't proclaim we are to the public. Besides, I'm your boss."

My return to work mode breaks the spell between us. "People meet at work and date all the time."

His reply sets me off-balance. I get to my feet and walk away from his scent, which tries to lure me back to him. Crossing my arms, I open my mouth but nothing comes out. On my second attempt, I reply, "You're right. About other people, but not us." *Please contradict me. Say you want to be in a relationship with me.*

He leans back in his chair, fixing his dark blue gaze on me. "You're right." *So much for my plea.* "How should we issue our own statement? Reporters aren't going to disappear. If anything, they'll more than double, vying for a scoop."

I break our eye contact. "I guess we could say we were simply out celebrating a pitch made to a potential new client?"

He nods. "Good idea. We don't have to say which one, so as not to put undue pressure on Friends For Fun."

"Right. And we can say we were discussing strategy, which is why our heads were together throughout the dinner."

"I like it. My kiss can be played off as a friendly gesture for all of your guidance."

His suggestion stings but makes sense. "Yeah. And walking out hand in hand was, ah—"

He completes my sentence. "Also friendly."

My breath hitches, although his spin is the right one. "Makes sense. I'm thinking we write up this statement ourselves and send it out to the magazines."

He shakes his head. "I like it. Should stem the tide. Although, the real possibility exists that at least some of the reporters won't buy what we're selling."

"I know. But we have to try. I think the bigger, more reputable magazines will lay off. It's the bottom feeders, like *Spill It*, that will keep coming our way. But I doubt we need a more robust public relations plan to combat them, as their reputation precedes them."

"Very true. Have I ever told you that Theo's girlfriend used to work for them?" When my brows form a question, he dives into Amelia Bellamy's story.

"Wow. It's amazing they ended up together."

"True. She says the magazine has no journalistic integrity."

"No debate there. What do you think of sending our story to Amelia at her new magazine, *Fact Expo*?"

His eyes light up. "I like it."

I stand, looking down at his mouthwatering body. Reigning in my rampant desire to repeat what we did in my apartment, I say, "Want to try writing the statement we discussed? I'll work up a full PR distribution list, in addition to Amelia."

He rubs his hands on his thighs. "Sure thing, boss." Rising to his full height, his baritone runs through me. "Thank you, M." He kisses my right cheek, over my scar, then leaves my office.

Heart hammering, I return to my desk chair. Palm covering my cheek where his lips just were, I run through his reasons for not wanting to date me. One thing's for sure. Darcey Abbott is on my shit list.

Although, if she were nice, I wouldn't be spending any time with Xander now.

If only this thing between us were real.

17

Xander

Sitting at my desk, I flip through the magazine articles about M and me. I stop on a photo that's been broadcast multiple times —where we're kissing. A weird thrill casts throughout my body.

Madison's the real deal. Hell, if she were anyone else, her parents would've given her plastic surgery right when the attack happened. But not her. She chooses to live her life on her own terms, scars and all.

Knocking on my door raises my attention and a guy built like a Mack truck walks through my doorway. Leaping to my feet, I give him a bro hug. "Theo. How the hell are you?"

"Keeping busy. This writing gig's a lot harder than you might think."

I pat his shoulder. "I bet. Same can be said for the PR biz, too." Pointing to my guest chair, he lowers his bulk into it and I return to my office chair. "So what brings you all the way downtown?"

Theo rubs his palm over his short beard. "Saw some stuff online and wanted to see how you were doing."

Online? Shit, why didn't I check there when I saw the magazines? I shrug. "All good here."

Theo's eyebrow raises. "Really? I would think being called a 'pity hire' would've set you off."

I sit ramrod straight. "What are you talking about?"

"Haven't you seen the coverage about you and your boss?" I point to the magazines scattered across my desk. He shakes his head. "I mean the digital ones?"

I swallow as my head shakes from side to side. How could I have made this rookie mistake?

He palms his cell phone and turns the screen to face me. "The print magazines were polite."

Grabbing the phone from him, I read the article he pulled up. "Fuck." Grabbing a pen, I run it through my fingers.

"Want to go somewhere else and talk about it?"

"Yeah." My voice comes out as a croak, and I clear my throat. "Yes." Pushing away from my desk, I add, "But I do want to tell Madison first." I stare at the industrial brown carpet. "And I'd like to introduce you. Okay?"

His expression morphs into a positive one. "Thought you'd never ask." He extends his arm. "Lead the way."

We trek through the halls, and I introduce my "brother" to everyone. When we approach M's office, I debate whether to give Theo a heads up about her admin. With a smirk, I decide against it. "Hey, Dev."

He glances up at me and does a double take, his mouth falling open, and he jumps to his feet. Stifling a chuckle, I introduce the pair. Gotta tip my hat to Theo. He shakes Dev's hand like the poor guy wasn't drooling.

Interrupting their moment, I ask, "Is Madison available?"

"What?" Dev shakes his head. "Oh. Yeah. Yes, she's not on the phone or anything. But I want to announce you."

He scurries around from his desk and opens M's door with a loud, "Madison, Xander is here. And he brought a friend."

Dev's antics took me a little while to get used to, but he's a hard worker and M values his input. "Thanks, Dev," I say as we pass.

For her part, Madison gets to her feet. "Oh. Theo Hansen, I presume." She extends her hand.

"A true pleasure." Theo grabs her hand and instead of shaking it, he lifts it to his mouth for a kiss, earning pink cheeks from Madison and a push on his back from me. Theo turns and faces me, his hands raised as if to say "what?"

Ignoring my best friend, I address M. "Theo stopped by after reading the articles about Friday night." Better give her the fuller picture. "Online ones."

I can see when she registers my meaning, as her eyes widen. "Oh."

"And I don't believe a word I read, especially since my girlfriend used to work for one of those rags and I know how they twist things around to suit their fake storyline." Theo's words seem to calm her.

"Pity hire" rings in my brain. I understand how these tabloids work, too, but this nickname really stings. I need to get out of here. Inhaling, I let the air fill my lungs. "Theo stopped by to take me out to lunch, but I wanted him to meet you first." I pause. Even though I didn't clear this with him, I add, "And invite you to join us." *What am I thinking?* If we're seen out in public again, reporters will have a field day.

M tucks some hair behind her left ear, all the while keeping her scar cleverly hidden. "That's very nice of you to think of me, but you two should go. There's a good place on Sixth and Twelfth, if you're looking for a recommendation."

Relief surges. How am I so all over the place with this woman? Positive he's already made reservations for us at Union Square Cafe, I offer her a nod.

Before I can push him toward the door, Theo asks, "How is Xander here working out for you?" He leans forward. "Do you need me to have a word with him?"

M's tinkle of laughter lightens my mood and calms my riotous thoughts. "I think he'll do."

A broad smile crosses my face. "Nice try, Theo. Like I told you in my office, I'm really loving this PR stuff."

"Just wanted to make sure your contributions were living up to your hype, dude."

"Thanks." I lock eyes with Madison, her blue eyes twinkling.

Pulling me into their depths. Seducing me. I want to tell her we'll talk later, but I'm too caught up in her aura.

Theo clears his throat. "If you can tear apart from each other, it's time for us to leave. I promise to bring him back in one piece, Madison. It was a pleasure to meet you." He tugs on my arm, breaking our silent exchange.

"See you later," I offer, then turn and follow my best friend.

When we're ensconced inside the elevator, he gives me a smug look. "Seems the paps got some things right."

I cross my arms across my chest. "Dude."

"It's all good. Remember who you're talking to." Reaching inside his jacket, he pulls out a pair of sunglasses. I follow suit. We step out onto the sidewalk and into one of our family cars. "Thanks, man. Didn't really feel like running from reporters."

"I know the feeling."

He instructs our driver to take us to the Union Square Cafe like I thought, and we remain silent for the short trip. Soon, we're seated at a quiet table away from the windows. The waiter brings us a bread basket, but Theo waves him away, asking for him to bring us waters with lemon instead.

"Hope you don't mind. Now that I'm back at the rink, I'm watching what I eat more."

Amelia got him into a local ice hockey league, which has worked wonders for his positive attitude. "No worries."

Squeezing the slice of lemon into his water, Theo glances at the menu and closes it. I decide on the salad with chicken breast added. Within seconds, our attentive waiter reappears and takes our orders.

Theo takes a sip of his water. "She's not your usual type."

"Maybe that's a good thing? She's not vain or vapid or fake."

He rubs his trimmed beard. "I can see that. I liked her sense of humor, too, from the little I got from her."

My lips tick upward. "She is pretty damn funny." I tip my glass to my lips. "So tell me, how are you and Amelia doing?"

"We're great."

He dives into a soliloquy about their new life together and I've never seen him this extroverted. Or happy. "This is great to hear."

Even though I'm truly happy for him, my mind reverts to the snide comment in the online article. I sit back. "I wasn't a pity hire, you know."

"I'm sure you weren't." He picks up his napkin and places it on his lap.

"I have an MBA. I'm qualified. And I landed the very first client I pitched."

"You did? Tell me about it."

I launch into a description about the Preserve and my plans for how to raise their profile. When I'm done, I focus on him, seeking approval. *What?* M already okayed everything, as did the client. Why do I continually look for validation?

Needed or not, Theo offers it. "I never could do what you do. Your plans are brilliant. I'm sure everyone around here will soon be name-dropping the Mahigan Preserve."

I study the tablecloth. "Thanks, man. I sure hope so."

The waiter brings our meals and we tuck in. "Have you heard anything about how things are going over at VOW-cubed? Or with the case? Since I've been gone, I've taken myself out of the loop."

He takes a bite of his lunch. "Honestly? Not much. From what I understand, our fathers have been bickering over the motion to dismiss. It's due to be filed soon, so I guess they have to get it resolved."

"I know they've been working on it." I spear some lettuce. "What's the gossip about the people in the office? Like Felicia or—"

"Are you sure you never banged her? She was hot."

I picture my former admin. "One-hundred percent. I never felt anything more for her than a working relationship."

"Oh, right." His fork clatters to his empty plate. "I seem to recall your telling me never to dip my wick where I work." He rubs his nose. "How's that going for you now?"

My shoulders slump. "Damn. I said that, didn't I?"

He takes a long drag of his water, his brown eyes peering over the rim at me, filled with mirth. "Yep."

For want of something to do, I raise my napkin and pat my

mouth. Then I play with my fork, even though there's nothing left on my plate.

"It's okay, Xander. You're allowed to be happy. And if Madison makes you happy, I'm all for it."

"You know Darcey threw me for a loop."

"She's a bitch. She was using you, and your dad was manipulating you with her. I'm actually rooting for you and Madison to make a go of things. I can tell she's not angling to get on a stupid reality television show."

Did Theo notice her scar? "You only talked with her for a few minutes. How did you get all that?"

"Madison has a *joie de vivre* about her that most people we've grown up with don't. Plus, her office is homey. I think she could be good for you."

I let his observations sink in. "You think so? Madison sure does tell it like it is. She's definitely a straight shooter."

He sips his water. "Somehow, I can't picture Uncle Vince being thrilled about Madison."

I wipe my mouth. "You know what? He's ruled my life for too long. I don't care that M's not runway ready. She makes me happy and she's beautiful and pure to me. Plus, she thinks my ideas are worthy."

"They always have been."

I tap my glass. "I'm trying to believe that."

"All I can say is that I like this emancipated Xander Turner. And your father won't." He runs his finger around the water glass. "Which is a good thing, in my book."

While I assimilate his comment, the server stops by and clears our table. Theo puts his muscular arm onto the table. "To change the subject, my sister is back living with us. I love her, but she's so aimless. You haven't heard about any houses that need to be flipped, have you?"

"I wish I could help. I'm not aware of any properties. But she must be clued in to the market, right? She hasn't found anything?"

He knocks on the tabletop. "No. Well, to be honest, I know she has found properties for sale but there's always something wrong with them. Wrong neighborhood. Not enough work to do. Too much work to do. Too expensive. She always has an excuse. I think if she got involved with another house, then she would get out of Mum and Father's way. And find some peace."

"I can't imagine living with my parents, especially under these circumstances." The fact that M lives in Brooklyn, where Paige did her last flip, gives me a little sense of hope I might hear of something. But I don't want to raise Theo's hopes. "I promise to keep my ears open."

"Thanks." I steer our conversation toward the twin's graduations, which are coming up. We brainstorm some ideas, but everything hinges on our fathers' criminal case as to whether we should plan to leave the area to celebrate.

Our server returns and we both shake our heads as to coffees or dessert, so he leaves us the check. Theo waves his hand. "My treat. I showed up in your office and dragged you out. It's the least I can do."

"I appreciate it. Let me text Jimmy." While Theo pays, I reach out to our family's vehicle concierge, who tells me the car is caught up in traffic but should be here in twenty minutes. Standing, I say, "The SUV is delayed. While we wait, let me show you the Green-Market. It's right around the corner."

We leave the restaurant and enter the throngs of people checking out the foods and crafts available at this fantastic open-air market.

"Wow. This beats anything we have on the Upper East Side."

We pass the pickle kiosk. Stopping, I reply, "I know. It's great." I buy us two pickles and give one to Theo. "You have to try this. Best damn pickle I've ever eaten."

Holding it up to his mouth, he jokes. "And how many pickles have you had?"

"Douche." I take a bite and enjoy the salty brine that explodes in my mouth.

He crunches on his own pickle. "Shit. This is fantastic."

"Told you."

Theo returns to the booth and gets six more. "Amelia's going to love these."

"Yeah. M introduced this place to me."

Finishing his pickle, he says, "I said this before. I like her, man. I have a good feeling about you two."

"Don't jump ahead of yourself. Despite what the tabloids are reporting, we're not even dating." Although our kisses in her apartment were mighty hot. "Well. Not really."

He puts his hand on my shoulder. "I have faith in you." The SUV stops in front of us and drops me at the office while continuing uptown to bring Theo back to his apartment.

I spend the afternoon going through all the online articles featuring M and me. Sorting their truths from the lies. In the end, I draft a statement I believe Madison will approve. When I turn the corner to her office, Dev's on the phone. I point to her door and he nods, so I enter.

"Hey, here's what I have. Let me know what you think." I drop the papers on her desk and turn.

"Xander." The way she says my name is like a caress. I face her. "Thanks for writing this up. I've worked out a complete campaign, which I just sent to the printer. I'd like your feedback."

"Of course. I'll pick it up." I leave her office and retrieve the document.

Dev's standing by his desk as I return. "Hey, I'm closing up here. Do you need anything before I go?"

"No. Thanks, I'm good."

He offers me a salute, yells goodnight to Madison, and leaves. My watch reads five-thirty. Hopefully, this won't take too long. I'd rather be doing much more enjoyable things with M. I focus my attention on her plan as I re-enter her office. "This looks amazing. You did all this while I was out to lunch?"

"Among other things."

The next hour speeds by as we refine her approach to handling the press. First stop, Amelia, to whom we send my revised statement. We're going to let her run with it and do our dirty work, so to speak.

"Done." Remembering my lunch companion's positivity toward

our relationship, I wrap a lock of Madison's hair around my pointer finger.

She removes her hair from my finger and tucks it behind her ear.

Undeterred, I ask, "May I interest you in dinner?"

She sighs. "I want to, but I'm swamped."

She obviously means the tabloid attention. I lean toward her. "Don't let them win. We can go to my apartment and order in." *Am I begging?* I amend, "We don't have to if you don't want to."

"Believe me, I'd love to. But I had to put aside my other work today, so I need to review plans for other clients plus there's a meeting with my accountant on Friday for which I have to prep." Her eyes drop to her desk, which is littered with more paperwork than normal.

"I get it. Can I help out?"

She shakes her head. "I wish. But all this requires my attention. Raincheck?"

Her last question soothes my heart. Reporters aren't driving her away from me. From us. "You got it." I lean down and kiss her lips. Her response is immediate and makes me want to lay her down across her desk and toss all the paperwork on the floor. My stomach drops as I realize we're not there. *Yet.* "See you tomorrow."

"Bye." Her breathless reply swirls in the air and keeps me warm all the way to the SUV.

As I'm sitting in the back being driven uptown, I replay my conversation with Theo. My leg bounces like a metronome on speed. "Please take me to my parents' house," I direct the driver.

When we reach their place in the Upper East Side, I enter the spacious lobby and wave to the concierge. Soon, I walk out of the elevator, which opens into their apartment. Their housekeeper rounds the corner. "Mr. Xander, it is so nice to see you again."

Entering the apartment, I reply, "Good evening, Luna." She takes my jacket. "Are my parents in the family room?"

"No, they're in the solarium. Dinner will be served in an hour. Want me to set you a place?"

I didn't come here to eat, but I guess I could. "Yes, please. Thanks."

Luna nods and turns toward the hall closet while I make my way deeper into the apartment. Floor-to-ceiling windows overlook Central Park, which I stop to admire for the first time in ages, remembering Madison's admiration at The River Café. Even though my apartment faces the Park as well, their view is more expansive. It's an impressive sight. After several moments, I enter the solarium. Originally, this room was a library, but Mom thought we needed a place for a piano so she remodeled it when we were kids. None of us played except Gabrielle, but it makes a statement nonetheless.

I scan the room. Dad's sitting in his spot—a brown leather chair next to the fireplace—with a newspaper in his hands. Mom's on the divan with her knitting needles whirling. She's reupholstered it since the last time I was in here, and it now sports an equestrian motif. One would think everything was normal but for the oversized metal "bracelet" around Dad's ankle.

"Mom. Dad."

Four eyes turn to me. Dad's blue ones bounce back to the newspaper before he folds it. Mom rises, drops her knitting onto the divan, and opens her arms. I walk to her and give two air kisses, my hands floating near her shoulders, per usual. "You're looking great, Mom."

"It's so nice of you to visit, Xander. Are you staying for dinner?"

"I told Luna I would."

"Great," she replies. "So nice to have company for our meal."

Leaving her, I approach Dad. "Hey." I extend my hand, which he takes without standing.

Mom's returned to the divan and is fussing with her yarn when she addresses me. "So tell me, what's been taking up your time, honey?"

Remaining standing next to Dad's chair, I drop my arm. "I've been working at a PR firm downtown, actually."

"That sounds nice," Mom replies while Dad tosses the newspaper onto the ottoman.

"I'm surprised by how much I love it."

"Did you just leave the office?" Dad stands, his gaze skimming over my full length. "They must do things differently downtown, considering what you're wearing."

I didn't have any pitches today, so I dressed like everyone in the office—a pair of khakis with a light sweater. "The office has a casual dress policy. I have two suits in the office, in case."

"Fascinating." His sarcasm is thick, but I refuse to take the bait. "Hope you don't run any town halls for them."

I meet his gaze. "I did what I thought was best for VOW-cubed."

He bends over and rummages in a basket next to his chair, picking up a couple of our magazines. "What you did was royally screw things up. We've had so much backlash from what you spewed during those stupid things. What were you thinking?"

I pull away from Dad's harsh words. Then in a rush, I regain my proper stature. "I was *thinking* that the employees needed to know what was going on so they would stay and not jump ship as many were talking about."

"Well, Ward and Ogden and I have had to deal with the fallout from your little rah-rah sessions. We've held our own meetings via Zoom, telling them what they need to know."

Which I'm sure isn't close to the truth—only what the execs want people to believe. My chest rises and falls faster as how poorly they treat their employees comes into focus, especially in comparison with how Madison operates. What do I care about VOW-cubed anyway? I don't work there anymore. Not my responsibility.

Deciding it's best to change the topic, I ask, "How's the bankruptcy going?"

Dad sinks deeper into his chair. "We're almost ready to file our motion to dismiss. Ogden added a few more things to the papers today."

"When's it due?"

"Next week."

My chin bobs in acknowledgment. "I hope it wraps up this whole interlude." I turn my attention toward Mom. "Then we can focus on the important stuff, like planning the graduation celebration for the twins."

"You're right, Xander. You're always looking out for the family, isn't that true, Vince?"

Dad makes an offhand noise. Ignoring him, I reply, "Thanks. I know we've always celebrated graduations, and they're going to be the last in the family to get their degrees. Have you spoken with Uncle Ward about this?"

"Ward's tied up right now." Dad's pronouncement lands like an atomic bomb in the middle of the room. We all know he's referencing my former Aunt Yvette, the twin's money-hungry blackmail-attempting mother, who's been splattered all over cable spewing venom against her ex-husband. Tried to extort a million bucks from me when I was at VOW-cubed, but I turned her down. Hence her cable appearances.

Casting about for a new subject, I say, "I've been working with Theo on some ideas for the graduation. We hope to have something to present soon. After all, May is right around the corner."

Mom approaches and puts her hand on my forearm. "That's great, honey."

Dad, obviously finished with this conversation, waves a magazine in the air. I catch the title and brace myself for what's to come. "Who's this Madison Welch?"

Straight to the punch. "She's my boss."

He flips through *Spill It Magazine*, opening it up to the story they printed about our dinner at The River Café. "You don't kiss your boss."

Not when it was my father, I supply in my mind. "It's not what it looks like." I offer him the cover story Madison and I formulated this afternoon.

Dad doesn't react to my story. He barrels on, "And look at her. How can you be seen with someone who looks like *that*? I will not have the Turner name tarnished by the likes of her." He flips the page and points. "Darcey Abbott, now that was the proper match for you."

My tenuous grip on my temper slips. "She threw my ring back at me when you were arrested by the FBI."

He waves the magazine. "Whatever. That should've been a temporary setback. Having the Abbotts on my side would've been helpful right now. But you didn't want to help, did you? No. You'd rather hold those stupid Town Halls."

I bite the inside of my cheek. Mom steps in. "Now, Vince. That girl made her feelings perfectly clear the following week with her articles. I don't think she was the right fit for our Xander."

"Well, I can tell you this schlub isn't the right fit either," Dad booms, tossing the magazine into the air.

My last thread snaps. "Madison Welch is one thousand times better than Darcey ever could hope to be. She's brilliant, an astute businesswoman who's built a fabulous Agency, and has a loving relationship with her family. Which is more than I can say about this." I refrain from pointing at my parents, but instead, motion around the room.

"Alexander—" Dad reacts as Mom utters, "Honey."

I'm done. I stride across the room, turning at the threshold. "Enjoy your dinner. It was something seeing you both."

Dad's voice booms down the hallway. "Xander, get back here!"

My steps don't falter. Snatching my coat from Luna, I leave their opinions where they belong. In the dust.

18

Xander

The next morning before work, interested in finding out how my statement was received, I boot up my laptop and do the one thing I've avoided doing for ages. I google my name. "All," "News," and "Images" tabs across the top are filled with results about me. As well as Madison. Information about VOW-cubed and Dad's prosecution round out the panoply. *Great.*

I click on "News," and am greeted with such headlines as "Xander Turner Goes Slumming," "All About Xander's New Fling," and "How Far the Mighty Have Fallen." I release my jaw when my teeth protest the pain. Fucking bottom feeders.

Ignoring the shit they spewed against me, I focus on the awful things they say about M. From comments about her appearance— her hair, her height, her face, her scar—to dissecting her business, the tabloids are ruthless. She did nothing to deserve this.

I click on *Fact Expo* and read Amelia's article. At least her magazine got it right. Or, as right as we want them to get it. Grateful for her support, I shoot her off a text of thanks. Then I return my attention to the other sites that aren't as positive. And fear things will get worse. Much worse.

Maybe I should work from home today? After all, I need to deal with the Preserve's campaign and don't need to be in the office to do that. Then I wouldn't get to see Madison.

My eyes land on my screen again, my lips pressed into a straight line. I shouldn't be seen with her anymore. Reporters will go away if we don't feed their stories.

I pick up my phone and call the office. Madison answers like I knew she would since it's too early for anyone else to be there. "Hey, M, it's Xander."

"Hi there. Everything okay?"

"Yeah, I'm fine. But I'm calling to ask if I can work from home today? I think it would be better for me to lay low, so Amelia's article can percolate and hopefully call off the other paps."

"Oh. I was hoping we could meet to go over the Preserve's campaign. I wanted to discuss the budget and your ideas."

"I still need to finish that up. I can do it from here."

"If you think that's best. But I don't want you to hide. Reporters will make up whatever they want to print." Her slight chuckle reaches my ears. "I should know. I've fed them enough lines over the years, and they've run with them."

I click through a couple more results. "You're right, I guess. I've been the subject of many articles throughout the past decade, but never has the spotlight been so harsh."

"Well, you have a leg up on me. I've never been in the headlines until now. Although, analytics on the website show a major spike in clicks. And visitors are staying on the website a lot longer than ever before."

As she speaks, her words ramp up faster and faster, showing how excited she is for this positive side-effect. The only positive one I can see. "That is some much-needed good news."

"Yeah, so don't stay away from the office because of me. Promise?"

But I *am* staying away to protect her. Perhaps I'm being overly so? "You don't mind the attention?" How could she not? They've basically portrayed her as some sort of grotesque monster.

"All press is good press, remember?"

Her use of the well-known axiom sounds a bit too upbeat. As if she's trying to convince herself. I want to be able to hold her, to reassure her that the reporters' portrayal of her is one-thousand percent inaccurate. If I stay home and hide, I'll be leaving her at their mercy. This final thought snaps me out of my own self-pity.

"You know what? I've changed my mind. I will come into the office today."

"Great. See you soon."

I end the call and text Jimmy requesting a car. Throwing on some black pants and a long-sleeved white shirt, I grab my windbreaker and lock up. Soon, I'm entering the office, ignoring the group of reporters who were camped out front. At least both Madison and I arrived separately. There is that.

At my desk, I make some tweaks to the campaign for the Preserve and email it to Madison. Proud of my work, I skim the websites M showed me when I first started, checking out companies seeking PR help. Some of their RFPs are straightforward, while others are more detailed. And more intriguing. This part of the job is exciting to me. Each submission is filled with hope for much-needed help to get their name out there. And I know we are up to the task. Madison fosters creativity amongst her reps, which fuels even more imaginative ideas. I click on one submission that calls out to me and start working.

"Xander, I'd like to review your campaign for the Preserve. Is now a good time?"

I look up and Madison stands in the doorway, pulling her hair concealing her scar into her mouth. So adorable. "Of course." I point to the guest chair.

"Great." She hands me some papers. "I've gone over your campaign and made some comments, which you can look at later. I'd like to discuss your proposed budget."

"Sure thing, boss." I lean forward to kiss her, then realize we're on company property, during the workday. "Ugh. Sorry."

Pink-cheeked, she waves her hand. "I liked your ideas a lot. I thought they were unique, and I bet the Howells will love them. However, we need to scale back due to the budget."

I pick up the first document. "I thought I was staying within it?"

"Overall, you were. But some routine items were missed that we have to account for. Things like an email service, for example. I remember them telling us that they don't currently send out newsletters."

I point to a line item in the budget. "That's right. Which is why I added this item."

She smiles. "That's only part of the expense. If they don't have a system they use, we're going to have to set one up for them." She goes on to explain the costs associated with adding newsletters into their marketing mix.

After discussing all of the budget items, I have a firmer handle on what we will be able to do for the Preserve. Which has been reduced by half, given all the expenses I hadn't anticipated. My admiration for M kicks up two more notches. She really knows her stuff.

Bonnie walks by my open door. "Bye Xander." She stops. "Oh, hey Madison. Have a good night."

I wave to Bonnie as she leaves, and realize how much time Madison and I have spent together. A few more reps walk out and give similar exchanges.

My boss stands. "I should get back to my office. Take a look at the rest of my comments and let me know if you have any questions."

I offer her a salute and spend the next hour revising the budget. Frowning, I turn to her comments on the campaign, which scale back my ideas to conform with the revised budget. How will the client get the needed attention on such a small budget? To be sure, their overall budget is a fair amount, but it was whittled down with all the small costs. So frustrating.

Standing, I rub the back of my neck. I've been at this all day and need to move my body to shake things up. Besides, I missed my workout this morning. Seeing as I'm the only one in the office, I close my door, take off my shirt and pants, and look for my gym bag with my workout clothes. Which isn't here. Shrugging, I hang the clothing on the hook behind my door and begin my routine. Twenty push-ups, followed by the same number of sit-ups, then ending with burpees. When I finish this set, I repeat it. And once more.

"Xander, I wanted to ask—"

Madison's words cease when I turn to face her, breathing hard. "Oh, hey." I take three quick breaths, becoming aware I'm standing in the middle of my office in only my boxer briefs. "Hope you don't mind. I needed to clear my head," I pant.

She bites her lower lip, her cheeks a gorgeous shade of pink. "No. It's fine." She stumbles over her words. Spinning toward the door, she adds, "Go back to what you were doing."

"Stay here."

Grabbing my pants from the hook mere inches from her body, I'm aware of her following my every move in her line of vision. Her chest rises and falls almost as fast as mine.

The desire to reach out and touch her rises. As does my lower half. *Can this brilliant woman truly be interested in me?*

"Why don't you come to my office tomorrow?" Her whisper is throaty. Like a purr. Sexy.

"I don't have anything to do tonight. Can we meet now?"

"Oh. Okay. Alright. See you there." She scampers out of my office.

I collapse against the wall. *Note to self: Keep an extra set of workout clothes in the office at all times.*

Second note to self: This attraction with M is real and captivating and undeniable.

Once I cool down and get dressed again, I walk over to Madison's office. "I'm here and dressed." My lip ticks up.

"Rats. I mean, I'm glad you're here." She tucks some hair behind her left ear. "I wanted to discuss your idea about adding the Preserve to various local tours. I think it's a great idea. But I'd like to expand as well as contract it."

I take a seat in her guest chair and put my notepad onto my lap. "How so?"

"Well, uhm, I thought we could reach out for larger tours. I mean, stick with the ones Upstate, but perhaps talk with the folks here in New York City. Like how the Great Escape Mountain House got itself known around here." Her eyes remain fixed on the papers on her desk.

I cross my now pant covered ankle over my knee. "That's a great idea. And we can publicize the Preserve to City Slickers as a place to donate their money, even if they can't visit in person."

She smiles at my old-school movie reference. "I love that. Since the Preserve isn't that far away, I bet we could hook up with some bed-and-breakfasts up there and create getaways from the City. I'm sure those businesses would appreciate an influx of cash."

"Love it." Her idea, expanding upon mine, is fantastic. I bet if I reached out to some of my friends, they'd at least donate. Remembering the cold shoulder I got at the club not too long ago, I amend my thought process. I'm sure my family would donate. Probably.

She lifts her head. "Great."

An idea crosses my mind. "How about we take a road trip to the Preserve and experience it first-hand, to see if any changes need to be made before we invite all of New York City up there?"

M waves. "This is your baby. Call up the Howells and make an appointment. Looks like you have some work to do. And a trip to take."

Am I being too presumptuous in wanting her to go with me? After all, she does have plenty of other clients to handle—not to mention other employees. I do know that if she came with me, she'd be able to give me pointers. I might give her some as well … in bed. *Head out of the gutter, Xander.* "I'll see when I can set something up. I'll make it for a couple of weeks from now so there's plenty of time to change your mind."

Her alarm goes off, and she hits the screen on her phone. "It's seven. I promised Ma that I would stop working at this time to pick up dinner and go home." Her stomach rumbles and her hands fly to her belly.

"Guess you didn't need that timer after all," I chuckle.

She pats her torso. "I do have an inner alarm clock."

I want to spend more time with her. Discussing marketing and PR tips. Exploring other things as well. "Want company?"

"After all the publicity, I don't think it's a good idea."

"I can have a car pick us up at the door and take us straight to your apartment. Dinner can be delivered. That way, we can avoid the reporters." I pause. "I'd invite you to my apartment, but my guess is some reporters are camped outside the front entrance."

Her fingers trace her right cheek. "Don't feel like you have to come over. I can eat my dinner alone, no problem." She opens her mouth as if to continue, but her lips shut.

I lean forward. *She's not a schlub.* Eschewing Dad's derogatory words, I say, "I want to spend as much time with you as possible, M."

A smile expands across her face until she's grinning from ear to ear. "I'd like that."

"Perfect." I rise to my feet. "Let me get my stuff and I'll meet you here in five." I saunter out of her office and proceed into mine. Preparing for all the work I need to do tomorrow, I text Jimmy to order our car and I return to her door, which is still open.

"I hear you, Macy. I think he's the real deal too."

A slow smile spreads across my face. This smart, sassy woman *is* interested in me. I don't care what she looks like on the outside— which I think is beautiful— but it's what's inside that matters. If nothing else, Darcey taught me that. To be fair, Grandma Lucia tried to get me to understand this truth. It only took me twenty-eight years after her death to finally learn this lesson.

I knock on the doorframe and Madison holds up her pointer finger. Nodding, I turn and go to the front of the office, where she joins me minutes later. I grab her briefcase out of her hand and open the door for her.

"Thanks for waiting. My sister was on the phone."

"The one who's pregnant?"

"Yeah." Madison turns and locks the front door, then we take the elevator and hop into the waiting SUV. "What would you like for dinner? We have a great Italian place by my house. Unless you want a burger. We have this local place that makes the best ones from ground filet mignon."

She's practically salivating at her mention of burgers, so I give in and agree. After all, I did manage to get my workout in today.

"You're going to love them. I'm not even going to let you order as I know the absolute best things on the menu." She whips out her phone and puts in our order. The only question she asks is my temperature preference. "Can we swing by and pick them up? It'll be much faster than delivery and I'm kinda hungry."

"Of course." She gives the driver the address.

Sitting in the back of the SUV, in the stop-and-go traffic that punctuates all of the City no matter the time of day, I study her profile. Since she's sitting to my right, her scar is on her opposite cheek. I wonder if she deliberately chose this seating arrangement. Reaching over, I play with her blond locks, tickling her unblemished cheek with it.

She swipes her hand over the offending hair. "Stop it." Her shoulders hunch.

"Is the adorable Madison Welch ticklish?"

"You don't have to do that, you know."

I tip my head to one side. "Do what?"

"I have a firm grasp on how I look. I'm not adorable or beautiful or any of the other adjectives you've used with your prior girlfriends." She turns and looks out the other window.

I place my hand on her shoulder. "Listen to me, Miss Welch." Beneath my fingertips, her spine straightens. When she doesn't respond, I continue, "I don't use these words with you as a throwaway. Or to entice you into bed with me. I mean them." I can hear Grandma Lucia clapping around us.

She turns toward me. "I have mirrors, Xander."

Taking her small face in my palms, I pull her hair away to expose her scar. "Darcey showed me that beauty comes from within. You can be as gorgeous on the outside as Miss America, but if your insides are filled with jealousy, mean-spiritedness and other morally corrupt ideas, then you're one of the most grotesque creatures to ever walk the planet. And you," I pull her forward and kiss her forehead, "are filled with the exact opposite. I'm continually awed by your brilliance, and how well you treat everyone in the office. So what if you're not over five-feet."

She smacks my shoulder. "Hey! I'm five-foot-two, I'll have you know."

Chuckling, I rub where she hit me. "I stand corrected." I glance around us. "Correction. I sit corrected. Any way you put it, your beauty shines from here." I place my palm on her chest, over her heart. "Not to mention that I could get lost for days in your eyes, you have the cutest nose I've ever seen—surgically enhanced or not—and your lips are eminently kissable." I move my finger upward and trace them.

"But you're a BP."

Retracting my hand, I blink. "I'm a what?"

Her blues cast downward to her lap. "It's a term I heard ages ago, and it sort of stuck in my mind. It stands for 'Beautiful Person.'"

I lean against the leather seat. "I've been in *People*'s 'Sexiest Man Alive' issues a few times, but I've never heard this phrase." I let her moniker soak in. "Well, if you think I'm a BP, then you're right there with me."

"What?" she squeaks.

"Did you just hear me? I think you're totally gorgeous, inside and out. So we're both BPs." I nod.

In contrast, her head shakes from side to side, her hair flowing with the movement. "I'm not a BP."

I can tell you this schlub isn't the right fit either. Dad's condemnation rumbles throughout my body again, but I shove it away. What the hell does he know anyway? He picked the hideous Darcey.

I mean, I picked Darcey. Dad only encouraged the match. *Right?*

I lean forward. Madison needs to see herself as I do. "You. Are."

Her exhale tickles my lips as I close the gap between us. The touch is intoxicating, and I pull her to me.

Our driver clears his throat. "We're at the restaurant, sir."

M pulls away from me. "Oh."

I grab her hand, not willing to let her go. "Thanks. I'll run in and get our dinners, then you can take us to Madison's apartment." I kiss the back of her palm and open the vehicle's door.

Ducking into the small restaurant, I pay for our dinners and rush back to the SUV. When I enter the vehicle, Madison's chatting up the driver. Something I've never bothered to do.

"You must have fantastic reflexes to drive in the City all day, Ben."

"Thanks, Madison."

Madison? She must've given *Ben* permission to use her first name. He always calls me "sir" and I've not corrected him. I clasp her hand while they chat all the way back to her apartment.

When we pull up to her building, M opens her door and exits onto the sidewalk. The driver—Ben—asks, "Do you want me to wait for you, Sir?"

I consider his question and allow hope to surge. "No, thanks. I'll text Jimmy if I need a ride home." I slide across the SUV. With one foot on the sidewalk, I add, "And please call me Xander from now on." Ben doesn't respond, but his smile says it all.

I trace Madison's steps into her building and take the stairs two at a time. Turning the corner, her key's already in the lock. "Ben's a nice guy."

"Yes, he is." I don't want to talk about my driver anymore, so I hold up the bag and point to the kitchen. "Let's eat while it's still hot."

"Sounds good to me." She drops her briefcase next to the door and hangs up her jacket while I walk into the kitchen and take out our dinners. Her hands land on my shoulders. "Here, let me take your jacket."

Letting my arms fall to the side, she slides the material off my arms. "BPs have muscles like these," she murmurs.

I spin around. "And other BPs ask drivers for their names." Circling my jacket-free arms around her, I enjoy how her body presses against mine.

She allows our closeness for a minute, then steps away to hang up my jacket while I finish unloading our dinners. Madison opens some cupboards and produces plates and a whole bunch of napkins. We set out the food and bring our plates into the small dining room with a round table covered with a blue plaid tablecloth.

Since the hamburger feels lumpy, I take off the top of my hamburger bun. "Shrimp?"

She smiles. "Yep. It has ground filet mignon with shrimp on top." Her mouth surrounds the burger, and she takes a big bite. Try as I might, I cannot picture Darcey doing the same thing.

"I've never mixed the two." Chewing, she motions for me to try it, so I do. Flavors explode in my mouth. This unique version of surf and turf is beyond delicious. Not bothering to swallow, I say, "Holy shit. This is great."

Giggling, she nods. And takes another bite.

We finish our dinners—the burgers plus Cajun onion rings—with nothing more than murmured delight in the food. Satiated, at least as to our physical hunger, we load the dishwasher. Patting my stomach, I admit the truth. "That was absolutely delicious. Decadent, to be sure, but still great. Thank you for this treat."

She elbows my side. "Stick with me."

"I plan to."

And just like that, the atmosphere changes from playful to electric. "I like you, Xander," she admits. "You're nothing like I thought you'd be."

"Food-conscious and snobby?" I offer, taking hold of her hand and leading her over to the sofa. Where I had my hands on her half-naked body not too long ago.

"Maybe. You're a hard worker with great ideas. You don't skate by on your name."

"Wow. You didn't have a high opinion of me, did you?"

"I didn't know you, only what I read in the newspapers. You were the privileged son poised to take over the family business. With Theo."

Her mentioning my best friend as someone who would take over VOW-cubed with me is laughable. "Is that what you thought? That Theo and I would take over the magazines?"

She shrugs. "That's how it came across in the press."

Reaching out, I cup her cheeks. "You couldn't be farther from the truth, but I'm not interested in talking about Theo now. Or any other man, for that matter."

Her light blue eyes eat me up. "I can do that."

Pulling my hands back, her scar is uncovered, but I ignore it. "Good." I lean forward and kiss her again like I did in the SUV. Pulling a centimeter away from her lips, I add, "I want to be the only man you think about."

She runs her hands down my chest. "You already are." Her fingers tangle with the hem of my shirt and I raise my arms over my head. Obliging, she skims the material off my body and tosses it onto the floor.

Bending down, I pick her up, but she tries to squirm away. "I'm too heavy for you."

"I've got you," I reassure her. This woman worries about me, never thinking about herself. Time to flip that switch. "I want to make you feel good." I kiss her as I walk over to the sofa, a compliant Madison in my arms. "Like real good."

I sit with her across my lap. Nibbling on her earlobe for a second, I then lick where my teeth were. Her right cheek pressed against my naked chest, she extends her neck. I dot open-mouthed kisses down to her collarbone.

She moans. "You're off to a good start, Xander."

"There's much more where that came from, M. May I open your shirt?"

"Please." She twists in my lap to give me better access to the string of buttons on her light blue shirt. Which matches her eye color. Soon it hangs open, and a light blue bra greets me. "You're my blue nymph today, huh?"

She giggles. "I've never been called a nymph before." Her finger traces my pec muscles. "But I like it coming from you."

I bet she's going to enjoy more of what comes from me. While I like making out with her on the sofa, I want the ability to explore her body from head to toe. Divesting her of her shirt, I kiss her boobs through the bra. "More. I need more space to explore all of you. Can we take this to your bedroom?"

She swallows. I pray she wants to be with me and give her time to make her decision, as I don't want to force her to do something she doesn't want to do. But, damn. I haven't been this turned on in what feels like forever. I want Madison to torpedo my born-again virgin status.

"Are you sure?"

"Positive. If you want to be with me, that is."

"You have no idea." She crawls off my lap and extends her hand.

When I intertwine our fingers, a shot of pure adrenaline rushes through me. I've never wanted to be with someone as badly as I want M. She opens an interior door and her bedroom appears. Ignoring the other furniture, the color of the walls, and the designs on the curtains, I focus on the queen-size bed with its purple comforter. Purple. Makes sense. She is royalty, in my book. Maybe not by birth, but definitely by spirit.

She stops by the end of the bed and looks at me. I want to put her at ease. "I'm honored you've decided to share this with me. It means more to me than you know. Although," I stop talking.

She kisses the center of my chest. "Although what?"

Dare I confess this? Gathering up my courage, I admit, "It's been a while for me. Since Darcey——"

She places her finger across my lips. "Shhh. It's been longer for me, but I trust that we both remember how."

"I think we can muddle through." My eyebrows flash. "Let's start with this." Reaching over, I unclasp her bra and guide it down her arms. "Now we're even."

M kisses my torso again. "Not exactly. You're sculpted and I'm, well, just me."

"Open and honest and smart. I'll take it."

I bend down and kiss her again, our tongues tangling as we re-explore each other's mouths. My hands land on my pants and I shuck them, together with my shoes and socks. In front of me, she does the same so that we're both in only our underwear. Instead of the tiny thongs Darcey favored, as have all my former girlfriends, M's wearing light blue cotton bikinis that match her bra. Which is now on the floor.

My hands land on her hips. "I'll never look at light blue the same way again."

Her head drops for a moment, then rises. When I apply pressure, she takes a couple of small steps to me so that we're touching from chest to toe. Although her chest is much more interesting than mine. And lower.

Her arms snake around my waist. Mimicking her, I reach down around hers, then drop my hands lower and squeeze her delicious butt cheeks.

"Oh!" M's head pops up, her eyes squinting. "Two can play that game." Her hands descend. Before she reaches her destination, I tighten my lower cheeks. "Holy shit, Xander."

I laugh. I've never been in this position before—mostly naked, ready to hop into bed for some serious sex, and enjoying the wit of my partner as much as I am right this second. "You like?"

She runs her fingers over my ass, so I remain flexed. "I've always wondered how a seriously buff guy would feel."

I like where this is going.

"I never thought I'd say this, but I think I prefer a little jiggle in the trunk."

What? Every other woman I've ever known has expected me to be all hard planes. Everywhere. Although M seems to appreciate my six-pack. I raise my hands off her plump butt and, using my thumb, direct her chin upward to face me. Her comment doesn't compute. "You don't like my body?"

Her eyes widen. "Oh, hell no. I mean, yes, I do." Her eyelashes sweep downward, then her blue eyes return to meet mine, accompanied by pink cheeks. "Like I've said before, you're sculpted. I was surprised that you feel like marble from the back. That's all."

Somewhat mollified by her response, I release the tension from my butt. Should I confess my little trick? Grabbing her hands and pulling them around my body, I plant them on my ass and flex one cheek, then the other.

Her giggle soothes my somewhat wounded pride. "Oh my! You're multitalented."

At her exclamation, my restraint breaks. "You have no idea. Yet."

Ensuring the bed is right behind her, I slide my arms to her back and kiss her with abandon. Our tongues duel as I keep pushing forward until she lands on the purple comforter. Standing, I reach for her hips and tilt my head. At her nod, I slide her blue panties down her legs so that her entire body is on display for me.

Her glorious boobs.

Slightly rounded tummy.

Short but shapely legs.

All waiting for me to explore. Without another thought, I strip off my underwear. "Slide up. I want to get acquainted with every aspect of your body."

Her palm goes to her right cheek, where her finger circles what I know to be her scar. I point toward the headboard and her chest rises on a deep inhale. She nods and squirms up the bed. I grab onto the comforter and pull it off. Don't need the purple distraction.

Giggling, her hand flies over her face. "Are you some sort of magician?"

"You're about to find out."

On my hands and knees, I stalk up the bed and kiss her ear, not missing the shiver that runs through her body. I trace her legs with my palm.

"Xander."

"Mmmm?" I kiss a line from her ear to her cheek, ending by closing my lips over hers. When I pull back, I ask, "Did you have something you wanted to say?"

Her palms slide down my chest, her fingers outlining each muscle ridge. "Are you sure?"

I blink. She said she wanted this, and we're both naked. My cock is so hard it could print its own magazine. "I'd say I'm one hundred percent in." I glance down at our bodies, then meet her gaze. "Well, not 'in,' in."

Ignoring my quip, she whispers, "I know I'm not like any of the other women you've been with—"

"Shhh." I place my finger over her lips. "I don't know where this insecurity is coming from. I'm exactly where I want to be. Hell, I've been fantasizing about being with you for a long time now. Why are you questioning my motives? When we're both naked, I might add."

Air blows up from between her lips. "I like you."

"I don't make it a habit of sleeping with people I don't like." Well, I've had a few random hookups in my past, but even then we always had a loose connection. And many more who I regretted afterward, like Darcey. Something tells me Madison will tire of me long before I get my fill of her. Which I can't imagine. Especially right now as her hand slips lower onto my rock-hard erection.

She curls her fingers around me and my hips rock forward. "He likes you, too."

Eyes hidden beneath long lashes, she mumbles something I can't hear. Rocking once more, I suck in my breath. "He really does."

She tightens her grip on me and I see stars. Instead of hiding, this time she locks her gaze with mine. "I think I'm going to like him a lot more."

When she tries to move her hand up and down, I pull away. "Darling, if you keep doing that, this little interlude will be over before we begin." I lie over her and plant my lips on hers, soaking in all her goodness while skimming my fingers down her torso and ending by rubbing her hard little nipples between my fingers.

"Oh."

Beneath me, she squirms, which I take as my signal to continue doing what I'm doing. A second later, I drop my hand lower while my mouth gets acquainted with the nipple it just left. Laving it, I say, "I love these." Not a lie. Her boobs are full and plump and real, with nipples distended because of me.

For her part, M grabs the back of my head, keeping me attached to her nipple. I give it a nip and she squeaks. Her reactions aren't calculated, nor over the top. What they do is give me a huge sense of satisfaction.

My hand lands on top of her thigh, and I rub up and down. When she doesn't move to open for me, I pull onto my forearms and look down at her. Face flushed, rapid breathing, she's a bundle of arousal. Shifting my weight off to the side, I kiss down her torso to the top of her thigh. Her scent is intoxicating—the need to taste her overwhelming. Kissing a path toward her center, I lick her inner thigh, then jump to the other one.

"I want to taste you." Looking up, I ask, "May I?"

Her mouth drops open as she shakes her head up and down. "Please." She sucks in her breath and opens her legs. Exposing her slick, pink folds. Now it's my turn to suck in my breath. My gaze travels up her body and locks with hers. Without breaking our eye contact, I dip my finger into her body, causing both of us to suck in air.

Simultaneously, she says, "Yes," while I yell, "God!"

Dipping back to her other nipple this time, I suckle all the while exploring her wet pussy. Pulling my finger away, I bring it to my mouth and finally sample her goodness. But it isn't enough. I dive between her legs and taste her firsthand, thrusting two fingers inside her while encircling her clit with my tongue.

"Xander. Don't stop!"

Like there's a chance in hell of that happening. I continue my attention on her pussy, enjoying every nuance—from her moans of delight to her delicious flavor. I'm lost in bringing her to pleasure, awash in her genuine reactions.

When she clenches around my finger, I know she's about to come so I don't waste a single movement. Beckoning her to come to me with my fingers deep inside her body, I give her one more lick and she screams.

Not my name.

Not a deity's.

She lets out a long moan while her head thrashes on the pillow. I've never heard a more glorious sound. While she comes down from her high, I kiss her stomach and force my body away from hers. Grabbing my wallet, I take out a condom and leave my pants on the floor.

In the minute I've been away from her, M hasn't moved a muscle. Still looking debauched, she watches me as I roll on the condom and reposition myself above her body. "Feel good?"

She nods. "More than." Lifting her head, she greets my lips with an open mouth. Her tongue pops out and traces the outline of my lips. With each swipe, I get more and more turned on, if that were possible. "I want you so much, Xander."

And the proverbial straw breaks. My hand goes to her pussy, ensuring she's ready to accept me. Which she definitely is. Taking my cock in my hand, I line up with her entrance and push in, relishing the way her body accepts me.

Instead of entering her with one long thrust, I take my time, savoring my glide into her warm channel. Fully seated, I place my forehead onto hers. "You feel divine."

Her hands slide down my back and squeeze my ass, encouraging me to move. I rock into her. Not with the fast pounding my body demands, but rather with a measured pace we both deserve. It's been too long for each of us, and I don't want this to end fast. Well, I do so I can start again. But, our first time deserves to be special.

Funny. I've never cared before.

I kiss her eyes, her nose, and her mouth, while my hand plumps her boobs. M's legs encircle my waist, giving me broader access to her body. Which I take full advantage of.

My balls pull back, indicating I'm seconds away from hitting the point of no return. Taking her nipple into my mouth, I give it a bite, then console it with my tongue. That pain point was all she needed to fall over the edge once more, again moaning incoherently in her completion.

Proud of how I gave her another screaming orgasm, I pull back and focus on pounding into her body with a relentless rhythm. A few more thrusts and it's my turn to yell my climax as I come and come and come into her body. Finally finished, I collapse onto her for a few seconds before rolling to the side so as not to crush her.

For her part, M hooks her ankles over my shins and turns to the side when I land on the bed. Wrapping her in a hug, we both fight for our breathing to return to somewhat normal.

I reach for the spent condom. "Let me take care of this."

"Oh, okay." She pushes back and sits against the headboard, covering her body with the sheets since the comforter still resides on the floor. As I'm walking toward the bathroom, she kicks off the sheet. "I'll gather your clothes. They're all over."

I halt as if I hit a brick wall. Does she want me to leave?

19

Madison

All of my relaxed energy vaporizes when Xander pulls away from my overheated body. He got what he wanted and is ready to escape. Why am I surprised? This is how all of my other "sleepovers" ended. My past boyfriends—all three of them—never stayed over, and I always returned to my apartment if we had sex at their places.

Stupid heart. I always hope things will be different, like what my parents and siblings have found. I focus on Xander's backside as he walks toward the door. At least *he* was different from the other guys I've slept with. For starters, he made me feel cherished for the first time in my life.

"Oh, okay." Leaning against the headboard, I kick the sheet off my legs. Better get this over with. "I'll gather your clothes. They're all over."

I cross to my closet where a robe hangs so I can cover my less-than body and retrieve his clothes. Before I can remove it from the hangar, Xander's voice booms. "I don't expect to leave here until you have at least five more orgasms."

Mouth open, I turn toward him, only to see his tall, sexy figure walk toward the bathroom. "What?" My whispered question goes unanswered.

I'm still gaping in front of my closet door when he reappears and strides toward me. My brain cannot comprehend that this god of a man still wants to be in my bedroom after we've done the deed. Yet here he is.

Hands on my shoulders, he dips down a foot so we're of equal height. His dark blue eyes search mine. "Are you on board with that, M?"

My brain is so scrambled I can't remember what he said before putting his hands on my body this time. *This* time. Oh my God, he —we—had sex. "What?" My voice sounds as if it was raked over gravel.

With a tender tone, he asks, "Are you alright with my staying? I'm not ready to leave you when we're only getting started. But I don't want to overstay my welcome."

"I want you to stay." I squash the urge to scream that I never want him to leave. Ever. He's beyond my wildest imagination, and I want to hold onto him for as long as I can. Because I'm sure he'll be out the door long before I've even finished chapter one with this amazing specimen.

The smile he graces me with lands at my feet and races up my spine. I wiggle my toes. "Right answer." He pulls me toward the bed again. Settling us into the cocoon of my covers, he asks, "Why did you think I was going to want to leave after what we just did?"

Although I'm embarrassed by the truth, he deserves to know what was going on inside my head. Or at least a sanitized version of it. "That's how it usually goes." I shrug, trying to play it off.

He picks up a lock of my hair, on the *right* side, and twirls it around his finger. The fact my scar is on display is almost as exposing as lying next to him without either of us wearing any clothes. I cross my right foot over my left ankle.

"Then you haven't been with the right guys." He tugs on my hair. "You obviously haven't, since this is only our first time together. Of many, many more."

This man wants to keep having sex? With chubby, scarred me? I shake my head. "Are you for real?"

"Ten by ten."

Equals one hundred. His use of this phrase brings me back to Kansas faster than barbeque ribs. "My brother used to say that phrase all the time."

Xander tugs me tighter to his muscled frame. As we snuggle, he says, "Tell me about him."

I describe Mark and Macy and share some of the antics we got into as kids. Rather, they got into and I watched. I was too goody-goody back then to do anything as crazy as they did. "Ma and Pops always praised me as their smart one."

Xander kisses my good cheek. "They weren't wrong about that. You're honestly one of the smartest people I've ever met." I scrunch up my nose, which he taps with his forefinger. "Sounds to me like you loved Kansas. Why did you leave it and come all the way out here to the City? I want the truth, please. Don't repeat the flippant answers you've given me in the past."

To get away from the people who tormented me my entire life, thanks to my ugly scar. Keeping this truth to myself, I reply with another. "Well, Kansas is great, but it doesn't have this vibe, you know? As soon as I walk out of my apartment, the buzz of the City invigorates me."

"I get that."

"Not to mention all the big clients are here. Not in Kansas."

He brings my hand up to his mouth and kisses it. "True. But your market isn't the truly high-end clients. My guess is Kansas has the sort of clientele you've cultivated out here."

"You're right. But I'm hoping to level up and snag bigger clients eventually."

His head bobs, although he seems to be in thought, so I keep my mouth shut. I've given him more than enough reasons why I left Kansas. When he remains silent, I can't help myself. "I do miss it, though. I love my family and now I only get to see them in person once a year for the holidays. My nieces and nephew grow like weeds." I chuckle, remembering our last visit. They're good kids.

"I have to say that I'm so happy you decided to move out here. Otherwise, I doubt we would've ever met. And I can't imagine my life without you in it."

"Oh, Xander."

Not knowing how to process his confession, I lean across and kiss him. Our kiss turns carnal in two seconds flat. Pretty soon, I'm splayed across his chest with his hands fitting my hips over his huge erection. The realization that my body's hanging over the sides of his makes me pull back.

"Oh no. You're not going anywhere. Unless it's to ride."

Part of me wants to do exactly that, while the other, larger part screams at me to hide my oversized body. I place my knee on the bed. "No, I—"

Xander traps my hips in his hands and brings me over him once again. "I've decided for the both of us." The sound of foil ripping punctuates his statement.

The next thing I know, his arms reach down between our bodies and he rolls the condom on. Then he holds his erection upright and uses his finger to tease my core. As he's pushing upright into my body, he brings his finger to my lips. "Taste yourself, darling."

I've never done this before, yet I do what I'm told. I suck in his tangy finger, running my tongue around and around. When he seats himself into my body, his moan bounces off the light grey walls. His hand leaves my mouth and lands on my hips, where he directs the pace of this coupling. Which is so much faster than the last time.

The last time? I've only had sex twice in one night with one of my boyfriends. Once. And Xander did promise me five more orgasms...

So I ride him like the stallion he is. Deep inside of me his large cock fills with promise. A promise it already fulfilled once today. Keeping up his punishing pace, a tingle begins at the tips of my toes and spreads like wildfire all over my body. An explosion radiates throughout all my limbs, which causes him to stop moving for an instant and then growl his completion. Which sets off another orgasm across my body. It's like a rolling climax that never ends. Until I collapse onto the god in my bed.

Sweat-covered, our breathing decelerates a bit before he reaches between us to take care of the condom. He maneuvers out of bed, pointing at me. "Stay right there. I want to get back into this bed and I expect you to be here."

Too tired to do anything more than nod, I watch his tight ass disappear out the door. *Holy crap on a cracker*. Not only is Xander Turner a perfect specimen, but he also knows how to use every one of his God-given muscles to elicit maximum pleasure.

I sound like a bad Hallmark card. But I don't care. He can rock my world whenever he wants.

He strides back into the bedroom, still as naked as the day he was born. Pulling back the sheet, I pat the bed and he slips in next to me. Wrapping me in his body for the best bear hug I've ever had, he whispers, "I'm so glad you were still here. I don't think I would've had the energy to bring you back if you tried to run off again." He finishes with a chuckle.

"There's no place on earth I'd rather be."

"Not even Kansas?"

"Definitely not there." He pulls my hair away from my bad cheek and kisses my scar. Because I'm more languid than probably ever in my lifetime, I divulge, "That's another reason why I left Kansas as soon as I could. Kids can be awful."

With a frown, he looks at me. "Did they torment you about your scar?"

Not wanting to see the pity I'm sure is written across his face, I keep my eyes trained on his sexy Adam's apple. "Yeah."

Xander shocks me for the millionth time tonight by flipping me onto my back and holding my wrists by my ears. "They were young and stupid. And they're in your past now. You saw how the kids with Friends For Fun loved on your scar. They thought it was super cool." He kisses it again. "I told you it's a mark of your past that shows how far you've come. You own your very own fucking PR firm in New York City. You're making a splash out here thanks to your smarts and determination, not to mention the great group of people you have working with you. How many of those in Kansas can say the same?"

Some of my classmates have gone on to find success back home. But none of them left to make their mark in the City. "You may have a point."

"I know I do." Sliding off my body, he tucks my head under his chin. "And because you've been so open and honest with me, I want to reciprocate." His finger races up and down my arm. "I'm scared that Dad and his partners are going to be sent to prison and I don't know how to stop things."

Because of the position I'm in, I can't move, so I plant a kiss on the back of his palm. This time, the tension in his body isn't from flexing. "How bad is it?"

His chin moves over the top of my head. "I'm not sure. They're getting ready to file a motion to dismiss, but they all seem to be fighting all the time. They never agree anymore. Maybe they fought like this before and I wasn't privy to their in-fighting." He pulls away from me, resting his head on the pillow. "I don't know what I can do to help."

The raw pain in his voice hurts me, so instead of lying next to him, I scoot over and rest my chin on top of his chest. "When was the last time you talked with them?"

His chest rises. "I went over to my parents' apartment the other day. We ended up fighting." Beneath his cheek, his jaw moves like he's clenching his teeth.

Laying my fingers on the side of his face, I try to offer him solace. I'm so out of my depth here. "You have a brother and sister, and the other execs have kids. Perhaps instead of trying to insinuate yourself into a situation that involves lawyers, why don't you try to help out your generation of the family?"

He raises onto his forearms. "You know, that's a good idea. Theo's one of my best friends. He was there after Hudson—"

When he doesn't continue, I nudge him with my shoulder.

He maneuvers against the headboard. "When that asshole came into my office and basically made me quit."

I push myself up and rest against the headboard, like him. "How could this Hudson guy do that?"

Xander slants me a look. "He's the head of the Creditors'

Committee. Told me he would be filing a 'motion to reject my employment contract' if I didn't leave VOW-cubed."

His fingers make air quotes around the name of the motion. While I don't speak bankruptcy law, I'm able to put two and two together and arrive at the real reason why he left his family's business instead of the sanitized version he gave at his interview. "He sounds like a nasty jerk. Seems to me you're much better off without having to deal with the likes of him. Or the upper echelon of the company."

"Yeah." He turns and stares out the window. Given it's dark outside, he can't see much of anything, but I doubt he'd notice the view in bright daylight.

Latching onto what I hope to be a positive relationship, I say, "I'm glad Theo was there for you."

He half-chuckles. "He quit too."

"I know." I reach out and run my palm over his naked shoulder. Which carries the weight of the entire Turner and Hansen families. "It seems to me that you need to be an example of how to handle this whole situation. You used to work for your father, and now you're not. Do any of the other kids work for VOW-cubed?"

He shakes his head.

"I think you told me Theo's writing a biography now?"

He nods in the affirmative.

"I bet his career change suits him." I lean over and kiss Xander. "Like yours does for you. You're amazing at PR, you know. Your gut instincts are great, and I love your ideas. As do our clients. You were wasted over at VOW-cubed, if you ask me."

His forehead wrinkles. "You really think so? I mean, you're not saying this to me because I'm lying naked in your bed and just gave you four orgasms?"

"Three," I correct him. Assuming the last one counts as an extraordinarily long one.

If possible, his body expands and makes my queen-size bed seem like a twin. "That means I owe you two more."

He reaches for my body. Conversation over, I let him play me like I was his personal amusement park, blowing my mind with my two "missed" orgasms.

———

Despite Xander keeping me up until the wee hours, my internal body clock wakes me up at six on the dot as usual. Knowing additional sleep will be fruitless, I turn over and study the man in my bed.

He's gorgeous. His dark hair is so grabbable, as I learned last night. His bright white smile is something I relish. Not to mention his mesmerizing eyes, perfect nose, and ripped abs. I grab my cell phone from the side table. Setting it to camera mode, I snap several shots. Next, I zoom in on his long eyelashes. Women would kill for these. I take another couple of shots and return the phone to the table.

His family is so unlike anything I'm used to, but I really hope he can rally his generation of Turners and Hansens. Something tells me his father's level is too preoccupied with their problems to care. Judging from what he told me, I wonder how close they ever were with their kids. At least Xander has Theo, who showed himself to be loyal by following suit when Xander was essentially forced out of the family business.

I want to do something nice for him, but what can that be? He has more money than I would ever have, so nothing I could buy would mean anything to him. No, I need to come up with some sort of amazing New York City experience. Grabbing my phone again, I do a quick Google search.

Several ideas researched and discarded, I click on my home screen without having made a decision, and a bunch of articles are recommended for me. Without thought, I flip through them. Until I stop on the headline in *Spill It Magazine*. "Darcey Abbott versus Madison Welch: Hit This Not That."

My hand raises to my mouth. "Oh my God."

I must've said this out loud because next to me, Xander turns over. "Hey, M." His hand runs down my flabby arm and I pull it away.

"What's up?" He raises onto his elbow and tries to peer at my screen.

Might as well let him see. I need one more photo of this man before he runs for the hills—this time with his eyes open. Holding up the phone and taking a sexy selfie, I open the article again and pass the phone to him.

His head tilts, then he looks down at my phone. "Fuck."

"About sums it up." I push the sheets down my legs and swing them over the side of the bed, intent on getting up and putting on my robe.

A soft thud sounds as my phone hits the bed. Xander's hand lands on my shoulder. "Wait."

I don't move. "Why? Looks like the magazine article says it all."

"Who the fuck cares what this stupid rag prints? You are worth a million Darcey Abbotts. To anyone who knows the two of you. And, believe me, I do."

Still sitting on the bed, his words soothe me somewhat, even though I know he's wrong. I scoop up my phone and stare at the screen. Hell, all the people in *Spill It* voted for her over me. All. Of. Them.

I check out the photos, and the comparison is almost laughable. There's Darcey, with her long, blond hair, perfect *tall* body that's a size zero soaking wet, and clear complexion—not a zit, never mind an ugly scar. Which this awful magazine caught in one of my unguarded moments and put on full display.

To torture myself, I click on the comments. Before I can even read one, Xander snatches the phone from me. "Stop tormenting yourself. What other people think doesn't matter. All that matters is what's in here." He pats his chest, then mine, not touching my breasts but rather over my heart. Which is pounding a shallow rhythm. "Please know I think you're beautiful."

He's not vision impaired, yet what other explanation can there be for his last statement? "I need to take a shower." Without looking back to log Xander Turner in my bed one final time, I grab my robe and trudge down the hallway into the bathroom. The water heats up fast. Dropping the robe onto the toilet seat, I walk into the spray and, like an automaton, start to scrub.

The shower curtain opens and Xander's head pops in, then his whole body. I pass him the body wash while putting some shampoo into my hair, not caring whether he sees the scar or not.

Crap. What if my clients saw this article? I need to do damage control. My fingers scrub my scalp, trying to wash the image of the poll away.

A gentle hand lands on mine. "Stop."

I respond to his command without thought, simply dropping my arms. Xander turns me around to face him, but I don't see the sexy beast towering over me by a foot. I do notice one droplet of water as it descends from his throat, winding a path down his chiseled chest. I keep my vision above his waist, not wanting to find out for sure if he's turned on.

Or not.

"This is the downside of publicity. The media only wants a story. They make shit up all the time, you know that. Don't let this get to you, M."

I turn my head away from him. Some pair we make. His family is going through legal persecution, while I'm being subjected to public shame. Irrational laughter bubbles up.

Xander pulls me to his wet body. "The best thing we can do is create our own offense."

My mind bounces from incoherent thoughts to undeveloped ones, never landing anywhere solid. I do know I need to get ahead of this. Pretend like their poll didn't strike a direct blow. Xander's right. I can't wallow.

I didn't when I was five and attacked by the pit bull. I'm not going to start now.

"That's my girl." His palm runs up and down my back. "I can feel your spine straightening. Let's finish up in here and get changed. Looks like we have some work to do." He bends down and kisses me, whispering, "Don't let them win."

He's been dealing with this type of shit for all his life, although the majority of the articles painted him in a positive light. Guess I need a crash course in what I preach—PR.

An hour later, we're both dressed and sitting around my dinette table. Well, at least I'm in clean clothes. Xander didn't have a change with him, and I don't have any men's clothing here. So now he's in his dress clothes from yesterday and we're working on a strategy to combat this negative press. Which, he reminded me, does bring attention to my firm. In some weird way, any press is positive, I guess.

He sniffs under his arms. "Hate to say this, M, but I need to run home and get a change of clothes."

I close the lid on my laptop. "No worries. Thanks so much for trying to help me get this under control."

"Hey." He stands and kisses my forehead. "Want to come with me? A change of scenery may be what the doctor ordered."

Should I go with him? Is he right? "What if—"

"Shhh." He silences my worries with a kiss. "I'm calling for a car."

If we hop into a car here and get out at his doorstep, how bad can it be?

As soon as he gets the text that the car is out front, he picks up the overnight bag I packed "just in case," and we leave my apartment. When we open the door to the sidewalk, I realize I was overconfident.

A bunch of reporters spring into action when they realize their prey is emerging. "Xander!" "Xander!" "Xander!" None yell my name.

For his part, he tightens his hand at my elbow and propels us forward. Without a word to the reporters, he nearly launches me into the car, for which Ben had thoughtfully opened the passenger door. It slams shut and, once he's behind the wheel, the outside noise disappears.

"Thanks, Ben." I rest my head against the leather cushions.

"Yeah, appreciate your help out there," Xander agrees. Scooping me up into his arms, he pulls me onto his lap. For the entire ride to his Upper East Side apartment, I'm wrapped in his steady embrace.

We stop at a light on Fifth Avenue, with Central Park to our right and a row of stately apartment buildings to our left. Across the street, there's a group of people milling about in front of one of them.

"Shit." He pulls me tighter as if protecting me.

Although I know the answer, I find myself praying for another as I ask, "Is this your place?"

"You guessed it."

At least twenty reporters are stationed here. Knowing this day has turned out to be one nightmare after another, I offer to go back to my place.

"No. You belong with me. Besides, once we get inside, we're home free." He nudges my overnight bag with his foot.

"Alright." I scramble off his lap. He says he wants me with him, so we're in this together. "Then we have no other choice. Let's keep our heads up. Try to ignore whatever the reporters shout. And, I guess we should look happy to be together."

"Sounds like you're getting the hang of the paparazzi business." He kisses my cheek. "And for the record, I am *very* happy to be with you."

His words soothe the ache deep inside. "Me, too."

Ben rolls to a stop in front of Xander's building. It has an ornate set of gargoyles guarding it, which I ask to send protection. Placing my hand on the door handle, I ask, "Ready?" My question is more directed at myself than Xander.

He smooths my hair from the back. "Whatever happens out there, know I'm very proud you're on my arm."

My skin tingles where his palm strokes. I can do this. Without responding, I open the door and get out of the SUV, then pivot to take my overnight bag, which Xander doesn't allow.

The crowd realizes who's arrived and swarms around us. Flash-bulbs erupt in my face, blinding me. I reach out seeking Xander, and his arm wraps around mine. With him steadying me, I'm ready for the short walk.

Or it would be short if people weren't rushing to stand directly in front of me. The yelling begins.

"Xander, what made you choose Madison Welch as your new girl toy?"

Girl toy?

"Xander, did you see the poll in *Spill It?*"

"Xander, how can you compare Darcey Abbott with Madison Welch?"

I'm standing right here. He squeezes me, offering the only support he can. I keep pushing forward.

"Xander, are you sleeping with the boss to pass the time? Is that how you got your new job?"

This last zinger lands like a bomb in my chest. Judging by the crushing grip Xander now has around my shoulders, I know it hurt him too. I take another step, but he's not coming with me. I turn my head in time to see an annoyed Turner face this group of paparazzi.

"Ms. Welch hired me on my own merits. She's an amazing boss, and I'm grateful for the opportunity she offered me when no one else would. Check out her PR firm's website and see what I mean."

He never responded to the "pass the time" comment. Why would he? I know I'm only a dalliance until he's back in his normal position in society—and I'm in mine. At least he directed them to the website. I tug on his hand and he faces his apartment building again.

Once inside the foyer, I close my eyes. He kisses my forehead, then using my overnight bag as a pointer, he directs us to the elevator. When we're on his floor, he brings me to his front door, and soon I'm sitting on a leather sectional in front of a modern, electric fireplace. His windows overlook Central Park. Of course they do.

What am I doing here? I'm a Kansas girl by way of Brooklyn. He's a BP who travels amongst high society royalty. And is one.

When he emerges from the bedroom in a pair of low-slung jeans and a long-sleeved navy blue shirt, I permit myself a moment to savor the thirst trap before me.

He crosses the room and sits next to me. "I'm happy you're here. I want to show you my place like you showed me yours. I want to laugh again." He wiggles his eyebrows. "And maybe even do some more indoor gymnastics."

My body screams for me to agree, while my brain warns of impending disaster. Shutting my brain off for the first time, I give in. Who could resist Xander's blue eyes anyway? Biting my bottom lip, I reply, "I would like to check out your digs. What I've seen so far is amazing."

He pops to his feet, hand outstretched. When I take it, he says, "Let me show you around." We walk through all of the rooms, which include a designated guest bedroom and a media room. He notes there's a gym and pool in the building, together with a rooftop bar. Since it's still early spring, the weather's a bit too nippy to visit. "We'll go to the rooftop when the weather's better."

Instead of responding and furthering the fantasy, I follow him into his massive commercial-grade kitchen. Ignoring the elephant in the room—rather, the reporters stationed outside, we enjoy our day together.

As the sun sets, we step outside onto the wraparound balcony. I lean back into his chest, fiddling with his fingers clasped together around my waist. Together, we gaze out at Central Park, with its streetlights dazzling. "The Park looks amazing at night."

His lips appear at my ear. "I think you're more amazing than any stupid park or building in this City."

My heart leaps at his sentiment, although I know his slick words cannot be true. More like what *Spill It* posted, or even what the paps screamed at us hours before. I don't reply, but rather twist in his arms until we're facing each other. Placing my palms on his cheeks, I pull him down and our lips meet. No need to keep spewing nonsense. And I want our interlude to continue a little while longer.

We're walking inside his apartment when his cell phone rings. Ignoring it, his lips lock onto mine and fingers explore beneath my shirt. As soon as it stops, the ringing starts again.

Xander pulls away from me and sighs. "Let me shut my phone off."

Despite all the emotions screaming through my body, I don't

want him to blow someone off because of me. "Check who it is first."

He looks at the phone and his hand swipes through his hair. "Shit. I should take this."

I motion for him to answer. After all, this is a fairy tale, and everyone knows they all come to a bitter end in real life.

20

Xander

I sit on the sofa next to Madison while Uncle Ward's daughter relays her roadblocks in getting a job in her field—she graduates in May with a degree in Human Resources and is the only student in her class who can't get an interview. Closing my eyes, I admit how crazy this is. None of us kids were involved with anything our fathers allegedly did. I grab M's hand and hold it, rubbing my thumb against the back of her palm.

"I wish I could give you a job, but I'm not really in any position to do so anymore. Ever since I left VOW-cubed."

Chloe says she understands and asks me for some pointers. I'm out of my depth, as I've never had to look for employment. Hell, this job at Madison's firm landed in my lap, as Jesse reminded me. "Have you checked with the placement office at your college?"

While she regales me with how she's been applying to all sorts of companies, I move our joined hands to my thigh. I flip them so that M's hand is directly on top of my leg, which allows me to enjoy her touch more. When Chloe finishes, I ask if she's been in touch with her parents and I tighten my grip on M's hand with her response. Seems like her mother's ditched her in favor of doing interviews on cable, and her father is wrapped up with the lawsuit. Although he does lend her an ear, much like a friend would do. I offer her as much guidance as I can and promise to see what I can do for her, then we click off.

Chloe's mother, ex-Aunt Yvette, has been a thorn in my side ever since the arrests and her failed blackmail attempt. I run my fingers through my hair. Whatever she spews can't directly impact my life anymore considering I no longer work in the family business.

"Everything okay?"

Madison's voice brings me out of my own head and I focus on her lovely frame. I don't care what the stupid reporters said out on the street, or about that awful poll pitting her against Darcey. She's a glorious real deal, radiating beauty from the inside. But I do know this—whatever *this* is—is only temporary. Until M realizes this emperor has no clothes, I want to remain in our bubble for as long as possible. She said I have good ideas and a great instinct. Yeah, not letting her go so long as I can help it.

"Chloe's having a hard time finding a job. She's graduating college in a couple of months and hasn't even landed an interview. Thanks to her last name being 'Turner'."

She winces. "Sucks being judged on what others in your family have done rather than on your merits. What's her degree in?"

"Human resources."

She taps her bottom lip. "I don't know anyone, but Stefanie works for a headhunting firm. I'll reach out to her if you'd like."

Overwhelmed by her generosity, I grab her and pull her to me. "Thank you so much. Even a simple ask is very appreciated. Especially, well, considering…" I don't finish my sentence. No need—M is aware of everything about the status of my family.

One kiss leads to another, and pretty soon we're naked and recovering from another round of amazing sex on the rug in front of the fireplace. Which isn't even lit.

Stroking her bare arm, I admit, "You're amazing."

Turning so her right cheek rests on her inner arm, she says, "You're not too bad yourself." Her satiated smile warms me to my toes. The fact I brought her to this state amazes me. That such a plucky, smart, driven, passionate woman finds me worthy spurs me to do better with my life. I want to deserve to be with her.

"As much as I enjoyed our interlude, I'm getting a bit chilly." Her stomach rumbles. "And a little hungry."

We both laugh. I sit up, kissing her until she melts into my arms. "Let's order food. Can't have you passing out on me."

Dazed eyes meet mine. "What?"

"Food. Then more of this." I stand and offer her my hand and help her become vertical. After we put our clothes back on, I place an order for delivery. For the rest of the weekend, we remain inside our bubble. Mostly naked.

Several days later, I'm in my office working on some details in preparation for a visit to the Preserve. The Howells were excited with my suggestions. Well, as modified by Madison.

My pen lands on top of my desk. M is so much more than I ever dreamed possible. She's giving. Smart. She makes me want to be a better man.

With a little time on my hands, I do a quick internet search to see what the paps wrote about Madison and me today, considering they were all over us this morning. Again. I click on the first article, which portrays me as using Madison—personally as well as professionally—until a better offer comes. As if. I only want to be with her. For as long as she'll have me.

Plus, I've never been this happy in my professional life, either. Working for M's Agency is a joy. The other employees are cool and accepted the fact that Madison and I are dating with happiness for us. I want to stay here and learn from these amazing people.

The next several articles dive into Madison's life, which makes me feel terrible. She didn't sign up for this treatment, especially their dismissal of her physical appearance as not being a good match to mine. Pfft. If they only knew what she was like on the inside—and what *I'm* like—they'd be writing their stupid stories the opposite way.

My phone rings, displaying Madison's name. Picking up the receiver, I lean back in my chair. "Hello, Ms. Welch. How may I service you?" Myriad options dance in my brain.

"We didn't get the Friends For Fun account."

I jerk upright. *Shit.* Without a word, I drop the phone back into its cradle and race to M's office. "What?"

She motions for me to take a seat in one of her guest chairs. Her sigh fills the air. "Vanessa called to tell me our firm was gaining notoriety they didn't want associated with the charity. We're no longer in the running to do their PR."

Me. She means I've rained the paparazzi down on the Madison Welch PR Agency. I try to swallow but my mouth is dry. "Madison, I'm so sorry. I can reach out to some other contacts to try to call them off. I can sue. I can—"

She holds up her hand. "Stop." Her voice is weary but firm. "We both know we can't stem the tide about us. I'm implementing our own PR strategy for the firm, but it's hard to combat the reporters who are on us like a cat chasing its tail. All we can do is wait for another scandal to mesmerize them and pull them away from us."

She's right. "This sucks. I'm so sorry I caused us to lose out on Friends For Fun."

"You didn't do it alone. I knew what I was getting into with you." She tucks her hair behind her left ear.

I'm not ready to give her up, so I rush forward. "Still. Do you think we could meet with Vanessa again and try to change her mind? We already have a connection with the kids. She didn't say she hired another firm, right?"

"Well, she didn't say that." She pauses. "No. I think we need to let this die down."

My mind races. "Well, just because they passed on the Agency doesn't mean we can't continue to volunteer. When they're ready to seek more bids, we'll be in a better position."

"That's a thought." She pulls her hair from the right side across her mouth.

I hope she didn't see the online articles. "What is it? Did something else happen?"

"Well, it's more like what hasn't happened. Remember that we submitted bids to pitch five new clients over the past couple of weeks?"

I sit up taller. "Yes."

"We haven't been asked to meet with any of them. And that's unusual. Normally, we get calls for most bids we submit. As you know."

"Maybe they're still collecting bids?" Even to my own ears, my hope sounds hollow.

"Maybe."

Dev pops into the office and deposits mail onto M's desk. Turning around to leave, he stops short. "Oh, hey, Xander. Didn't see you there."

I offer him a half-wave. "Hi, Dev."

He walks over to me, towering above me since I'm still sitting. Getting all up in my face, he warns. "Don't fuck her over and we're solid." Without waiting for my reply, he bounces out of the room.

"At least he's protective of you."

Looking up from an envelope she's opening, her lips tick upward. "That he is." She pulls a letter out of an envelope and smooths the document on top of her desk. Picking up the next envelope, she sighs. "Sorry, Xander. I better pay attention to all this." She motions toward the mail.

"I get it." I rise and stifle my urge to give her a kiss. "I need to put the finishing touches on my campaign for the Preserve anyway." On my way to my office, I pass the break room, where a couple of employees are sitting. From the threshold, I wave. "Hi."

Bonnie waves me in. "Hey, Xander."

Welcoming the distraction, I take a step inside the room and go to the coffeemaker. With my mug filled, I turn and Elisabeth pats an empty chair next to her. "How's it going?"

As I take the proffered seat, I reply, "It's okay. Working up a campaign for the wolf preserve in upstate New York. Have a meeting in two weeks." I blow on my coffee. "I'm excited about it. I think we can help the Preserve make a big splash."

"Awesome," Elisabeth replies. She sips from her mug. "We're trying to come up with a cross-promotion for our clients."

"We both think the boutique grocery store and upscale florist have great crossover potential," Bonnie adds. "We're just trying to make it happen."

I fiddle with the handle on my mug. "I'm sure you've already thought of this, but do you have a couple of items from each store in the other's? With a sign indicating where to get more like them."

The two women exchange glances. Elisabeth answers, "You know, we hadn't thought about that. We've been so focused on social media and their newsletters that we haven't gotten to the physical spaces." She holds her mug toward me. "Great idea."

"I can picture a couple of beautiful floral arrangements welcoming patrons into the grocery store now," Bonnie adds. "Thanks."

Warmth spreads throughout my limbs at their approval of my suggestion. Dev appears in the breakroom, his eyes focused on me. The warmth turns into a frisson of nerves. "What is it, Dev?" I half-stand. "Is M okay?"

I don't even realize I've used my nickname for the owner of the company until Dev's mouth drops open. "M?"

Shit. I reach my full height and look down at him. He's not a short guy, but at least four inches shorter than my six-foot-four, which has helped me throughout my professional life. And it works this time as well, as Dev doesn't pursue this line of inquiry. Instead, he says something worse. Much worse.

"I think you should put on NewsTime."

Oh no. What is this cable news network airing now? They're reputable, so whatever it is, they've vetted it. "Crap."

I rush over to the television and turn it on. My former Aunt Yvette's face takes up the screen. Beneath her, a "Breaking News" chyron tells the world that my father and his partners filed their motion to dismiss. Not having a pen handy, I rub the back of my neck.

"There's no way any judge in his right mind would grant this ridiculous motion," my former aunt says. "But leave that to my ex-husband and his partners. Always looking for an easy way out." She continues to spew, hinting at financial misconduct including how Uncle Ward used to wine and dine potential advertisers then increase the company's advertising rates before they signed on the dotted line. And recording his successes in a "secret" journal.

Wonderful. This is the first I've heard such an allegation, although it does comport with the FBI's allegation that Dad and his partners had a second set of books. The 2019 ledger I found at the cabin tickles my mind.

The interview ends and the show's hosts come back on and discuss the motion to dismiss. According to them, it's pro forma. As will the court's eventual denial, according to the talking heads.

"I better go." Not waiting for their responses, I dash back to the refuge of my own office. I may no longer be on the fifty-second floor, but an ingrained desire to do damage control materializes. My first call is to Theo.

"Hey, did you see the interview?"

"Yeah. Amelia called me about it. Yvette is unbelievable."

"Totally. I spoke with Chloe yesterday but she didn't mention her mother was up to this. Why can't she disappear and never return?"

"I hear you, bro. I don't know what to say. But when she talked about Uncle Ward taking notes about the advertisers he fleeced—that brought me back to what the FBI was alleging about the double books."

"I thought the same thing." I take a deep breath. "Remember when Madison and I spent the night at the cabin?"

"Yeah."

"I needed some paper so I went into Dad's office. In his drawer, I found a ledger from 2019 hidden in his desk." I suck in my breath. This sounds so much worse out loud. My eyes slam shut.

Theo whistles. "Shit. Well, here's the good news: we're no longer at VOW-cubed. We don't have to bother ourselves about what our dear old former aunt has to say anymore. Or whatever our fathers were doing throughout the years."

"I wish." I pick up pens with both hands, flipping them through my fingers. Theo may be right, factually, but my need to manage this added disaster is strong. "At least the motion to dismiss was filed."

"Again, not our responsibility. Besides, it'll probably linger for months before it's decided."

"Listen, I'm going to reach out to Gabrielle. Since Chloe didn't have much to say about her mother, I'm hoping her twin will."

"Good luck. But, Xander, remember; this isn't your circus anymore."

"Yeah." Disconnecting this call, I press send on the next. Gabrielle's phone goes right to voicemail. Of course it does. Modulating my voice so as not to show how stressed I am, I ask her to call me back.

"Xander." Madison's voice enters my office while she remains standing in the hall.

"Oh, hi."

She takes a couple of steps into my office. "I saw the news about the motion to dismiss your father and his partners filed. Sending you good wishes."

"Your wishes aren't for me, but thanks. And remember when I was speaking with Chloe the other day, but she didn't have any info about her mother? Now we know why her dear old mum was avoiding her. I left a message for her sister Gabrielle to call me to see if she knows anything about her mother's latest interview, but I doubt she does." M rubs her right cheek, a sure sign I'm not going to like whatever it is she has to say. "What?"

Madison purses her lips and takes a seat across from me. "I'm sorry to say this, but I also got a few calls from reporters wanting our reaction to both the motion to dismiss as well as the information Yvette Newman shared."

"Our?"

She nods.

Fuck. I glance at my phone and for the first time realize my message light is blinking. If I still were at VOW-cubed, Felicia would've fielded these calls. Or at least warned me of their existence. I tilt my head up to the ceiling. From this position, I reply, "Give me the messages and I'll get back to them."

"Xander, I feel terrible about your family business hounding you, especially since you don't work for the company any longer. But you are family. If you want to take some time off to handle this, I'd understand."

My fist lands on top of the desk. "No." I echo Theo's sentiment. "This is their mess. I'm sorry it's intruded in here, but it's not my job to clean up for them anymore."

"Are you sure?"

I leap out of my chair, unable to remain in one place. Pacing across the small office, my adrenaline dips to normal as I start to accept the truth. I stop next to her chair. "I'm sure. I want to focus on the Preserve's strategy. I want to work on new pitches. I want to be productive. For you."

M pushes her chair backward and comes to her full height. Such as it is. She cups my cheek. "I get it. Just don't let your family's mess overtake your well-being. They made their beds, but you don't have to lie there with them."

Dragging her into my arms I plant a small kiss on her lips. "I'll do my best." And I will. For her.

21

Madison

Returning to my office, I ignore the pile of work that needs my attention, focusing on my boyfriend's current demeanor. Raking my fingers through my hair, I sigh. Today's been a shitshow. The Friends For Fun was decidedly *not* a fun call. The new television interview with his former aunt. The paparazzi snapping our photos and yelling awful questions at us. I can only imagine what horrors they've posted.

Don't check, Madison. Stay away from the internet.

I make it through another piece of mail before caving and Googling my name. When I click on "images," way too many shots of Xander and me greet me. Knowing I shouldn't—but doing it anyway—I flip through them, assaulted with nasty memes and "lovely" comments comparing me unfavorably to the women who have previously been on his arm. And in his bed. One even says he'd do better with Miss Piggy.

Step away from the computer.

Compartmentalize.

For once, I heed my own advice and pull up the spreadsheet my accountant requested. Despite the intensive work, I can't complete more than two lines without thinking of Xander. The real man. The one with insecurities about his self-worth, which I can't understand. The one who tells me I'm beautiful, which I can't believe.

Then there's HIM. Naked. In my bed. In his bed. On the floor. My legs rub together at the memories. If only the media would lay off.

Bonnie walks in, closing my office door behind her. "Hey, Madison. I'm getting ready to leave but wanted to ask if you needed to talk? I'm here."

Bonnie was my first hire and is a great producer. I like her ideas and clients rave about her. But we've never really had this type of relationship. *I've never been in a situation like this one before, either.*

"Thanks so much, but I'm good."

Her head leans to one side. "Are you sure? I've seen the media coverage about ..." She sucks in her breath. "The articles have been brutal."

I sigh. "Yeah." Waving, I continue, "Nothing I haven't heard before—or said to myself."

Bonnie walks over to me and sits on the corner of my desk. "Please don't let this get you down. We both know the media makes stuff up for ratings."

"Yeah." I make myself busy by straightening up the documents on my desk.

"For what it's worth, I think Xander's darn lucky to have you at his side. He seems like a lost puppy."

She's picked up on that, too? I test the waters. "He's confident and suave. Prospective clients love him." At least before the media turned their scrutiny against him.

Her lips twist from side to side. "Maybe on the outside. But I see the way he hangs on your every word, absorbing your suggestions like you're the Dalai Lama of marketing."

I scoff. "He does not."

"Oh yes, he does." She adjusts her seat so that her left foot swings. "Not only that, he defers to you on everything. Like where to go for lunch, which client to pitch. Elisabeth and I both think it's cute. We were so happy when photos surfaced showing you two together."

"The media's blowing this all out of proportion."

She holds up her hand. "Ignore them. You guys make the cutest couple. I'm rooting for you two."

Heat infuses my cheeks. "Xander is model-worthy, isn't he?"

Bonnie shrugs. "If you like the tall, dark, and gorgeous-as-hell type."

I snort. He does fit the bill. Still, I can think of plenty of other women who should be on his arm. "If you believe he's so into PR, then he should be with Kelsey."

She frowns. "Are you talking about Kelsey Hughes? The redhead?"

I nod. "She's pitching the same charity we did. They just told me they wanted to steer clear of the drama surrounding our firm." My shoulders slump.

"Okay. Ignoring Kelsey for the moment, I'm positive the charity missed out by not choosing us. I bet the pitch was fantastic."

"Xander did a great job. It looked like he had them eating out of his hand."

"And they didn't want to go with us because of all the buzz surrounding the firm? That's nuts. If nothing else, they could use the press to their advantage."

"I tried to tell her that, but their mind was made up." I move a pen from one side of my desk to the other.

"I'm sorry, Madison. Hopefully, they'll change their minds." When I bow my head, she says, "Now, what's this about Kelsey? Why on earth would you think Xander would be interested in her? She has a good PR mind, yes, but I've always found her to be a wet blanket. No personality at all. You have that in spades."

I lay all my cards on the table. "But she's beautiful. And taller than me. And thin." I do omit she has a perfect complexion. I can't confess that to Bonnie. It's bad enough Xander's well aware of my scar.

"Oh, Madison. Beauty is only skin deep, and the prettier you are on the inside, the more gorgeous you become. So what if she's objectively pretty? She needs to loosen up. Smile once in a while."

My lips curl upward.

"Like that. Your smile pulls everyone in, wanting to know the secret you're hiding."

I roll my eyes. "I hardly think I'm the Mona Lisa."

She hops off my desk. "All I'm saying is that you and Xander Turner are equals. Never doubt yourself." With that, she picks up her briefcase and walks out of my office.

My voice carries throughout the empty room. "I'll have what she's on."

Dev sticks his head into the room. "What?"

"Nothing. Are you on your way out?"

"I am, but wanted to invite you to walk out with me. You know, in case reporters are camped out."

If Dev wasn't the best damn admin known to womankind, I'd never let him leave for this reason alone. He's always so protective of me. "I wish, but I'm not ready to leave."

He strolls into my office. "Can you bring some stuff with you and work at home? I don't want you to have to brave whatever's waiting for you outside alone."

My heart melts. "Thanks for your concern, but I need to reference invoices and other documentation here. I'll be fine. I bet there's no one out there anyway."

He walks over to the window. "Baby doll, neither one of us believes that. You're the new 'it' couple."

I push away from my desk and join him at the window. From this vantage point, we can't see the front of the building, although a couple of people holding cameras walk by and my posture wilts. "Guess you're right."

"If you can't leave with me, at least promise me you'll wear a hat or some sort of disguise when you get out of here."

I make an X over my heart. "You're too good to me."

We discuss upcoming meetings, then Dev leaves, shutting off the lights in the main area of the office. Although Xander hasn't stopped by my office, his family drama probably pulled him away ages ago. Trying to block all the internal noise, I focus on finishing up reviewing the data for the accountant. About an hour later, I shut down my computer. Done.

Packing up tonight's work, I make sure everything is ready for another workday and turn off my office overhead light. Before I leave, I grab the hat Xander picked out for me in what feels like ages ago. Walking into the main part of the darkened office with my disguise, I glance down the hallway and stop. One office still has its lights on. No matter how many times I ask people to turn them off, invariably someone always forgets.

I drop my bag and hat onto Dev's desk and walk down the hall. Xander left his lights on this time. *Great.* I walk into his office looking for the switch.

"Hey, M. Fancy meeting you here."

My hand flies in front of my face, my heart pounding. "Xander. I didn't expect you to still be here."

He gets to his feet in one graceful move. Walking around his desk, his hands land on my shoulders. "Hey. You didn't think I would leave here without you, did you?"

"Oh, well, it's late."

"And I've been working. I've finished up another bid proposal that I want to read over in the morning before sending it to the boss." He dips his chin while maintaining eye contact.

With that, my heart beats faster and not from fright. "I bet your boss will love it." Without thinking, I rise onto my tippy toes and kiss his glorious mouth. The one that brings me more ecstasy than I ever thought possible. That says the most wonderful things. That I wish I could kiss when we're old and grey and sitting on a porch swing somewhere.

Whoa.

I try to pull away, but Xander must have other ideas, given the fact his arms tighten around my waist. He rubs his nose against mine. "I was going to suggest we wait until we find a proper bed, but I can't. I need you now."

He *needs* me.

Who am I to argue?

His hands find the hem of my shirt and he pulls it up and over my head. I dressed a bit more casual today. Within seconds, he's stripped me and is only wearing his navy blue boxer-briefs. Which I know is covering a necessary part of this puzzle. Bending forward, my teeth latch onto his waistband and I pull downward, his erection springing in front of my eyes. The material flutters to the floor as I open my mouth and accept him.

Due to our height difference, I only have to bend my knees slightly to get the perfect angle. His palm comes to the back of my head and his hips pump forward. I've given blow jobs before, but they've never been this carnal. And I like it.

My tongue circles his head, and he lets out a long groan. Before I can repeat this motion, though, he takes two steps away. Holding his erection, he says, "No. Not like this. I want to be buried inside of you."

Well, when he puts it like that. I reach my full height—making me even with his little, hardened nipples. He grasps my hand and drags me over to his desk, where he pushes the papers over to the side with his computer and picks me up. My bare butt lands on the wooden desk, causing a ripple of excitement to run through my body.

I open my arms and legs and he steps between them, his cock now sheathed in latex. His hand goes to my butt, where he pulls me closer to the edge of the desk. Satisfied as to our position, he inserts his finger into my center.

"Damn. You're so wet. Maybe I should let you suck me off more."

"Or maybe you should stop talking and get down to business."

"I like the way you think."

Without further talking, he rushes forward and fills me. "Oh my!" escapes on an upward gasp. Xander doesn't stop. He begins with a fast rhythm that only increases, sliding in and out of my body. His teeth latch onto my right nipple, causing my back to arch.

Locking my ankles around Xander's waist, I lay down so our bodies form a "T." Standing, he holds my boobs and throws his head backward. He pistons into my body.

So fast.

So hard.

So deep.

An orgasm washes over me out of nowhere, causing me to scream into the otherwise empty office. At the same time, Xander emits a low roar and stills before collapsing on top of me, his lips seeking mine.

With languid movements, his tongue brushes against my lips. "You. Are. Amazing."

"Back at ya." I run my fingers through his hair, tugging at the ends.

With deliberate movements, I unlock my ankles and let my legs drop to the side of the desk. *Holy crap! We just had sex on one of my office desks.* My hand steals over my mouth as heat infuses my body.

He removes my fingers from my face. "Not that I'm complaining, but what brought on this delightful shade of pink?"

"We did it on the desk."

He chuckles. "We sure did."

I struggle to my forearms. "But you work here."

"And now I have the best memory to inspire me." He puts his hands around my body and lifts me to sitting. Running his palm down my back, he continues, "You're the best quitting time whistle I've ever heard."

When he says silly stuff like that, I can't help but fall deeper in love with him. *Oh, no! How did this love stuff happen? We're only supposed to be a fling.* Shoving my wayward thoughts aside, I settle for a quick kiss.

He handles the spent condom while I jump off the desk and put my clothes back on. "Let me help you," his baritone wafts directly into my ear. Shooing my hands away, he clasps my bra and settles my shirt over my head.

"Thank you." With my top half covered and wearing only my panties again, I dip into a curtsey.

Still naked, Xander makes a flourish with his palm and bows. My heart does a little flip, but I keep my mouth clamped shut. Instead, I pick up his underwear and slide them up his legs in the reverse move I did earlier. He tucks himself into the boxer briefs, so my eyes stray upward to check out his ripped abs.

"I amend my earlier comment. You're much sexier than a statue."

He gives me a hug. "And a lot warmer than a slab of marble." He punctuates his statement by biting my earlobe.

In response, I giggle. "Hashtag truth."

As we finish dressing, he asks, "Want to come back to my place? I didn't pack a change of clothes."

"Me neither." Given the reporter situation, I know we need to spend the night apart if, for no other reason, than to throw them off our scent. "We should sleep at our own apartments tonight."

My statement lands like an oversized piece of luggage on the tarmac.

"No. We should do what we damn well please, paparazzi be damned."

I close my eyes because looking at this model-like man could make a nun forget her vows. "Xander, the press has been all over us. Photos, articles, polls." I pause, trying to forget the "Hit This, Not That" venom from *Spill It*. "And the Agency's gaining a bad rep, judging by Friends For Fun passing on us. We can't give them more fodder."

Scowling, he replies, "The paps will write lies if we don't give them anything."

"Lies I can handle. You know as well as I do that spinning truths is much more difficult."

His cheek moves, the only indication he heard what I said and is processing it. "I don't like this. I want more time with you."

This will be good for you, Madison. Get away from the spell he weaves. Get some perspective. I shake my head. "I understand, but it's for the best."

"How are you getting home?"

"The same way I've done it for years. The subway."

"How do you expect to avoid the paparazzi on mass transit?"

Shit. I didn't think of that. "I'll call an Uber."

"I can drive you home."

Where he'll persuade me to change my mind. "No, that's fine. I'll see you back here tomorrow." My eyes stray to his desk, and heat rushes into my cheeks.

He follows the direction of my gaze. Smirking, he replies, "I think we need to christen your desk next."

Jutting out my hip, I reply, "We'll have to see about that." I give him another kiss, escape from his office, and order an Uber.

Back in my apartment, I replay all the places Xander and I have been naked in here. On this sofa, in my bedroom, in the shower. Seeking a safe haven, I settle into my dining room chair. How am I going to handle my gorgeous employee?

Sighing, my true feelings for him are undeniable. I'm in love with him. Although, I'm all sorts of wrong for him, as the reporters have oh-so kindly pointed out. Over and over. A huge part of me wants to keep him all for myself, while my brain screams to run away before I'm picking out china patterns that'll never be set on a table.

I pull out my phone and stare at the photos I took of him sleeping next to me in my bed. I could submit this photo as Exhibit A for a Wikipedia entry about BPs. My phone rings, causing me to almost drop it. Seeing "Ma" on the screen causes me to giggle. "Hi. How's everything out in Kansas?"

"We're all doing well. I haven't heard from you in a little while, so I thought I'd call to check in."

Mom guilt. I forgot to call her over the weekend like I normally do, as I was *otherwise occupied* with Xander. *Shoot.* "Oh, sorry. I was crazy busy this whole weekend. I'm fine."

"What were you up to?"

I can tell from the tone of her voice that she knows something. Macy probably blabbed to her. Through the years, I've learned it's easier to come clean rather than try to hide something from her. "I was spending some time with a guy I met." I check out my manicure. "It's really nothing. Only a fling." *Remember that, Madison.*

"I'm happy to hear you're getting out. I worry that you're getting lost in the big city, and all you do is work. There's much more to life, you know."

Says the woman who only wants the best for her kids. "I know. We've tried out a couple of restaurants." Takeout.

"That's great. Have you gone to any theatre? New York has

Broadway, I've heard."

I offer a quick laugh. "It does. But, no, we're keeping everything quiet. As I said, it's not going to be anything more than it already is." When she doesn't press, I'm compelled to add, "We're really not in the same league."

"Madison Lauren Welch, what the hell does that mean? You're equal to everybody in that city."

Her indignant tone brings a sad smile to my face. "Ma, things are a little different in New York. This guy is a member of the upper echelon of society. His family's worth millions upon millions." Or at least it was before the arrests. "He's photographed when he goes to buy a cup of coffee, for heaven's sake."

"And he's choosing to spend time with you. Shows he has good taste."

That's one way to look at it. Another is to recognize the fact that our lives won't intersect for much longer. His dad will get out of jail, he'll return to VOW-cubed, and date the Darceys of the world once more. All the while, I'll remain in lower Manhattan, trying to pick up the pieces of my battered PR Agency. Not to mention heart.

"Thanks. I'm not sure he's the one for me, though." I cross my fingers. "We're only having fun."

"If that's your choice, then I'm all behind it. I don't want to hear you belittling yourself, though. You're smart and funny and beautiful, and deserve to be with whichever lucky guy catches your fancy."

"Thanks, Ma. I'll remember that."

Hours later, I lie in my bed, replaying her words. More like picking them apart. Smart and funny, okay, I can agree with those two assessments. Beautiful? My right hand rubs the raised keloids on my cheek. Hardly. If I style my hair the right way, and a photographer catches me at the correct angle, I could be considered passable at best. Bonnie's assessment from earlier pops into my head, which I also dismiss.

These people don't have a clue.

Before I fall into slumber, Xander's words float into my consciousness. "Please know I think you're beautiful."

Dare I believe?

22

Xander

Sitting at my desk, I put the finishing touches on another proposal. I've created four of these over the past week, but we haven't been called in to do an actual pitch for any. I'm sure the calls will come—sometimes it takes a while. At least that's what I've been telling myself.

In my drawer, my cell rings out. Opening it up, I pull it out and see Jesse's name across the screen. Smiling, I pick up my friend's call.

"Hey, buddy," he begins. "I'll be by you tomorrow. Want to grab some lunch and catch up?"

"Sounds good. I need to check in with Madison to make sure it's okay."

"Bring her with you. Her suggestions have been working wonders with my new business."

"She's filled with great ideas." I replay this past week, which has been one of the best—and worst—of my life. The best? Spending more time with M, mostly naked. I want to take her to see a show on Broadway, or even check out my favorite museum, Natural History, but the paparazzi have been relentless. My eyes land on my desk, which we christened last week. Hell, we've found some *pleasurable* ways to spend our time in each other's apartments.

"I also wanted to ask you both how you're holding up with all the press scrutiny."

I push back in my chair. "Dude. The shit they're writing about her is brutal." Which brings me to the worst of this week—all the nasty headlines being written about us. Saying I was using Madison for a job. Calling me a "wannabe PR rep." But what they've printed about me has been nothing in comparison with Madison. "I honestly believe she is one of the most beautiful women I've ever seen. She takes my breath away. But the reporters—"

"I know. They're all fucked up. Did you see the one with side by side photos of her and Darcey?"

A shudder runs through my body. There was a glamour shot of my former fiancée next to the worst photo imaginable of Madison, with her scar exposed. In a strangled voice, I respond, "Yeah. Madison puts on a good face around me, but I know this has to hurt her."

"I can only imagine. She's lucky to have you at her side."

Lucky? "I'm the one who rained all this shit down on her. I don't know if I'm her rabbit's foot, or a circling crow."

He chuckles. "I'll bring a four-leaf clover keychain when we meet up tomorrow."

Phone down, I reread the proposal one final time and email it to Madison. My conversation with Jesse lingers, and I do another Google search for our names, hoping nothing new has been written about us today. Of course I'm wrong. Instead of decreasing, the chatter seems to be amping up. *Fuck.* Clicking on several articles, my fingers weave through my hair and I tug on the ends.

One sticks like glue to me. "How the Mighty Have Plummeted: Xander Turner's Fall From Grace is Complete." A photo of Madison and me holding hands accompanies this article, noting our height disparity in unflattering terms, which I don't bother to read.

First and foremost, why does everyone dwell on the physical? I was blessed with good genes, but so what? It's what's on the inside that counts. Don't the reporters understand that? If only they'd take a couple minutes to talk with Madison, I'm sure they'd rewrite their headline to remark on how much she's lowering herself to be with the likes of me.

Working here, I've learned more about PR than I ever thought possible. The way we all bounce ideas off one another is unlike anything in my experience. Check egos at the door, as one person's success reflects on the whole company.

Standing, I go to the break room and grab a cup of coffee, not even willing to brave going outside to the GreenMarket. The sting of being called a "wannabe PR rep" doesn't wash away with my first sip.

Dev enters the room. "Hey there. Having a good day?"

I blow on the mug in my hand. "Pretty good. Sent in another proposal for Madison to review. Hope we hear back soon from some of the ones we've submitted recently. I'm ready to get out there and pitch."

The admin's eyebrow quirks. "I don't think there are any outstanding proposals. I'm glad you sent in a new one, so hopefully, they'll call us in."

"What do you mean? I haven't heard anything."

His eyes bounce throughout the room. "We got our last 'Thanks For Coming Out' email this morning."

I freeze, the mug halfway to my mouth. "Come again?"

He busies himself at the coffeemaker. "I'm fairly certain we've gotten rejections from all the proposals we've sent out."

Why hasn't Madison shared this information with me? It's not like I don't have a vested interest in them, as they were my babies. I straighten. Picking up a mug that says, "Life's a Pitch," I fill it with coffee the way M likes it. Raising it, I nod toward Dev. "I'm going to bring this to Madison."

He gives me a salacious wink, which I ignore. Although his gesture felt forced. All the way to her office I ponder why she hasn't told me about our rejected proposals. Am I not good enough to share the bad news? Does she just think of me as a good-looking bedwarmer?

What else do you have to offer?

No. I know she thinks more highly of me than that. She's told me so. I need to hold onto that. Dev must've misunderstood the situation. Knocking on the trim of her door, I wait for her to look up. "Oh, Xander." She jumps up from her desk. "Did we have a meeting scheduled?"

"We didn't," I confirm. Entering her office, I elaborate, "I sent you my latest proposal and brought you some coffee to celebrate."

Her smile electrifies me. How can reporters write such stupid shit about her?

She extends both hands. Instead of passing the mug to her, I raise it above her head. "It's hot. Let me put it down." She nods, and her blue eyes follow the trajectory of the mug filled with black gold as I place it on a coaster on her desk

Madison swivels the mug around, picking it up by its handle. "You're right. This is super-hot." She blows on the brew and takes a tentative sip.

How should I go about inquiring into the status of my proposals? I choose a roundabout tactic. "Did you have a chance to read what I sent over? I think it's my best proposal to date."

Her finger rolls around the rim of her mug. "No, sorry. I haven't had a chance to look at it yet."

No bite. Guess I need to be more direct. "Have you heard back from any of the proposals we've submitted recently? I'm excited to work on pitches."

Her gaze doesn't leave her desktop. Which we've also christened. After a pregnant pause, she says, "I have, actually."

I place my coffee mug on her desk and approach her. Placing my finger on her chin, I lift it upward. "Good news, I hope?" *Please say yes.*

Her deep swallow tells me Dev was correct. I tighten my grip on her shoulder, which prevents her from moving. "Unfortunately, we seem to have hit a bad patch. All but one of the proposals were rejected for further consideration."

Even though I was prepared for this answer, I can't keep the disappointment out of my voice. "There's only one still in play?"

She nods, freeing herself from my grasp. Taking a sideways step, she hurries around the desk and falls into her chair. "Yes."

"All because of me?" I plop into the guest chair.

Her correction is above a whisper. "Us."

I raise my chin. "Then fuck 'em. We'll find new clients to pitch. Like the one I just sent you."

She rubs her scarred cheek. "If only it were that easy. Friends For Fun wasn't the only client you pitched who turned us down. Two of the other pitches were declined because of all the publicity surrounding the firm. I've deployed a PR offensive to combat the reports, but they only seem to spur the paparazzi on rather than get them to back away."

I pull out my phone. "Let me call Amelia. I'm sure she can do something for us."

"Don't bother. I reached out to her and she told me what everyone else has. We have to ride this out. Wait for another 'media star' to blow up. Her words, not mine."

A chill runs through my limbs. Using my fist, I hit my thigh to get my circulation going. And to vent my frustration. "So, because we're unable to deflect the media from us, potential clients believe we won't be able to either turn the spotlight on them or will be too busy to handle their account."

Her hand drops. "About sums it up." She brings her coffee to her lips. "I'm starting to agree with them."

My spine stiffens. *What?* "About what?" I ask, hoping her answer isn't something I don't want to hear.

She sighs. "Xander. Reporters are camped outside this office as well as both of our apartments. We have to be shuffled from place to place in tinted SUVs to protect our identities. We can't even dine inside a restaurant."

I rake my fingers through my hair. "But this will die down. It always does. Hell, I'm not the only one reporters hound. Theo and Amelia get bombarded too, as do Ryder and Halle. We're all in their crosshairs."

"Your whole family, yes. As well as celebrities, who try to be as normal as they can be, but at least they chose to be in the spotlight. I never did." She pauses. "I want my clients to shine."

"I know. That's our job, to focus attention on them."

"Right. But now it's on *us*."

She stresses her last word. My breathing accelerates. "What can I do? How can I make this better?"

"I don't think you can do anything. Except—" Her mouth clamps shut.

"What are you thinking? I want this business to succeed. And if we can figure out how to harness this glare and focus it onto our clients, they'll garner more attention than they ever dreamed possible."

"All my attempts have failed. You know it."

"But you just said you had one more idea that we haven't explored. What is it?" I'm ready to slay a dragon if it would deflect attention away from the company. And us.

Her next question takes me aback. "Where are you on the wolf preserve?"

Suffering whiplash at the change in direction, I fill her in about my plans to travel up there at the end of the week and how well our ideas have been received by the upstate community. When I finish, she says, "That's wonderful."

"Are you sure I can't convince you to join me for the road trip? We could get a room up there and make a weekend of it. I'm sure reporters won't follow us up there." This idea has more merit than anything I've come up with all week.

Absentmindedly, she replies, "You know I don't do dogs. And wolves are big dogs." All the while she's focused on her computer. "Shit."

I'm around her desk in an instant. "What happened?"

She sucks in her breath and points at her screen to her emails. The open one reads, "Why are you wasting your time submitting a proposal to us? Use your skills on yourself. When your Agency, your name, or Xander Turner's aren't in the headlines, we can talk. Better yet, contact us when you get rid of Turner."

"Shit." My hands land on her shoulder. Trying to reassure her, I say, "There will be more clients."

M remains still. Beneath my hands, her shoulders tense until it feels like boulders are beneath my palms. She tucks her hair behind her left ear, the one closest to me. Without her scar. For the first time, I wonder if she set up her office so that her "good side" would be visible to all her guests. My heart constricts for her pain.

She licks her lips. "Would you mind sending me your campaign plans for the Preserve?"

My pulse picks right back up. She doesn't mean to follow this email and get rid of me. Right? I drop my arms. "Why?"

She doesn't move. "I'd like to see them."

Maybe she needs time to assimilate this latest email. Hell, I need time. "Sure. I'll go to my office and send it right over."

"Thanks."

She doesn't turn toward me, so I take a step backward and leave her office. *Give her time, dude.* I don't wave to Dev on my way out and duck into my office. After reviewing my strategy one final time, I email it to Madison. The heavy air suffocates me until I jump to my feet.

Elisabeth passes by my office, putting on her jacket. "Hey, Xander. I'm heading out to grab a bite from the GreenMarket. Want to come with me?"

Actually, I do. I need fresh air. "Thanks, I think I will join you." I grab my hat and a new, ugly vest M picked up for me to use as a disguise, and join her in the hallway. Bonnie's waiting with her too.

"I have to get one of those pickles," Bonnie says.

I salivate at the idea. "Definitely." Because I want her to come with us, I can't help myself from asking, "Have you asked Madison or Dev to join us?"

"I did," Elisabeth responds. "She's too busy, and Dev's meeting some of his friends."

I nod, plop the newsboy cap onto my head, and enter the elevator with them, happy to be getting away. I open the front door for the ladies and follow them onto the sidewalk, where the paparazzi start hurling questions at me. Guess my disguise doesn't fool anyone any longer.

"Xander, are you stepping out on the Pit Bull?" *Pit bull?*

"Moving on to more women in the office, Xander?"

Flashbulbs go off, blinding me. At least they distract me from the rest of the reporters' questions. My stomach curls in on itself. I can't do this. Bending forward, I shout in Elisabeth's ear to be heard, "So sorry. I'll return to the office."

Her eyes flutter to the ground. "We'll get you a pickle."

With a half-hearted wave at my co-workers, I retreat into the building—my jail. Within minutes, I'm back at my desk. Caged, I walk around the office and soon find myself at Madison's open doorway. "May I come in?"

Madison looks up at me, her eyes guarded. I need to apologize for turning her life upside down. "I tried to go out to lunch with Elisabeth and Bonnie. Damn paparazzi wouldn't let me leave." I take a seat in one of her guest chairs, rubbing my palms over its arms.

"Xander, we need to talk."

Fuck. Nothing ever good follows this statement. Bracing myself, I force my eyes to meet her gaze.

"I reviewed your email."

Exhaling, I let the craziness of the past half hour subside. She wants to talk about work. "We're already getting buy-in from the community."

She waves her hand. "Great." Her shoulders rise to meet her ears. "Xander, your work is stellar. You have some amazing ideas, and your charisma holds the room for days. People fall all over themselves to hear you speak."

"Thanks." These are all good things. But why do I feel as if this conversation isn't going to end well?

"Your work product certainly isn't the problem. Hell, I wish I had more of you working for me."

I skim my hand over my body. "Sorry. I'm only one guy."

She closes her eyes. "That's the problem, though. You're one guy with a passel of rabid reporters. One of them did a deep dive and posted a lengthy article about my scar today. Now everyone's referring to me as 'Pit Bull.'"

"I'm so sorry. I'll sue whoever did that to you. They had no right—"

"No, they didn't," she cuts me off. "But that's beside the point. The Madison Welch PR Agency isn't about our clients anymore. One of our longstanding clients just pulled their account, due to all the media surrounding us. I can't, for the good of the company, keep doing this if I'm going to have a company next week. We do good work here. We get solid results for our clients. We're not flashy, but the reporters are turning us into something I don't recognize. I can't counteract them."

What is she *not* saying? My voice lowers. "I've told you, this will all die down. Very soon."

"We've waited for that to happen. For weeks." She shakes her head. "I only see things getting more intense, as your father's trial ramps up. There should be a ruling on the motion to dismiss soon, right?"

I stare out the window. "The hearing's set for the end of the month."

"Right. If he wins, that means more press. And if he loses, there will be even more press. Can't you see that?"

"What does this have to do with me?" Snapping my eyes toward hers, I grumble, "I'm not the one generating all this media attention."

"No. You're not." She moves various items around on her desk-top. "I don't know how else to say this, but your working here has put me in a difficult position. You're a fantastic employee, don't get me wrong. But I can't get ahead of the reporters, and the Agency is in the public eye, in a really bad way. Clients are leaving the firm, others won't give us even a shot to do a pitch. I'm sorrier than you can understand, but I need to ask you to clear out your desk."

I leap to my feet. "M. No. Don't do this. Don't let them win. I like working here. With you."

Palm cupping her scar, she admits, "I like it too. Only, it's too much. I can't continually fight all the media off and try to maintain a business."

Collapsing into the chair, my fingers bury themselves into its arm. "Maybe I can work from home? That way, no one will know I'm still your employee." That should satisfy the vultures. We'll have to figure out a way around them to keep seeing each other. Although not working with her daily, face-to-face, will suck.

"No. I don't think that'll work. Believe me, I've analyzed this from all perspectives, and I think it's best if we have a public break."

Public. Break? "You *are* talking about our work relationship only, right?" I can't compute anything else.

She rubs her right cheek. "It's better if you're with someone who's not me."

My voice raises. "You're firing and breaking up with me? Because of the *paparazzi*?"

"Given the situation, I don't see any other way forward. We'll each return to our own lives. You'll go back to living the high life on the Upper East Side. And I'll return to taking care of my bodega clients downtown—and my Brooklyn apartment." She moves a pen across her desk. "It's for the best."

I blink several times while her words settle into my bones. I'm not good enough for her. I should've seen this coming. How could I fool myself into believing otherwise?

Without saying a word, I stare into her liquid blue eyes, memorizing her perfect features. Perfect to me. My soul cries, absorbing the depth of my loss.

I rise. "If this is what you want."

She stares at her computer, palm on the mouse. "It's what has to be."

My heart leaps out of my chest and lands in her lap. Somehow, without it, I take stilted steps away from the only woman on earth who made me feel whole and wanted. Who saw me as a positive contribution to society. Who valued my opinions.

Stopping at her door, my hand lands on the handle. I can't bring myself to turn it. Swiveling on my heel, I rush back to her desk where her head pops up. Without a word, I fuse my lips to hers. Taking my final taste. Giving her all of me. Wanting her to change her mind.

When we part, I wait a beat. Neither of us says a word. Which says it all.

23

Madison

Following his farewell kiss, Xander strides out of my office without looking back. Like his whole world didn't just shatter into a million pieces.

Mine did.

My stomach rises with multiple shallow breaths. Devoid of a working soundtrack, Dev works at his desk. It's as if the buzz of the office disappeared when Xander left. Pain in my jaw relays to my brain, prompting me to unclench my teeth. As I open my mouth to relieve the pressure, the imprint of Xander's lips makes itself known.

Run. Away.

I push away from my desk, my eyes landing on the papers strewn across my desktop. I don't want any of this anymore. What's the point? If I can't work with the people I want to because the fucking press won't stop hounding me, why should I? Besides, no one wants to hire a PR firm that has more headlines than them.

Not to mention I can't be in a relationship with the one man who made the stars sing and shine brighter. Who actually made me believe I was beautiful in his gorgeous eyes.

The media calls me "Pit Bull." My story, one I've kept hidden since I left Kansas, is now available for public consumption. Everyone knows about how I was attacked when I was five. And they've seen the scar. Its ugliness compared with Darcey Abbott's beauty.

My tense thighs scream in pain. My breathing accelerates. *Flee!*

I stand and take a step toward the door. And stop. I can't leave this room and face Dev or Bonnie or Elisabeth. Or, oh God, Xander. No. My only other option is to hide.

If I'm stuck here, I can at least get privacy. With every step I take toward my door, pinpricks behind my eyes multiply. My breathing becomes more and more labored. I mime like I'm getting on a call to Dev, who nods as I snick the door shut.

I stumble to my desk and take the handset off its cradle. My shoulders droop. I purse my lips and stagger toward the table on the side of my office before the tears flow. My hand flies in front of my mouth to keep my sobs as quiet as possible.

Searing pain races through my body at what I've lost. Above all else, the man whom I've grown to love is out of my life forever. *You knew this was temporary*. Nothing ever changed his being a BP. For a while there, though, he was *my* BP.

And now he's not.

My fingers run over my lips, still tingling from his kiss. He had to leave me with one final taste of what I'll never know again. More sobs escape, which I try to stifle. Grabbing some tissues, I blow my nose in a vain attempt to stem the tide. I collapse into a chair and let my pain run rampant.

No more Xander. On a personal level. On a professional level. His PR chops were great. He far surpassed Ellen's presentations but at least she didn't come with enough negative press to scare potential clients away.

What am I going to do now? How can I save the Agency, since there's no hope for me personally? As I sit, my tears stem, and ideas about how to move forward as a business start to surface. I do what I've always done—compartmentalize. I focus on how to announce to the world that Xander Turner is no longer affiliated with my firm. Or my life. Gain distance from all the negative headlines. Become a reputable PR firm again.

Which means I also have to service the clients we already have. The Preserve. Xander's only client now falls on my lap. I can't ask any of my other reps to pick up the pieces following his departure. I simply can't.

Gathering a boxful of used tissues, I toss them into the trash and pick up his notes for the Preserve. They're solid. We've worked together on this campaign, so it's in good shape, although now that I'm looking at it, I can see ways to improve. Keeping my mind occupied with work, I begin to make changes.

A text chimes. Knowing it couldn't be Xander, yet stupid hope remains eternal, I pick up the phone. It's from Macy. When I open it, there's a photo with the caption "16 Weeks!" She's glowing, and her little baby bump is bigger.

Grateful she didn't call, I drop the phone and more tears fall. I'm happy for her, but why can't this ever be me? *Because you choose either losers or gods like Xander.*

"Madison, I'm going to head—" Dev breezes into my office, then stops on a dime. "Oh." He closes the door and crosses the room. "Are you okay?"

Sniffling, I can't bring myself to say a word. I haven't spoken since Xander left. Dev plucks a few tissues out of a new box and hands them to me. After blowing my nose, several times, I look up to my admin.

"Is this about Xander?"

I blink, and more tears flood my cheeks.

He drops to his knees. "I saw him leave here a few hours ago. He was carrying a box. What happened?"

"The press is writing about us all the time," I croak.

"That's been going on for a while."

I wave my hand. "And now the clients are catching on." I keep the fact one dropped us to myself. No need to worry the rest of the staff. As the head of the company, it's my job to do all the worrying.

Dev's silent for a few moments, which isn't a good sign. He's never quiet. "What are you planning to do to retaliate?"

I don't have any fight left in me, that's for sure. "We're going to keep on doing our thing. Our clients have been happy with our work for years, and will continue to receive the same great service."

"Uh-huh." He hands me another tissue. "Xander's not coming back, is he?"

Covering my face with the tissue, I shake my head. *Woman up, M.* I inhale at my private use of his nickname for me. Dropping the tissue, I reply, "No. It's for the best. All the press coverage was interfering with our work."

"I see." He stands. "Workday is over. Go home, eat a gallon," he pauses, "or two of Ben & Jerry's, and go to sleep. Don't come in tomorrow. You need to mourn."

"Mourn?" I repeat.

"Yes. You lost an employee today. A good one. Who also was your boyfriend. You need time to process." He pulls me up by my arm. "And then you'll know how you really want to proceed."

Dev gives me a quick hug and hands me my briefcase. I shovel the papers on my desk into it. "Maybe you're right. A change of scenery will do me good."

Squaring my shoulders, I escape out of the office and hop into an elevator. All I have to do is walk the two blocks to the subway, take the F train ten stops, and get myself into my building. Where I can curl up and nurse the gaping wound that is my heart.

Exiting the building, a crush of people spring forward. Flashbulbs shock my face. "It's the Pit Bull," someone yells.

"Where did Xander go?"

"Did you fire Xander?"

"Did Xander quit?"

I'm all alone, with no one here to protect me. No one meaning Xander. Without any other options, I turn around and race back into the building.

Pulling out my phone, I open the Uber app and press send. I have ten minutes before my ride's here. I approach the registration desk.

"Hi, Gracie. Lou. Any chance you might have an extra jacket or hat back there? I don't have anything to disguise myself, and the reporters out there are relentless."

"Sure are, Miss Madison," Lou responds. "They've been hassling all the employees as they exit the building." He opens a closet door behind him.

Rack up another reason in favor of my decision to let Xander go. Doesn't provide any healing salve, though. When he returns to the desk holding a jacket, I say "Sorry, Lou, for the inconvenience. I appreciate your jacket. I'll get it back to you, I promise."

He smiles, uncovering the gap between his front teeth. "Don't worry. I know where you work."

For her part, Gracie passes me an umbrella. "Sorry. I didn't have a hat, but thought you could use this as a weapon."

I take the green striped golf umbrella from her. "That's a good idea. Thanks."

Donning my borrowed jacket and umbrella, I check the app and it shows my Uber is arriving. Tipping the umbrella toward my friends, I take a deep breath and exit the building once more. As soon as I'm on the pavement, I open the green and white umbrella in front of my face and push forward, ignoring all of the pap's questions. When I reach the sidewalk, I find my Uber and dive into it.

Back in my apartment, I drop the borrowed jacket onto the floor and toss the umbrella on top of it, kick off my shoes, and toss my briefcase onto the sofa. The sofa that's seen more action than ever, thanks to Xander Turner. I pick it back up and place my work onto the dining room table. Safer. Less vivid memories.

Taking a seat in front of the briefcase, I dump its contents onto the table in a haphazard mess. "You look like my life. One big, jumbled disaster without any hope of anyone setting it straight."

The top document stares up at me. Of course, it's Xander's strategy for the Preserve. Which now will be my cross to bear.

Because he's never going to be in my life ever again.

I throw my arms down onto the table and let my forehead crash into them. *You're so stupid, Madison. Fall for a BP and you get what you deserve.*

More tears flow unchecked.

24

Xander

My driver—Ben—drops me off at my building's front door. Before M, I didn't know his name, and now all I can think about is how much she changed me. For the better. And now she's gone.

Ben opens the door for me. Forcing myself to get out of the SUV, I grab my box of stuff for the second time in a few months. Fired. Twice. Well, close enough to the truth.

Reporters stationed outside my door throw questions at me. I hear them screaming but can't register a single word other than "Pit Bull." Ben opens the building's door for me and only then do I realize he's been walking at my side this entire time.

As I pass him, I say, "Thanks so much, Ben. You're a lifesaver."

He tips his head so that the brim of his cap bows downward. "Wanted to keep you safe, Sir."

I don't deserve his loyalty. And don't have the energy to chide him for not using my name. What have I ever done for him, except fund his salary? At that moment, I vow to do better by him. Juggling the box on my knee, I clasp his shoulder. "I really appreciate all you do."

His cap bobs again, then he turns toward the outside. I grasp my box in both hands and walk to the elevators. Minutes later, I'm inside my empty apartment. It still smells like M. Madison. I have to stop thinking about her with a nickname if I'm ever going to get over her.

My lips flatten. Like that'll ever happen.

I put the box on top of the kitchen island and picture her lying against it as I pounded into her body. Her breathy moans spurring me on. Her incoherent screams as she came. Never one to yell out my name or use some fake string of words like the others I've been with. No. Madison was an original.

Abandoning the box, I turn toward the bar and pull out an unopened bottle of bourbon. It'll be a start. Before I open it, I place a call for three more bottles to be delivered. There. I won't have to leave for at least a day. When I can call for another delivery.

Opening the bottle, I walk over to the fireplace and flick the switch so it turns on. A grin flits over my face as I remember Madison being impressed with this showpiece. The fire dances as if everything were all right in the world. It's not. And never will be again.

I unscrew the top of the bottle and tip it to my lips. Maybe Madison wasn't such an original after all. Perhaps she was using me to gain notoriety for her PR Agency, and when it danced like the flames before me, she dumped me. I take another swig.

No.

I admit to myself Madison was nothing like that. She genuinely liked me. She supported my ideas—made me feel wanted and included for the first time in my life. Not because of some accident of birth, but as a result of my own contributions. She thought I was worthy.

Until the media made her see how unworthy I really am. The press hounded us relentlessly. Well, her more than me. As for me, they tried to make hay of the fact I left VOW-cubed and landed at her PR firm. But for her? They were unrelenting, even digging up her story about the dog bite when she was so young. How can people smear another human being without thought of the possible impact?

I want to help her deflect the reporters. I've already reached out to Amelia, but even a member of the media wasn't able to stem the tide. My mind comes up blank. The only possible way to protect her is to do as she asks and stay away.

From the only job I was proud to show up at every day.

More importantly, from the one woman who gave me unconditional support, unparalleled excitement, and real conversations. I pour about half of the bottle down my throat.

Wiping my lips with my fist, I wander to my island and start unpacking my box. Only when everything's laid out on the island do I realize I never took a photo of her. *Fuck.*

But I know where I can get one. Bourbon in one hand and my cell in another, I plop down on the black leather sectional and scroll through all the photos the paps have oh so generously taken of us. I stop on one at The Riverside Café. Our mouths are fused, and my palms are on her cheeks.

I don't care what the press says. She's the most beautiful woman ever to enter my orbit. I swipe my fingers over my wet cheeks and bring the bourbon back to my mouth.

Sometime later, knocking brings me to the present. I've stared at more photos of us than I could ever imagine existed. Even sent a bunch to a local store to be printed. I cannot live without having photos of this woman in my apartment. Or in my life.

Knocking sounds again. *Shit.* Must be the extra bottles of bourbon. I place the nearly empty bottle onto the table and swing the door wide open, stumbling a little. "Yes?"

"Whoa, there, man." Jesse comes into focus, grabbing my arm to steady me.

"Thought you were more bourbon," I explain.

"I bet."

He steers me into the apartment, slams the door shut with his foot, and physically points me in the direction of the sofa. I lope into the living room and pick up the bottle of my new best friend. Instead of obeying his unspoken command to sit—I'm so fucking done with doing what I've been told—I follow him to the kitchen, where he opens and closes cabinet doors.

On the second try, my elbow lands on the island and catches my chin. "What'cha looking for?" I don't bother to listen for his response, instead replaying memories of the creative ways Madison and I used this island. "Damn."

Jesse stops with the cabinet doors. "Damn what?"

I tilt my chin upward and stare into his khaki-colored eyes. "Your eyes are a cool color. Never seen any like them before."

He shakes his head. "Alright, let me take this from you." He pries the bourbon out of my fingers and puts it on the back counter. The next thing I know, I'm being planted into one of my bar stools and the fridge is open. "Eat this."

Laid out before me is a weird assortment of food. Olives, carrots, kale, hard-boiled eggs, and turkey. "What the hell is this?"

"All I could find in here that's edible." He turns from me and picks up a box of crackers, adding them to the unappealing buffet.

"Doesn't look like anything worth eating to me. Gimme the bourbon back. That's all I need." I try to stand, but he's behind me, exerting pressure on my shoulders.

"Sit down. I'll get it for you."

"That's what good friends do. Help each other get shitfaced when the world crashes in." I plant my ass on the stool.

More cabinets open and close, and he holds two glasses in his hands. He pours a minuscule amount of amber liquid into two of them, passing me one. "Here."

Picking up the glass, I down its contents in one gulp. "'Nother, barkeep."

He chuckles. "Give me a few minutes. I have to tend to other patrons. While you're waiting, why don't you tell me what brought all this on."

"I can show you." I reach for my phone, but it's not on the counter. I pat my shirt and pants, and still no cell. "Shit. Where is it?"

"Can I help you find something?"

"Yeah. My phone."

He turns his head in a few directions while I continue to pat my body and still come up empty. Jesse disappears and returns holding up a rectangular black device.

"My phone!" I scoop it out of his hands, unlock the screen, and turn it toward him. "See."

Jesse squints. "May I?"

"Sure."

Taking my phone out of my hands, he swipes through several of the photos I was looking at earlier. Which reminds me. I need to find out when my photos will be ready for pick up. "Hey, can you pass my phone back? I need to get a date."

Instead of handing the cell to me, he places it on the countertop behind him. "Looks like a date is what got you into this state to begin with."

I plant my elbows on the island, palming my chin. "She sure did."

"What happened between you and Madison? You better not have hurt her, or I'm not going to be responsible for what I do next."

A grin spreads across my face. Dropping my hands, I reply, "She's lucky to have guys like you in her corner. 'Specially after what the piranhas have been writing about her. Us."

He sighs. "I came over because I saw a cryptic article about you getting fired again. What happened? Talk to me."

"I did. Not again, tough." That's not right. Shaking my head, I correct, "Though." He stares at me and I remember his question. "I quit the first time."

He hands me a glass. "Keep talking."

I knock back the shot. Which tastes suspiciously like water. Whatever. "The press were awful to her. Terrible. Did all these comparisons between her and Darcey."

"I saw some of them. I assumed you told her to ignore everything."

I jump off the stool, which crashes to the floor. "Of course I did! Why can't the media keep their noses out of people's lives and stick to following the news?"

"I've heard this from the day I moved to the City."

I stomp around my apartment, getting pissed all over again at what they put M through. Madison.

Jesse, still by the kitchen island, asks, "So what happened? Why did she fire you?"

"Because they called her a Pit Bull."

"Excuse me?"

"That's not it." Steering clear of the downed stool, I plop onto another. "She fired me because I was a distraction for her firm. We submitted five proposals and didn't get one invitation to pitch. Plus, one of her clients fired her because the Agency is the story and they didn't feel like their store was going to be heard above the noise. Plus, the charity didn't hire us although I'm sure we gave them the best presentation." My verbal diarrhea comes to a halt.

"I see." Jesse rights my former stool and sits next to me, handing me another glass.

This time, I survey its contents. Smell it. "Is this vodka or water?"

His eyes bounce between my drink and me. "Vodka. You finished the bourbon."

Assured this liquid will take the edge off, I swallow the shot. Which tastes like water. "Are you sure?"

His hands raise. "Would I lie to you?"

Sighing, I reply, "I guess not."

"So, if I got this right, Madison's firm was suffering due to all the media coverage you two were getting."

I tap the empty glass onto the island. "Yup."

"She fired you to regain control over her business?"

"About sums it up."

"That sucks, man."

My hands climb into my hair. "I liked working there. It was a great atmosphere, and I was learning something. I felt like I contributed." And the owner? Simply breathtaking.

"What about you and Madison? I mean, I take it you were dating?"

Unable to support their weight, my arms fall to the island. "We were. We had a blast. We even went out to the Catskills with

Friends For Fun—you know, that charity in Brooklyn that pairs adults up with underprivileged kids and they do fun stuff together?"

His brow furrows. "I think I've heard about them."

I narrow my eyes. "I just told you they passed on hiring us because of all the negative press. Keep up." He makes a noncommittal sound and I barrel forward. "Well, we volunteered to chaperone a ziplining trip with them." I chuckle. "You should've seen Madison. She was petrified. But I got her to do her first trip, and then there was no stopping her. The kids loved her."

Me too.

"Sounds like a fun time."

Jesse stands, grabs my glass, and walks around the island. This time, I follow him. Better make sure he's pouring the real stuff. His gaze meets mine and he sighs. Bending down, he opens a cabinet door. "Oh look. I must've been wrong." He holds up a bottle of bourbon with about a quarter of the good stuff still in it.

"Great." I point to my glass. "Hit me."

His pour is barely a finger, but I'll take it. He won't be here too much longer and reinforcements from the liquor store should arrive soon. When we clink our glasses, I notice his is much fuller. Downing the tiny shot, I slam the glass down intending to ask for another, but I must've miscalculated the trajectory, and the side of the glass contacts the edge of the quartz. And shatters.

My hand opens and I stare at the mess.

"Crap." Jesse springs into action, rushing to the sink and ripping paper towels off the holder. "Don't move. Let me take care of this. You don't want any glass lodged in your hand."

Would it matter? Not like I have a job to go to and use it. But I do as commanded since he seems intent on playing Dr. Jesse.

He swipes shards away. Tossing the broken glass into the garbage, he asks if I have an emergency kit. *Do I?* Shrugging, I stare down at my hand, which is now a dark red. "If I do, it's in my bathroom. Let me check."

I take a couple of zig-zagging steps toward the master bedroom. Jesse appears at my side, plastering himself around me. I try to lose his grip around my waist, but he's tenacious. Using my bleeding hand, I motion, "This way."

We make it into my bathroom where I'm assailed with more vivid images of Madison and me enjoying each other. How can this be over between us?

Because you're not her equal, idiot. When you rain down paparazzi on a business owner, no way will she want to stick around. Besides, she should be with someone with at least half of her intellect. I collapse onto the toilet seat.

Jesse opens a couple of drawers and retrieves some bandages and a bottle of disinfectant. I start to slump to the right, but he brings me upright. "Watch it there. You don't want to get blood on your pants."

Who would care? Yet I obey his commands while he cleans the cuts and applies the bandages.

"Will I live, doc?"

His teeth bite his lower lip and he frowns. "I hope so." Laughing, he ruins his savage demeanor.

With my good hand, I push him. "Dick."

"Why don't we get you to bed, huh?"

I wiggle my eyebrows at him. "Are you trying to get in my pants? The ones you managed to keep clean?"

He rolls his eyes. "Sorry, dude. Don't swing that way." He pauses. "But if I did, I wouldn't want your sorry ass anyway. Now, come on. Stand up for me." He puts both of his hands under my arms and lifts me to my feet.

Walking toward my bed, I confess, "She's something special, you know? So smart it hurts. And she has a wicked sense of humor."

"Finally the truth is coming out."

I stop and point at his chest, the white of the bandages covering my palm. "And who cares that she has a stupid scar. She's beautiful."

His head tilts. Or is it the room? "I thought your type was catwalk-ready."

My hands land on my hips. "Why? What made you think that?"

Jesse supports my indignation by placing his hands on my forearm. While he exerts pressure for me to sink down onto the bed, he replies, "Oh, I don't know. Just that every woman I've ever seen you with was either a model, a celebrity, or someone off the society pages. And Madison certainly doesn't fit any of those bills."

Using my foot, I kick off one shoe. Rather, try to. It takes me three attempts, but finally, the offensive footwear is on the floor. "So what? They were all arm candy. Madison's so much more."

"More what?"

"Substantial." I manage to get the other shoe off with only two attempts.

"You know I think Madison is fantastic. Only trying to verify you agree."

I flop down onto my back, my injured hand over my forehead. "Damn straight."

The bed dips as he parks next to me. "Then what are you going to do about getting her back?"

"What can I do? My proximity ruined her life. Got her reputation shredded. Hell, reporters call her 'Pit Bull' because of the dog that gave her the scar." I shake my head. "Should be a badge of honor."

He joins me looking up at my coffered ceiling. "I've seen some articles that have been downright awful."

"To put it moody." I run my swollen tongue over my teeth. "Not moody. Moldy. Mildly." Working through this word choice has been exhausting, so I close my eyes.

Rustling next to me registers, but I can't bring myself to move. "Sleep it off, Xander. I'm sure things will be much clearer in the morning."

S unlight streaming through the edges of my shades rouses me. Opening and closing my cotton mouth several times, I blink. I'm in my bedroom. Turning my head on the bed, I verify I'm alone. And my sock-covered feet are on the floor. Seems my shoes are the only thing I took off last night.

Groaning, I bring myself to a sitting position. What the hell happened? Memories of yesterday's debacle become clear, including being fired and losing the best woman I've ever known. My head pounds. On my nightstand, a humongous glass of water sits together with a piece of paper. Rolling onto my stomach, I notice a bottle of aspirin next to the glass, so I take three and chug down the entire glass. Turning my attention to the note, I recognize Jesse's handwriting.

Sleep it off. Make sure to change the dressing on your hand. And for Pete's sake, get Madison back in your life. ~Jesse

Slumping onto the bed, I lift my hand and stare at the bandages before throwing my forearm over my eyes. *Crap.* I must've blabbed everything to him like a schoolgirl. If only following his order was remotely possible.

I loved working with Madison, and not only because I was attracted to her. She valued my ideas—which spurred my own belief in myself, for the first time. I'm damn proud of how my ideas transformed our clients, for the better.

The smell of lilac tickles my nostrils. The scent of my Grandma Lucia. It invades my pores and urges me to grab onto what's good in my life. Like how she taught me to ice skate—find your balance and keep moving forward. What was it she used to say? "Looking around will only distract you."

I slam my arm onto the soft mattress and rush to a seated position, woozy at the sudden movement. I refuse to be distracted. I don't want the press to keep me from my goal. Which is to keep my job. And my girl. Woman. A slight grin touches my lips. Definitely a woman.

Picking up my phone, I press Madison's contact. It rings and rings and rings. With each tone, my determination slips farther and farther away.

Maybe Jesse is wrong. Maybe she doesn't want to be with me.

When M's voicemail picks up, I don't bother to leave a message. If she wanted to talk, she would've answered.

It's best if I let her soar.

25

Madison

I watch my cell as Xander's name disappears from the screen. My body begs for me to call him back, but I can't. I spent all night crying over the BP who made my body sing. Not to mention stupidly staring at the photos I took of him in my bed. If I cave and hear his voice again, I'd beg him to come back to me.

The papers around my office and messages on my desk tell me that's impossible.

Not to mention the headlines today. "Xander Turner Returns to His Senses" is the kindest of all of them. Shutting my eyes, I refuse to dwell on the harsher ones.

Dev's discombobulated voice comes over the intercom. "Madison, I've been holding all of your calls like you asked, but it's Mr. Howell on the phone now. Do you want to talk with him?"

No.

Strike that. Hell no.

The professional side of me overrules my immediate rejection, however, and answers Dev in the affirmative. Clearing my throat, I swipe a tear off my cheek. "Hello, Mr. Howell. Did you like the campaign strategy I sent over to you?"

"We did, very much. Although, we feel it's missing something."

Of course it is. I bite back my frustration. "Really? What would you like added?"

"We're not sure. We think it might be clearer to all of us if you join Xander on his trip up here on Friday to tour the Preserve. Experience it for yourself."

If I wasn't almost throwing up over the possibility of being cooped up with a pack of wolves, I would've screamed hysterically at the thought of spending another minute with my former super sexy employee.

My finger traces my scar. *Crap.* I'd forgotten Xander had made this appointment. Taking a deep breath, I share he's no longer affiliated with the Agency.

"I'm sorry to hear that." *Not as much as I am.* "I'll switch the schedule for Friday to your name for eleven a.m. That's after the wolves wake up and before they're fed, so they'll be excited to see you."

My body twists itself into knots at the prospect. My head shakes from side to side, which he can't see. I painted myself into this corner, with no other option but for me to accept. "Great," I mumble. Hanging up the phone, I take time to deposit the receiver into its cradle.

How am I ever going to do this? I picture a wolf, taller than me, with his mouth open. Rows of sharp yellow teeth line his upper and lower lips. He advances toward me. My breathing accelerates. Sweat breaks out on my brow.

"Madison, do you need—"

Panting, I register talking but can't make out the words.

Someone touches my hands. Guides paper into them. "Take this and put it over your mouth." Dev's voice penetrates my haze, and I do as instructed.

"Lean forward and put your head between your knees."

He rubs my back as I take deep breaths. A bag inflates and deflates with every breath I take. My heart rate decreases to a normal rate and I sit up. Depositing the paper bag onto my desk, I look at my admin. "Thank you."

Dev continues to rub my back. "What brought that on?"

Might as well tell him. After all, he's going to have to help me prepare anyway. "A meeting came up for Friday that I don't want to attend."

Tossing the bag into the trash, he sits in my guest chair. "Talk to me. What can I do?"

I try to swallow over the sawdust in my throat. "It's at the Preserve." I give him detailed instructions as to what paperwork I'll need to take with me, and Dev offers to prepare a binder with all of the documents.

The next day, Dev sits in front of me and we review the binder for tomorrow's meeting. At. The. Preserve. Once we're done, I sit back in my chair. It feels like forever ago that Xander left here, but it's only been a few days. Working on his client has made me miss him all the more.

Who am I trying to kid? He's left a void in my life that permeates every single second of every single minute of every single day.

"Xander did a good job with the Preserve," Dev remarks.

I force my lips to tip upward a fraction. "He did."

"And he was good to look at." His eyebrows rise and fall, and a leering expression crosses his face.

Truth wars with devastation. "That he was."

"Why did you fire him again?"

I roll a pen on top of my desk. "You know exactly why I had to let him go. New prospects wouldn't even let us pitch. The firm *was* the story rather than promoting our clients." The pen falls off the side of my desk, and I catch it. "He was bad for business."

"Are you aware of how many inquiries I've been fielding? People who are interested in hiring the Agency simply because we are in the headlines?"

I drop the pen. "What?"

"Yup. I told them to send us an RFP and we'd submit a bid. So you see, all the press wasn't bad."

If something sounds too good to be true … "Have any followed up?"

He picks lint off his trousers. Like I thought. "I know you're all prepared for the meeting at the Preserve tomorrow since I created this binder for you." He grins. "What are you wearing?" His sudden change of subject confirms that the callers were only looky-loos.

"One of my suits, I guess."

"No, no, no. Not upstate. They're all granola up there."

A smile graces my face for an instant before I realize what I'm doing and I temper my expression. "We met the Howells, remember? They were wearing suits."

"That's because they came here. When you're up there, you should wear something casual chic. Says you're there to do business but not a stuck-up suit from the City."

I glance down at my navy blue trousers and white blouse. "I don't dress stuffy."

"Girlfriend, you may not know this, but your clothes scream you're all about business." He claps. "You should go shopping."

Maybe Dev does have a point. After all, he's all about fashion. Plus, I don't have much to do other than stew about tomorrow, so perhaps a shopping trip isn't a bad idea. I stare at the papers on my desk without seeing a word. "Maybe you're right."

"Great." He leaps out of his chair. "I'll send an email to the team letting them know you're going to take an extended lunch and will be at a client meeting tomorrow."

"Thanks." After he leaves my office, I give my shopping buddy Stephanie a call and we agree to meet. Raising my briefcase to my admin, I escape from the building at this off-hour without attracting any media attention. Which, admittedly, has dropped since Xander's not been working here.

My body collapses. *It was the right decision.*

I join up with Stephanie at the mall in Brooklyn and she helps me pick out a pair of brown trousers with a lightweight red sweater boasting a scoop neck and an almost invisible diamond weave from the petite section. "You look amazing. I couldn't carry off that ensemble, but it's like you walked off the pages of *Womanhood*."

At her mention of the VOW-cubed magazine, all the enjoyment of our trip flees. I clack the two hangers together. "Thank you."

Oblivious to what she said, Stephanie asks "What shoes are you thinking for this fab outfit?"

I wave. "I can wear my booties."

"What color? Do they have a heel?"

I can't focus on my wardrobe, so I shrug. Taking my nonverbal answer as a yes, Stephanie pulls me over to the shoe department and picks up a pair of dark brown ankle-high short boots with a wedge heel. "Try these on. They'll be perfect, especially if you're on uneven ground."

Although I've lost the fervor for shopping, I try them on and take a few steps. "What do you think?"

"I think you're going to wow them." She gives me a quick hug. "Thanks for inviting me today. I needed the break, and I love hanging out with you, although I am jealous of how you can wear anything off the rack and look amazing. Me? I have to bring whatever I buy into the tailor."

I point to myself. "Me? I'm hardly a fitness model. I was lucky today, that's all."

"You're always so put together, Madison. Your new outfit looks like it was made for your body. Almost wish those stupid reporters would take a photo of you in it, but I'm sure they're too busy fawning all over Xander's exes to see the beauty he has on his arm."

"Had."

"What?"

Surprised she hasn't heard, I explain the painful reasons why we ended things. "And besides, all of his other girlfriends were gorgeous, like him." I pull the hair away from my right side. "None had this on them."

Stephanie studies my scar, which makes me feel as if I'm under a microscope, so I drop my hair back in place. "Honestly, I forget you have a scar most of the time. Usually, your hair covers it, but it's not that bad anyway. Your pores are flawless."

They are? I blink several times. "In addition to my scar, though, I'm shorter than Xander by like a foot. And I probably weigh more than two of his former girlfriends put together."

She waves her hand. "So what about your height difference? People probably try to figure out how you do it." She giggles.

Of course, all I'm thinking about now is how Xander played my body as if I were designed for him. Shows how much experience can be put to good use.

Stephanie slips her arm through mine. "Let's get something to eat and mock everyone eating a salad." We go to a burger joint and order some cheeseburgers and fries, to spite all the waif-like models out there.

Back at home, I lay out my new clothes on the chair in my bedroom. Dev was right. I'll be more in place wearing this outfit than one of my usual suits. When this task is done, I ignore my need to get out of my bedroom. Xander is everywhere. For added torture, I plop onto the bed and pull up the photo of him sleeping right here. My fingernail traces his gorgeous features.

Ma's FaceTime call replaces Xander's picture, and I almost drop my cell. "Hi, Ma. I was holding my phone and your call startled me."

She gives me the once-over. "Did I catch you at a bad time?"

Wallowing over my ex-employee? "No. I wasn't doing anything important."

"How was today?"

I've been speaking with Ma every day since The Day My World Imploded. "It was fine. I actually went shopping with a friend for a meeting in upstate New York tomorrow."

"I'm happy to hear you're getting out. How far away is your meeting tomorrow? Did you rent a car? Who are you going to see?"

Turning, I flee my bedroom toward the kitchen, intent on making myself a cup of tea. "Thanks. About three hours. Yes. The Mahigan Preserve." I respond to her rapid-fire questions. At her tilted head, I add, "It's a wolf preserve. It was Xander's only client and no one else was able to take it on, so here I am."

"Wow. I'm very proud of you, honey, for taking this on yourself."

She doesn't mention my dog attack and resultant fear of dogs. No need. I busy myself by pouring water into my mug and placing it into the microwave. "Thanks."

"I'm sorry you and Xander have had to take a break to allow the media to die down."

I pause from picking out a teabag. "Ma, I told you we're on more than a break. We're done. If there ever was an 'us,' that is."

"I went online and I've never seen you look as happy as in the photos of you two. Not that you confided in me about him, that is."

I take on her Mom Guilt head-on. "There's a reason for that. I knew, right from the start, that we weren't meant to be. If you've seen pictures, you know why."

"All I saw was my daughter over the moon. And a man totally besotted by her."

A *pfft* escapes my lips. "Besotted? Who says that word?" She's wrong. She has to be. Doesn't she? "I was only someone to pass the time for him."

It looks like she just sucked on a lemon. "What makes you say that?"

I plop the teabag onto the counter and take out the sugar. "Ma, did you actually *look* at him? He's tall, built, and so good-looking it hurts to be in his presence. It took me a couple of days to be able to put more than two words together around him. Plus, his family's rich. Like super rich. I was never going to be anything more than a fling to Xander Turner." The microwave goes off so I remove the steaming mug and add the teabag to steep.

"Madison Lauren Welch. I raised you to be better than this." Her commanding tone underpins her disapproval of what I said. "Simply because this guy's rich and attractive, you're judging him as not worthy of you. You never liked it when people discriminated against you for your scar, yet you're doing the same thing against him—only in reverse."

I pause mid-air holding a teaspoon. "It's not like that at all. Reporters hound his every move. Publish unflattering comparisons about me with the trail of other women he's had in his life." And bed. Throwing away the teabag, I dump two heaps of sugar in the mug and stir, creating a whirlpool.

"So what? You've never allowed what people said to influence your decisions before."

Only fled the state to get away. A memory surfaces of him calling me brave and kissing my scar. Shoving it aside, I reply, "The press has been brutal."

"This guy deserves the chance to prove himself worthy." Unlike mine, her tone becomes more clipped the longer this conversation continues. "Think about what I said." She disconnects.

I haven't heard her so angry since a teenaged Mark and his friends had a secret, massive party at the house while she and Pops were away for a weekend. Taking my tea into the dining room, I drop into a chair and take a sip. Xander's more than worthy. Have I been guilty of reverse discrimination against him, judging him as an unsafe bet due to his appearance and status?

I check my voicemails. Nothing new. If Ma were right, he would've left a message. I bring my mug to my lips and blow.

26

Xander

"I'm downstairs. Meet me for coffee."

I stare at my cell, which no longer has Theo attached to it. His call wasn't an invitation, more like an order. Throwing a NYU sweatshirt over my grey sweats, I finger comb my hair and pick up the pair of sunglasses Madison ordered me to buy what feels like ages ago. Not caring that my goatee needs trimming, I grab my wallet and lock up.

Ignoring the paparazzi shouting questions and taking photos, I join my "brother" on the sidewalk. "Here I am."

"Jeez. You look like crap." He pulls me in for a bro hug.

"Kick a man while he's down, why don't ya?"

He smirks. "That's what I'm here for. Let's duck the vultures and go to the café around the corner." Soon we're settled into a booth far away from the windows, our coffees and omelets on the table. "Talk to me. How are you doing?"

"I can't. Not right now." I rake my fingers through my hair. "Tell me about you."

An understanding Theo launches into the status of his biography about Uncle Daniel. The buzz for it is phenomenal. Pride at his accomplishment wells inside and, for a moment, overtakes my own pathetic life.

"I'm stoked for you. If you don't go all the way to the bestseller charts, I'll be shocked." I offer him my fist, which he bumps.

"Thanks. I don't want to jinx anything, but Amelia says the same thing."

"She's still liking her new job, right?"

Theo's face softens. "She loves it. Finally doing the hard-hitting investigative journalism she's been craving."

"That's great." Like Madison's doing PR work. I drop my fork onto my half-finished plate.

He leans forward. "Listen. I know how much you were into that Madison chick. You even abandoned your 'born-again' virgin status for her. Are you sure there's no way for you two to get back together?"

He knows all about my "second" firing and our separation. The empty feeling in the pit of my stomach refuses to budge. Shaking my head, I reply, "No."

"Remember when everything came to light about Amelia's hidden identity? You were there for me, encouraging me to try to work things out. Now it's my turn to repay the favor."

I wipe my palms on the napkin on my lap. "The big difference between us is that you were head-over-heels in love with Amelia."

He scoffs. "And you're not?"

My eyebrows come together. "What? No way would Madison want to hitch her wagon to the likes of me. I bring the press down on her like a ton of bricks. Cause her firm to lose clients as well as opportunities to get new ones."

His pointer finger taps on the rim of his coffee mug. "But how do you *feel* about her? When you talk about her—even right this second—your whole face lights up. I've never seen you look like that, even with Darcey." His nose crinkles.

"My feelings are irrelevant."

"Dude. If I've learned anything over the past year, it's that you have to go for what you want. And I think that's Madison Welch. Don't let some stupid headlines get between you two."

"You've misread this whole situation. I'm not in love with her."

Liar.

"If that's true, then I hope you find your real match soon."

When we part ways on the sidewalk, I can't bring myself to return to my apartment so I walk aimlessly. My damned feelings toward Madison are irrelevant. Posts pop into my mind showing ugly, unflattering photos of her juxtaposed against the women I've dated. Yet looks are superficial. Hell. I've been approached to do modeling more times than I can count, but always turned the offers down. So what if my external features catch people's eye, when nothing's beneath the surface?

I find myself standing outside my parents' building. We haven't talked since our disastrous last encounter, so perhaps now is a good time to clear the air. Luna lets me into the study where Dad's staring at the unlit fireplace.

"Hey, Dad."

Startled, he swings toward me. "Oh. Xander. Your mother's gone out for lunch with some friends."

Seems like some things haven't changed. "That's okay." I pull a wingback chair over closer to him so we don't have to shout to be heard. "How are you doing?"

His shoulders rise and fall. "We got a date for the hearing on our motion to dismiss. It's in a few weeks."

Much sooner than anticipated. "That's great." The 2019 ledger I discovered in his desk at the cabin pops before my eyes, but I bury it. I didn't come here to discuss legal issues. Instead, I put on a happy face. "Then this will be behind you and things can get back to normal."

He nods. "Assuming that asshole Hudson hasn't decimated VOW-cubed in the interim. He's been running roughshod over the company, ignoring everything Ogden, Ward, and I have been telling him."

I rub my goatee. Well, more like a full-fledged beard. "Why is the bankruptcy court allowing this?"

His hands fly up in the air. "I don't know. I talk with our attorneys daily to try to stem the tide, but it seems the judge can't keep up with his lightning-fast changes." His fist contacts the table in front of him. "I want my fucking company back."

I can sympathize. *But not about VOW-cubed.* "Well, once the judge grants your motion, you'll be able to kick Hudson out. I'll be able to come back to work for you and help." There. Let him know I'm a free agent. Again. Even if just the *idea* of returning to work in the family business is repugnant to me.

His eyes find mine, the same dark blue gaze that I inherited boring into me. "What do you mean?"

My lungs expand. "I was fired from the PR Agency. Seems the press scrutiny was too much for the company to bear." That's a truth.

He nods. "Good. No Turner should have to resort to working *downtown.* And for such an unattractive company."

And by "company," he means its business owner. My spine stiffens. "Madison is brilliant, Dad. Her Agency was a pleasure to work at. I learned a lot."

He snorts. "You could've learned a lot more from Darcey's father's company. Now there's someone who's connected to all the right places. She looked fabulous on your arm. Not like that schlub of a PR agent."

"Darcey broke off our engagement due to your *arrest.* Plus, Madison's worth more than one hundred times as much as the superficial Darcey could ever hope to aspire."

Dad waves his hand. "Darcey was shrewd and knew how to navigate in the right social circles. But it doesn't matter any longer, since reports are talking wedding bells for her and the quarterback."

"He can have her."

Dad continues as if I hadn't spoken. "But once I get VOW-cubed back, I'm sure she'll drop him like a hot potato. You're a much better catch than the dumb jock."

"I don't want her back."

Once again, he barrels on. "If only this were already over. I hate all the time it takes in the courts." He raises his leg and pulls his pants leg up, uncovering the ankle monitor. "And this damn thing. Can't leave this prison."

I glance at what he describes as a prison, complete with views of Central Park and staff ready to fulfill his every whim. I disengage from his rambling discourse, fully acknowledging that he doesn't really care about me. He's only in it for himself.

If he truly was interested in my life, he'd understand I left Darcey in the rearview mirror ages ago. She's a bitch wrapped in couture. Not like Madison—with her empathetic eyes, brilliant mind, and kind soul. Who only wants to help people succeed.

My father continues babbling while I ponder Theo's question anew. Do I love her? Snippets from our conversations about marketing strategy bring a smile to my face. A remembered touch of how our bodies fit together makes me shift in the overstuffed chair. Laughter threatens when I remember slipping away from the paps into a department store by the office.

But do I love her? I loved Darcey and look where that got me. A Tiffany ring she thought wasn't in the right setting. Grandma Lucia's tutting still haunts the evening of our engagement when she asked if she could get it reset.

My former fiancée blabbed lies to every reporter who would listen, painting me as a lackey for my father, who was running a crime syndicate. My breathing hitches. Maybe Darcey's assessment wasn't so far from the truth. I glance at Dad, who's stopped talking and sulks in front of the fireplace. He wants me to get back with that bitch?

Do I love Madison? She righted my skewed perception of what success means. Who taught me my ideas have merit and they matter. *I* matter. *Hell yes!* The answer hits me like a bolt of lightning, causing me to leap out of the chair.

Dad tilts his chin up at me. "What got into you?"

"I've been a fool, and it's about time I did something to fix it."

"What?"

I stare into his eyes, our similarities ending there. "I'm done following your dictates. I wasn't meant to be a pawn for your magazines, but rather to help small businesses achieve their potential." I stand straighter. "I'm finally going to create my own path. With the woman of my heart, if she'll have me."

He bellows, "I will not have any son of mine—"

Not allowing his bluster to rule my life another second, I rush out of the room and into the elevator. Ideas about how I can get Madison back dart into my mind.

When I get back to my apartment, I grab my phone and sit on the sectional. I pull up a photo of Darcey and me right after I proposed, still wearing that God-awful ugly holiday sweater. We're smiling at the camera. Fake. It was all fake. At least on her part. I post the photo to Instagram and begin my tirade:

"Many of you have commented about how wonderful Darcey is, and how Madison isn't fit to breathe the same air as her. I'm here to tell you that you're wrong. Darcey is a manipulative liar who steps all over anyone she needs to in order to get ahead. She only wanted me as her fiancé so she could get on reality television. And I was the stupid schmuck who proposed. All I can say is I'm fortunate the engagement didn't last even twenty-four hours. Believe me when I say Madison Welch is the complete opposite of Darcey, and I couldn't be happier. Where Darcey is two-faced, Madison shows herself to be beautiful through and through. Darcey wants only what's good for her, while Madison works to promote others. Madison believes the purpose of PR is to spread the wealth, not to beat the competition—and all Darcey sees is competition. I don't care if you disagree with me. Scratch beneath Darcey's brittle veneer and all you'll find is an empty, ugly shell. Madison is the real deal. #lifegoals #madisonwelchrocks #isupportmadison"

Without rereading my post, I press post.

And spend the next several hours working on ways to right all my wrongs with Madison.

I wake up on the sectional, the sun just starting to come through the drapes. Jumping awake, I review all my notes, determined to get to Madison through her business. Once that's righted, things will be clear for us to explore our relationship. I hope.

Even before making a coffee, I hop onto the computer and send an email to Amelia promoting the Agency and all the good work it does. When that's done, I race into my bedroom, take a quick shower, and don a pair of jeans and long-sleeved collared shirt.

Since it's eight, I make a cup of coffee and take a fortifying sip before placing my next call. Vanessa answers on the first ring. "Xander. I'm surprised to hear from you. We spoke with Madison last week and told her we're unable to move forward with your company."

"I understand your position. However, would you have a different perspective if I were to tell you things have changed? I have it upon good authority that the media is going to be running a story about the positive way Madison promotes her clients as opposed to some of the underhanded dealings that have become the norm in the City."

"I'm listening."

After we hang up, new appointment in hand, I raise my fist into the air. "Yes!" Friends For Fun has agreed to give us a second chance. Like I hope Madison will for me.

Taking a deep breath, I place my most important call of the day. "Madison Welch's office, how may I help you?"

"Dev. Hey. It's Xander."

"Oh. Hello." Disapproval oozes out of his voice.

I need to enlist Dev's help if I have any chance of pulling this off. Deciding to be upfront, I say, "I know I'm *persona non grata* over there. But I'm calling with good news."

"You're moving to Alaska?"

Chuckling, I reply, "Not that." Gotta give him props. He definitely has Madison's back. "I got us another meeting with Friends For Fun. I pitched a new angle to them and they're intrigued. Can I make an appointment with Madison to discuss this with her?"

Pages flip on his end. "I might be able to fit you in a week from Tuesday for thirty minutes."

Almost two weeks? I shift my weight between my legs. "I was thinking more like this afternoon."

He emits a dramatic sigh. "Why? What do you have to say to Madison that's so important?"

I love her. I can't go on without her in my life. I want to work for her again —and forever. I choose the most uncontroversial. "I need to fill her in about Friends For Fun. The meeting's on Monday."

"Why don't you send her an email?"

My response is rapid-fire. "Because I want to see her in person."

"Not good enough."

I rub the back of my neck, trying to contain my anger at Madison's fortified gatekeeper. At my wit's end, I say, "Because I love her, alright?"

"I saw your post. But you can't see her today. She's not here."

Shocked that my burning admission didn't even earn a blip on his radar, I blurt, "Where is she?"

"Right now? I'm guessing about an hour outside of the City. She's meeting the Howells at the Preserve at eleven."

"Holy. Shit."

I don't realize I've uttered the epithet until Dev answers. "It's true. Mr. Howell called and wanted to have an in-person meeting up there to review the finer points of the new campaign."

My campaign. My client. One she never would've touched with a ten-foot pole but for my pushing. And when I won the client, she was both excited for me and relieved she'd never have to do anything with them. Once I found out about her dog bite as a child, I understood her aversion to wolves. "Couldn't Bonnie or Elisabeth go?"

"Nope. They're both tied up with their own clients. Madison even bought some new clothes for the occasion."

Probably laced with steel. But she overcame her fears to take this meeting. My body clicks into gear. Madison has an hour's head start on me. "Thanks for the information, Dev. Gotta run."

I swear I hear him say "I'm rooting for you" before the line disconnects.

27

Madison

I put the rental car into park in the dirt parking lot. Pressing the button to turn off the ignition, I survey the fenced-in acreage with several huge penned-in areas. A farmhouse-red building sits off to one side, appearing welcoming. But I know the truth. This place is filled with humongous dogs waiting for the opportunity to take off a person's arm. Or leg. I trace my scar. Or eat someone's face.

My body becomes rigid. *I can't do this.* Over the three-hour drive, I gave myself a pep talk, the benefits of which evaporate in the face of impending death. I can call the Howells and tell them my car broke down. Better yet, I'll reach out to Kelsey and give her this awful client. I'm sure she'd love to take another client from me, and I'll willingly pass this one to her.

The firm is hemorrhaging clients, Madison. Get a grip.

Knowing I have no other alternative, I slip the handles of my briefcase over my shoulder and open my car door. My brown ankle-length wedges hit the dry ground like a shovel chipping away after an ice storm, the shock ricocheting up to my hips.

A woman appears at the front door of the farmhouse, waving her arms. "Madison, is that you?"

Caught. Because I'm incapable of doing anything else, I offer

Isa a slight wave. In response, she motions for me to enter the building. That's my safe place. No wolves will be inside. Right?

Slamming my car door shut, I manage to cross the parking lot in record time, refusing to look anywhere but at the red building in front of me. When I reach the front step, Isa greets me, "Chauncey and I are so happy you're up here. Can I take your coat?"

Despite it being late spring, I'm chilled to the bone but have no other option but to accept her offer. She ushers me into an oversized kitchen, which appears to have been remodeled not too long ago with white cabinets, quartz countertops, and a large farmhouse sink. A grey island with seats for at least five is the focal point.

I take a seat at a stool where Isa offers me a cup of hot tea. I'm going to need all the chamomile I can get to make it through this meeting. Chauncey joins us and sits at the stool next to mine while Isa remains on the other side of the island, keeping an eye on something she's making in the double ovens.

"So." I clear my throat. "I brought all of the paperwork about the new campaign." I reach into my briefcase and pull out three copies of the campaign and pass the extras out. "As you can see—"

Chauncey puts his hand over my stack of papers. "We've examined the campaign. It's solid, although a bit impersonal. That's why we wanted you to come up here and experience the Preserve for yourself. I bet it's not like anything you've envisioned."

"Oh, I don't know about that, Chauncey. We've done extensive research, compared your, ah, preserve with others in the area as well as performed a SWOT analysis." At their confused expressions, I explain, "Strengths, Weaknesses, Opportunities, and Threats. It's a marketing tool we use to evaluate a client's business." My use of this acronym without explanation shows me how far off my game I am.

The couple exchanges a glance. "That sounds nice, dear. But nothing can beat firsthand experience."

My head shakes in the negative. "I think our plan addresses everything."

"It may." Isa walks around the island and stands next to me. "But it's missing a bit of the heart we heard from Xander during his presentation. Such a shame he couldn't make the trip today."

I swallow over my pain. I thought I told Chauncey? "Well, he, ah, left the Agency."

The couple exchanges another glance that communicates volumes in its silence. Chauncey opens his mouth, but Isa zooms in. "I thought Chauncey misheard you during your last conversation. That's a shame. Xander had great ideas, and his presentation style is captivating."

I pull my hair across my cheek. "I used his work to springboard some additional ideas, like partnering with local Airbnbs to exchange rack cards with their guests."

"We liked that idea. A lot," Chauncey says.

"See. We'll be able to do this without Xander's input." I rest my back against the stool for the first time.

"I'm sure we will. It's that Xander had this flair that drew us to him. He seemed to have a connection with our preserve. And the wolves."

One I definitely don't have. I put on a brave face. "He mentioned how much he appreciated the hierarchy the wolves maintain. It provides a sense of stability when each dog—excuse me, wolf—knows its place in the herd."

Isa corrects me. "It's a pack, dear."

"Oh. Right. Well, Xander explained it all to me, which I'm sure you read in the campaign."

"Have you ever been on a farm before?"

My right hand steals over my cheek. I address Isa. "I have."

"And was it a working farm?"

"Well, more like a petting zoo." With an insane pit bull.

"I see." She addresses her husband. "You should take her on a tour so she gets a better understanding of what we do here."

"I agree." Chauncey gets to his feet.

Trapped, I must go along with this farce. I don't need to tour their stupid wolf farm to market it, for Pete's sake. Perhaps I can cut this short. Getting off my stool, I examine the objects on open shelves. "I'm sure a quick walk around in here will acquaint me better with your product."

"We wouldn't dream of shortchanging our PR person. We

simply must give you the full tour."

That's what I was afraid of. I force a smile. "Lead on."

We start in the house, which is modern by all accounts. It has a state-of-the-art office setup, complete with several desks for employees who monitor the health of each individual wolf on the Preserve.

All dozen of them. They've grown by half since our initial meeting. Somehow, I have to figure out how to avoid meeting any of them.

We loiter in their office while I toss out question after question. When I get down to the type of ink toner they use, I know the jig is up.

"Chauncey, why don't you take Madison out back? I'll make us lunch in the meantime."

"Please don't go all-out on my account, Isa. I ate." Yesterday.

"It's no problem at all. You and Chauncey go pet the wolves and when you're done, I'll have a hearty lunch prepared for you. That way, you'll be able to return to the City on a full stomach."

If she thinks whatever food she's making will last all the way to the City, she's on crack. Chauncey takes my elbow and escorts me toward the front door. As we pass a bathroom, I ask for a moment.

Inside the half bath, I hold onto the sides of the pedestal sink and stare at my terrified face in the oval mirror above it. How am I going to get out of this? If Xander were here, he'd be all about playing with the death creatures. Me? All I want to do is curl up into a ball and put my palms over my eyes, pretending if I can't see them, they can't see me either.

A knock on the door breaks my panic attack. "All good in there?"

"Yes." I cough. Trying to inject positivity into my tone, I say louder, "I'll be right out!"

I stare into my pale blue eyes. *This is it. You got this, Madison. You're a strong, thirty-year-old woman, not a five-year-old child. You're taller than these wolves. They're not going to eat your face. Stand up straight and show them who's boss. Be their alpha.*

Fortified with as much backbone as I can muster, I flush the toilet, run the water, drag myself out of my last refuge. Chauncey stands by the front door, holding up my coat. "There you are. I thought I was going to have to send in the cavalry." He chuckles at his joke. I join in, even though I know he wasn't far from the mark.

While I put on my coat, all I can think of is my repeated mantra —*delay, delay, delay*. "Can we take a tour of your property?"

"You want to see the whole thing?"

"Since I'm here," I shrug. "I think I should."

He grabs keys off a hook and instructs me to follow him. We get into a pick-up and soon we're going around the outskirts of his land. We leave the cleared area and drive into an overgrown part.

I point. "Oh wow. Is that a river?"

He chuckles. "Right now it may appear to be a river, but come in the summer months and it'll only be a trickle." He maneuvers the truck on dirt roads, explaining about the vegetation and wild animals who call this area home.

He pulls to a stop at the top of a small hill overlooking his entire farm. Surveying his property, I admit, "I'm actually happy you took me on this tour. I had no idea all this land was yours. I bet there are several hiking trails people can take. If a local bakery could prepare a nice picnic lunch, your guests would love to explore out here."

"And there she is."

I turn my head. "What?"

"Isa and I knew you'd find your footing once you got out here and on our land. I thought the wolves would've given you inspiration, but I can see it's nature that calls to you."

With a start, I realize I'm enjoying this tour. "I absolutely love it out here. Where I'm from, Kansas, we have lots of trails. This kind of reminds me of home."

"It sure is peaceful. I come out here when I want to get myself centered."

"Centered. That's an excellent way to put it. I bet we can incorporate that into our marketing." Chauncey places his hand on the stick shift, but I'm not ready to leave. "Would you mind if I stepped out?"

"It's your tour."

With a little wave, I walk away from the truck and turn until I feel like I'm the only person for miles. Chauncey said he comes here to get centered. For me, it's freeing because I can breathe. Like in Kansas, the land here promises to cleanse all my worries. About the Agency. About living so far from my family. About missing Xander. *God, I miss him.* Dev coined the right word—mourning.

If only he were here to experience it with me. I wonder if he even knew about all the land since he never once mentioned it. Or included it in his campaign. As I allow myself a moment to grieve the fact he's out of my life forever, an ache sears through my body. With a loud exhalation, I release all my heartbreak into the clean air. An owl hoots in the distance, as if accepting my troubles.

With a lighter heart, I return to the truck and Chauncey navigates back toward the pens where the wolves live. Trying to divert my thoughts, I pepper Chauncey with all sorts of questions about how the Native Americans honor the land. His responses provide further fuel for how I want to tweak the marketing plan.

We pull to a stop outside the front of the building. No more time to delay. I have to meet the wolves. An idea pops into my mind. "I can walk around and see the wolves in their natural element." Sounds reasonable to me.

"Oh no. You really have to interact with them to get the full flavor of how magnificent these animals are." He exits the truck.

I can't make myself open the door and step willingly into the proverbial lion's den. My head shakes from side to side as the door opens and Chauncey appears next to me.

"Now, don't you worry about a thing with these wolves. They're as tame as kittens."

I snort. "I doubt that."

"Come on. I'll introduce you to them." He pulls on my arm as he whistles and shouts for a sheriff.

My feet stop moving. Why is he calling for law enforcement? Are the wolves attacking someone? I search the pens but don't see much going on other than some wolves taking in the sunny day behind the fenced-in area. Wide-eyed, I ask, "Why are you calling for a police officer?"

Chauncey chuckles. "Sheriff is the leader of the pack. The alpha."

"Oh." I try to play off my stupid question as if it were a joke, but my insides protest every step I take toward the wolf's lair.

He opens the fence and steps inside the pen. It's now or never. From across the way, a wolf the size of a horse runs toward us. My hand flies to my mouth. "There he is. Isn't Sheriff beautiful?"

"Beauty's in the eye of the beholder."

Chuckling, he replies, "Step inside the pen so I can close the door. We don't want any wolves getting loose."

"Of course you don't."

I shuffle my feet across the dirt far enough that Chauncey's able to close the fence. It locks us inside with these deadly animals. Chauncey enters the main area of the pen as Sheriff bounds to him. They start roughhousing.

I take a step backward. And another. Until my back is against the fence. Holding my breath I try to become invisible. I can't stay here. My eyes slide to the left and I calculate how quickly I could escape from certain death. Five steps and I'll be in the clear. Without thought, I race for the fence and am outside slamming it shut, my breath coming in rapid pants.

At the noise, Chauncey disengages from the wolf. "Oh, hey Madison. I hope this little display didn't scare you away. Sheriff here is friendly to all humans, but he has a spot all his own in my heart."

From the safety behind the fence, I offer, "Enjoy yourselves. I didn't want to be in the way."

Taking the wolf's head in both his hands, he shakes, causing the animal's head to bounce. Laughing, Chauncey bends down and kisses the massive beast's forehead. Or snout. Or whatever you call that place hiding its teeth.

For several minutes, the two play together. Chauncey's laughter punctuates their rambunctious shenanigans and I, improbably, find myself laughing at their antics. The other wolves let this pair enjoy their time, as they remain lying down across the pen.

Man and wolf look like a pair of teenage wrestlers grappling on the ground. Sheriff hasn't shown his teeth yet. Well, unless you count the time Chauncey extended his arm right in front of his mouth, and the wolf rubbed his face against it. I saw his teeth then, but he wasn't about to bite Chauncey—his black lips simply pulled away from his pointy teeth.

Head thrown back, Chauncey laughs and smacks his hands on his thighs. Without my knowledge, I smile at this unlikely pair. He waves at me. "Your turn."

My hand lands on my chest. "That's okay. You're having enough fun for the both of us."

"Don't you want to feel how soft his fur is?"

"I'm fine." This response is lower than before, my smile fading.

He pats the wolf on its head and walks over to me. "Listen. I know you're afraid, but wolves are wonderful creatures. Come here and I'll introduce you. Sheriff won't bite."

My confession tumbles out of my mouth. "I've had a bad experience with a dog."

"All the more reason to try again. Sheriff is wonderful, as you've just witnessed. And he wants to play with you. Look."

I follow the direction he's pointing and, sure enough, the wolf sits upright with his tongue lolling out of his mouth. Amber eyes— inquisitive, intelligent, inviting—seemingly call out to me.

"I promise you'll enjoy this. Nothing bad will happen, but I bet you're going to fall in love."

"Doubt that," I pant.

Chauncey tugs the fence open. "Why don't we find out?"

Given their playtime, it seems safe. My brother's words spring forward about being the time to overcome my phobia. Like my reverse discrimination against Xander—if our time together taught me one thing, it's not to judge any living thing by its looks. Even if I'm too late to fix our mess, at least I know this truth going forward.

I step forward. "So long as you're right there with me."

He places his palm over his heart. I manage to get inside the pen and don't freak out too badly when the fence closes us inside. My body trembles, but I hope the wolf doesn't notice. Sheriff stands when he sees us walking toward him, his tail wagging. Chauncey speaks in a soothing tone, introducing us as if we both were humans. And it hits me. Chauncey treats this animal with as much dignity as if we were equals. Maybe we are? Different species, but we both breathe the air, eat food, and drink water. The Native American's respect for all things living spurs me on to cross the final gap.

Chauncey takes my hand and puts it on top of Sheriff's head. My fingers stroke his fur, which feels like coarse silk beneath them. "He's so soft."

"He is."

Chauncey takes a couple of steps backward so he's standing behind me. His hand slides up to my shoulder and he gives me a gentle push. "Talk to him."

Inhaling as much as possible, I begin. "Hello, Sheriff. I like your name." With a trembling hand, I stroke his head. Soon my other hand gets into the act. When I lean forward to pet the wolf's side, Chauncey's hand falls off my back.

He's so lithe. "You are beautiful, Sheriff. And I never thought I'd say that to a dog. Ever. Well, you're not really a dog though, are you? No, you're a mighty wolf, protector of the animal kingdom."

More words trip from my lips, most not making any sense. But Sheriff doesn't seem to mind. In fact, he head butts my arm as if to say I'm not petting him enough. Chuckling, I say, "Demanding thing, aren't you?"

The wolf turns his head toward my face and I freeze. Closing my eyes, I concentrate on breathing. *He's not going to bite your cheek. He's not a poorly trained pit bull from years ago.*

Strong hands close around my shoulders. A warm body provides silent strength from behind.

My eyes pop open and I focus on Sheriff. Who nuzzles the side of my neck.

The clanking of a triangle rumbles behind the wolf, and he goes on high alert. When someone yells "Feeding time!" Sheriff takes off at a full-on run toward his dinner.

I stand and lean back into the man whose hands never wavered from my shoulders. On an exhale, I murmur, "Xander."

28

Xander

If I weren't so attuned to this brave woman, I might have missed the way she sighed my name. But I didn't.

Over my pounding heart, I whisper, "I want to talk with you. Please."

In response, she drops her head onto my chest. For the moment, everything is right with this world. My gorgeous woman faced her fears and pet a massive wolf as if he were a housecat. And she agreed to talk with me.

After a brief meeting with the Howells in which I have no idea what was said, we each drive to a local restaurant they recommended. In the parking lot, I race over to her car door and open it for her. I don't know what to expect but intend to share everything with this amazing woman.

Tucking her hand into the crook of my arm, I say, "Let's get a table. I have a lot I want to say to you."

Pale blue eyes meet mine. "And I you."

We're seated at a window, overlooking lush, green rolling hills. She points. "There's the Preserve."

The server responds. "Yes. It's a lovely place. Have you been?"

"We're coming from there," I reply. "The wolves are magnificent." Not as much as the woman sitting across from me, though. Nothing is.

The server brings us a couple of glasses of water and leaves us with menus. Madison grabs one and opens it, studying the selections as if her MBA were riding on it. I get her nerves. With my bouncing knee, I'm not the picture of calm myself.

I flip through the menu and select a juicy burger, needing some culinary encouragement. Tossing the menu off to the side, I wait for her to close hers, which she doesn't do until the server returns to take our orders.

Finally alone, I take Madison's hand. "You're so brave. When I saw you petting that beast, I knew you'd conquered your biggest fear."

A wistful smile crosses her face. "I was shocked at how gentle he was. And you could tell how smart he is from his eyes." She dons an adorable grin. "Plus, Chauncey wasn't going to let me leave without touching him."

Using my thumb, I rub the back of her palm. "Still, I know how much bravery that took for you to do. You continually amaze me."

Her gaze meets mine. "Me? You were the one who showed up here out of the blue. Why?"

Three simple letters form a question of epic proportions. So many answers float through my mind, but I choose to start with the biggest truth. Grandma Lucia would be proud.

I take a deep breath. "Because when you realize you're in love with someone, you don't want to waste a minute before you tell them. And I love you, Madison Welch. You're the most beautiful woman I've ever met. Your outsides are gorgeous, but it's the positivity radiating from deep inside that ensnared me. Always wanting the best for everyone. Seeing possibilities where others only see ugliness. You're the best thing that ever happened to me, and I didn't want to spend another day without telling you the truth."

Disconnecting from me, her hand covers her mouth. "Oh."

Needing the connection, I retake her palm, enclosing it in mine. "It's all true. I told the world on Instagram but thought it was a better idea to tell you in person." I inhale. "So here I am. I'm all yours, if you'll have me."

My last statement hangs in the air. I've been so focused on the fact I'm in love with her, I never considered she might not feel the same. As much as every fiber in my being wants her to reciprocate, I prepare myself for the distinct possibility that she doesn't.

My stomach roils.

My teeth worry my bottom lip.

My hands grip hers tighter.

She extricates herself from my grasp, wiping her hands on her napkin. "But I'm not tall and thin and picture perfect all the time." She cups her scar. "Ever."

I dismiss this line of reasoning. "What are you saying? You don't have to wear a shit ton of makeup to appear natural. And you eat like a real person, not just lettuce."

Case in point—the server delivers our matching meals. She picks up her cheeseburger.

Breaching the silence, I add, "I'm all for rabbit food, but not all the time." She takes a bite of the burger when I do, the beef hitting a much-needed spot. I chew, waiting for her to continue. Praying she feels the same way about me.

Her burger lands back on the plate. "I'm flattered, of course, that you feel this way. And I have an admission that may change everything."

My burger slips from my hands. This is where she tells me I'm not good enough for her. "You don't have to say anything, Madison." I chug some water. I'd rather she keep her mouth shut than say the words.

Her hand lands on top of mine, causing my brain to short-circuit. Some other lucky dude will be the recipient of all her touches from now on. *Fuck.*

"But I do." She sighs. "I've been horribly unfair to you, Xander. I judged you on your looks and upbringing well before we actually said more than two words to each other. When we met at the b-school networking event, the aura of you sucked up all the energy in the room. Every woman wanted to bed you, while the guys all wanted to be you. Press followed your every move. You set trends. If you ordered tea, baristas wept. You're … you."

Is she saying all the media hype that intruded into our relationship cannot be overcome? "I'll do more to shut the reporters up."

I have more to say, but her index finger covers my lips. I resist the urge to take a nibble.

"Shhh. Listen. Ma pointed this out to me, but I didn't believe her until I thought about it. I've been reverse judging you. Thinking someone like you wouldn't ever want to stay with a nobody like me. I mean, you have it all."

How can she think that? "My father is under indictment, remember?"

"I know, but that's beside the point. I didn't give you a chance to prove my hypothesis wrong. I always felt we were destined to be a simple fling until you got your feet back under you. Plus, all the media attention was, uhm, unflattering to say the least." She lifts her water glass. "The thing is, I fell in love with you along the way. I never would've gone ziplining, or tried The River Café, or ridden in a limo, or stayed in a cabin that looks more like a castle, without you. All the while, I couldn't understand what you were doing with me, so I buried my feelings."

At her admission she's in love with me, my ankle bounces up and down. *She loves me!* "You're the real deal, M. All the ugly comparisons with my former fiancée showed me how much you're worth. No matter how empirically pretty Darcey is, she has a mean streak through and through that only will get worse over time. On the other hand, you're going to become more beautiful. Fuck. Look at what you did today. Conquering your fears is a huge turn-on, and you did that in spades."

She dons a smirk. "I was sort of a badass, wasn't I?"

She giggles, and my heart soars. I could hear her giggles forever. Which is what I want. I grab her hands and pull them toward my face, dropping kisses on her knuckles. "You're the biggest badass I know."

"I love you, Alexander Turner."

Her use of my full name is the last straw. Leaning over the table,

I give her a full-on kiss, not caring who might be watching. Hoping many people are. Taking all the pictures and posting them. I want everyone to know Madison Welch is mine.

The server clears her throat, which causes me to pull back. M touches my cheek and I have to fight not to reclaim her lips. Above our heads, our server says, "I'll take this when you're ready." A light thud indicates she left the bill portfolio.

I pull her hair away from her left side. "Can I interest you in a bed and breakfast? We need to move this reunion to a more appropriate venue."

Her wide smile causes my breath to hitch. "I think I can be persuaded."

"Great. I'll take care of the bill while you scout out a place." I sit back. "Somewhere nearby." I bring the bill up to the register, my mind racing with joy at the fact Madison wants to be in my life. We're going to have to figure out a better way to handle the press, but for now, I'll settle on having her at my side. *Or under me.*

Grinning, I return to the table, where M holds up her phone. "What about this one?"

I don't bother to look. Instead, I stare at this amazing woman. "Perfect."

"You're such a sweet talker."

"Only if it'll get me into your pants that much quicker." I let my gaze skim over her real curves. She's not rail-thin, but model looks don't interest me anymore. Truth be told, I was tired of hearing about salads for days—on top of cocaine and booze—and appreciate M's true zest for life.

I follow her to the place she selected and check us in. Soon we're ensconced in a nicely-appointed suite, complete with a balcony overlooking rolling hills. But I'm not interested in any of that. My attention is laser-focused on the woman standing next to me. I place my hands on her shoulders.

"I know we have a lot to discuss, but if I don't get you naked and beneath me in five minutes, I'm going to lose my mind."

She giggles again. "We can't have that happening now, can we?"

She pulls her red sweater up and over her head. Not one to be outdone, I reach behind my neck, grab the back of my collar, and lift—causing my own shirt to sail off my body.

"You look so sexy when you do that."

"If that's all it takes, darling, I'll take my shirt off for you every day." And I will. But for now, I have more important things to do. Like, divest her body of her new brown trousers. She kicks off her shoes while I shove my jeans down my legs.

Standing in front of me in only a white cotton bra and blue panties with the word "Imagine" written across her ass, she crosses her arms across her body. "Sorry. If I had known this might happen, I would've worn something more appropriate. I mean sexier."

I place my index finger under her chin and lift so that our gazes meet. "Don't apologize. Your underwear is sexy because you're wearing it. And all I'm doing right now is imagining what I can do to you when your naughty panties come off."

"Oh." She shakes her booty. "When you say it that way—"

I can't take this any longer. "Stop talking."

I swoop down and capture her lips with mine. All finesse forgotten, I wrap her in my arms and yank her against my naked torso. My hand reaches up and tugs at the bottom of her hair, causing her neck to extend backward. When she exclaims in surprise, I don't hesitate. My tongue swoops in and mates with hers. My free hand slips around to her back and I unclasp her bra with a flick of my fingers, then I slide the straps off her arms.

Her boobs make contact with my chest, which makes my stomach leap. "You feel so good."

M's fingers slip between our bodies and she traces the muscles on my chest. "So do you."

Bending down, I pick her up and walk over to the king-size bed, and deposit her in the center. "I'm happy you're getting all this bad press. That way, no one will know how fucking sexy you are and try to steal you away from me."

"Not possible. I worry all the time that some starlet or model will turn your head."

Hands on my hips, I level her with my most ferocious look. Well, as ferocious as I can in only my underwear. "That's it. I

258

never want to hear you talk this way again. I'm in love with you—all of you. Your height, your hair, your skin, your intellect. Your *scar.* I've been with starlets and models and socialites, and where do I choose to be? Right here, with you. Got it?"

She swallows but doesn't say anything. I hope this is the last time I'll have to set her straight, yet I'm sure allaying her fears will take many more conversations.

That's for another time. Now, I need to make her scream. "If that's all settled, it's time for me to make you yell so everyone in upstate New York will hear how I make you feel."

I remove my boxer briefs and lay out a few packets of condoms before turning my attention to her last scrap of clothing. Placing my hands at her waist, I tug her "Imagine" panties down her legs and toss them over my shoulder.

Running my lips up her leg, I drop a quick kiss on her pussy before giving her other leg the same treatment. Joining her on the bed, I know this should be a soft and loving coupling, but I can't hold back. I dip my finger into her center, pleased she's more than ready for me. Pulling it out, I smell her scent and bring it to her mouth.

"Taste."

She opens her lips and sucks my finger, causing her hips to squirm with need. My breathing turns harsh. "I can't wait."

Her hand flops around on the bed until she retrieves one of the foil packets. With a rip, she opens it and sits up. "I want to put this on you."

Who am I to argue? I flip onto my back, my cock straining toward my bellybutton. Arms outstretched, I instruct, "I'm all yours."

A delightful grin crosses her features. "I'm so lucky." Instead of rolling the condom down my erection, her mouth covers the tip of my cock, licking the pre-cum off. She sits on her heels, looking smug.

"Like that, did you?"

Nodding, she confesses, "Very much."

I roll my hips. "Put the damn condom on, and I'll show you something you're going to like even better."

She stares into my eyes for a prolonged moment before doing as instructed. Sheathed, I realize I'm too excited to delay this any longer. Plus, I want to be the one in charge. Grabbing her around the waist, I flip our positions and surge into her in one smooth move.

"Oh, Xander!"

This is the first time she's said my name during sex, and I want more. I want her to scream it as she comes. Placing my palms on her cheeks, I kiss her with everything I have. My love for her oozes out of my pores and seeps into this kiss, all the while I pump in and out of her warmth.

"You're so amazing." Dropping down, I flick her nipple with my tongue.

Her legs go around my waist, but they're not long enough to connect around my body in this position. Before I can give her a suggestion, her heels drop to the bed and her hips move in time with mine. Could she be any more perfect?

I need her to scream my name. Moving my lips next to her ear, I encourage just that. "When you come, I want the world to hear who's giving you all this pleasure. Scream my name for me. *Please.*" I nip her earlobe.

She pushes against my body and her sex clenches around me, which makes stars shoot from behind my eyelids. "I'm so close."

"I know you are." I pump into her faster, adding one final admonishment. "My name, Madison."

Beneath me, her body tightens like I'm the only thing protecting her from a pack of wolves. Her body ripples around mine. At the top of her lungs, she screams, "Xander!"

A feral roar of "M!" releases from the center of my body as I empty myself into her convulsing body. I stiffen above her, then collapse to her side, still intimately connected. Pulling her close, we hug from head to toe.

Finally, our breathing returns to a more normal pace. She plants kisses along my jawline, her arms encircling my neck. I could stay like this forever, but duty calls. Grabbing my waning erection, I pull out of her body. "I'll be right back. Don't go anywhere." I kiss her once more for good measure.

Her giggle provides the backdrop as I dash into the bathroom and take care of the condom. Stopping at the sink, I wash my hands and check my reflection. Which looks more relaxed than I've ever looked, in my opinion.

When I stroll back into the bedroom, she's under the covers. Flipping one side of the blankets when she sees me, she pats the empty spot next to her. I slip into my side of the bed, pulling her close. "You're amazing, M."

"So are you, Mr. Scream-My-Name."

"A guy wants to hear his name sometimes."

She raises onto her forearm and traces my jawline with her tongue. "Well, you certainly deserved it." She settles in next to me again.

Playing with her hair, I admit, "I'm honored you want me in your life, but we do need to address the elephant in the room. How are we going to handle all the press coverage of our relationship? Because I'm not about to hide us from the world."

She thinks for a little bit, then responds with a strategy that should put them off. It's brilliant. And it's the simple truth—we fell in love and aren't interested in outside opinions. We bounce ideas off each other while taking nibbles on each other's bodies.

"Brainstorming has never been this exciting before," she says.

Ignoring her teasing tone, I opt for another truth. "Honestly, I've never felt a sense of self-pride in my work before I came to your firm. Working as an advertising exec for VOW-cubed was a different animal, where my ideas weren't appreciated. Dad and his partners would listen and then do whatever they wanted without further discussion." I pull her close and rest my chin on top of her head, needing her support for this final truth. "I've tried all my life to get Dad's approval. Went to the schools he chose. Worked for the family business, even if my passion wasn't advertising." I take a huge breath and confess, "Got engaged to the woman he chose."

At this acknowledgment, M's arms tighten around me.

Accepting her support, I continue, "But I never got his approval. And I won't. I've finally accepted the truth that Dad doesn't care about anything other than himself and VOW-cubed. I'm ready to put myself first, for a change. I'm not here to do Dad's bidding any longer. Don't get me wrong, I want the indictment to go away and for him to get back to the business, but I'm looking out for myself. What I want. *Who* I want. And it's all wrapped up in you. I love PR, and how you run the Agency. Most of all, I love you. My father's opinions no longer govern my decisions."

"I'm so proud of you and can't imagine how hard this has been. I wish I'd been there to have helped you through it." She kisses my cheek.

"Are you crazy? You're the reason I finally figured this all out. Because of you. Of us." I kiss her again, and all talking ceases.

The next morning, we put our clothes back on for the trip back to the City. Since we were naked all day yesterday, we can survive another three hours in them. At her car door, I can't stop kissing her.

"If we're ever going to get back home, we have to stop doing this." She looks like a woman who's been well loved. Because she has been. Is.

"Three hours. We have to make it three hours before I get to do this to you again." I lean down and skim my palms over her cheeks, pulling her hair back.

She sucks in when she realizes I've exposed her scar. We've talked all night long, but this issue remains. "You know, if your scar offends you so much, you could have it removed." I kiss the raised skin. "But I wouldn't do it because it shows the world how much you've overcome. It's your superpower, like the kids at Friends For Fun said when we were ziplining."

M pulls her head backward, and I let her hair fall to her shoulders. When she looks at me, it's as if a different woman is inhabiting her body. Much more self-assured, ready to tackle whatever shit the world's about to sling at her.

"You're right. I've spent my entire life hiding behind this disgusting scar, blaming it for every evil visited upon me. I'm done.

The kids thought it was cool, and you—Mr. Perfect on the exterior and all mushy inside—agree. If people judge me harshly for this scar, then so be it. I want to show the world my badge of honor. I may be scarred on the outside, but I'm not going to let it define me anymore."

She pulls her hair into a ponytail, throws her head back, and yells, "See me, world? I've been bitten before by worse than you can ever dream of, so bring it. Know I'm never going to back down. And since I have Xander Turner in my corner, you can suck it!"

Laughing, we get into our cars and spend the entire drive talking over Bluetooth, planning our next steps with Friends For Fun and discussing PR strategy for the Agency, all of which is interspersed with comments about how deeply we love each other.

Dad be damned, this is my life and I'm finally living it on my own terms. Out loud.

Epilogue - Madison

"Hey, look at this. Kelsey won the Doorman's Association account." Xander points to his computer screen.

Walking around his desk, I check out the announcement. "Good for her." Not a lie. Over these past few months, with Xander's help, I've come to understand Kelsey does excellent work and I'm happy for her success—like how she's been supportive of the Madison Welch PR Agency. We've both picked up steam with our new client base. Feels like we're finally hitting our strides. My hand reaches out and cups my amazing boyfriend's cheek, stroking his goatee with my thumb.

Xander turns his face and kisses the inside of my palm, which sets off an explosion of desire throughout my body. *Not here. Not now.*

Retrieving my hand, I reach for my cell phone. Holding it up, I explain, "I want to call and congratulate her."

He settles his hands on either side of my hips. "I love how encouraging you've become of each other. There's plenty of work out there to keep one hundred PR firms busy."

"True. A rising tide lifts all boats." I press Kelsey's contact icon. When she answers, I say, "Xander pointed out your latest win. Congrats."

"Thanks. We've wanted to branch out to these big associations for a while now, and we're excited to be working with the Doorman's group. This is a cottage industry that needs more attention."

"And you're just the woman to do that."

"I hope so. Oh, and before I forget, I saw you scooped up two new reps. That brings your firm to what? A total of twelve?"

"Yeah. We needed to hire them to handle all the work Xander's bringing in." He squeezes my hips, and I bestow a soft smile on him. We make a fantastic team. He loves pitching and schmoozing, as well as handling an occasional client—like the Mahigan Preserve, which we actually handle together. I like to oversee the work by all the reps and pop into various meetings. On the whole, we're a pretty well-oiled machine.

It only took a month for all the negative publicity surrounding us to die down. A very loooooong month, but we weathered it. Xander and I drew closer than ever, presenting a unified front to fend off whatever unflattering thing they threw at us. We also became more adroit at recognizing possible problems before they blossomed. The fact Darcey got married two months ago didn't hurt. Although the headlines suggest her marriage is already on the rocks. Whether that's true or not, we don't care.

Kelsey clears her throat. "I saw the company that owns the new buildings by the Highline is looking for PR representation because they've been selected to be on HGTV. I've never worked on something like this before but was thinking of pitching. Have you ever worked with a cable network before? Any tips?"

"I haven't, but you'd be fabulous for them." Xander and I considered the listing but decided to steer as far away from media publicity as possible. "I'd love to help you brainstorm some ideas."

"Oh, wow. I'd appreciate that. How about I take you out for lunch and we can talk?"

"Sounds great." We set up a date for next week.

When I disconnect the call, Xander says, "I'm in awe of you. Remember when I started working here and we first went to the GreenMarket? I thought you were going to blow a gasket when you saw her!" He chuckles.

My, how things have changed. I reach to tug on my hair, only remembering I put it into an updo today, so I end up patting it instead. "I was super jealous of her until a certain someone convinced me I needn't be. And look where we are now. Friendly rivals who help each other out."

He stands, towering over me. Bending down, he kisses me with a ferocity that serves to spur on my own need for this man. A knock interrupts us before we can get started.

"Excuse me, lovebirds. Madison, your next appointment is here and I set them up in the conference room."

Shit. I pull away from Xander's lips. In a throaty voice, I murmur, "We'll have to pick this up later."

"One for the road?" Our lips fuse together again, but Dev's noises break us apart.

Using my palms to push him away, I get to my feet. "Later." Trailing my admin, I leave Xander in his office and walk down the hallway.

"He has no clue, does he?"

"Nope."

Dev's laughter echoes throughout the office. "Can't wait 'til he finds out. Can I please, *please* bring him into the conference room?"

He's like a little puppy wanting a treat. Guess I can throw him a bone, considering he's been helping me plan this over the past month. "Sure. I'll let you know when it's time."

We part ways at the conference room doorway. Squaring my shoulders, I enter the room, where two people in black suits sit, sipping water. "Martin. Allison. Thanks for all your help getting this ready."

"Of course," Martin says, standing to shake my hand. "We've done a lot of revisions to partnership agreements, but never without all parties active in the negotiations. I'm sure Mr. Turner will be shocked."

"It's what I want. I know it's the right thing for the Agency."

"Do you want to look it over?" Allison asks, passing me a stack of documents about an inch thick. At my raised eyebrows, she flips a few pages and points. "Here are the relevant portions, explaining that Alexander Turner is now a full partner in the Madison Welch PR Agency."

I skim over the words, which are in line with what I asked them to draw up for me. "Your firm has always done right by me, so I know it's perfect." I've been their client since I started the business and while other law firms have bad reputations, theirs has always been on the up-and-up. "What's next?"

Martin replies, "You both need to sign this, and we'll notarize it for you. Then you'll be all set."

Butterflies, which I thought I had banished way back at the Preserve, decide to do loops in my stomach. I haven't mentioned this to Xander out of fear he wouldn't want to stay with the Agency. I also don't want him to think of this as a handout. He's earned his place here—hell, if not for him, we wouldn't have all the work that's piling up. Yes. This is the right decision. The fact he's the best boyfriend I could ever have dreamed of is beside the point.

"Great. I'll ask Dev to bring him in." While my admin retrieves Xander, I ask my attorneys, "Can you please lead this part of the meeting? I want it to sound official."

Martin chuckles. "If the title 'Partnership Agreement' doesn't sound legitimate, I don't know what will."

He has a point. As a single-member limited liability company, I didn't need an actual agreement before. Now, though, it's a necessity.

"What's up, M?" Xander breezes into the conference room and stops. "Oh, hello. I didn't see you there." Behind him, Dev rubs his hands together.

Martin stands. "Hello. I'm Martin Porter, and this is my wife Allison. We're the attorneys Ms. Welch has been using for her business since she started it."

Xander's brows furrow and he throws me a questioning look. Instead of answering him, I suggest we all sit down. Like the gentleman he is, he pulls my chair back and helps me get settled in before taking his own, despite not knowing what's going on. Dev leans against the back wall.

Allison ends his misery with a simple statement. "Ms. Welch

asked us to prepare a new document for the Agency, a Partnership Agreement. You and she are the named partners."

His inhale ricochets throughout the conference room. Wild-eyed, he turns to me. "You what?"

Placing my hand on top of his, I explain, "What you've done for the Agency is amazing. You've been closing seventy percent of all the proposals we've submitted, which means you're responsible for our expanded team here. Not to mention the accounts you've been personally working on, which have generated four times the amount of projected revenue. All of this hard work deserves recognition."

Martin draws our attention. "We've converted the Agency from single-member into a formal partnership." He passes Xander the document, opened to the page we were reviewing prior. "As you'll see, all the relevant information is contained on these few pages. Of course, so that your own lawyer can review the agreement, we made an extra copy." Allison holds up the spare.

Xander reads the pertinent parts of the Partnership Agreement without saying a word. My butterflies have multiplied and it's all I can do to remain seated. I hoped he'd be ecstatic, but his silence doesn't bode well. I gnaw my bottom lip.

His first words since this all was set into motion make my breath catch. "Would you mind if I had a word with Madison about this? Alone?"

My attorneys share a look. "Of course." They stand. "Take all the time you need. When you're ready, give us a call and we can make whatever changes are necessary."

Before they can take a step, Xander says, "There's a great farmers' market a couple of blocks away called the Union Square Green-Market. Why don't you go there and pick up some food, then come back to the office?"

"I love open-air markets," Allison replies. Holding up her phone, she adds, "Call us when you're ready." Dev escorts them out of the conference room, leaving the door open.

Now I'm the dumbstruck one. He wants them to come back? I need to get ahead of this. "Xander, I—"

"Shhh." He puts his finger across my lips.

Beneath his warm index finger, I open my lips but remain silent when he says, "Hear me out."

I thought I was doing a good thing here, but WOW, I never anticipated a rejection. At my slow blink, he releases his finger and takes me by the shoulders. Staring into my eyes, he says, "Madison, I never dreamed in a million years we would come to this. That you want me to become your business partner. That you actually believe I'd be worthy of helping to drive this amazing machine you've built. I cannot explain what your faith in me means."

"You deserve—"

"Hush. It's my turn. I'm beyond honored you want me as your partner, and I will gladly accept your offer."

My shoulders sag as all of the butterflies in my stomach fly away.

"On one condition."

And the butterflies return. "What do you want?"

"A *real* partnership."

I kept fifty-one percent of the company, at the Porters' recommendation, but will gladly change it to fifty-fifty. I'm amazed at the work he's been doing, and how much he brings to the table. He's more than worth it. "I can up your percentage, no problem. The fifty-one wasn't my idea in the first place." Because he's still silent, I add, "And we can change the name. I only kept it the way it was because people know it. But—"

His smile unfolds, which still captures my fascination even after all this time. "That's not what I mean. Both the percentage and the name stay." He inhales. "My brave M, do you realize how much you've affected me? You've helped me find my place in the exciting world of PR. I love pitching our services to businesses who need our help, tackling their accounts, and seeing them prosper. Working with you has brought a level of self-confidence to my professional world that I never had before. For that, I am eternally grateful to you."

He kisses me, pulls something out of his pocket, then drops to one knee.

One. Knee.

My hand flies in front of my face.

Taking my hand, he says, "So, yes, I am flattered to become your partner here, but only if you agree to become mine in life. I want every square inch of you, Madison Welch. Be it work, home, or on vacation somewhere. You belong to me as much as I belong to you, and I want the whole wide world to know this."

"You want," a tear rolls down my cheek. "To *marry* me?"

"If you'll have me."

If *I* will have *him*? My old doubts about not being enough for him sneak into my thought process, and vanish. We are equals in every sense of the word. He's taught me that. There is only one possible answer. "Yes! I'd be honored to become your wife!"

Grinning, he reveals what he took out of his pocket—a diamond ring pin. "I've been waiting to give this to you for a while." Squealing, I snatch it and affix it to my shirt with trembling hands.

Xander rises to his feet, his arms encircling my back, his lips covering mine as if they were his sole means to acquire air. I understand the feeling and reciprocate.

Our lip-lock is interrupted by clapping. Pulling apart an inch, our heads turn toward the door, where Dev stands, still applauding. "I take it he said yes?"

My admin's been in on the planning of our corporate merger. Hell, he was the one who prodded me forward when I had my doubts Xander would accept. My smile gives him the answer he knew I'd receive.

My fiancé's baritone rumbles. "And so did she."

I give him another kiss. In the background, Dev splutters, "What? Hey, what did I miss?" When we don't break apart, he wheedles, "Guys? Give me something here."

Laughing, our lips separate, and I spin around in Xander's arms. With my back to his delicious front, I display my new piece of jewelry. "Xander's going to be my business partner, and I'm going to be his life partner."

My admin's hands fly in front of his face. "Does this mean? Are you two?"

Xander takes pity on him. "Yes, Dev. I asked this gorgeous woman to be my wife and she accepted."

"Oh my!" He rushes at us. "I'm so happy for you both. I knew from the very start there was something between the two of you." His arms come around us.

Xander kisses the top of my head. "And now, if you can escort the Porters back in here when they return, I have some documents to sign."

Once my attorneys leave with all the paperwork in order, Xander takes my left hand. "I'm sorry I didn't have a proper ring for you when I proposed. Let's take the afternoon off and go to Tiffany's where you can select any one you want."

My heart bleeds for my fiancé as I remember the debacle of his prior engagement. How the press made a big deal over Darcey's accusation that he refused to reset the ring to meet her preference. But I'm not his ex. "Why waste money? Let's go to the Diamond District instead."

His eyebrows disappear into his hairline. I allow him to process my statement. When his eyes turn a liquid azure and his palm cups my right cheek, I know he understands. "You, Madison Welch, are beyond anything I ever dreamed I'd deserve. I'm the luckiest man on earth. Let's go."

Ben drops us off on Forty-Seventh Street and we peruse the storefronts, entering Landsberg Jewelers. A nice woman helps us select the most gorgeous diamond I've ever seen—not that I've seen too many of them. And never for me. I let Xander take the lead, and he goes for a three-carat colorless one. In my opinion, it's way too extravagant, but he overrules me. When I state I want a simple setting, the clerk says they can do it in-house and it'll be ready for pick up later today. We seal our engagement with a kiss, or twenty, while his credit card is being rung up.

On the street, Xander asks, "Would you like to catch a bite to eat up here while we wait?"

"Sure. Restaurant Row isn't too far. Want to walk?"

My words are still floating between us when the paparazzi

appear out of nowhere, shouting questions about what we're doing in the Diamond District. I reach to pull my hair across my cheek, only to realize it's still in the updo I chose to wear for the attorney meeting earlier. Rising to my full height, I reply to the reporters before Xander. "Scoping out a new venture." I hear his chuckle beneath the reporters' disappointment. They'd never believe we were shopping for ourselves here.

Xander texts Ben, who pulls up to the sidewalk a minute later. With a wave to the remaining paps, we disappear into the car. "Sorry about missing our walk, but I figured we should make our escape."

"Always thinking ahead." I settle into his arms and let Ben take us to Restaurant Row. Dropped off at the corner of Eighth Avenue and Forty-Sixth Street, we stroll down the sidewalk. "Let's have Spanish," I say, pointing to a restaurant called Meson Sevilla.

"Whatever my fiancée wants, she gets." Soon, we're seated at a tiny table in the welcoming restaurant, and we place our orders for tapas. "I do have one more item of business to discuss with you."

Touching my new diamond ring pin, I reply, "Ask away."

His palm snakes over his goatee. "I was thinking. We share our time between our two apartments." He sits straighter. "It would make sense to combine our living arrangements like we're combining everything else."

I bite my lip. This is one conundrum I've been grappling with for a while. I don't want to leave my place in Brooklyn, but his multi-million dollar apartment on the Upper East Side will be impossible for him to leave. I can do this. For him. "What would you like to do?"

His eyes shift from side to side, finally landing on mine. He holds his palm up, on which I place my own. "I want to sell my apartment and move in with you."

My mind blanks. One word escapes my lips. "What?"

"I don't belong uptown any longer." He frowns. "I'm not comfortable there. I like it in Brooklyn. It's so—" He searches for the word. "Down to earth. But more than that, it's where you are. And that's where I want to be."

Could this man be any more perfect? Not caring that we're in a restaurant, I leap to my feet and race around the table, planting my lips on his.

Laughing, he breaks our kiss. "I take it that's a yes?"

Grinning, I answer in the affirmative before kissing him again, only breaking apart when the server brings our tapas. After a fantastic assortment of small plates, Xander pulls out his phone. "Would it be alright with you if I call Theo to let him know our news?"

"Of course!" Xander and I called my family on the drive over. While I know he's not particularly close with his parents, I'm thrilled he wants to share our engagement with his "brother." A newly-minted *New York Times* bestselling author at that.

Xander FaceTimes Theo. "Hey, I've got some news and wanted to share it with you."

"What's up?"

"I'm a double partner!" My head tilts in the same exact way Theo's does. When he remains silent, my fiancé explains. "Madison asked me to become a partner in the Agency."

"Dude. That's awesome."

"Thanks. I agreed on one condition."

Theo's brow wrinkles. "You wanted to pay her double for the buy-in?"

"No. The financial conditions were more than fair." He leans over and kisses me off camera.

"Hey, is your girl there?" He peers into the camera. "Where are you, anyway?"

I lean into the screen, waving. "Hi, Theo!"

"We're at a restaurant on Forty-Sixth. Celebrating."

"Interesting choice of location, but that's great." Amelia walks behind him and he catches her hand, pointing to what I assume to be his phone. She bends down and waves at us, her new diamond ring sparkling.

She asks, "Did I hear you're celebrating?"

I jump into the conversation. "We are! Two things." I hold up my left pointer finger. "Xander agreed to become my partner at the

Agency and—"

"Madison agreed to marry me!" Xander finishes my sentence.

Both Theo and Amelia beam at us. Amelia finds her voice first. "I always wanted a sister. I'm so excited."

I never thought of it like that. How cool. With Xander, I'm gaining a huge extended family. "Me, too!"

"Congrats!" Theo rubs his trimmed beard with his palm. "Hey, Amelia and I just hired your sister as our coordinator. What do you think of a double wedding?"

I turn to my fiancé, who's sporting a small smile. Like how my nieces look at a toy store window during Christmas hoping against hope that Santa will leave the must-have item under the tree. I can't deny him this. My family loves to visit New York City anyway, and will be excited to be here for not one, but two weddings. I nod.

He whispers, "Really?"

"Yes." Seems to be my word today.

We face the camera. "So, when's our wedding date?"

They emit a whoop and give us the date, which is the only thing they've set for the wedding so far. We've gone out with Theo and Amelia on several occasions, sometimes with his sister Paige, all of whom are awesome. Since Amelia doesn't have any family, I know mine will welcome her with open arms.

The server delivers our dessert plates, so we disconnect the call, all the while holding each other's non-dominant hands. He finishes before me, as usual, and sends texts to his brother and sister, as well as his generation of extended "cousins." He's soon engrossed in conversations, all the while beaming at me.

After I finish eating, I follow suit and call Stephanie, who is beyond thrilled at my engagement. When we disconnect and our table is cleared, a ping announces the arrival of a new text on my phone. With a smile, I hold it up for my fiancé. "It's from Jesse."

"Cool."

"Huh. His text says HGTV is going to be filming a house-flipping show on the High Line right here in New York City." I pause. "That's the account Kelsey is going to pitch."

"Right."

"Well, anyway, he says he's up to the task of being a carpenter on it, thinking it will give his new business some good exposure."

"He's not wrong."

Pride at how Xander's PR mojo is flowing, I type my reply, "Congrats on an excellent PR move."

I'm about to tell him about our engagement when Jesse's response arrives. "He's asking if I can recommend anyone he might be able to partner up with for an audition."

My fiancé's gaze meets mine. Without thought, we both say, "Paige."

* * *

Want to experience Xander's first meeting IRL with Madison's family in Kansas? Download this FREE Bonus Epilogue today ~ and enjoy!! https://BookHip.com/DGNGMSD

Next up is Paige Hansen's story, IDLE, which releases in summer 2022. Please pre-order it on Amazon, and add it to your Good-Reads TBR list! https://geni.us/Sins4

A Note from Arell

Dear Fabulous Reader,

Thank you so much for reading PRIDE, the third entry in the Sins of the Fathers series!

This is the story of the eldest child of all the executives of VOW^3 Media, Xander Turner. Up until this point, Xander's pretty much led a charmed life ~ reaping the benefits of fame, money, and his good looks. All that changed in Vice, of course. He's now confronting the reality that all of his pride was derived from trying to please his father: an impossible task.

Madison Welch is the very unlikely heroine who saves him. A downtown girl who certainly doesn't look the part offers Xander a job when no one else would. While this book follows his journey to find pride in himself, it also offers a glimpse into how his belief in Madison gives her strength as well. And I will confess here and now … my single focus in writing this book was to get to the scene with Sheriff. When he places his hands on her shoulders and she sighs his name, AHHH! I get tears just thinking about it!! And I hope you did too.

As usual, some of my own life experiences appear in PRIDE ~

• The jogging loop around Central Park that Xander and Theo take when he's sorting through the mess of his life caused by Patrick Hudson? While I'm not a jogger, at all, I have walked portions of this loop and can highly recommend it!

• The scene with the parents pushing a stroller in the mall, and the child screams about Madison's scar came from a story Big Mike told me about his younger brother's reaction to seeing someone, for the first time, with a disability. I could only imagine how horrifying it was for my mother-in-law, not to mention the person he was shouting about. I channeled all that angst and sadness into the scene.

• The GreenMarket in Union Square is a real place! While I did make up the booths, I'm sure there are wonderful foods for you to explore there. And I wouldn't be surprised to find a pickle!

• Ziplining with Friends for Fun was super-fun for me to write! I've actually gone ziplining twice ~ once in Mexico and another time in Costa Rica ~ and I highly recommend it! Be like Madison, pull up your big girl panties, and soar. You'll love it, I promise! (although, I can't guarantee Xander will be waiting for you on the other side.)

• Xander and Madison's going to the Diamond District to pick out an engagement ring? You guessed it! Big Mike (sans me, lol) worked with Landsberg Jewelers to get my diamond. And we celebrated my saying "yes" at Meson Sevilla on Restaurant Row! (Sadly, we visited this famed street not long ago only to find out this restaurant is now closed.)

Please stay in touch! Subscribe to my newsletter at geni.us/SinsNewsletter or join Arell's Angels, my reader group on Facebook (www.facebook.com/groups/arellsangels) ~ or both!!

If you have any questions, feel free to email me at Arell@ArellRivers.com. I love chatting with readers!

Thanks for devoting your precious time to Pride. I hope Xander and Madison's story left you cheering in your seat!

All my love,
Arell

Gratitude

PRIDE couldn't have happened without so many awesome people!

First off, as usual, a huge cheer to my at-home support system ~ my husband, Big Mike, and my Mom. They never cease to amaze me with their support, hugs, and positivity.

Pride wouldn't be what it is without my fantastic team. My plot coach, Theresa Leigh of Velvetfire Press, really helped me identify pitfalls before I wrote and gave me confidence to write about Madison's courage! Once I was thoroughly frustrated with my first draft, I handed it over to Trenda Lundin of It's Your Story Content Editing who immediately identified the problem! With her guidance, I turned it around and proudly gave her a second round, which she loved! From there, Rebecca Hodgkins of Rebecca Hodgkins Editing edited my prose with skill. And, finally, proofreaders Angel Nyx, the Proofreading Bayou Queen, and Roxanne Blouin caught all of my stupid errors. Big huge, virtual hugs!!

In addition, Pride Dar Albert of Wicked Smart Designs sealed the deal with this droolworthy cover! Hope you love it as much as I do!!

And so many friends gave their time and energy into making the blurb actually sound enticing, lol! The simple word "thanks" doesn't express my appreciation to Lilly Wilde, Taylor Delong, Libby Waterford, Mary E. Montgomery, and Aviva Vaughn. You lades are the bomb!

Huge hugs to my ARC Team!! Each one of you spurs me on to keep doing what I do. Thank you for taking the time to read, review, and share Pride!!!

My Facebook reader's group, Arell's Angels, is my go-to place to hang out, check out hot photos, and simply just vent! Shout out to "Arell's Insiders" who post daily and keep the group rockin' with your wit and devotion. To all the Angels who participate in our Hotties of the Month, daily games, my crazy Facebook Lives, sneak peeks, collaborative stories, and author Takeover Sundays ~ you make this journey so worthwhile! Remember ~ there's always room for more angels!

I'm so lucky to have met, in person and virtually, so many wonderful authors who are so giving of their advice, support, and friendship. Sophia Henry, Taylor Delong, Libby Waterford, Mary E. Montgomery, Nicole Locke, Aviva Vaughn, Lexi Rourke, Claire Marti, Lilly Wilde, Isabelle Peterson, Marika Ray, Joslyn Westbrook, Jessa York, SH Pratt, Nancy Herkness, Stacey Wilk, JB Schroeder, and Lori Matthews are more than amazing.

And to everyone who picks up this book, *I hope Xander and Madison showed you to look beyond the surface.* If you enjoyed Pride, please share it with your friends and write a review.

Blessings,
Arell

About the Author

For as long as Arell Rivers can remember, she has been lost in a book. During her senior year in college, she picked up a romance novel ... and instantly was hooked!

Arell started writing her first book because the characters were screaming at her to do so. The story came out in her dreams and attacked her in the shower, so she took to the computer to shut them up. But they kept talking.

Born and raised in New Jersey, Arell has what some may call a "checkered past." Prior to discovering her passion for writing romance, she practiced law, was a wedding and event planner and even dabbled in marketing. Arell lives with two adorable cats and a very supportive husband who doesn't care that the bed isn't made or dinner isn't on the table. When not in her writing cave, Arell is found cooking in the InstantPot, working out with Shaun T, or hitting the beach.

Want to keep up to date with Arell? Sign up for her newsletter at https://geni.us/SinsNewsletter. All new subscribers receive a special gift!

facebook.com/arellrivers

twitter.com/arellrivers

instagram.com/authorarell

Connect with Arell

- Subscribe to Arell's newsletter - https://geni.us/SinsNewsletter
- Join Arell's Facebook Group, "Arell's Angels" - http://www.facebook.com/groups/ArellsAngels
- Like Arell's Facebook Page - http://www.Facebook.com/ArellRivers
- Follow Arell on Instagram - http://www.Instagram.com/AuthorArell
- Hang out with Arell on Amazon - https://geni.us/ArellRivers
- Check out Arell on Goodreads - https://geni.us/ARGoodReads
- Follow Arell on BookBub - https://geni.us/BookBubFollow
- Head over to Arell's website - http://www.ArellRivers.com
- Email Arell - Arell@ArellRivers.com

Other Books by Arell Rivers

Sins of the Fathers

A series about the children of 3 notorious businessmen

Book #1: VICE (short story, originally published as "Tinsel Bomb" in the 2021 anthology TINSEL AND TATAS) - http://geni.us/Sins1

Book #2: ANGER (Theo and Amelia) - http://geni.us/Sins2

Book #3: PRIDE (Xander and Madison)

Book #4: IDLE (Paige and Jesse ~ pre-order now!) - https://geni.us/Sins4

The Hunte Family Series

A series about the dynasty created by rocker Braxon Hunte

Book #1: OUT OF THE RED (Brax and Sara) - https://geni.us/OOTR

Book #2: OUT OF THE SHADOW (King and Angie) - https://geni.us/hunte2

Book #3: OUT OF THE GOLD (Melody and Chase) - https://geni.us/OOTG

Book #4: OUT OF THE BLUE (Trent and Cordelia) - https://geni.us/Hunte4

The Hold Series

A series about rock star Cole Manchester, his publicist Rose Morgan, and their friends

Book #1: NO ONE TO HOLD (Cole and Rose trilogy, part 1) - https://geni.us/NOTH

Book #2: HARD TO HOLD (Cole and Rose trilogy, part 2) - https://geni.us/HtoH

Book #3: To Have and to Hold (Cole and Rose trilogy, part 3) - https://geni.us/THTH

Book #4: Hold On (series prequel novella) - https://geni.usHoldOn

Book #5: Take Hold of Me (Wills and Emilie) - https://geni.us/THOM

Book #6: Hold Still (Ozzy and McKenna) - https://geni.us/GDwdlls

Book #7: Hold Me: A Rock Star Box Set (includes Books 1-4 plus a bonus novella) - https://geni.us/HoldMeBoxSet

ANGER

Want to learn more about Theo and Amelia?

Read on to enjoy the first chapter of Anger,
Book #2 in the Sins of the Fathers Series!

The truth doesn't *always* set you free...

Theo

This isn't the life I wanted.

Being a reporter for my family's media conglomerate instead of a
pro hockey player was *never* my plan.

And yet, here I am with no other prospects.

What I *do* have is anger. The all-consuming, isolating kind.

Until I meet Amelia. She calms my mind, soothes my soul, ignites my body.

Still … I sometimes wonder if fate brought her here to save me—or break me once and for all.

Amelia

All I ever wanted was to be a journalist.

Working for an almost tabloid is *not* ideal. But for now, it's the best I can do.

I won't lose my integrity, though. I'll *never* be a liar.

Which makes my new assignment *that* much harder.

To keep my job, I need to use Theo for a story. It helps that my byline doesn't match the name by which he knows me. Still … I like him. I don't want to betray him.

And worst of all, he makes me want to extend our relationship past my policy of one-night-stands.

When the truth is spilled, will Theo and Amelia be able to take a shot at love? Or will their romance end up as nothing more than yesterday's news?

ANGER
Sins of the Fathers Series, Book 2
Arell Rivers
©2021 Tarnished Halo Publishing LLC

Chapter 1 – Theo

My fist slams down on my desk, causing all the mail on it to jump. "When will this end?" My griping goes unanswered in the empty office.

Chucking all the hate mail into the bin, courtesy of VOW3 Media's founders slash executives slash my father and his partners being hauled away in handcuffs at the Tinsel & Tatas Gala, I reach for my coffee cup and gulp the last dregs of the too-bitter brew. I already hit the company's gym earlier, yet the need for a second round looms. Dealing with Father's and my "uncles" indictments has taken over my life this past week. Had to duck a gaggle of paparazzi on my way into the building this morning, which prompted my early workout. This is freaking nuts.

Even though they—my bosses—pleaded not guilty, the judge slapped them with a five hundred-thousand-dollar bail, each, and confined them to their homes with ankle monitors. Since our families were all raised together as if we were siblings—we call each other's parents Aunts and Uncles, which seems like a curse now. Thankfully, I used part of my trust fund as the down payment on my apartment, so I have a respite from their shitshow.

Picking up the first magazine in the pile, I flatten it on my desk and check out the *Spill It Magazine* cover. The rag features a photo of Darcey Abbott in the bottom-right corner, sporting the sensational headline, "Grateful to Have Escaped." *Seemed plenty excited when Xander put a ring on her finger.* By my way of thinking, he's the one who should be "grateful to have escaped" *her* conniving ways. My heart rate dips. At least something good came out of this disaster.

Bracing myself for God knows what she said, I flip to the page highlighted on the front cover. It's an article by A. Bellamy—despite being a reporter here in New York City for the past four years, I've never heard of him. I skim through the piece, which makes the blood in my veins kick right back up. For the second time in five minutes, my fist pounds onto my desk. "The fuck!"

Slamming my eyelids shut, I inhale all the way to my diaphragm and hold. Exhaling, I reopen my eyes but the words don't change. Darcey blabbed lies to the magazine, and the tabloid ran with them. True to form, they didn't bother to double-check any of her so-called facts. Not even her spurious claim that Xander had refused to reset the ring to a setting more to her liking. I *know* he agreed to do just that, despite the red flare her request sent. Yes, he is much better off without her. Still, this article is whack. I need to tell Xander about this ASAP.

Leaping to my feet, I stomp toward my "cousin's"-cum-best friend's domain in the marketing department. As I march through the halls, the quiet is almost deafening. I guess it's to be expected. What are employees supposed to do when they find out their executives have been arrested for fraud, money laundering, and tax evasion?

Before reaching his office, I google "A. Bellamy." A shadowy profile photo appears on the *Spill It* website. Other photos similarly obscure his identity. Whoever the fuck this reporter is, he needs to grow some balls. If you're going to write crap like this, at least have the guts to show your face. Slapping the magazine against my thigh, I stop in front of Xander's door, which is closed. A week ago, that would've been unusual. Nowadays, though, he works in solitude. Rapping on the door, I call out, "It's me."

"Come in."

Leaving the door open, I enter his office, which looks like a tornado hit. Piles of papers are everywhere, two computer monitors are fired up, and he has pens behind both ears plus one in his mouth. "Too bad you have nothing to do."

His eyes dart from the screens and he slants me a dirty look. Removing the pen from his lips as if it were a cigarette, he taps it onto his desk. "If you came here to comment about my workload, dude, you can turn around and walk your ass right out."

"You know me better than that." I hit my leg once again with the magazine, move two piles from a guest chair, and plop into it. "How are you holding up?"

"Oh, peachy. Dad calls me every fifteen minutes with how he wants things handled. As if I have any say around here. I'm only an *assistant* vice president." His tone underscores his disgust at his situation. Perhaps he's finally getting out from under his father's thumb? A guy can hope.

Our fathers plus Uncle Ward are the only C-suite executives in the firm. There was talk about promoting Xander to Executive Vice President of Marketing when he got engaged to Darcey, and we all know how that turned out. As amplified by *Spill It Magazine*.

"Well, I'm not here to make things worse for you, but I just read this article and wanted to find out if you've seen it?" I open the magazine to Darcey's rant and pass it over to him.

He quirks his eyebrow at me before reaching out and taking it. When he finishes, his index finger taps his bottom lip. In an even tone, he notes, "This reporter, A. Bellamy, left me a message a few days ago, but I didn't bother to return it. Says here, 'we reached out to Xander Turner for comment, but he didn't respond to our request.' Guess this is what I get." He tosses the magazine across his desk.

"That's it? How can you not be mad at what she spewed?"

He shrugs. "I have bigger fish to fry than her twisted truths."

His nonchalance fuels my fury. "If you're not going to do it, I have half a mind to go over to that stupid magazine and tear all of them a new one. How could they print Darcey's shit? When you didn't respond to their message, they should've tried harder rather than put in a lousy disclaimer." My hands form fists on my thighs.

"I'm not letting it get to me, so you shouldn't either. People are going to say what they feel like—"

"Yeah, but she was your fiancée, man."

"For less than twelve hours." His hand flutters. "It's done." Xander's cheek twitches, the only sign that Darcey's words reached him. "Seriously, let it go."

While this article wasn't written about me, my rage toward his ex refuses to subside. How can he be so blasé over it? True, the indictments have turned both our home and professional lives upside down, but this is a personal attack on Xander. On his character. He can't let this go unchecked. "If you won't lay into *Spill It*, I'll write the correct version of the story that this A. Bellamy should've printed in the first place."

"Make sure you get a comment from him before printing."

I harrumph. "Yeah, I'll be right on that. Give this 'A.' person the same chance he gave you."

Xander's shoulders rise on his next inhale. "So, Dad wants to print an article about how the charges are bogus against him and the others. He swears they've done nothing wrong." My anger refocuses on his dear old father when he changes the subject.

For this, we need privacy. I stand and shut his door once more. Lowering back into the chair, I ask, "Do you agree?"

"To the article or to his assertion?"

"Either. Both?" I've been suspicious about how things were so rosy around here, given our late entry into the online sphere. I assumed our print circulation was covering our digital losses. From what I've gathered based on others' reporting about the company, though, seems like I was caught up in the classic meaning of "assume." And I don't like being made an ass out of.

"He claims the three have discussed it and agree on this course of action."

Feels like Father is leading the brothers in trying to control this whole situation, like how he ruled our household when we were growing up. With an iron fist.

Xander swivels his chair so he can look out the window. From the fifty-second floor, Manhattan almost looks magical. In a low voice, he replies, "I'm not sure what to think. Mom simply states that he's innocent and we should get on with our lives as if nothing's wrong. But Dad's on home confinement, for heaven's sake. The executives can't come into the office, as that would set off their ankle monitors. And the FBI tracks their computers, so they can't work from home, either."

"I know. While your mother's pretending like everything's normal, Mum's been a bitch on wheels. Thank God I don't live there anymore, but Paige reports back to me about how awful it's been with them." My sister complains nightly about the misery of her living situation. So far, though, she's refused my offer to let her stay with me. Why can't we all rewind a week before all hell broke loose?

"All this and Uncle Ward's at his apartment, alone. I'm grateful his twins are still on their college campuses." He returns to his chair and turns toward me.

I run my palm over my short beard. "Think their graduation celebrations will still proceed?"

He shrugs. "Don't see why not. I'm positive all of this will be well over by May."

"Let's hope so. This better not drag out longer than a month, for sure."

Xander's phone rings. His face twists in disgust. "I can't deal with him now." It rings out and goes to voicemail.

Before I'm able to make a comment about his father's calling, Xander's admin walks in and hands him yet another pile of documents. "All the articles from yesterday that mentioned VOW-cubed Media."

"Thanks, Felicia."

She smiles at me and walks out, closing the door behind her. His admin is smokin.' "Geez, if I had her working for me, I don't think I'd remember Darcey's name."

"Hold up, Mr. 'NYC's Ultimate Playboy.' Never dip your wick where you work. Besides," he tosses another pen into the air and lets it roll on the top of his desktop. "I'm off women."

I lean back into my chair. Ignoring Xander's use of the stupid media headline about me, I recall he always had chicks hanging off his arm. In fact, he cheered me on during my early ice hockey games when he was fifteen years old, and he had babes with him even then. "I'm sure there's a line a mile long of women ready to take your mind off Darcey."

He winces and shakes his head fast. "My life is complicated enough."

"Which is exactly why you should hook up with someone. Take the edge off." Like I should be doing, although no one has caught my eye as of late. Father's arrest put a wet blanket over my dating life, but I'm itching to throw it off. A more pleasurable way to get rid of this excess energy than hitting the gym all the time.

"I don't want to deal with the headaches women cause." He

rifles through the new stack of papers, effectively ending this conversation.

I let it drop, but vow to fix the shit Darcey spewed. Xander deserves so much better than her. I remember overhearing her discussion with her friend, Sloane English, about getting on "NYC Wicked Wives," and an idea about how to counter her venom forms. Which I'm not sharing it yet. "What are you looking for?"

He taps on the pile. "Not sure. But it's good to read what's being written about us and respond." He points toward *Spill It*. "Not in shitty little magazines like this one, but in law journals and hard-hitting ones. Always spinning everything is taxing." His hand ghosts over two of the piles on his desk. "It sucks to always play catch-up. I have to somehow get in front of this fucking mess."

"I can't imagine how much harder your job is now." That's the truth. Xander's position has always been challenging, but as of last week, it exploded. Before, he was in charge of staying on top of all the advertisers and keeping everyone happy. Now, he's sort of the *de facto* head of the company. Until our fathers come back. Considering how his father's calling him nonstop, Xander's not really in charge, though.

He removes yet another pen behind his ear and flips it in the air, catching it over and over. "I've heard the scuttlebutt around here. Way too many people are thinking of jumping ship. Crazy rumors pop up constantly." His hips shift as he switches his weight from side to side. "People say the company is going to go under."

I scoff. "As if. Our fathers are many things, but tax cheats and devious money launderers aren't one of them." I hope.

Xander nods. "I agree. I can't imagine what the feds think they have on them. I'm sure it's a misunderstanding." When I remain silent, he continues. "I'm trying to figure out how to calm the atmosphere around here and keep up productivity."

My fingers run over my beard. "What about a company Town Hall? You can explain the family's side of things. That might appease the sharks somewhat."

Xander stands and paces around his office. "That's a great idea.

We can do it in the conference room and plug in people who aren't here via Zoom." He spins and faces me. "I like it."

"Thanks. Just know you're the one who's going to be in the hot seat, not a lowly journalist me." I wink at him and he cracks the first smile I've seen out of him in over a week. Progress.

"I wish I knew what was going on. What precipitated this mess." He pauses. "What our fathers really did."

His last statement hangs over us. While I can't let myself believe they did everything they're accused of, a small part of me does wonder if they haven't been playing with the numbers. A larger part wonders if being a dick to your kids qualifies for an FBI investigation.

"I'm sure they didn't do as much as the government is accusing them of. They'll maybe have to plead to something stupid, pay a fine, and this will end. At the very most, they may have to do community service for like a day."

Xander places his hand on my shoulder and squeezes. "Better arrange for this Town Hall."

I stand, grab the *Spill It* magazine, and we both file out of his office. While he goes to speak with Felicia—who I still think he should bang—I return to my office and pull up a blank document on my screen. I'm going to fix the wrongs this A. Bellamy put out.

A little while later, with Xander's emailed invitation to his Town Hall written in my calendar, my hands cover my eyes and rub. I need lunch and coffee. And not the crap in the break room. Remembering the new coffee shop that opened a couple of doors down, I cross my office and take my coat. I make it a point to pass by Xander's office, but he's not around. Oh well, I'll give him a review after I've tried their lunch. I wave to our receptionist and amble toward the elevators.

———

Read the rest of Theo and Amelia's story on Amazon now!
http://geni.us/Sins2

Made in United States
North Haven, CT
04 April 2022

17850306R00186